big NATE
BLOW THE
ROOF OFF!

Complete Your *Big Nate* Collection

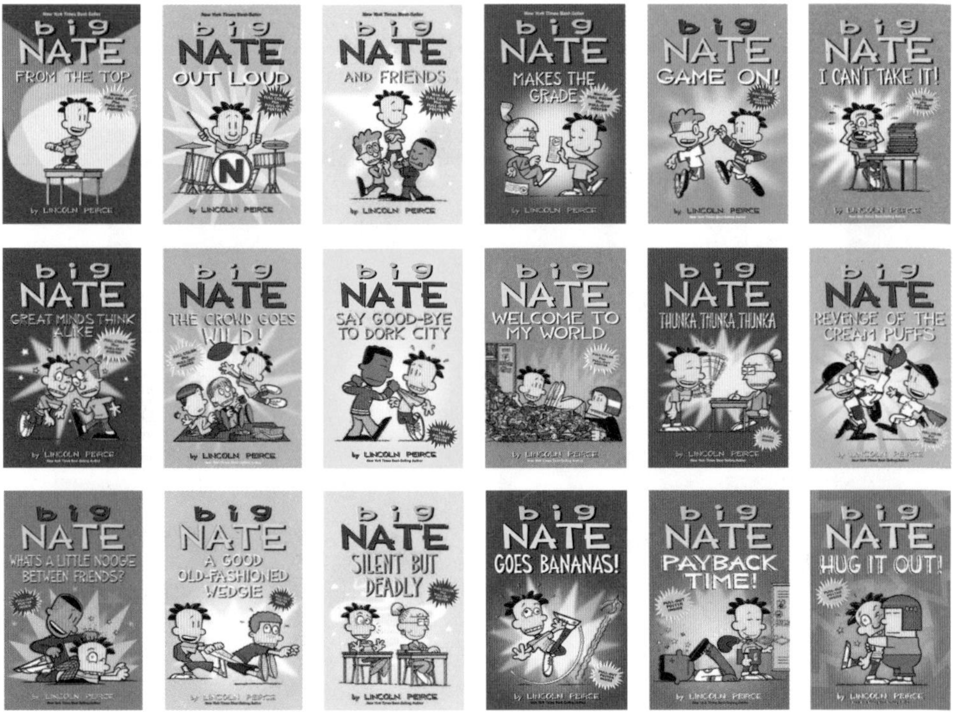
big NATE FROM THE TOP
by LINCOLN PEIRCE
big NATE OUT LOUD
by LINCOLN PEIRCE
big NATE AND FRIENDS
by LINCOLN PEIRCE
big NATE MAKES THE GRADE
by LINCOLN PEIRCE
big NATE GAME ON!
by LINCOLN PEIRCE
big NATE I CAN'T TAKE IT!
big NATE GREAT MINDS THINK ALIKE
by LINCOLN PEIRCE
big NATE THE CROWD GOES WILD!
by LINCOLN PEIRCE
big NATE SAY GOOD-BYE TO DORK CITY
by LINCOLN PEIRCE
big NATE WELCOME TO MY WORLD
by LINCOLN PEIRCE
big NATE THUNKA THUNKA THUNKA
by LINCOLN PEIRCE
big NATE REVENGE OF THE CREAM PUFFS
big NATE WHAT'S A LITTLE NOOGIE BETWEEN FRIENDS?
big NATE A GOOD OLD-FASHIONED WEDGIE
big NATE SILENT BUT DEADLY
by LINCOLN PEIRCE
big NATE GOES BANANAS!
by LINCOLN PEIRCE
big NATE PAYBACK TIME!
by LINCOLN PEIRCE
big NATE HUG IT OUT!
by LINCOLN PEIRCE

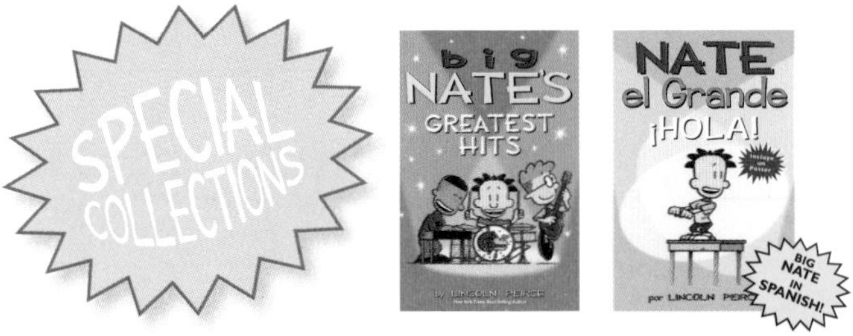
SPECIAL COLLECTIONS
big NATE'S GREATEST HITS
by LINCOLN PEIRCE
NATE el Grande ¡HOLA!
por LINCOLN PEIRCE
BIG NATE IN SPANISH!

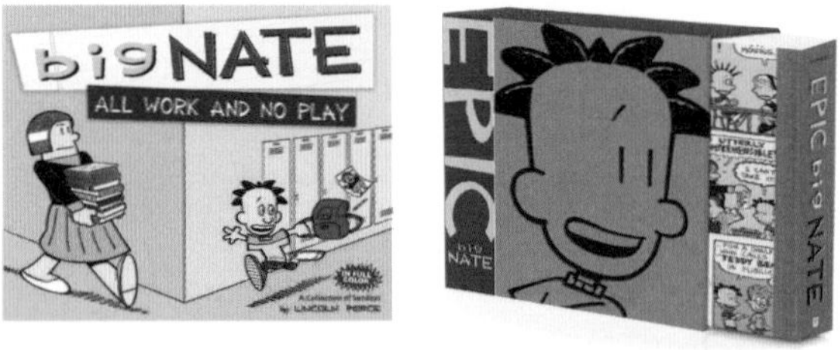
big NATE ALL WORK AND NO PLAY
by LINCOLN PEIRCE
EPIC big NATE

big NATE
BLOW THE
ROOF OFF!

by LINCOLN PEIRCE

Andrews McMeel
PUBLISHING®

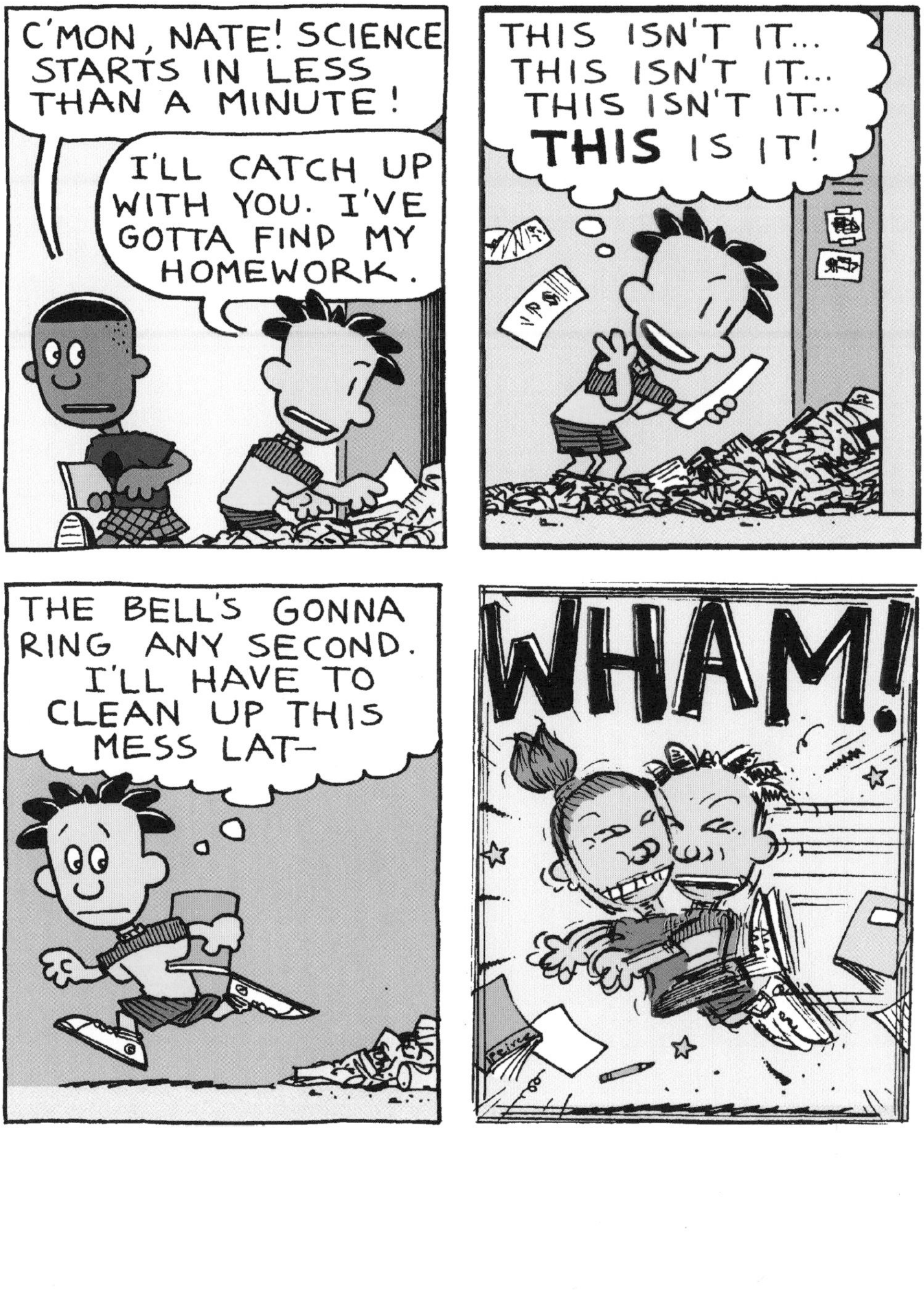
C'MON, NATE! SCIENCE STARTS IN LESS THAN A MINUTE!
I'LL CATCH UP WITH YOU. I'VE GOTTA FIND MY HOMEWORK.
THIS ISN'T IT... THIS ISN'T IT... THIS ISN'T IT... **THIS** IS IT!
THE BELL'S GONNA RING ANY SECOND. I'LL HAVE TO CLEAN UP THIS MESS LAT—
WHAM!

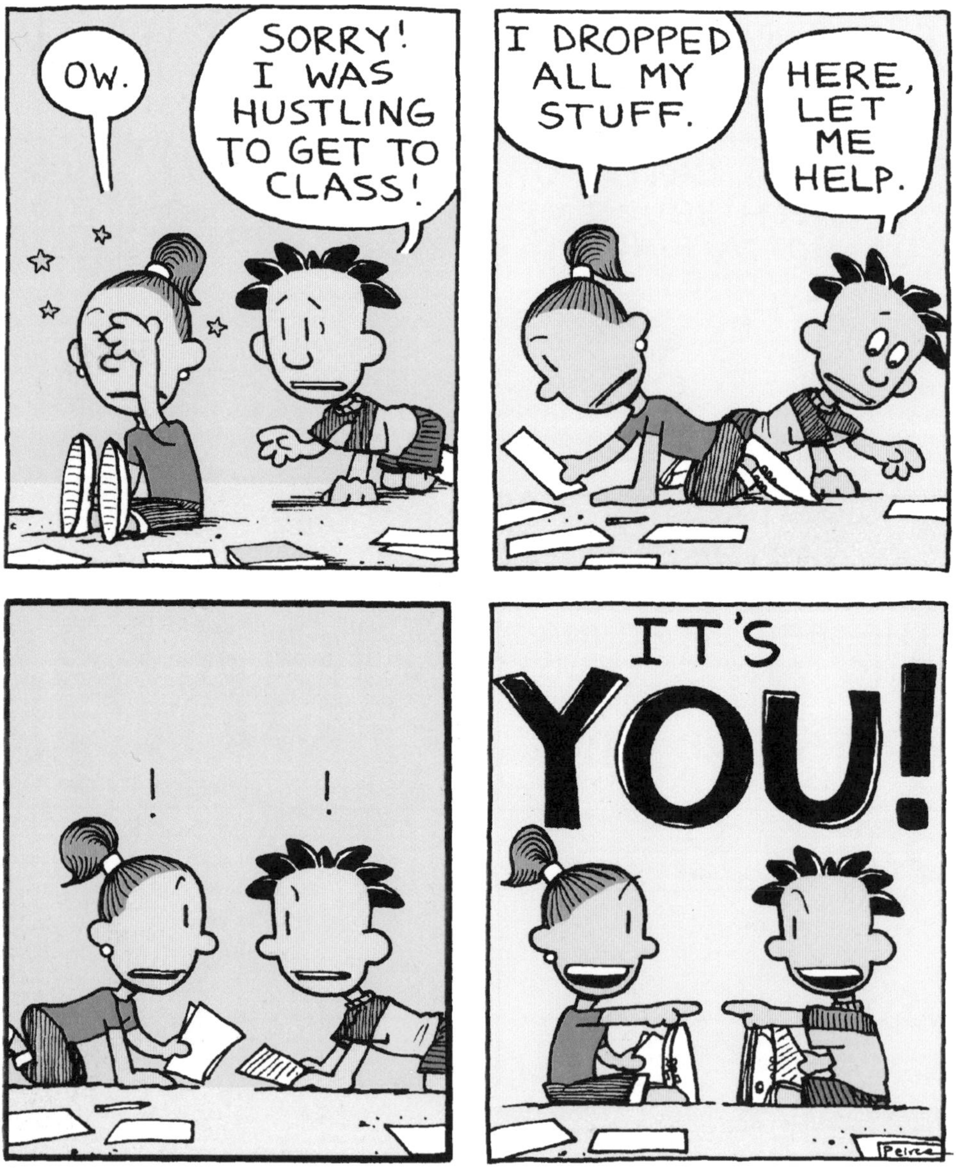
OW.
SORRY! I WAS HUSTLING TO GET TO CLASS!
I DROPPED ALL MY STUFF.
HERE, LET ME HELP.
!
!
IT'S YOU!
Peirce

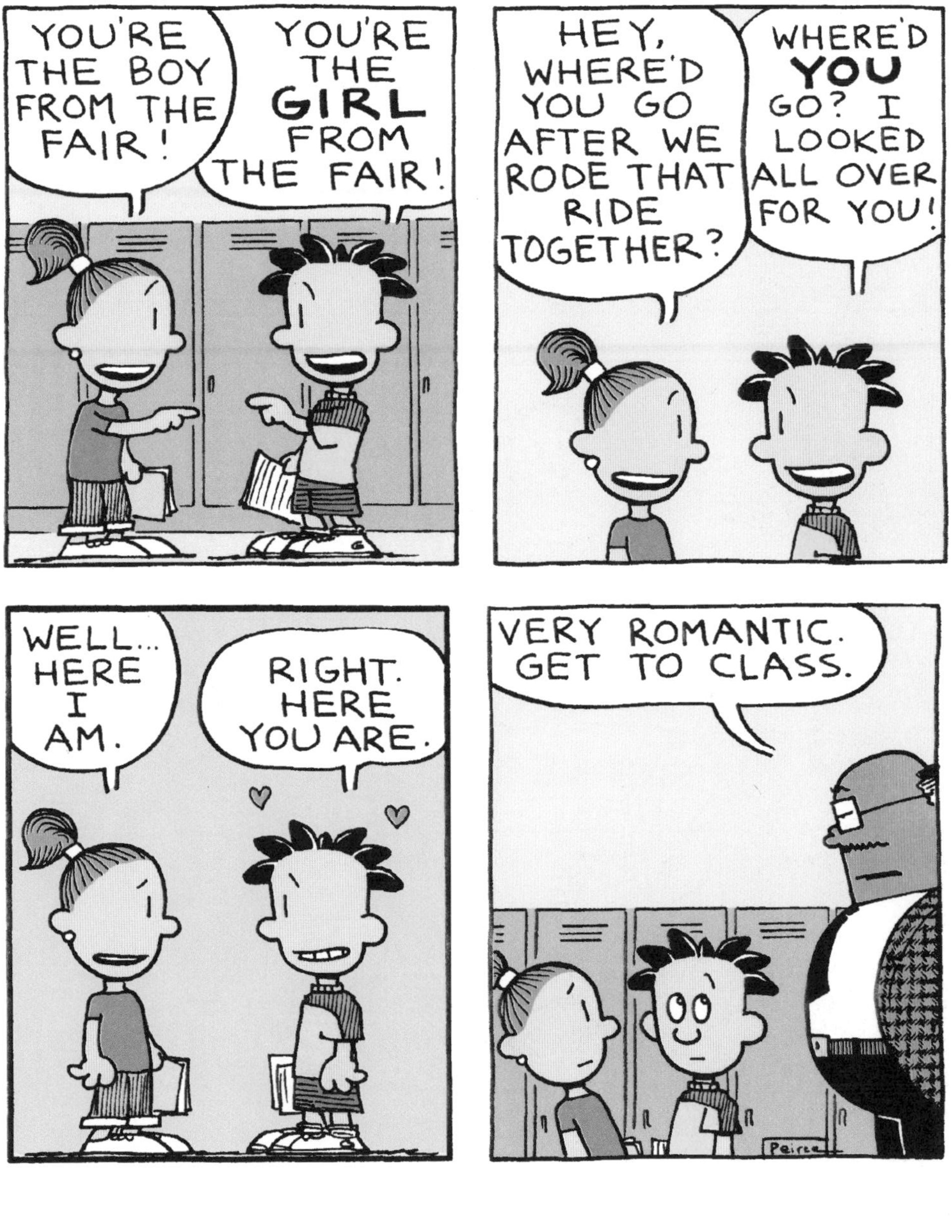
YOU'RE THE BOY FROM THE FAIR!
YOU'RE THE GIRL FROM THE FAIR!
HEY, WHERE'D YOU GO AFTER WE RODE THAT RIDE TOGETHER?
WHERE'D YOU GO? I LOOKED ALL OVER FOR YOU!
WELL... HERE I AM.
RIGHT. HERE YOU ARE.
VERY ROMANTIC. GET TO CLASS.
Peirce

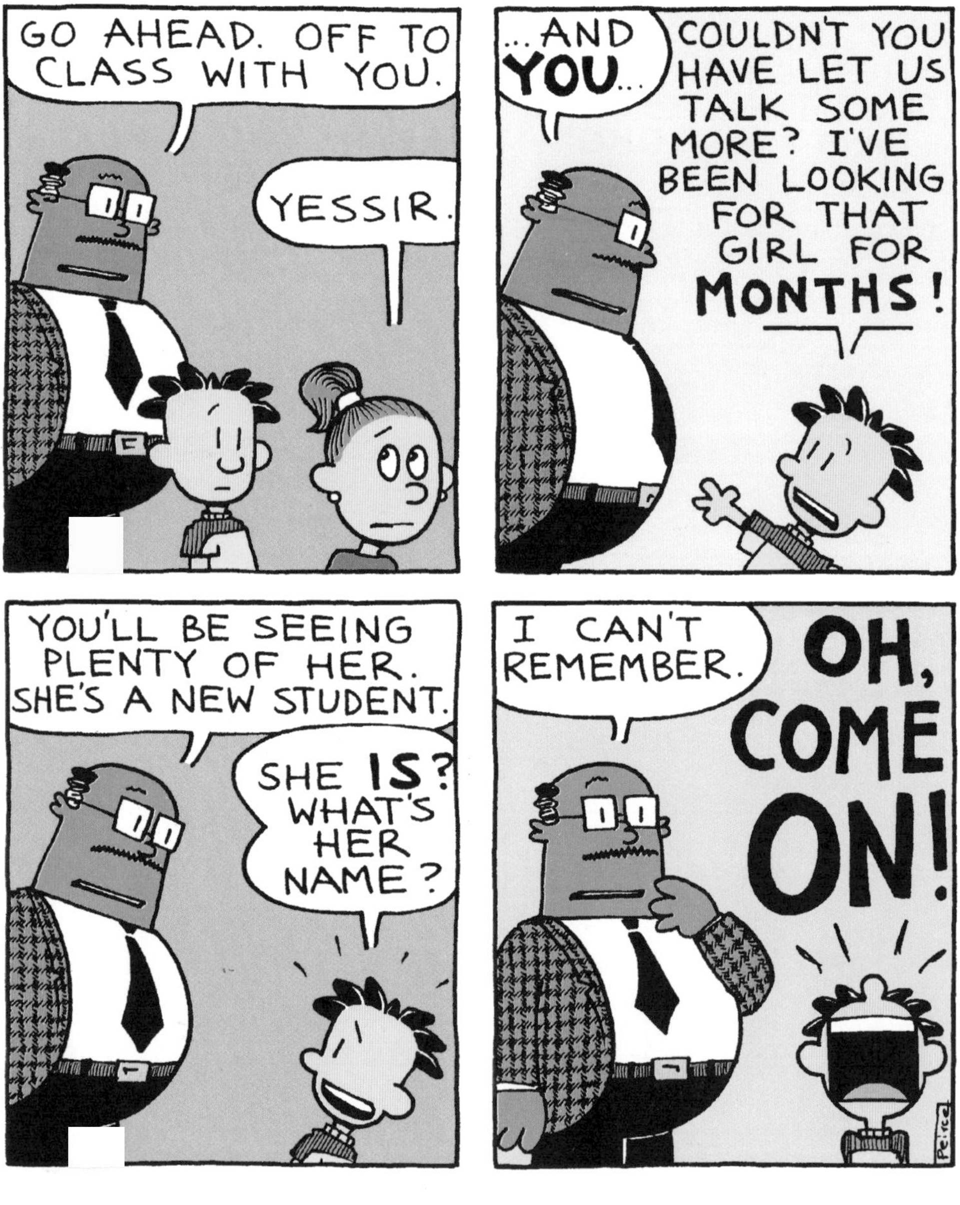
GO AHEAD. OFF TO CLASS WITH YOU.
YESSIR.
...AND YOU...
COULDN'T YOU HAVE LET US TALK SOME MORE? I'VE BEEN LOOKING FOR THAT GIRL FOR MONTHS!
YOU'LL BE SEEING PLENTY OF HER. SHE'S A NEW STUDENT.
SHE IS? WHAT'S HER NAME?
I CAN'T REMEMBER.
OH, COME ON!
Peirce

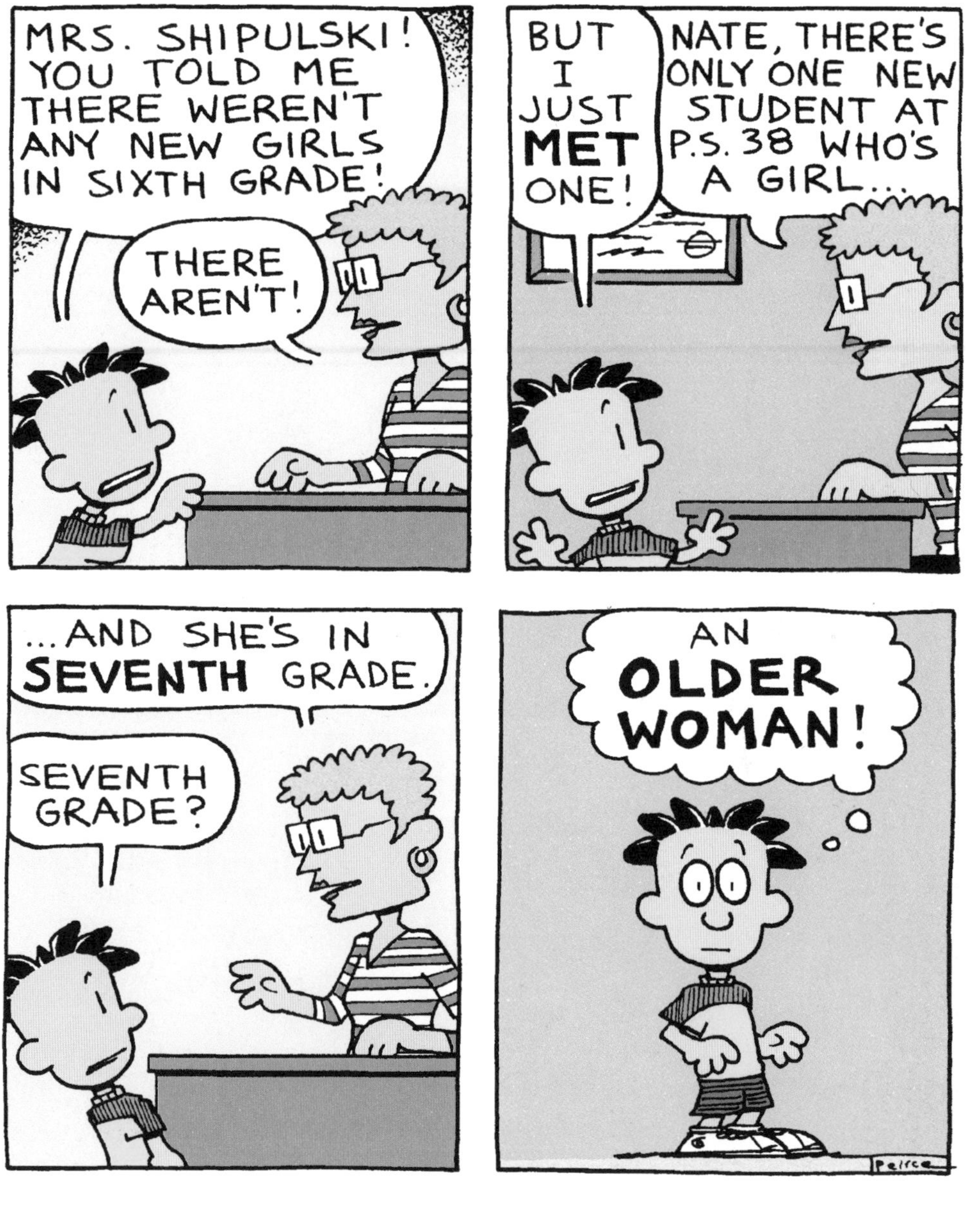
MRS. SHIPULSKI! YOU TOLD ME THERE WEREN'T ANY NEW GIRLS IN SIXTH GRADE!
THERE AREN'T!
NATE, THERE'S ONLY ONE NEW STUDENT AT P.S. 38 WHO'S A GIRL...
BUT I JUST **MET** ONE!
...AND SHE'S IN **SEVENTH** GRADE.
SEVENTH GRADE?
AN **OLDER WOMAN!**
Peirce

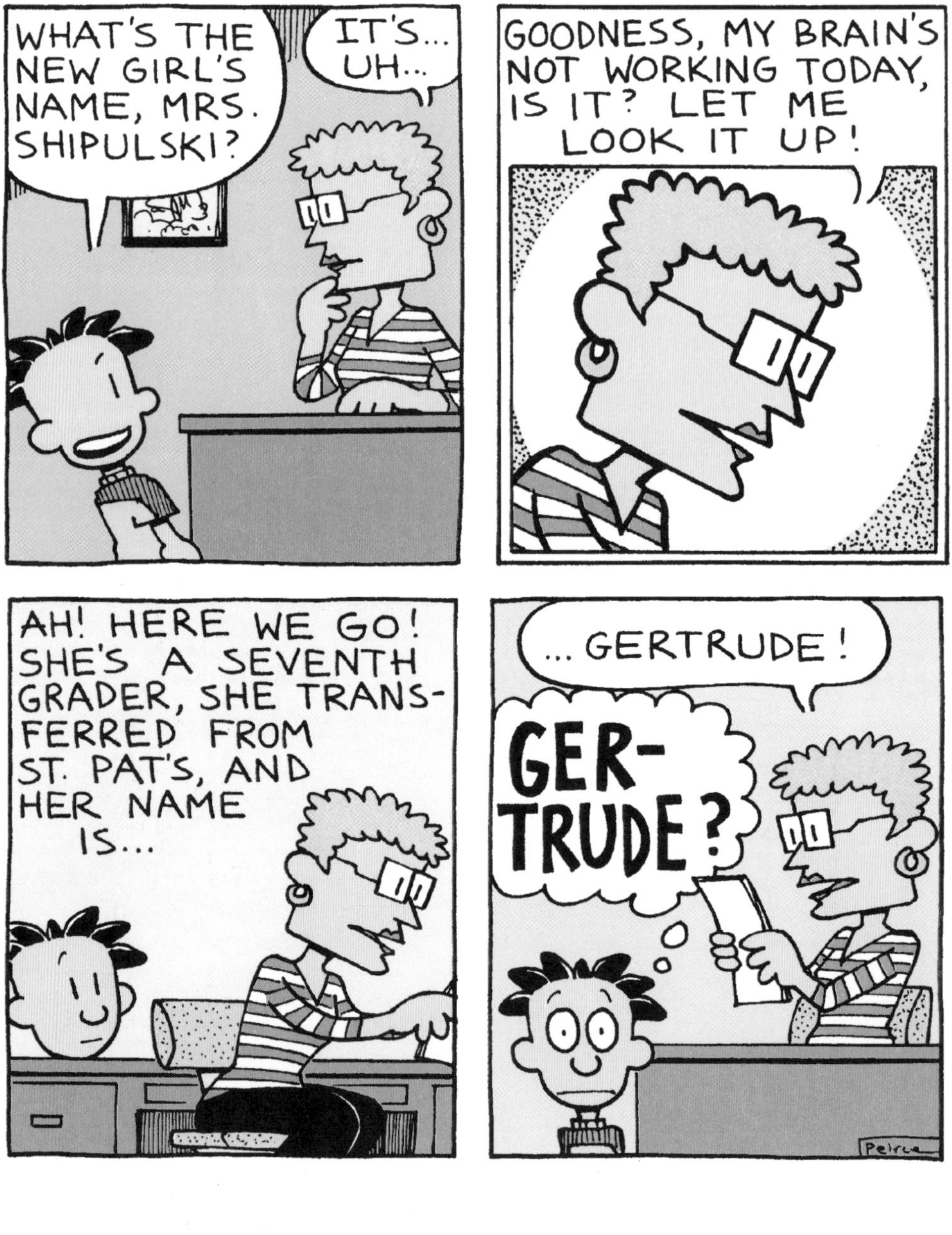
WHAT'S THE NEW GIRL'S NAME, MRS. SHIPULSKI?
IT'S... UH...
GOODNESS, MY BRAIN'S NOT WORKING TODAY, IS IT? LET ME LOOK IT UP!
AH! HERE WE GO! SHE'S A SEVENTH GRADER, SHE TRANS-FERRED FROM ST. PAT'S, AND HER NAME IS...
...GERTRUDE!
GER-TRUDE?
Peirce

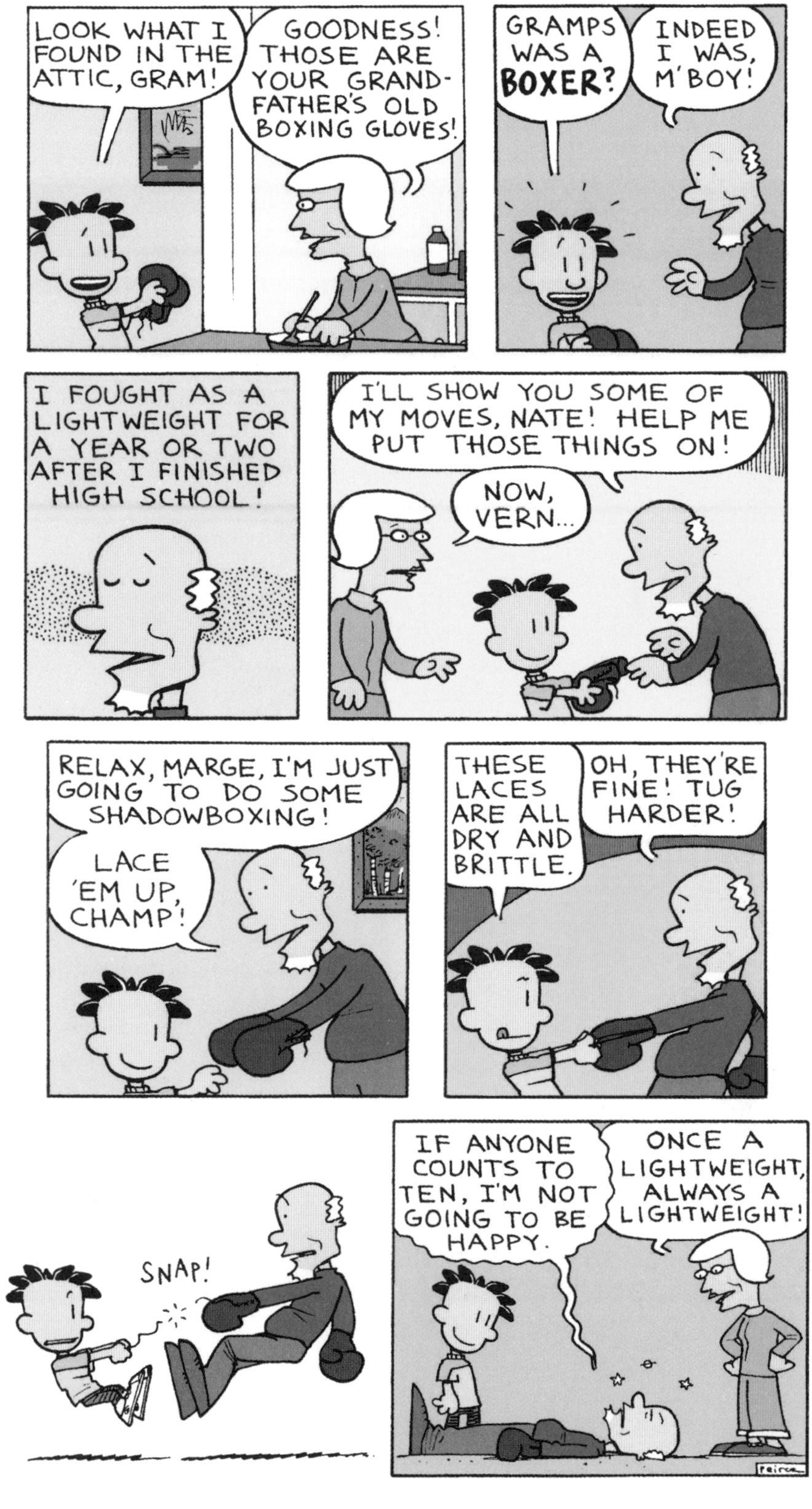
LOOK WHAT I FOUND IN THE ATTIC, GRAM!
GOODNESS! THOSE ARE YOUR GRAND-FATHER'S OLD BOXING GLOVES!
GRAMPS WAS A **BOXER**?
INDEED I WAS, M'BOY!
I FOUGHT AS A LIGHTWEIGHT FOR A YEAR OR TWO AFTER I FINISHED HIGH SCHOOL!
I'LL SHOW YOU SOME OF MY MOVES, NATE! HELP ME PUT THOSE THINGS ON!
NOW, VERN...
RELAX, MARGE, I'M JUST GOING TO DO SOME SHADOWBOXING!
LACE 'EM UP, CHAMP!
THESE LACES ARE ALL DRY AND BRITTLE.
OH, THEY'RE FINE! TUG HARDER!
SNAP!
IF ANYONE COUNTS TO TEN, I'M NOT GOING TO BE HAPPY.
ONCE A LIGHTWEIGHT, ALWAYS A LIGHTWEIGHT!
peirce

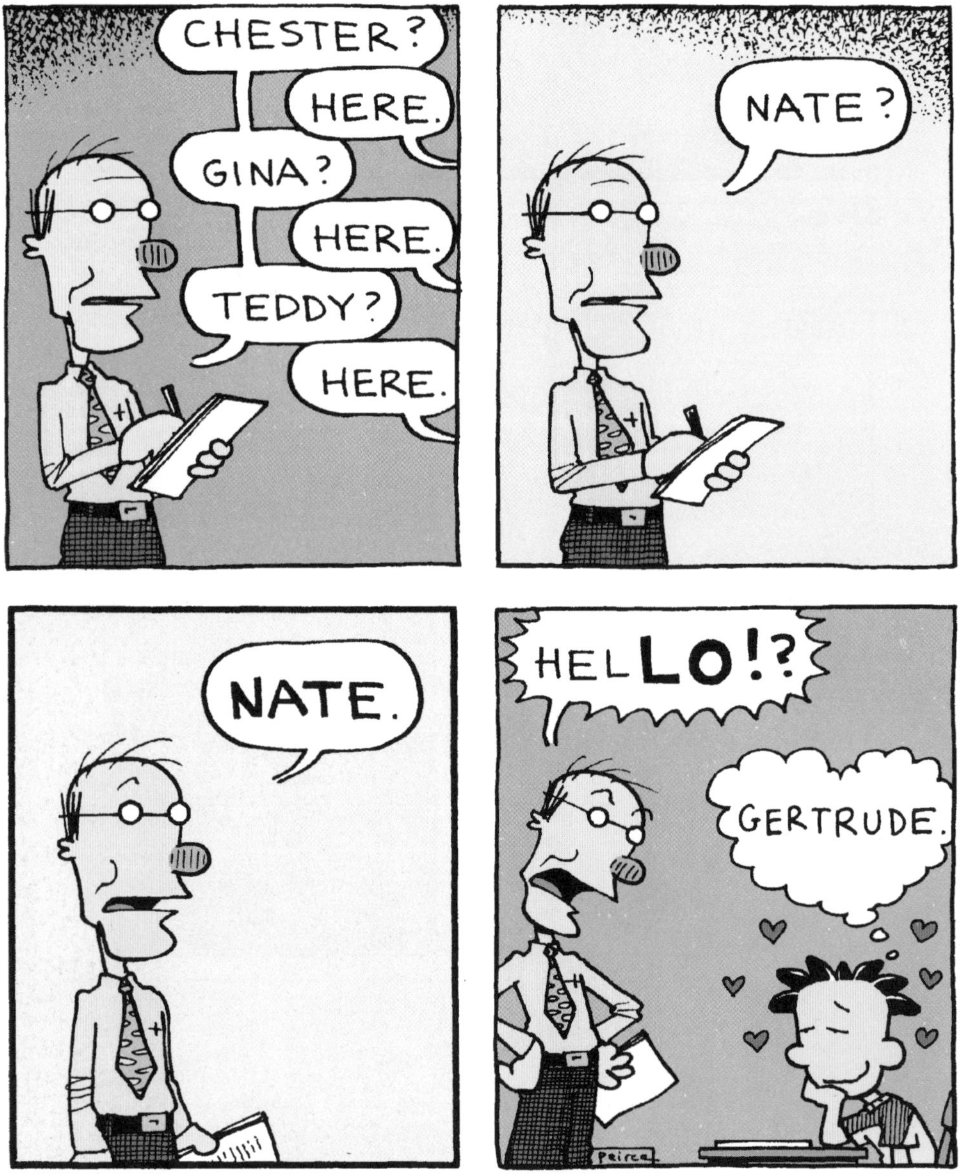
CHESTER?
HERE.
GINA?
HERE.
TEDDY?
HERE.
NATE?
NATE.
HELLO!?
GERTRUDE.
Peirce

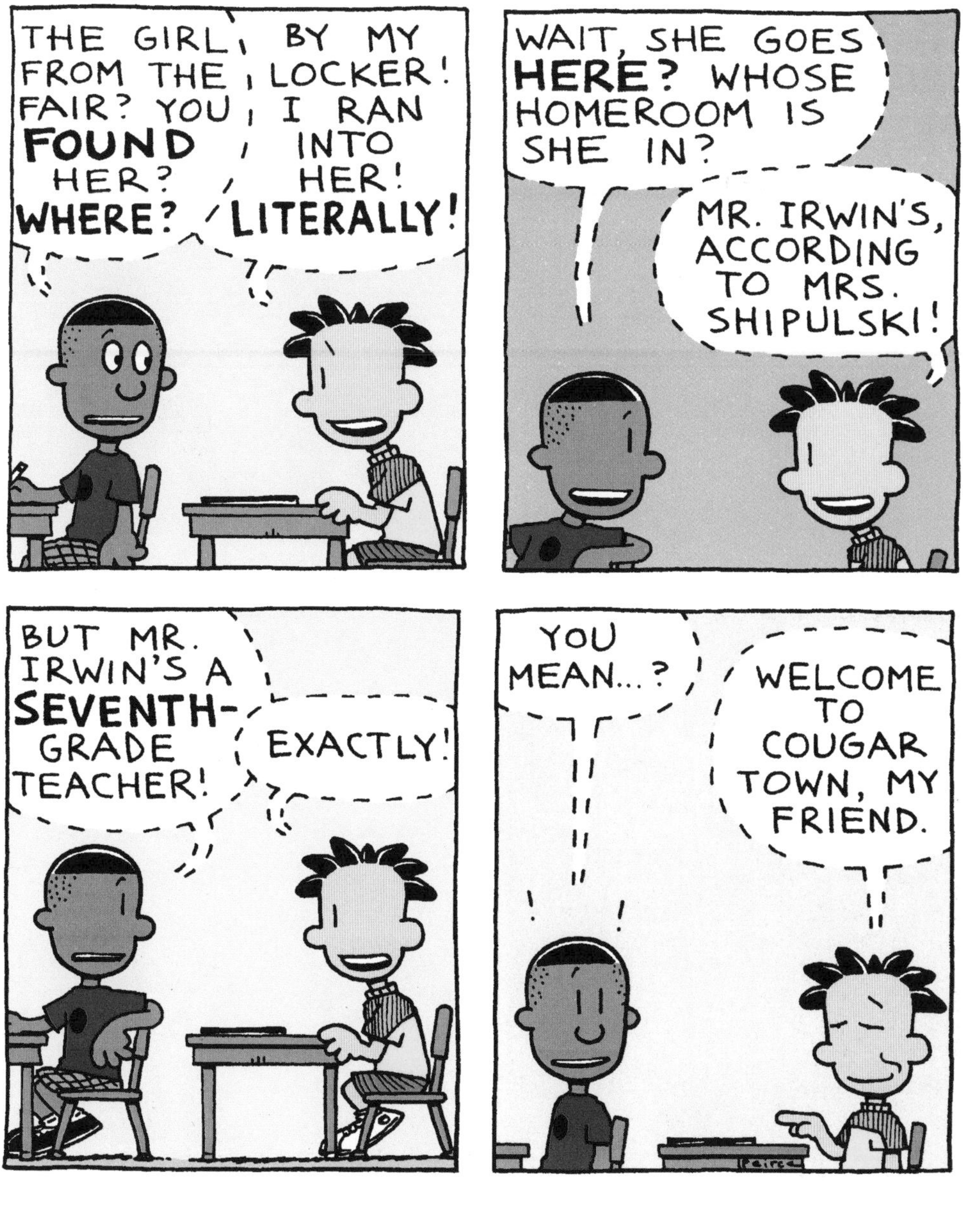
THE GIRL FROM THE FAIR? YOU FOUND HER? WHERE?
BY MY LOCKER! I RAN INTO HER! LITERALLY!
WAIT, SHE GOES HERE? WHOSE HOMEROOM IS SHE IN?
MR. IRWIN'S, ACCORDING TO MRS. SHIPULSKI!
BUT MR. IRWIN'S A SEVENTH-GRADE TEACHER!
EXACTLY!
YOU MEAN...?
WELCOME TO COUGAR TOWN, MY FRIEND.
!
!

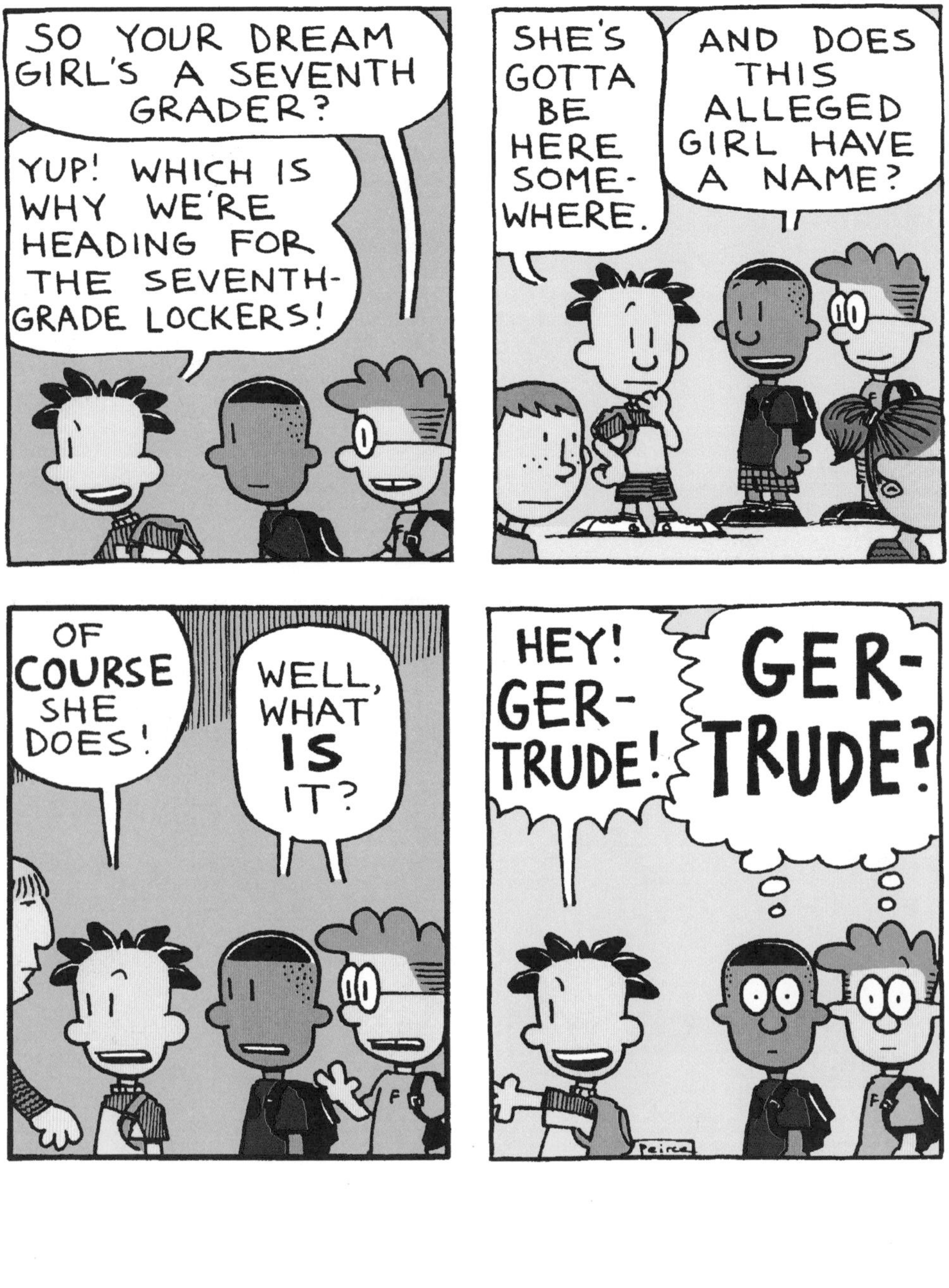

SO YOUR DREAM GIRL'S A SEVENTH GRADER?
YUP! WHICH IS WHY WE'RE HEADING FOR THE SEVENTH-GRADE LOCKERS!
SHE'S GOTTA BE HERE SOME-WHERE.
AND DOES THIS ALLEGED GIRL HAVE A NAME?
OF **COURSE** SHE DOES!
WELL, WHAT **IS** IT?
HEY! GER-TRUDE!
GER-TRUDE?
Peirce

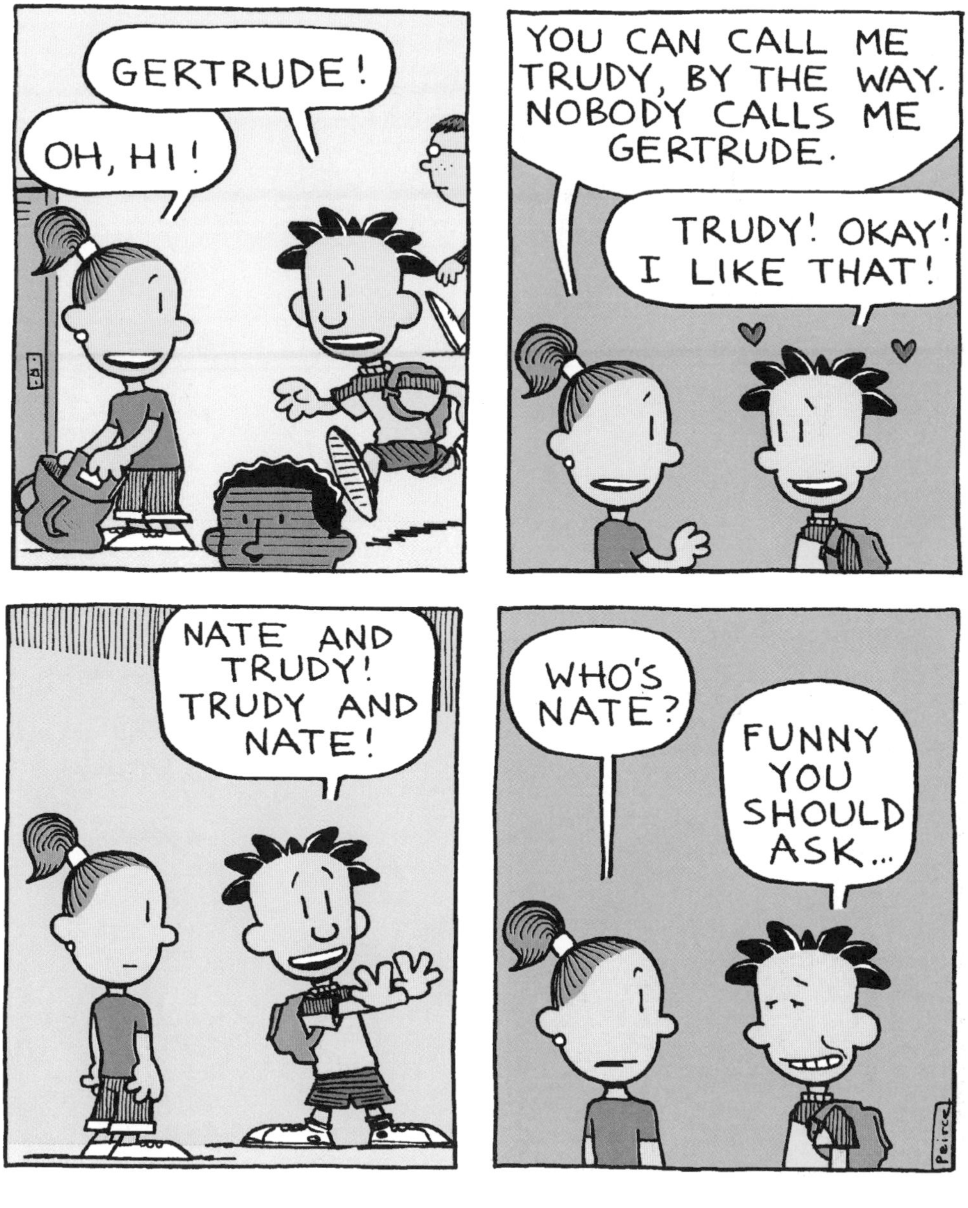
GERTRUDE!
OH, HI!
YOU CAN CALL ME TRUDY, BY THE WAY. NOBODY CALLS ME GERTRUDE.
TRUDY! OKAY! I LIKE THAT!
NATE AND TRUDY! TRUDY AND NATE!
WHO'S NATE?
FUNNY YOU SHOULD ASK...
Peirce

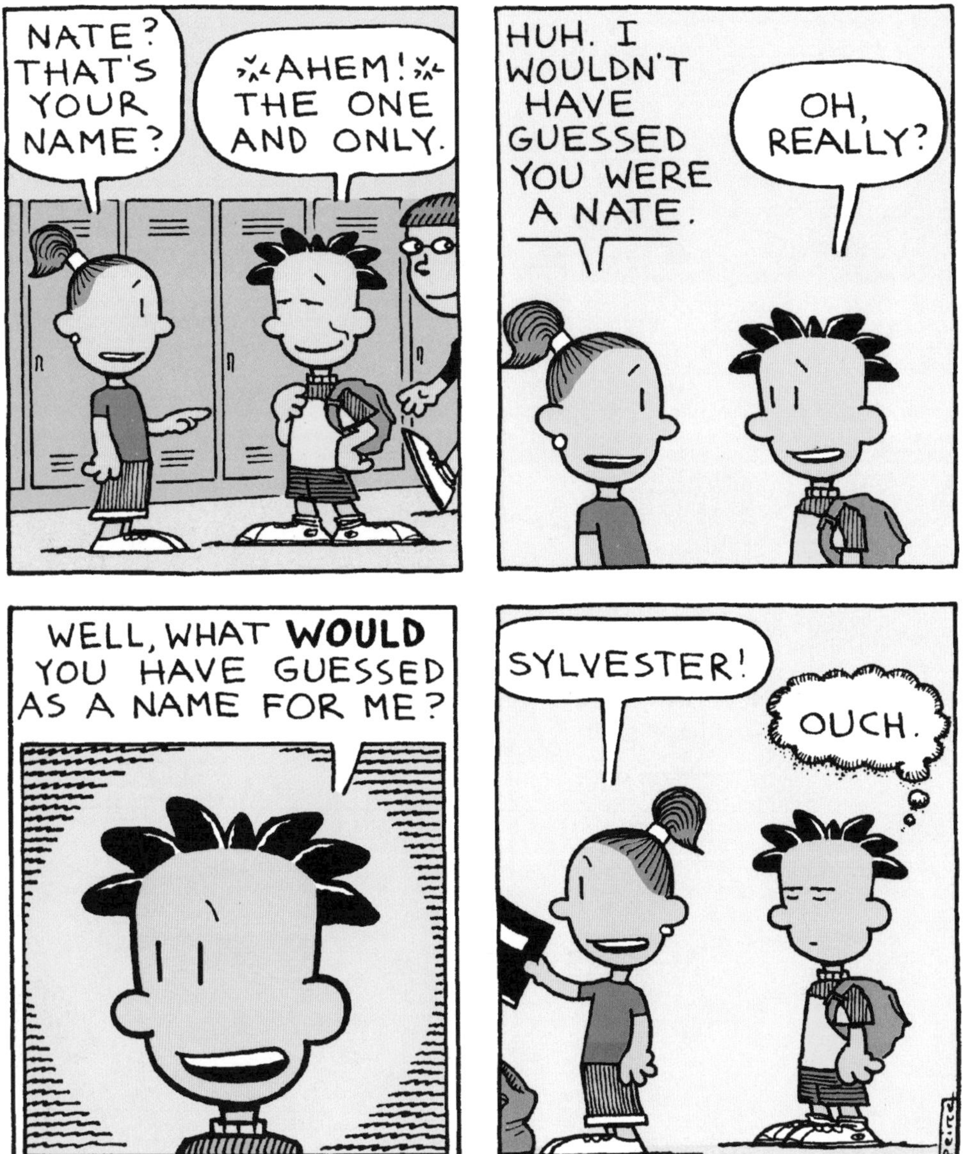
NATE? THAT'S YOUR NAME?
AHEM! THE ONE AND ONLY.
HUH. I WOULDN'T HAVE GUESSED YOU WERE A NATE.
OH, REALLY?
WELL, WHAT **WOULD** YOU HAVE GUESSED AS A NAME FOR ME?
SYLVESTER!
OUCH.
PEIRCE

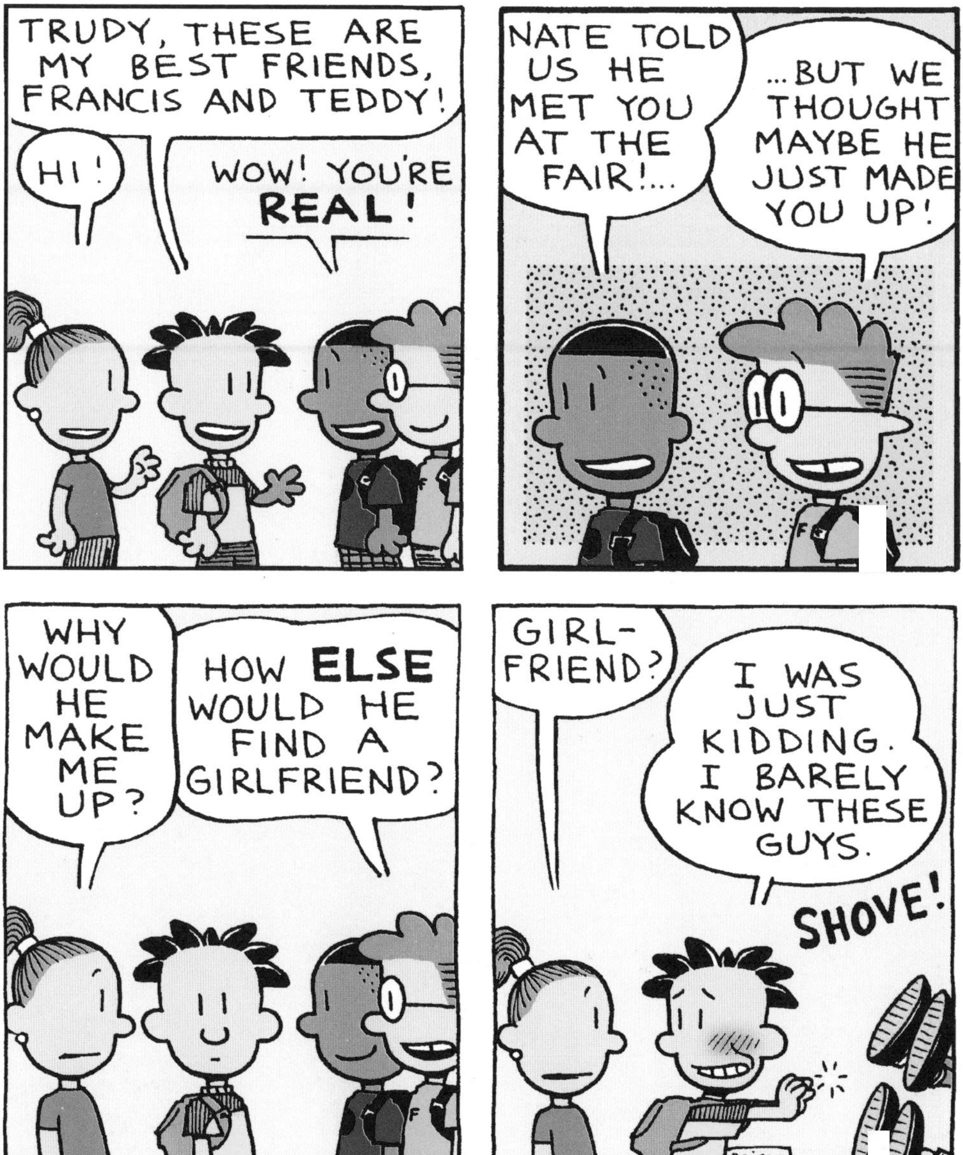
TRUDY, THESE ARE MY BEST FRIENDS, FRANCIS AND TEDDY!
HI!
WOW! YOU'RE **REAL**!
NATE TOLD US HE MET YOU AT THE FAIR!...
...BUT WE THOUGHT MAYBE HE JUST MADE YOU UP!
WHY WOULD HE MAKE ME UP?
HOW **ELSE** WOULD HE FIND A GIRLFRIEND?
GIRL-FRIEND?
I WAS JUST KIDDING. I BARELY KNOW THESE GUYS.
SHOVE!
Peirce

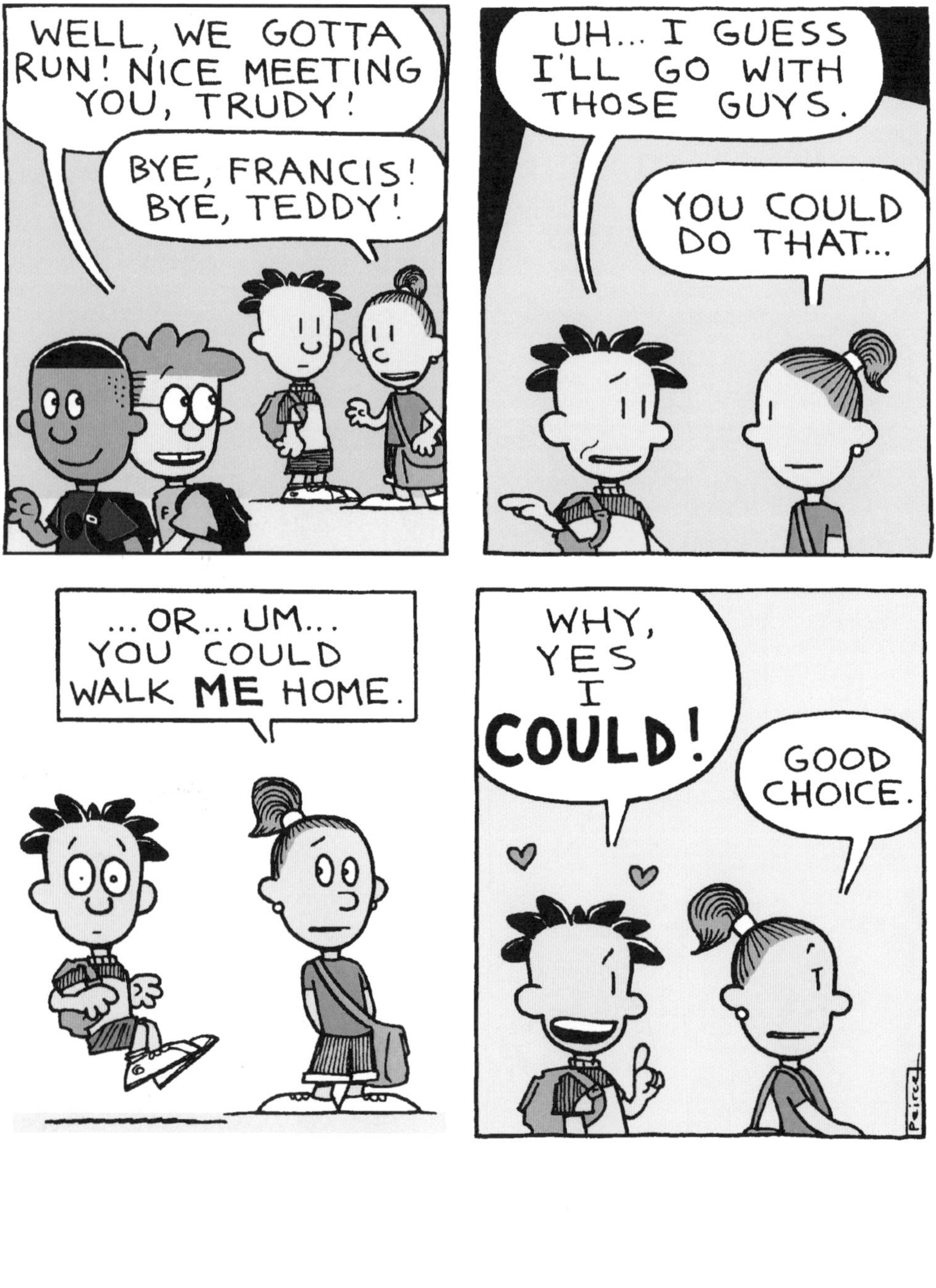
WELL, WE GOTTA RUN! NICE MEETING YOU, TRUDY!
BYE, FRANCIS! BYE, TEDDY!
UH... I GUESS I'LL GO WITH THOSE GUYS.
YOU COULD DO THAT...
...OR...UM... YOU COULD WALK **ME** HOME.
WHY, YES I **COULD!**
GOOD CHOICE.
Peirce

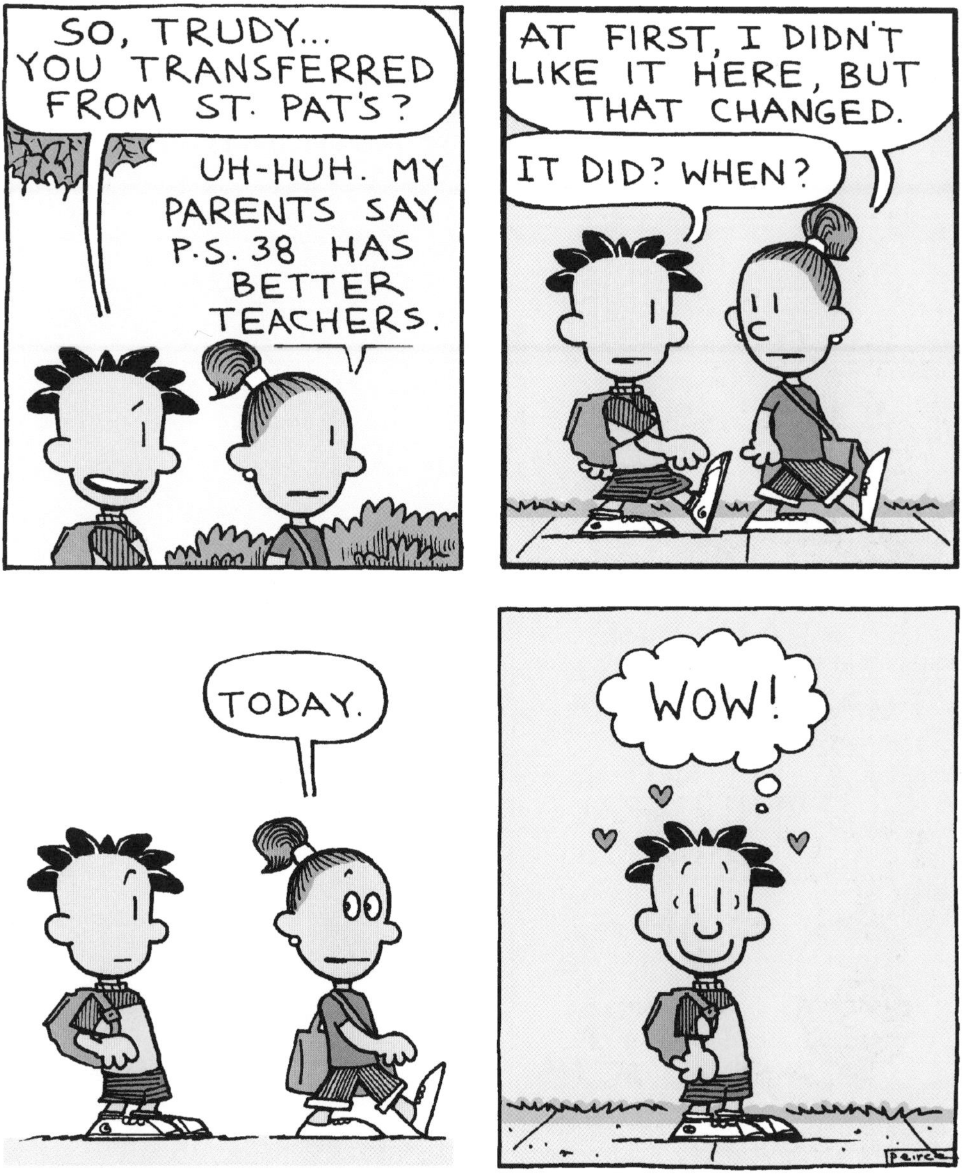
SO, TRUDY... YOU TRANSFERRED FROM ST. PAT'S?
UH-HUH. MY PARENTS SAY P.S. 38 HAS BETTER TEACHERS.
AT FIRST, I DIDN'T LIKE IT HERE, BUT THAT CHANGED.
IT DID? WHEN?
TODAY.
WOW!
peirce

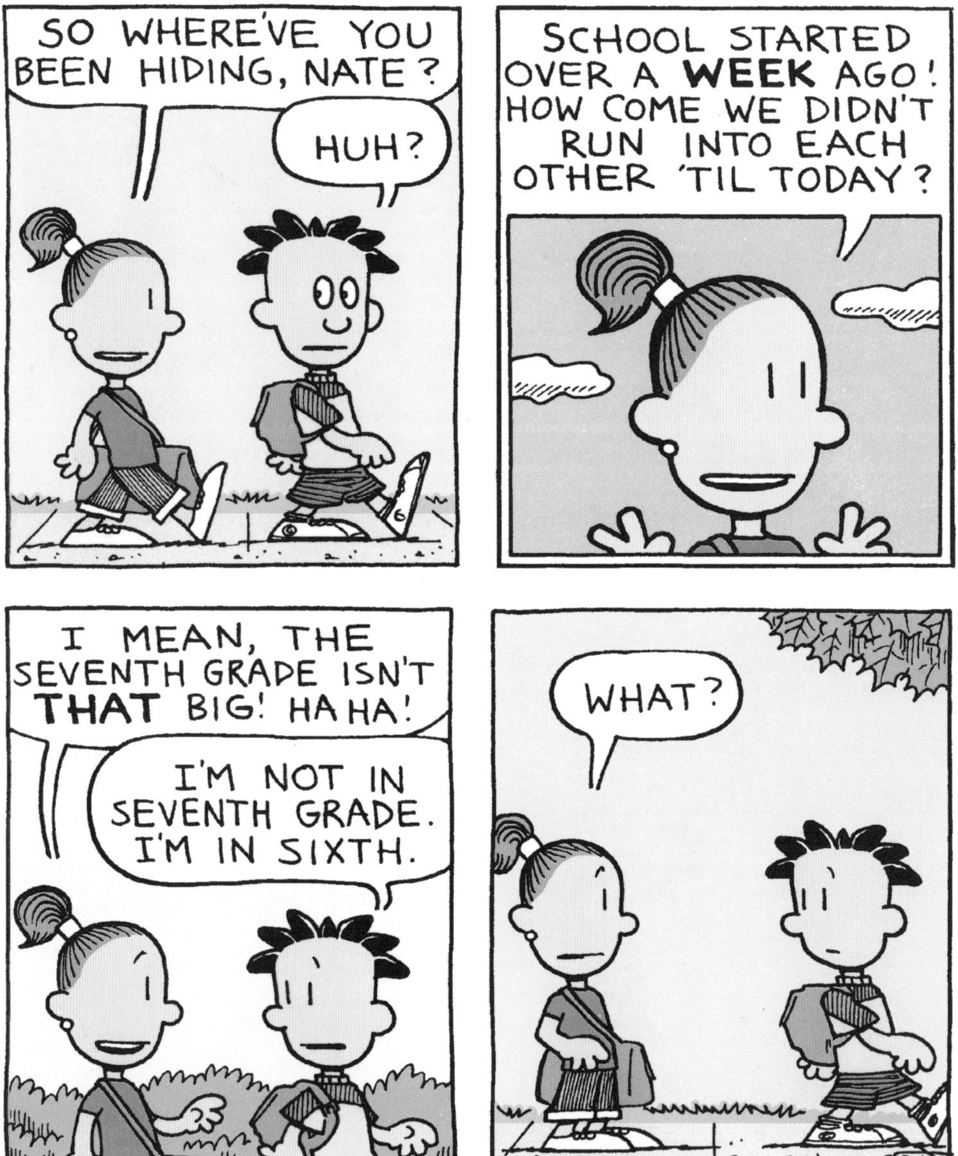
SO WHERE'VE YOU BEEN HIDING, NATE?
HUH?
SCHOOL STARTED OVER A **WEEK** AGO! HOW COME WE DIDN'T RUN INTO EACH OTHER 'TIL TODAY?
I MEAN, THE SEVENTH GRADE ISN'T **THAT** BIG! HA HA!
I'M NOT IN SEVENTH GRADE. I'M IN SIXTH.
WHAT?

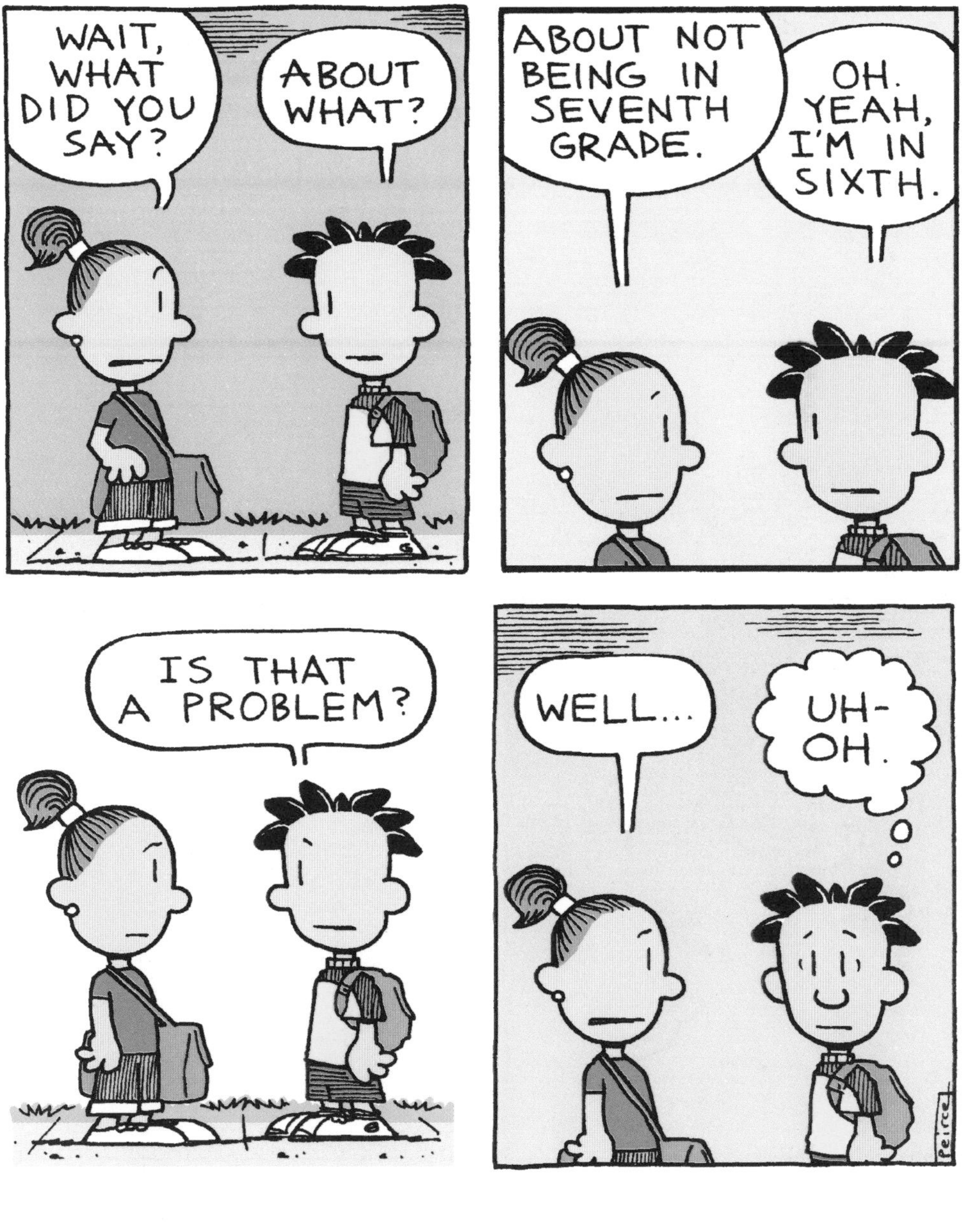
WAIT, WHAT DID YOU SAY?
ABOUT WHAT?
ABOUT NOT BEING IN SEVENTH GRADE.
OH. YEAH, I'M IN SIXTH.
IS THAT A PROBLEM?
WELL...
UH-OH.
Peirce

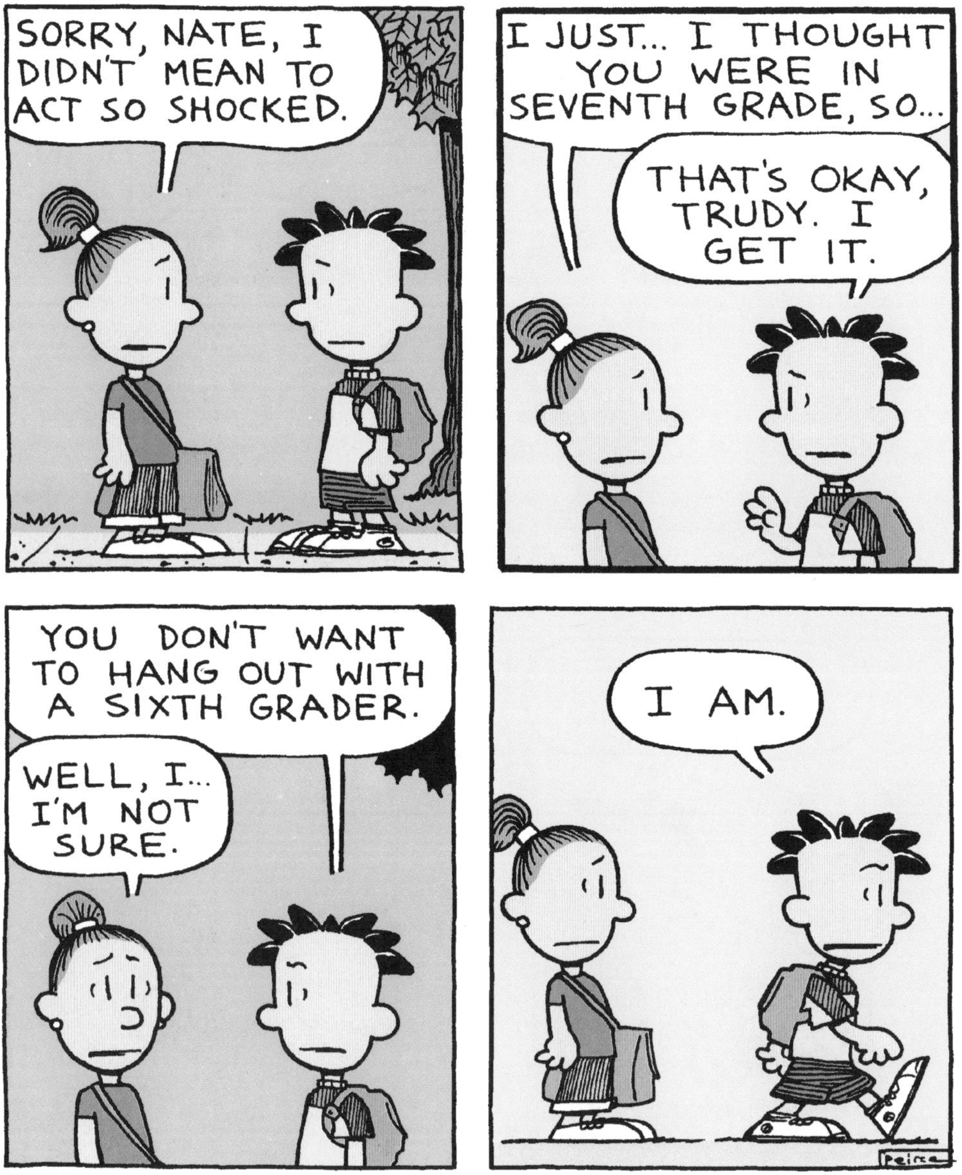
SORRY, NATE, I DIDN'T MEAN TO ACT SO SHOCKED.
I JUST... I THOUGHT YOU WERE IN SEVENTH GRADE, SO...
THAT'S OKAY, TRUDY. I GET IT.
YOU DON'T WANT TO HANG OUT WITH A SIXTH GRADER.
WELL, I... I'M NOT SURE.
I AM.

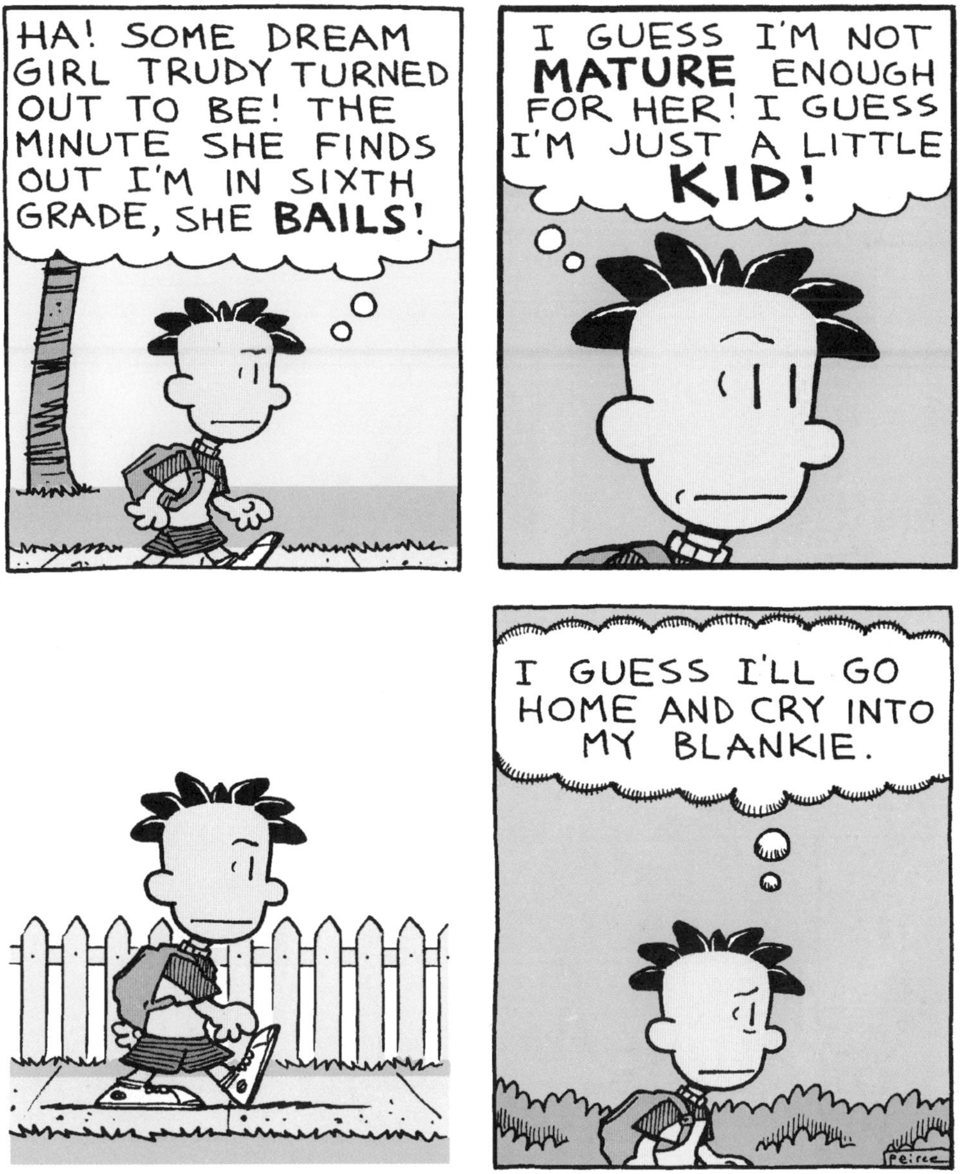
HA! SOME DREAM GIRL TRUDY TURNED OUT TO BE! THE MINUTE SHE FINDS OUT I'M IN SIXTH GRADE, SHE **BAILS**!
I GUESS I'M NOT **MATURE** ENOUGH FOR HER! I GUESS I'M JUST A LITTLE **KID**!
I GUESS I'LL GO HOME AND CRY INTO MY BLANKIE.
peirce

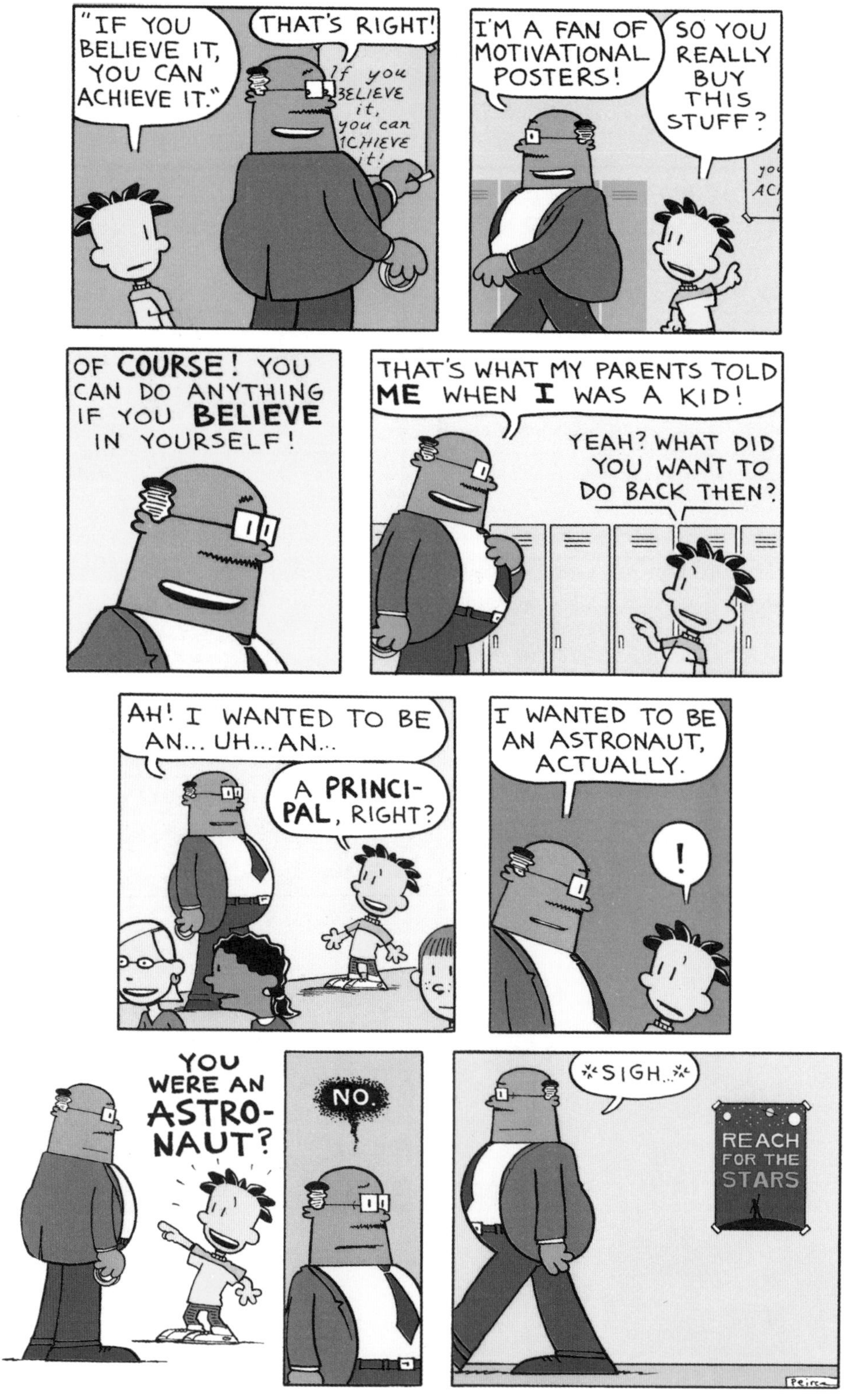
"IF YOU BELIEVE IT, YOU CAN ACHIEVE IT."
THAT'S RIGHT!
If you BELIEVE it, you can ACHIEVE it!
I'M A FAN OF MOTIVATIONAL POSTERS!
SO YOU REALLY BUY THIS STUFF?
OF COURSE! YOU CAN DO ANYTHING IF YOU BELIEVE IN YOURSELF!
THAT'S WHAT MY PARENTS TOLD ME WHEN I WAS A KID!
YEAH? WHAT DID YOU WANT TO DO BACK THEN?
AH! I WANTED TO BE AN... UH... AN...
A PRINCIPAL, RIGHT?
I WANTED TO BE AN ASTRONAUT, ACTUALLY.
!
YOU WERE AN ASTRONAUT?
NO.
SIGH...
REACH FOR THE STARS
Peirce

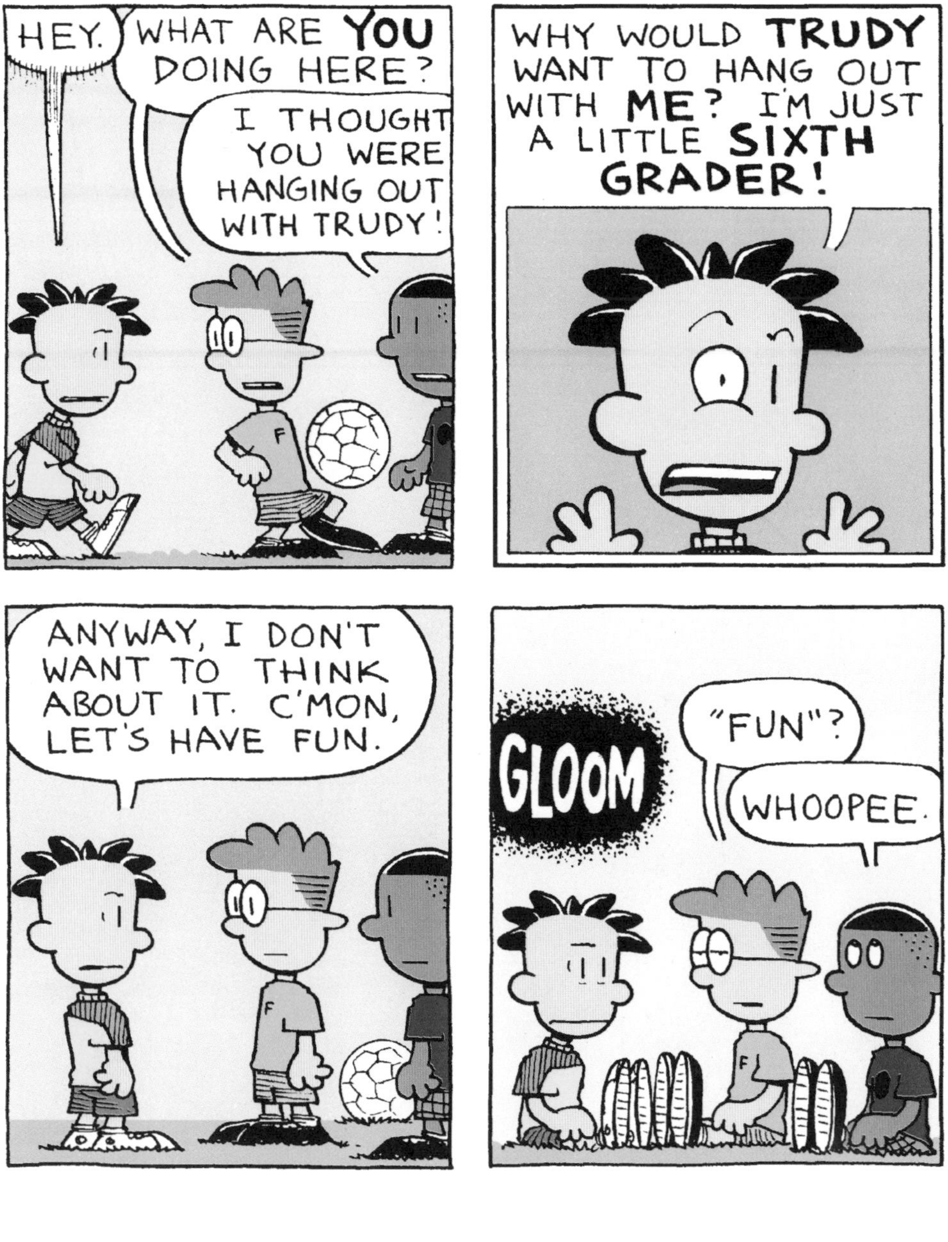
HEY.
WHAT ARE **YOU** DOING HERE?
I THOUGHT YOU WERE HANGING OUT WITH TRUDY!
WHY WOULD **TRUDY** WANT TO HANG OUT WITH **ME**? I'M JUST A LITTLE **SIXTH GRADER**!
ANYWAY, I DON'T WANT TO THINK ABOUT IT. C'MON, LET'S HAVE FUN.
GLOOM
"FUN"?
WHOOPEE.

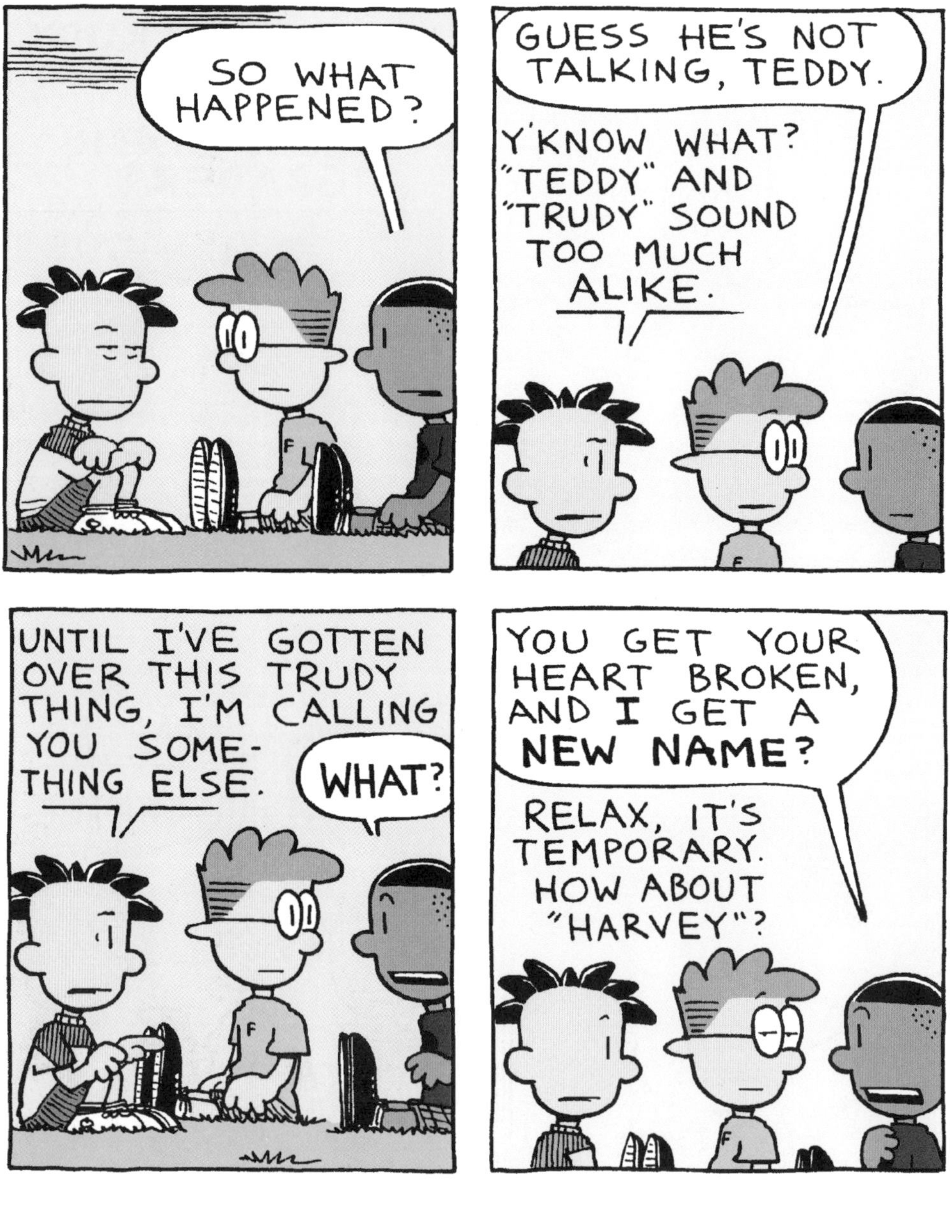
SO WHAT HAPPENED?
GUESS HE'S NOT TALKING, TEDDY.
Y'KNOW WHAT? "TEDDY" AND "TRUDY" SOUND TOO MUCH ALIKE.
UNTIL I'VE GOTTEN OVER THIS TRUDY THING, I'M CALLING YOU SOMETHING ELSE.
WHAT?
YOU GET YOUR HEART BROKEN, AND I GET A NEW NAME?
RELAX, IT'S TEMPORARY. HOW ABOUT "HARVEY"?

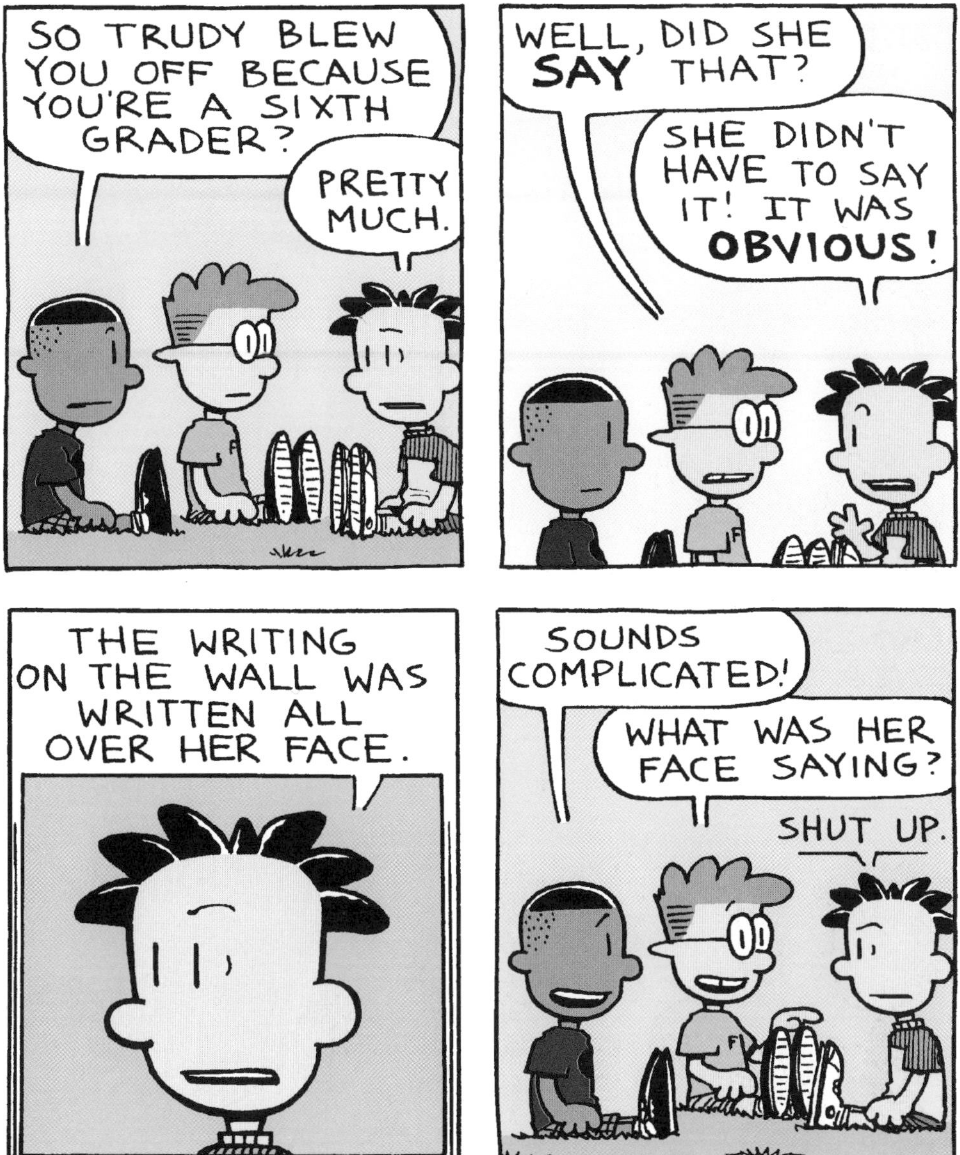
SO TRUDY BLEW YOU OFF BECAUSE YOU'RE A SIXTH GRADER?
PRETTY MUCH.
WELL, DID SHE **SAY** THAT?
SHE DIDN'T HAVE TO SAY IT! IT WAS **OBVIOUS**!
THE WRITING ON THE WALL WAS WRITTEN ALL OVER HER FACE.
SOUNDS COMPLICATED!
WHAT WAS HER FACE SAYING?
SHUT UP.

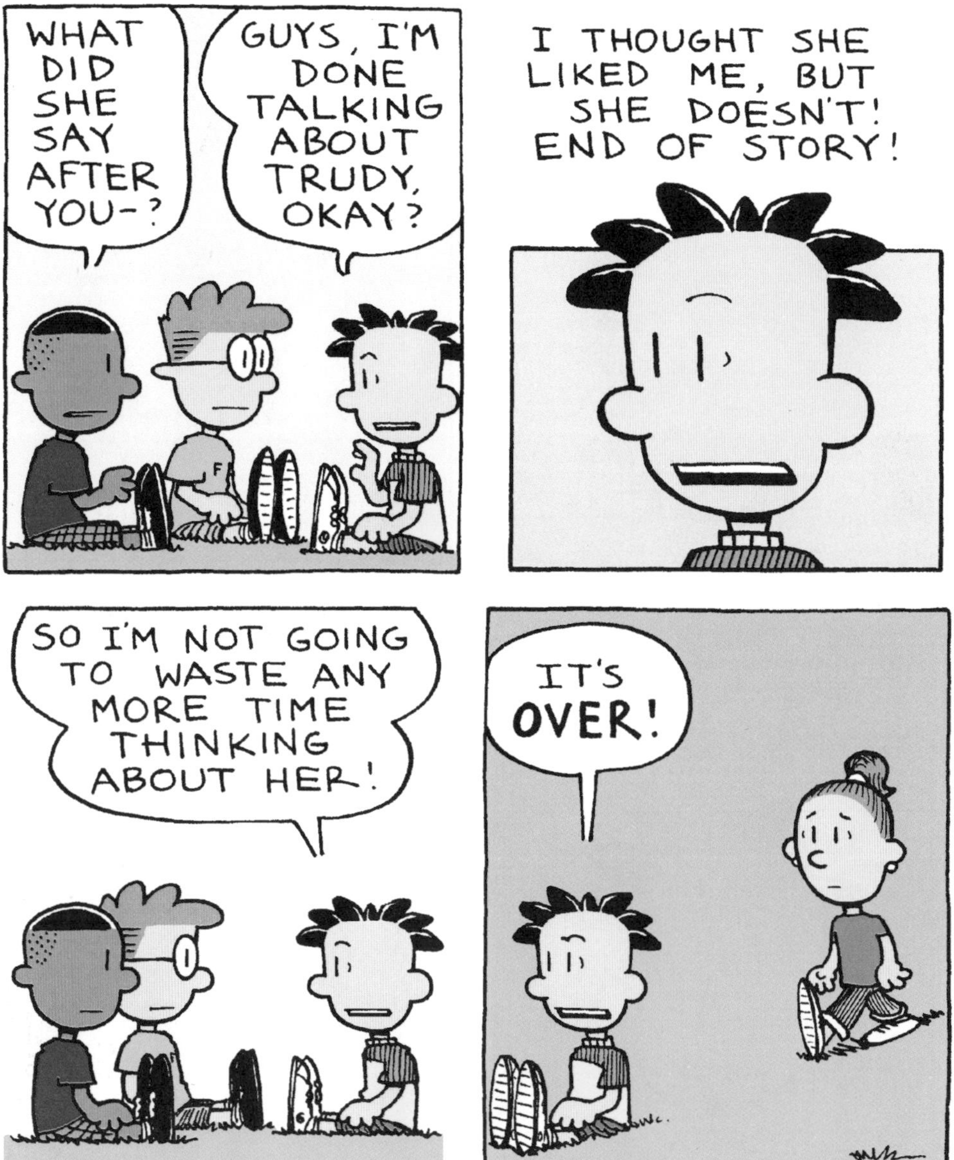
WHAT DID SHE SAY AFTER YOU-?
GUYS, I'M DONE TALKING ABOUT TRUDY, OKAY?
I THOUGHT SHE LIKED ME, BUT SHE DOESN'T! END OF STORY!
SO I'M NOT GOING TO WASTE ANY MORE TIME THINKING ABOUT HER!
IT'S **OVER!**

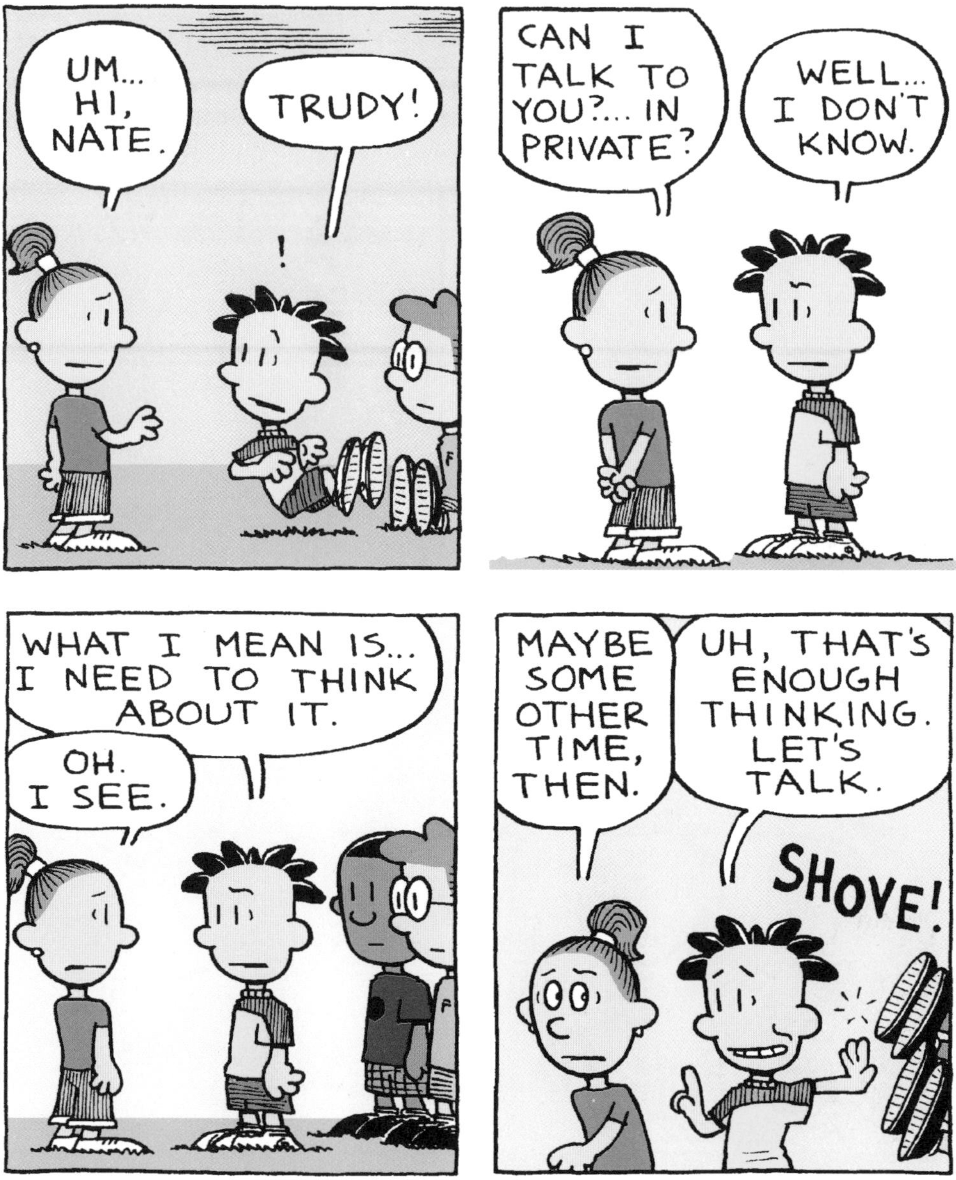
UM... HI, NATE.
TRUDY!
!
CAN I TALK TO YOU?... IN PRIVATE?
WELL... I DON'T KNOW.
WHAT I MEAN IS... I NEED TO THINK ABOUT IT.
OH. I SEE.
MAYBE SOME OTHER TIME, THEN.
UH, THAT'S ENOUGH THINKING. LET'S TALK.
SHOVE!

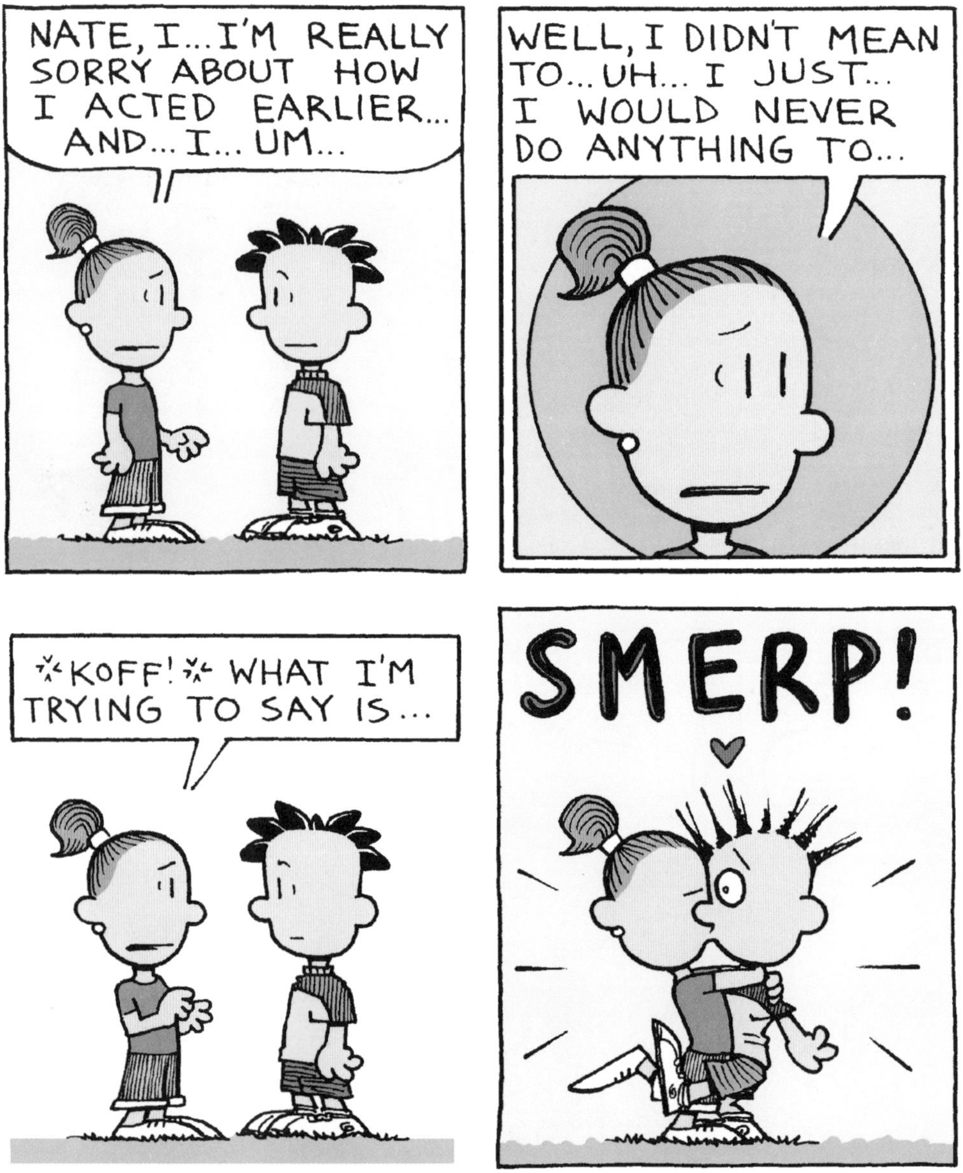
NATE, I... I'M REALLY SORRY ABOUT HOW I ACTED EARLIER... AND... I... UM...
WELL, I DIDN'T MEAN TO... UH... I JUST... I WOULD NEVER DO ANYTHING TO...
KOFF! WHAT I'M TRYING TO SAY IS...
SMERP!

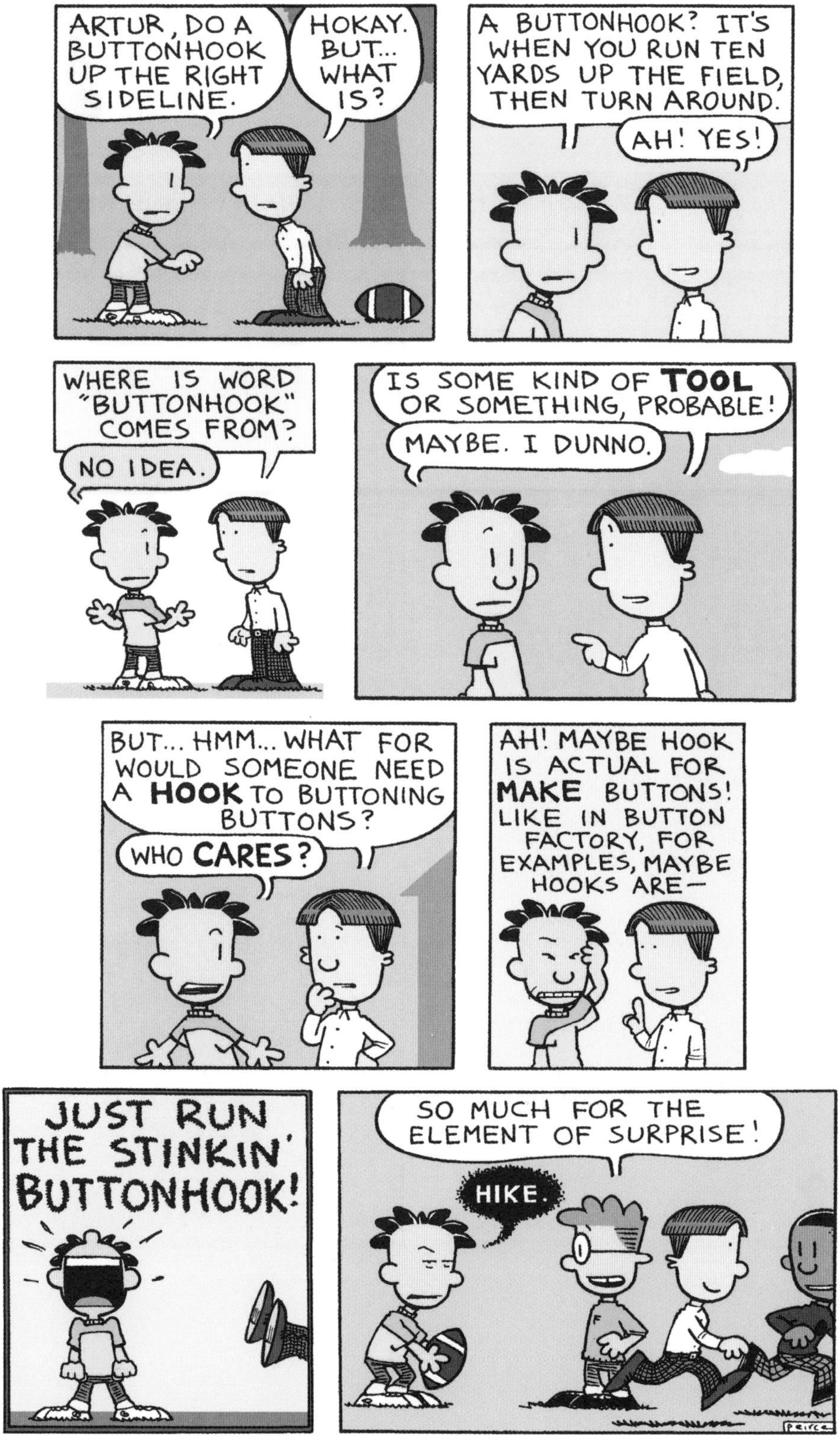
ARTUR, DO A BUTTONHOOK UP THE RIGHT SIDELINE.
HOKAY. BUT... WHAT IS?
A BUTTONHOOK? IT'S WHEN YOU RUN TEN YARDS UP THE FIELD, THEN TURN AROUND.
AH! YES!
WHERE IS WORD "BUTTONHOOK" COMES FROM?
NO IDEA.
IS SOME KIND OF TOOL OR SOMETHING, PROBABLE!
MAYBE. I DUNNO.
BUT... HMM... WHAT FOR WOULD SOMEONE NEED A HOOK TO BUTTONING BUTTONS?
WHO CARES?
AH! MAYBE HOOK IS ACTUAL FOR MAKE BUTTONS! LIKE IN BUTTON FACTORY, FOR EXAMPLES, MAYBE HOOKS ARE—
JUST RUN THE STINKIN' BUTTONHOOK!
SO MUCH FOR THE ELEMENT OF SURPRISE!
HIKE.
PEIRCE

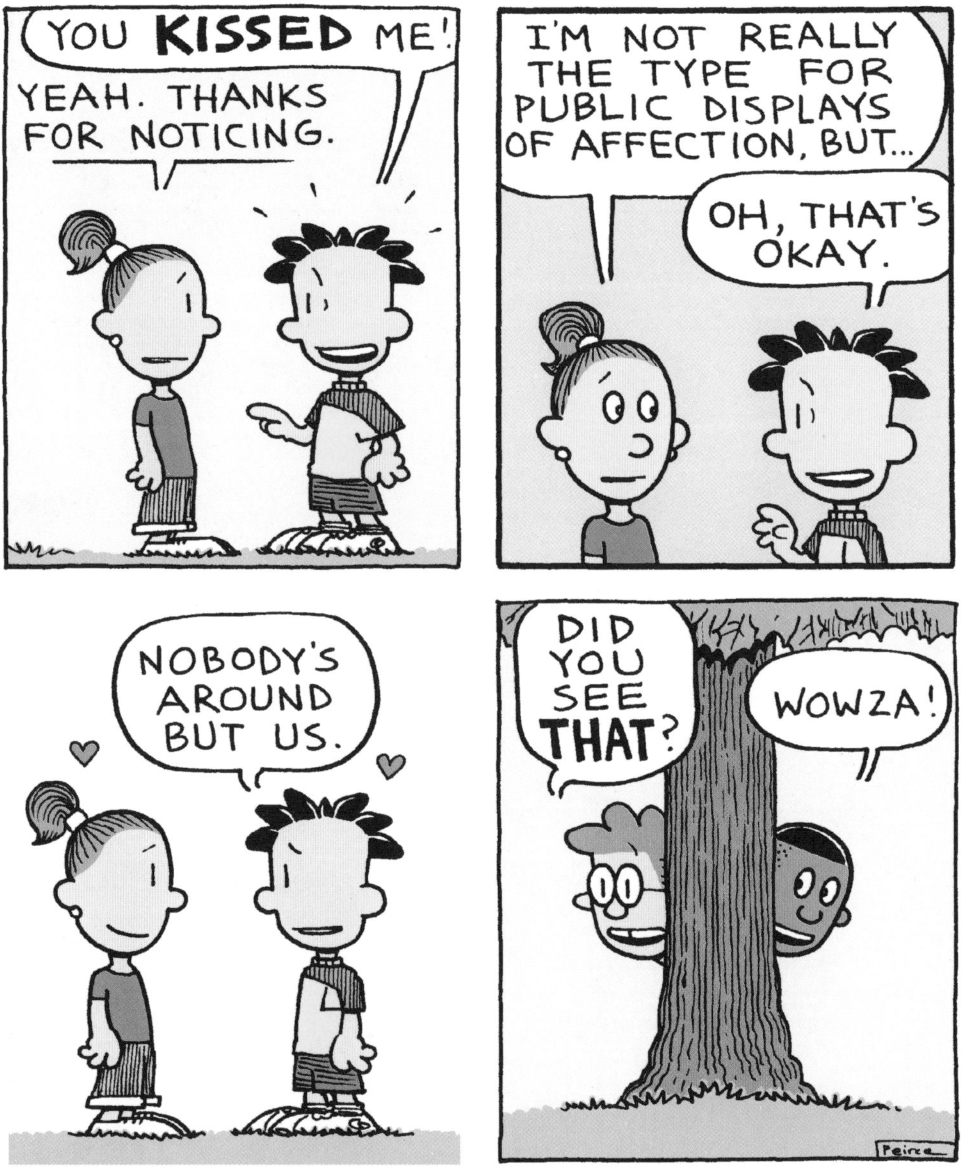
YOU KISSED ME!
YEAH. THANKS FOR NOTICING.
I'M NOT REALLY THE TYPE FOR PUBLIC DISPLAYS OF AFFECTION, BUT...
OH, THAT'S OKAY.
NOBODY'S AROUND BUT US.
DID YOU SEE THAT?
WOWZA!
Peirce

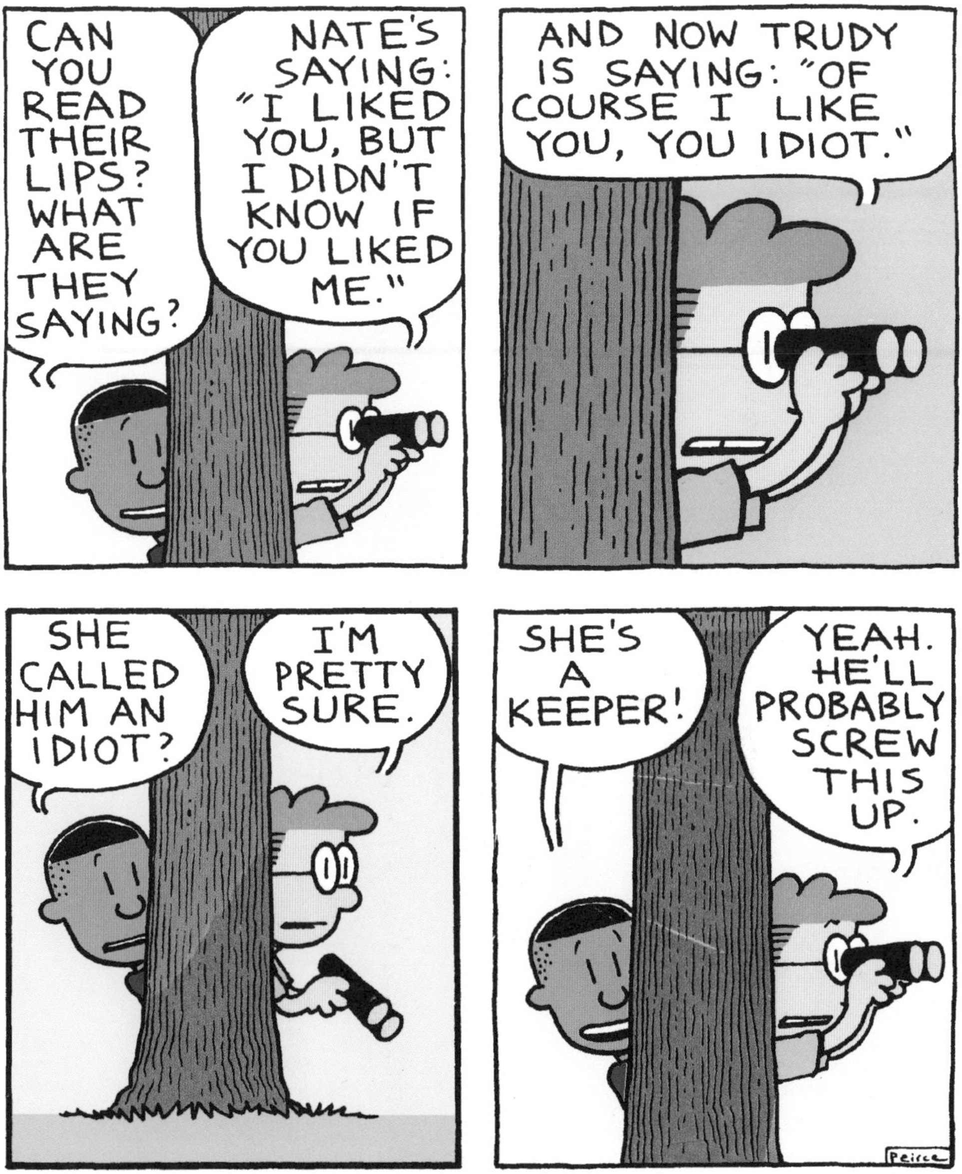
CAN YOU READ THEIR LIPS? WHAT ARE THEY SAYING?
NATE'S SAYING: "I LIKED YOU, BUT I DIDN'T KNOW IF YOU LIKED ME."
AND NOW TRUDY IS SAYING: "OF COURSE I LIKE YOU, YOU IDIOT."
SHE CALLED HIM AN IDIOT?
I'M PRETTY SURE.
SHE'S A KEEPER!
YEAH. HE'LL PROBABLY SCREW THIS UP.
Peirce

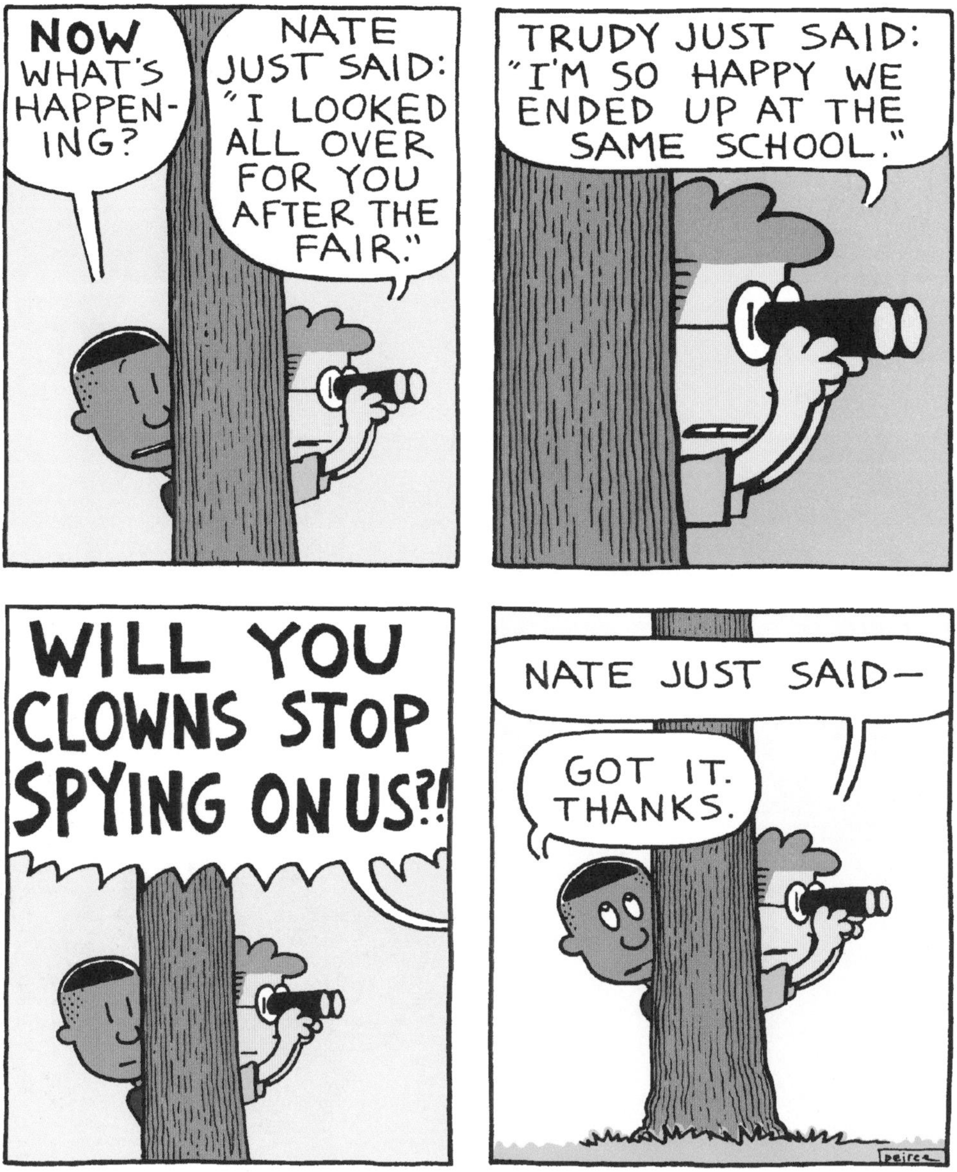
NOW WHAT'S HAPPEN-ING?
NATE JUST SAID: "I LOOKED ALL OVER FOR YOU AFTER THE FAIR."
TRUDY JUST SAID: "I'M SO HAPPY WE ENDED UP AT THE SAME SCHOOL."
WILL YOU CLOWNS STOP SPYING ON US?!
NATE JUST SAID—
GOT IT. THANKS.
peirce

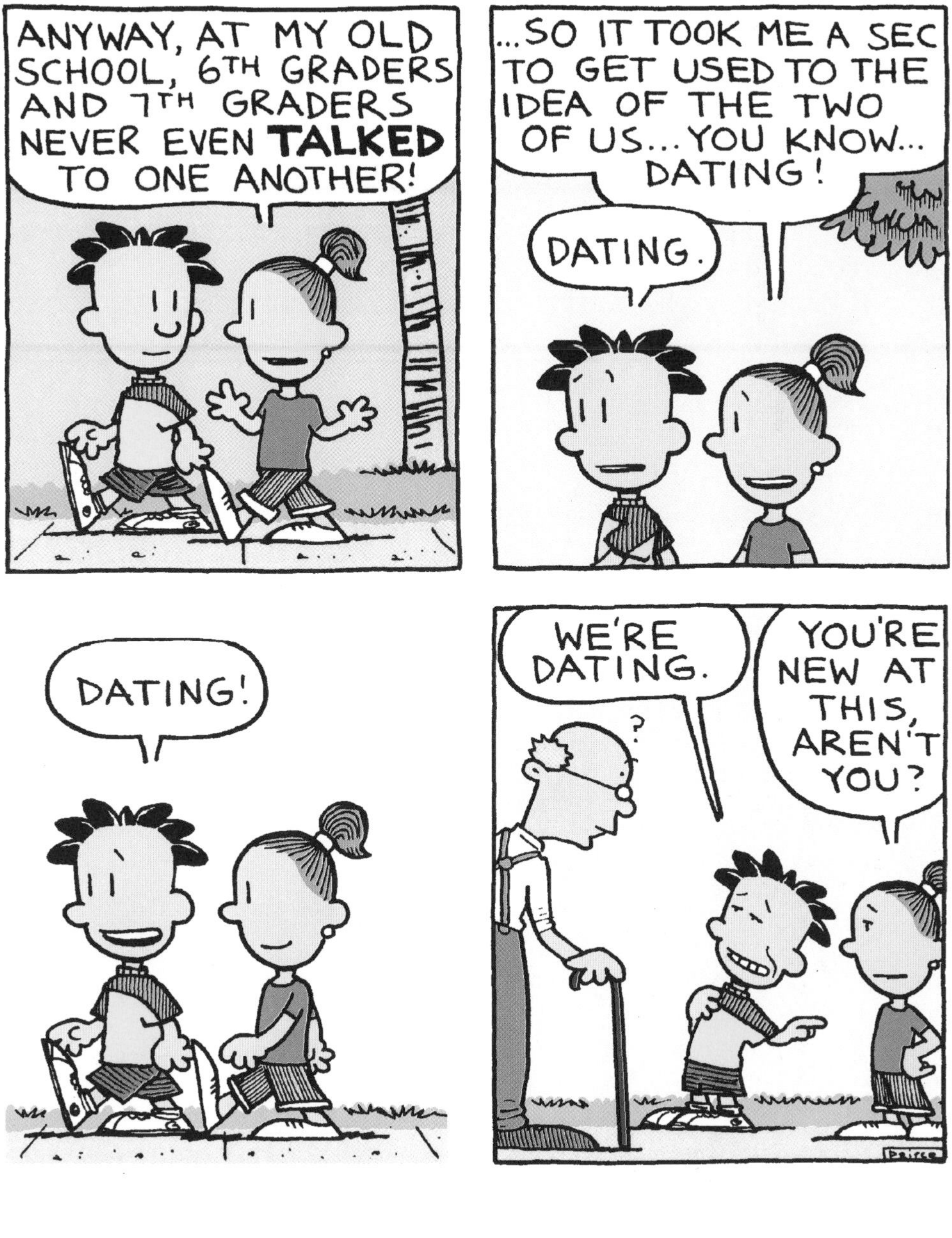
ANYWAY, AT MY OLD SCHOOL, 6TH GRADERS AND 7TH GRADERS NEVER EVEN **TALKED** TO ONE ANOTHER!
...SO IT TOOK ME A SEC TO GET USED TO THE IDEA OF THE TWO OF US... YOU KNOW... DATING!
DATING.
DATING!
WE'RE DATING.
YOU'RE NEW AT THIS, AREN'T YOU?
?
Peirce

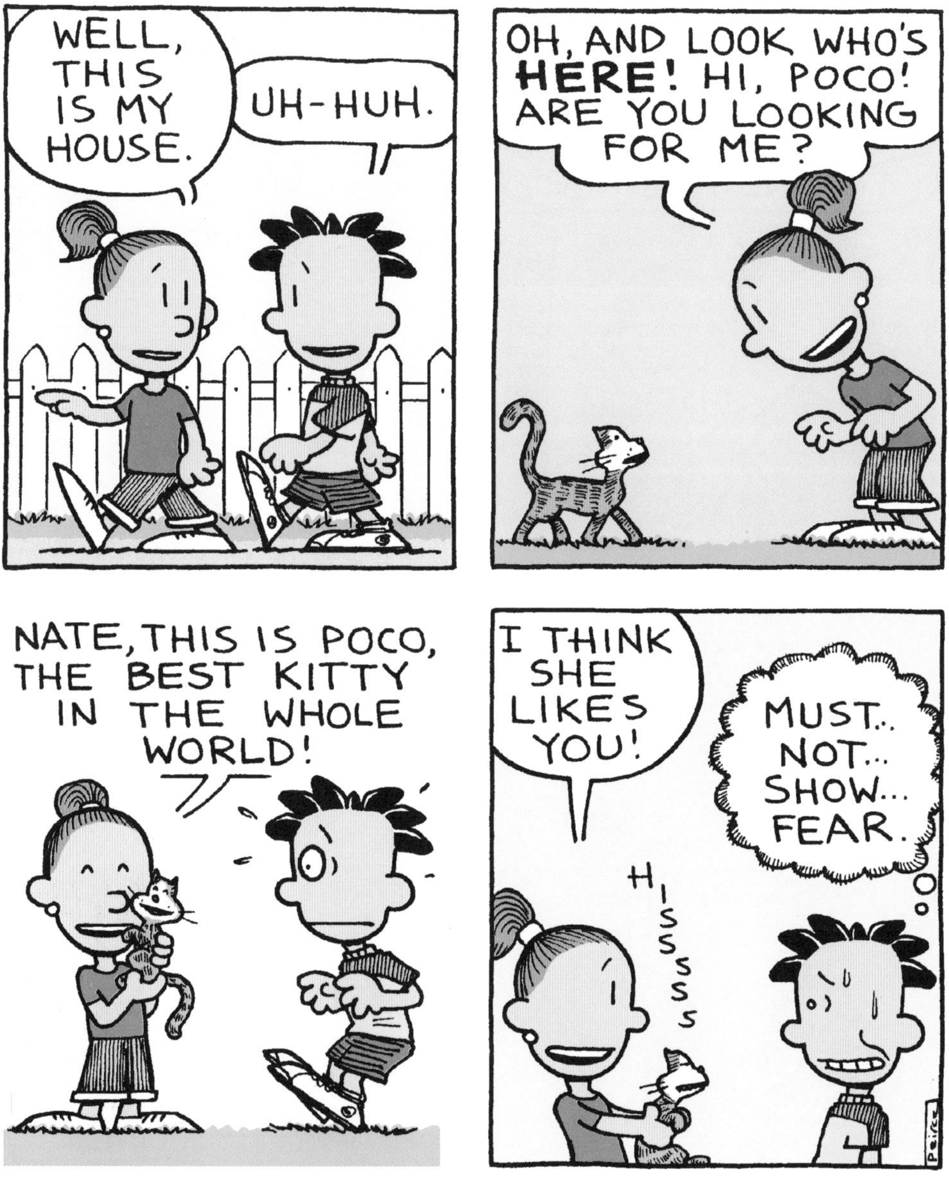
WELL, THIS IS MY HOUSE.
UH-HUH.
OH, AND LOOK WHO'S **HERE!** HI, POCO! ARE YOU LOOKING FOR ME?
NATE, THIS IS POCO, THE BEST KITTY IN THE WHOLE WORLD!
I THINK SHE LIKES YOU!
MUST... NOT... SHOW... FEAR.
HISSSSS

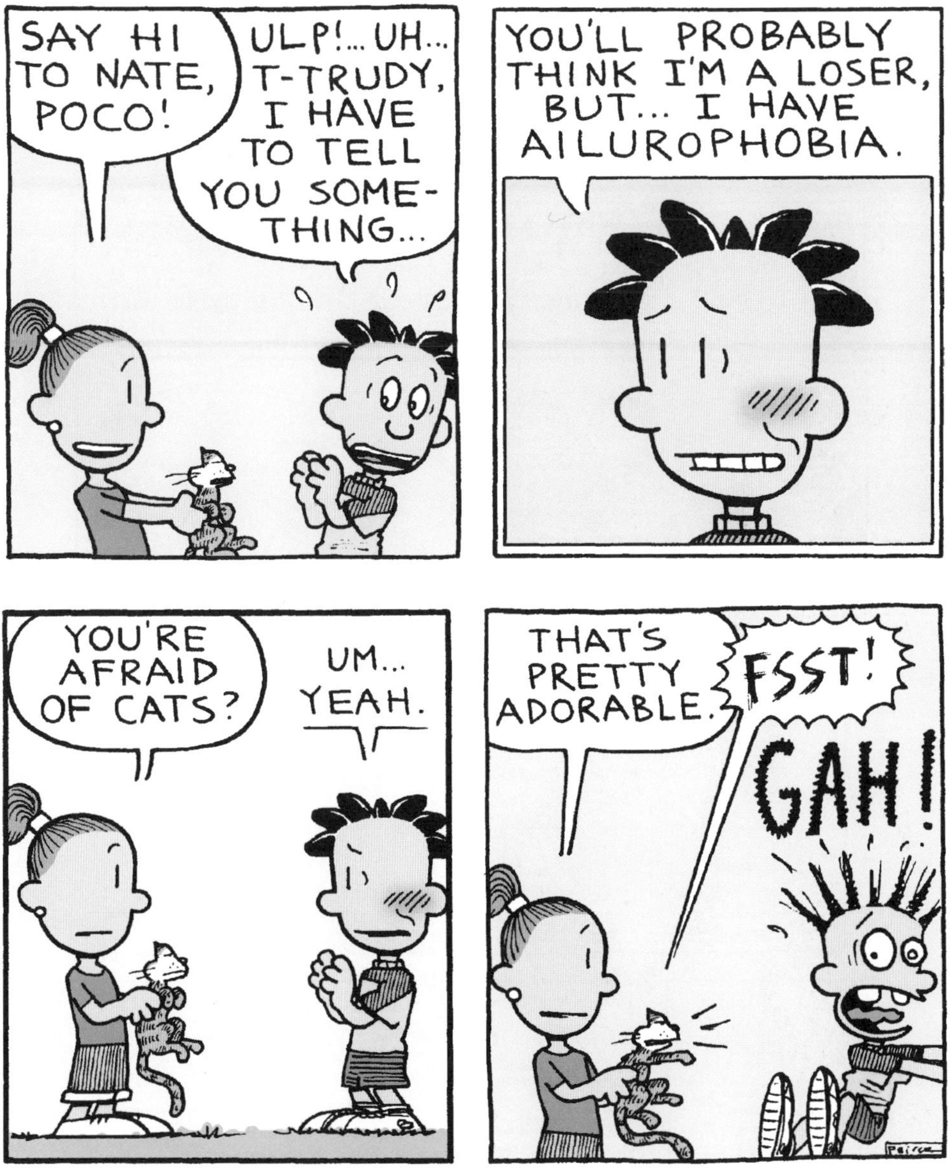
SAY HI TO NATE, POCO!
ULP!... UH... T-TRUDY, I HAVE TO TELL YOU SOME-THING...
YOU'LL PROBABLY THINK I'M A LOSER, BUT... I HAVE AILUROPHOBIA.
YOU'RE AFRAID OF CATS?
UM... YEAH.
THAT'S PRETTY ADORABLE.
FSST!
GAH!
Peirce

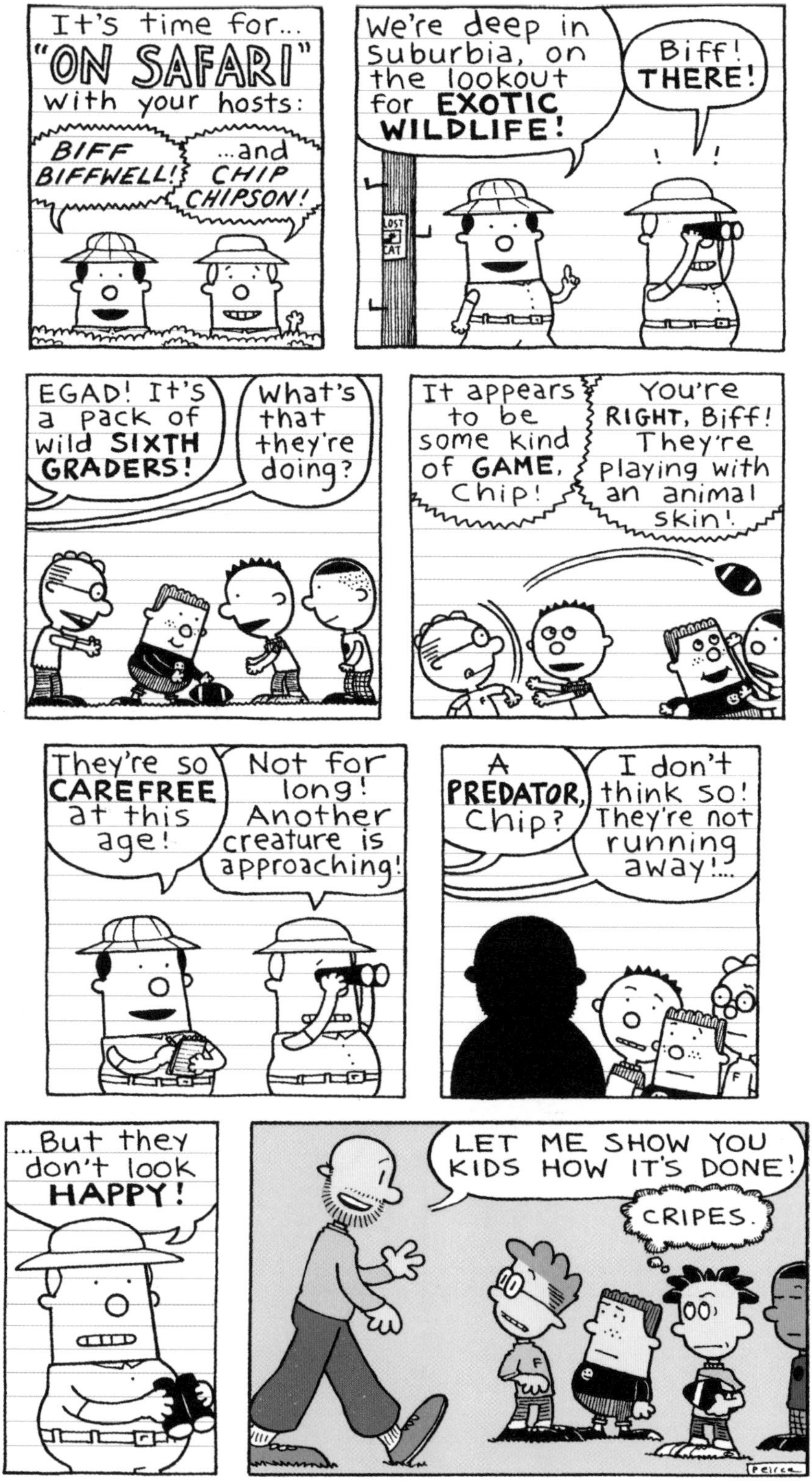
It's time for... "ON SAFARI" with your hosts:
BIFF BIFFWELL!
...and CHIP CHIPSON!
We're deep in suburbia, on the lookout for EXOTIC WILDLIFE!
Biff! THERE!
! !
LOST CAT
EGAD! It's a pack of wild SIXTH GRADERS!
What's that they're doing?
It appears to be some kind of GAME, Chip!
You're RIGHT, Biff! They're playing with an animal skin!
They're so CAREFREE at this age!
Not for long! Another creature is approaching!
A PREDATOR, Chip?
I don't think so! They're not running away!...
...But they don't look HAPPY!
LET ME SHOW YOU KIDS HOW IT'S DONE!
CRIPES.
Peirce

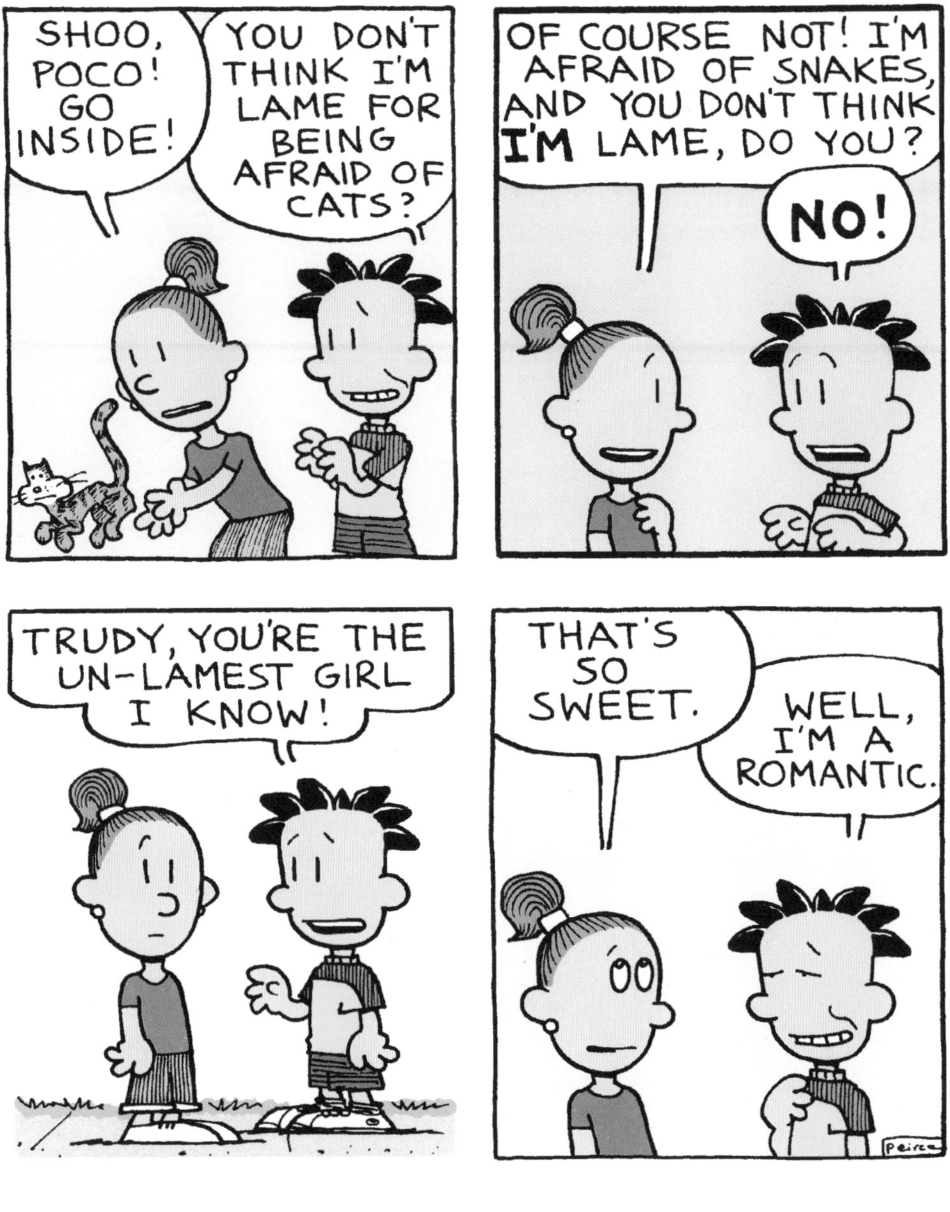
SHOO, POCO! GO INSIDE!
YOU DON'T THINK I'M LAME FOR BEING AFRAID OF CATS?
OF COURSE NOT! I'M AFRAID OF SNAKES, AND YOU DON'T THINK **I'M** LAME, DO YOU?
NO!
TRUDY, YOU'RE THE UN-LAMEST GIRL I KNOW!
THAT'S SO SWEET.
WELL, I'M A ROMANTIC.
Peirce

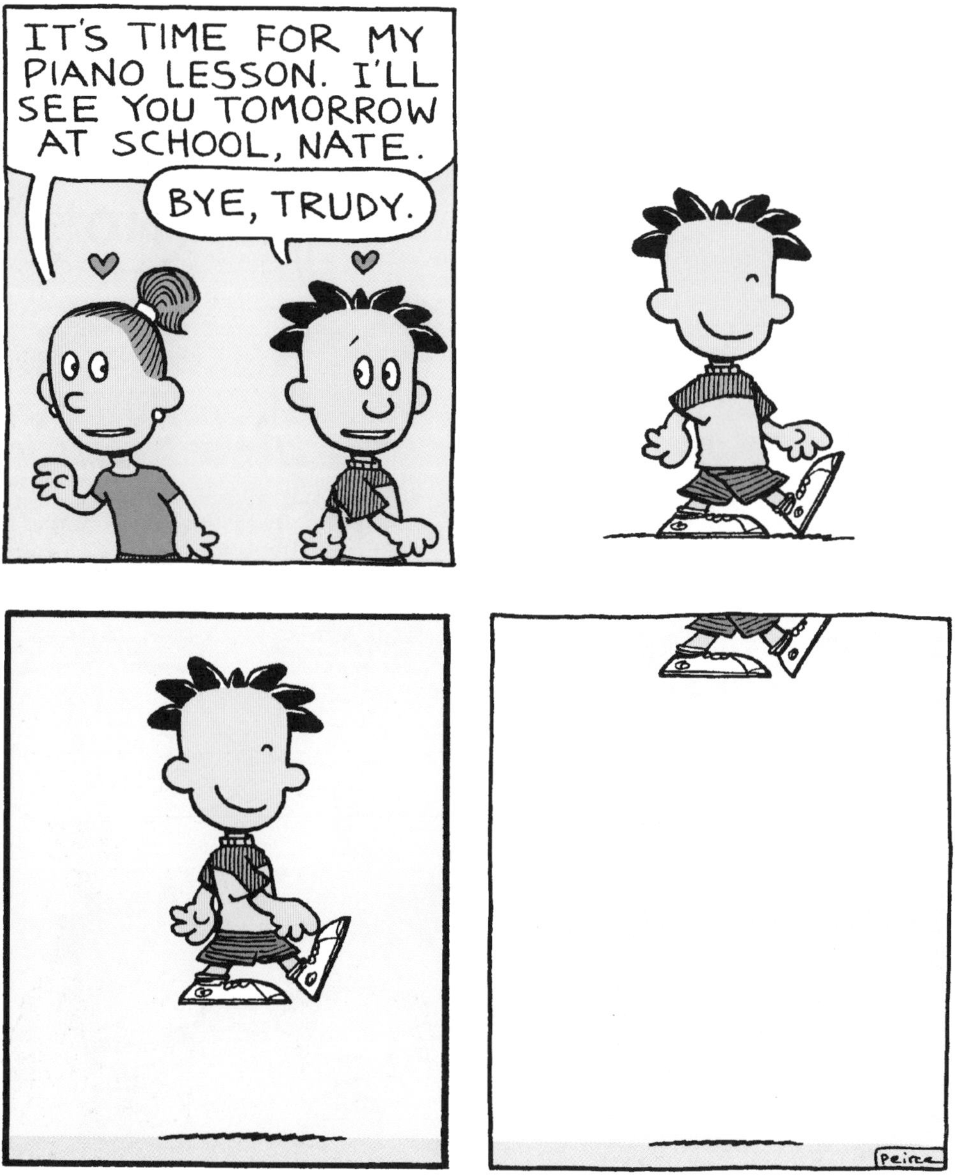
IT'S TIME FOR MY PIANO LESSON. I'LL SEE YOU TOMORROW AT SCHOOL, NATE.
BYE, TRUDY.
Peirce

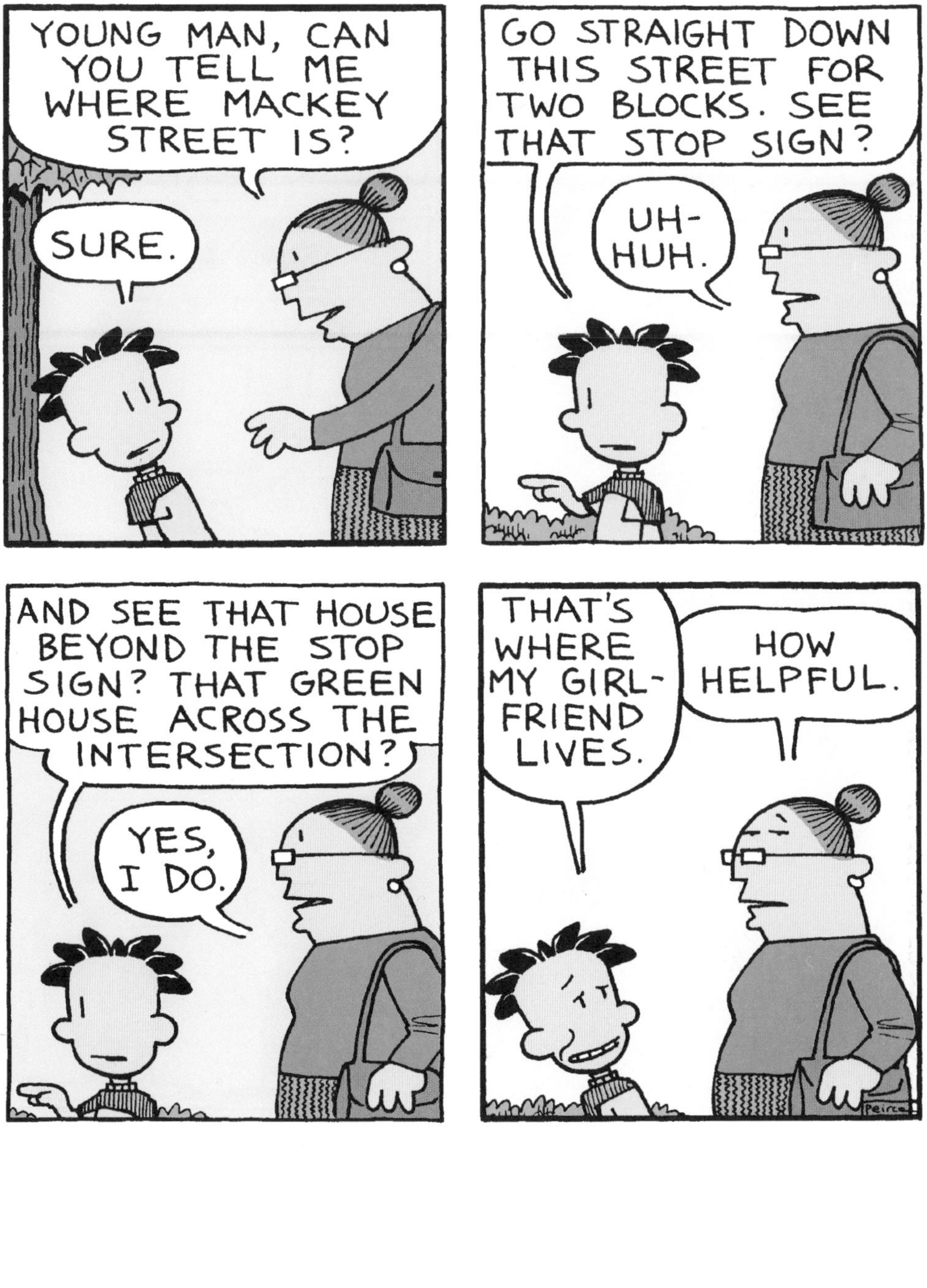
YOUNG MAN, CAN YOU TELL ME WHERE MACKEY STREET IS?
SURE.
GO STRAIGHT DOWN THIS STREET FOR TWO BLOCKS. SEE THAT STOP SIGN?
UH-HUH.
AND SEE THAT HOUSE BEYOND THE STOP SIGN? THAT GREEN HOUSE ACROSS THE INTERSECTION?
YES, I DO.
THAT'S WHERE MY GIRL-FRIEND LIVES.
HOW HELPFUL.
PEIRCE

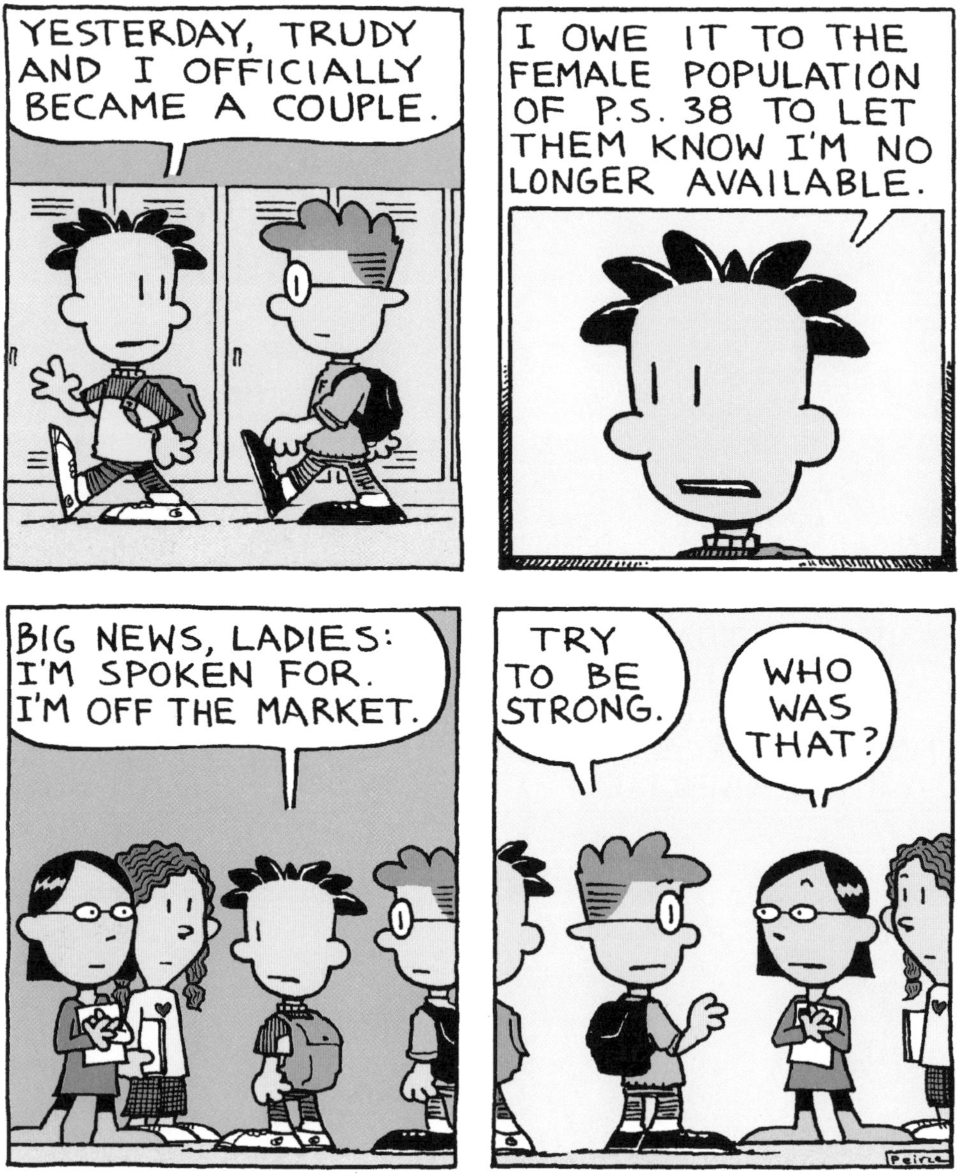
YESTERDAY, TRUDY AND I OFFICIALLY BECAME A COUPLE.
I OWE IT TO THE FEMALE POPULATION OF P.S. 38 TO LET THEM KNOW I'M NO LONGER AVAILABLE.
BIG NEWS, LADIES: I'M SPOKEN FOR. I'M OFF THE MARKET.
TRY TO BE STRONG.
WHO WAS THAT?
Peirce

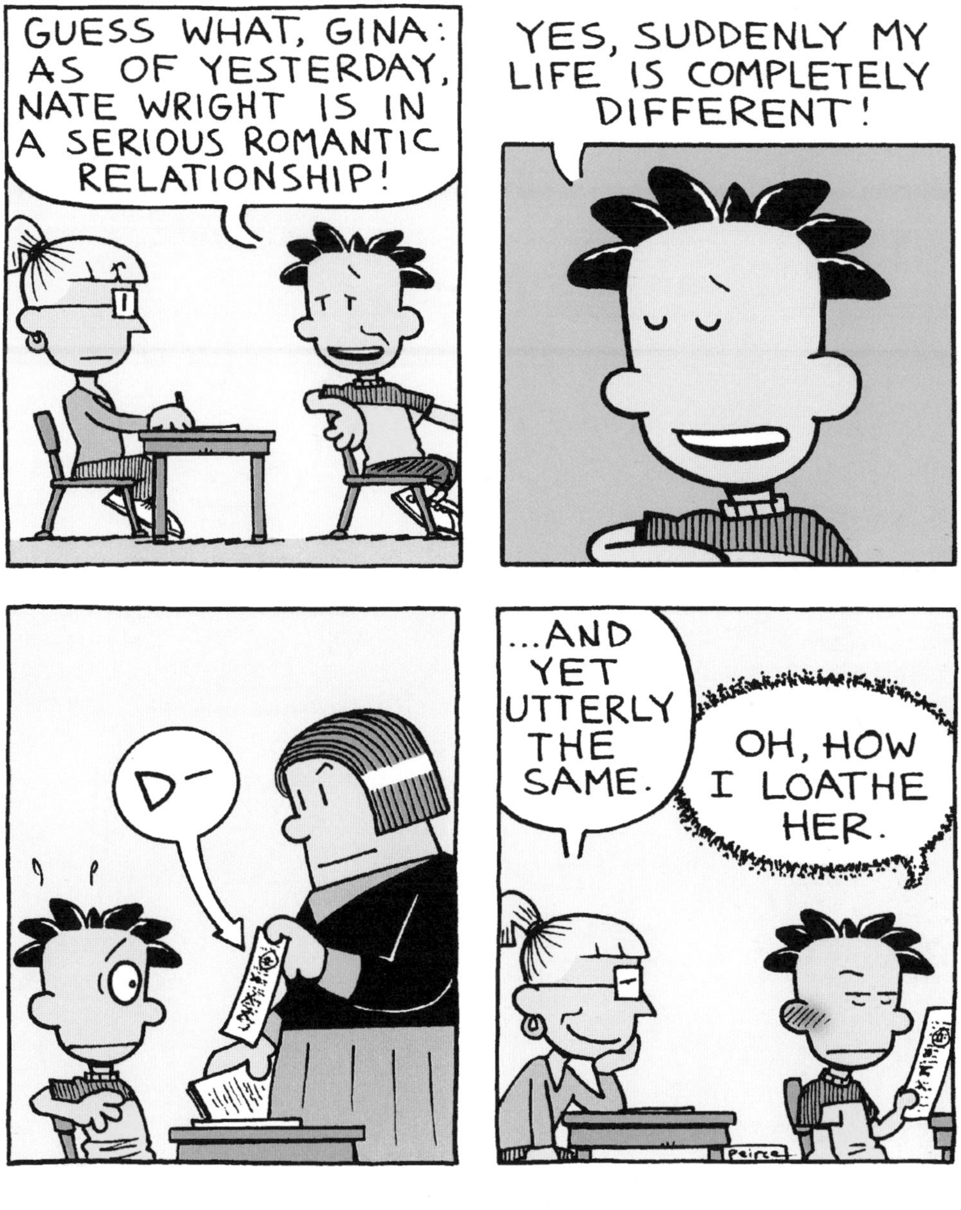
GUESS WHAT, GINA: AS OF YESTERDAY, NATE WRIGHT IS IN A SERIOUS ROMANTIC RELATIONSHIP!
YES, SUDDENLY MY LIFE IS COMPLETELY DIFFERENT!
D-
...AND YET UTTERLY THE SAME.
OH, HOW I LOATHE HER.
Peirce

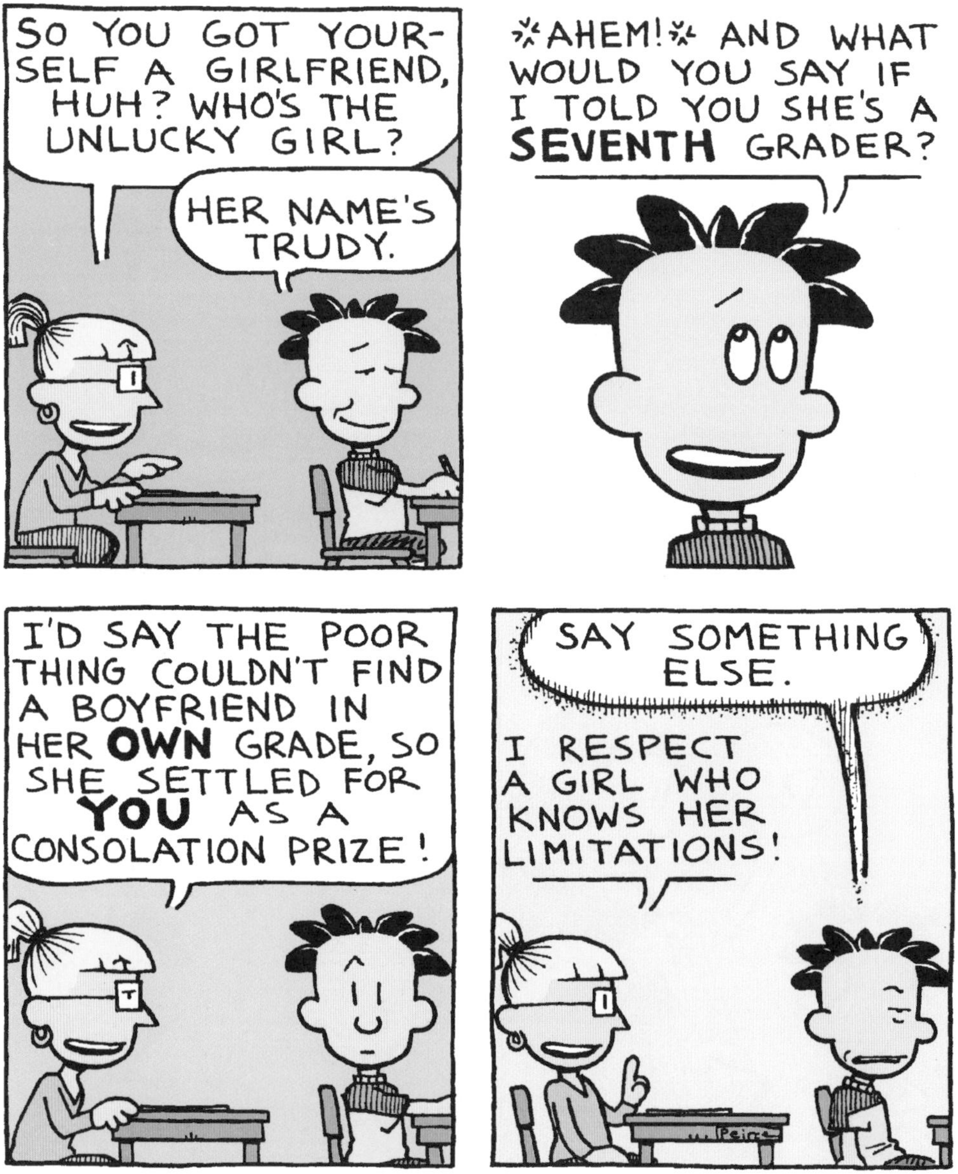
SO YOU GOT YOURSELF A GIRLFRIEND, HUH? WHO'S THE UNLUCKY GIRL?
HER NAME'S TRUDY.
AHEM! AND WHAT WOULD YOU SAY IF I TOLD YOU SHE'S A SEVENTH GRADER?
I'D SAY THE POOR THING COULDN'T FIND A BOYFRIEND IN HER OWN GRADE, SO SHE SETTLED FOR YOU AS A CONSOLATION PRIZE!
SAY SOMETHING ELSE.
I RESPECT A GIRL WHO KNOWS HER LIMITATIONS!
Peirce

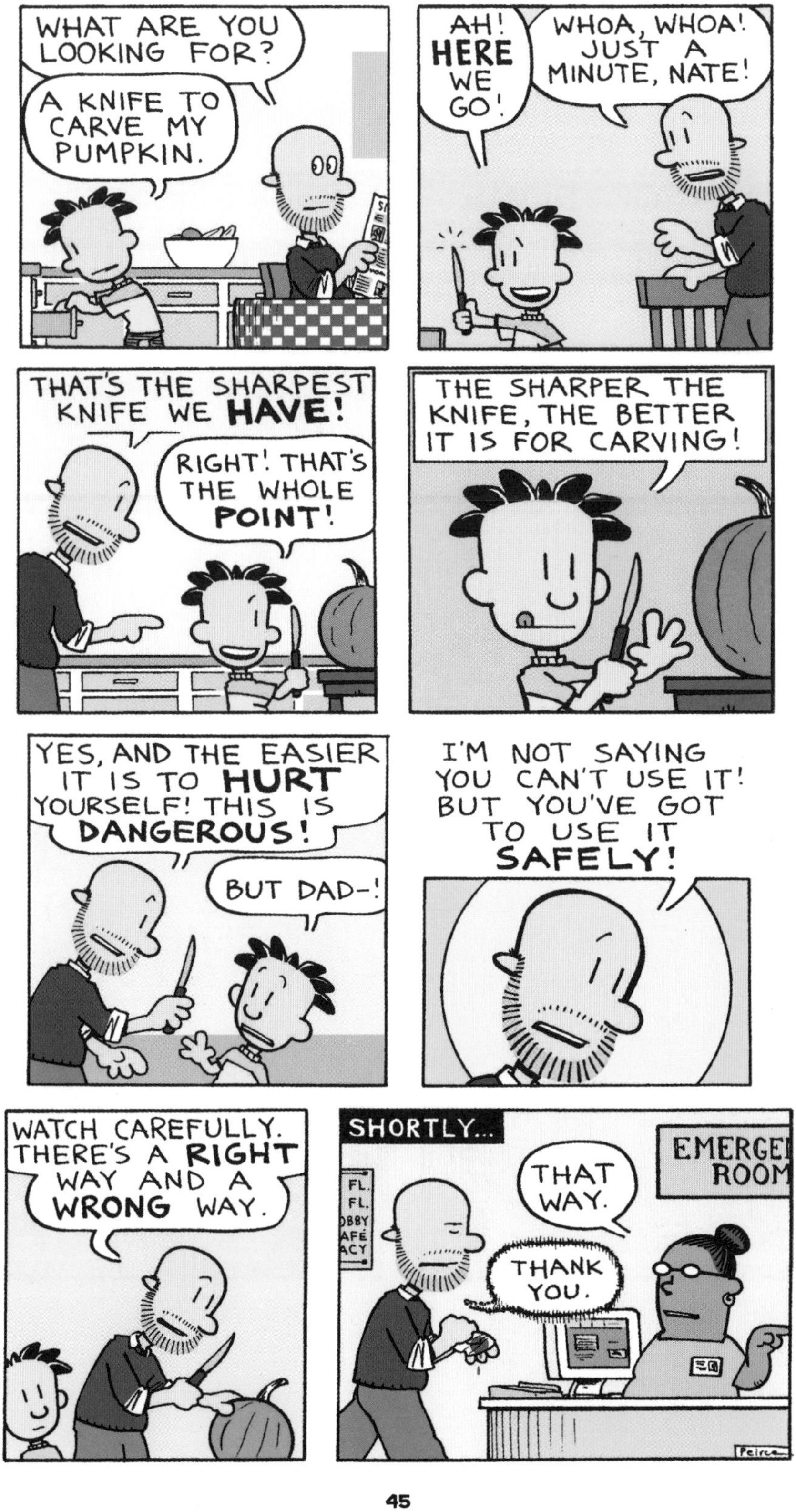

WHAT ARE YOU LOOKING FOR?
A KNIFE TO CARVE MY PUMPKIN.
AH! HERE WE GO!
WHOA, WHOA! JUST A MINUTE, NATE!
THAT'S THE SHARPEST KNIFE WE HAVE!
RIGHT! THAT'S THE WHOLE POINT!
THE SHARPER THE KNIFE, THE BETTER IT IS FOR CARVING!
YES, AND THE EASIER IT IS TO HURT YOURSELF! THIS IS DANGEROUS!
BUT DAD-!
I'M NOT SAYING YOU CAN'T USE IT! BUT YOU'VE GOT TO USE IT SAFELY!
WATCH CAREFULLY. THERE'S A RIGHT WAY AND A WRONG WAY.
SHORTLY...
THAT WAY.
THANK YOU.
Peirce

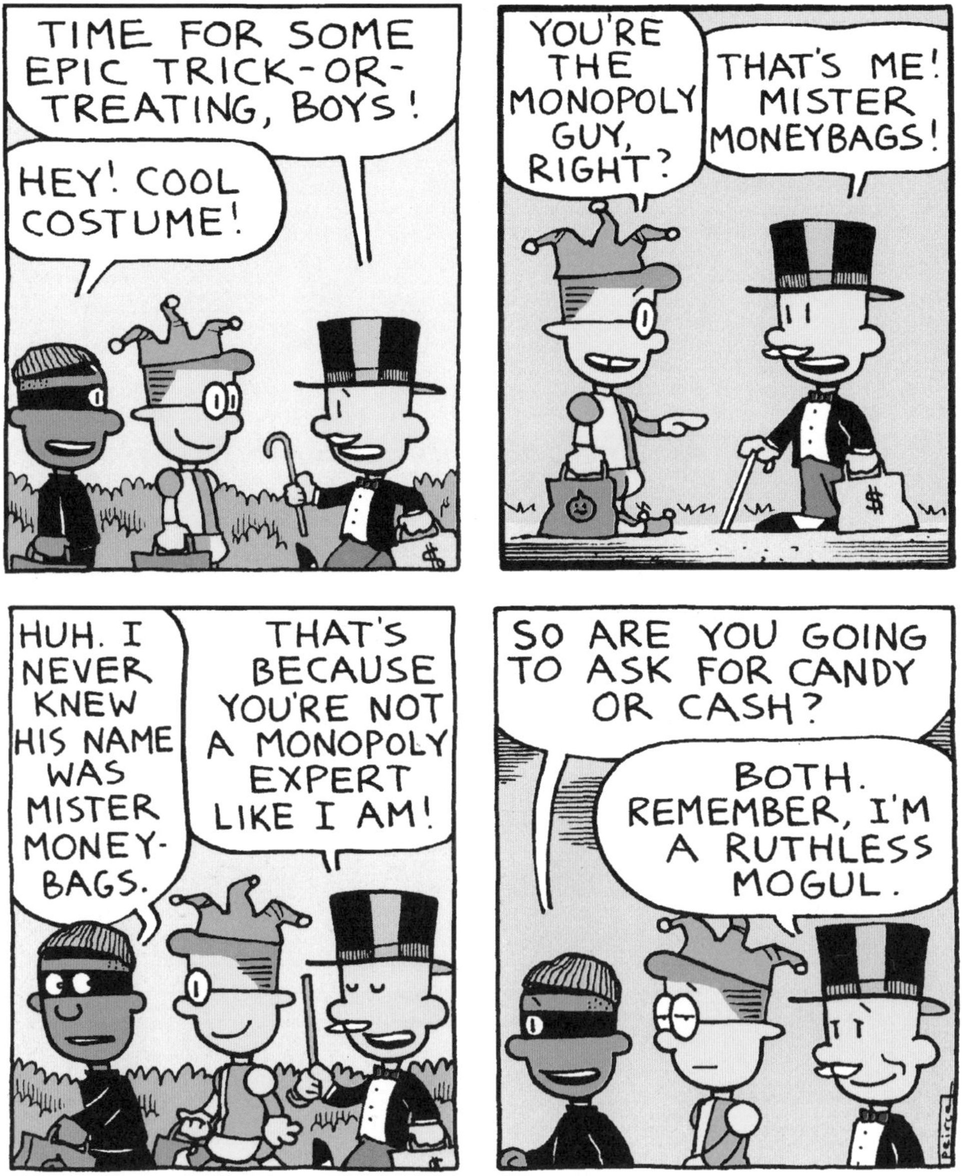
TIME FOR SOME EPIC TRICK-OR-TREATING, BOYS!
HEY! COOL COSTUME!
YOU'RE THE MONOPOLY GUY, RIGHT?
THAT'S ME! MISTER MONEYBAGS!
$
HUH. I NEVER KNEW HIS NAME WAS MISTER MONEY-BAGS.
THAT'S BECAUSE YOU'RE NOT A MONOPOLY EXPERT LIKE I AM!
SO ARE YOU GOING TO ASK FOR CANDY OR CASH?
BOTH. REMEMBER, I'M A RUTHLESS MOGUL.
PEIRCE

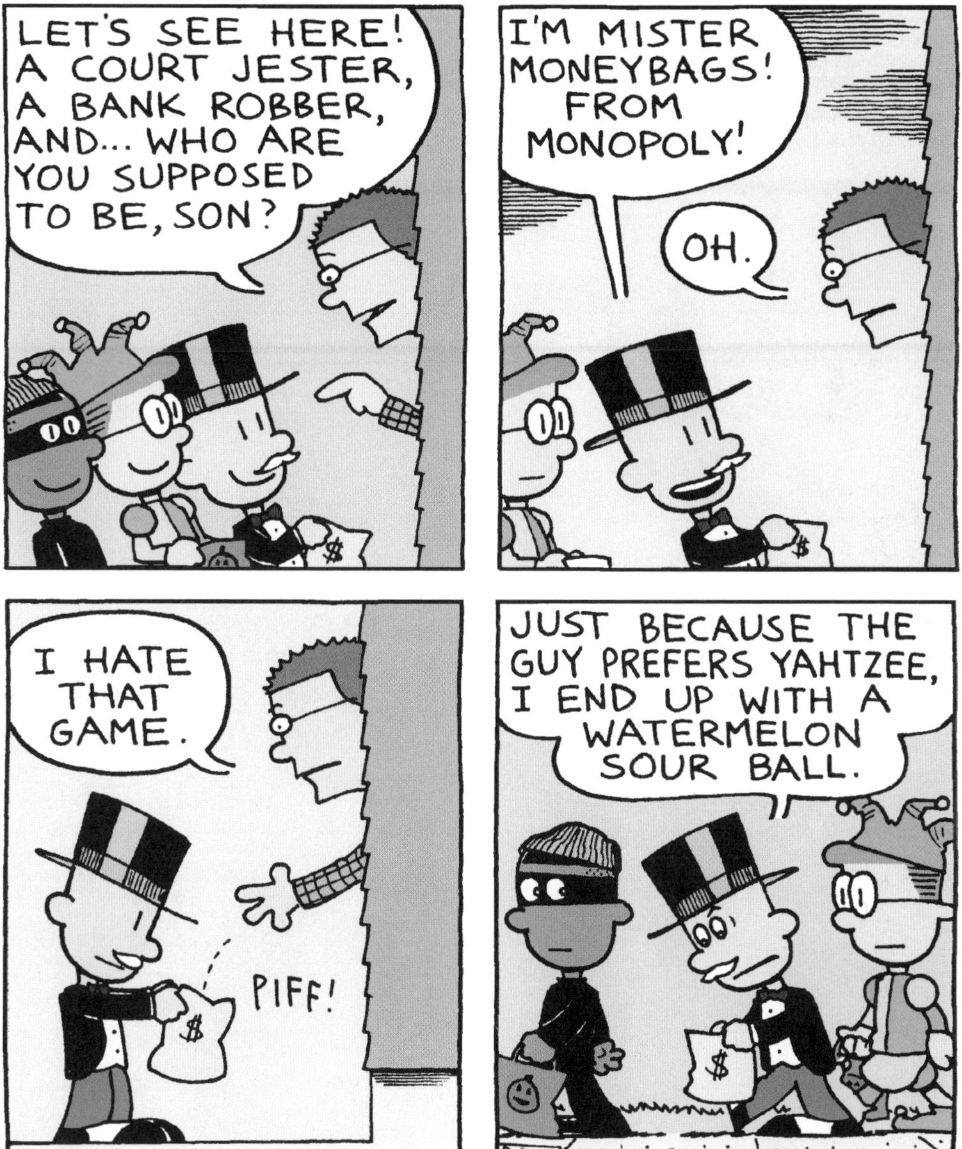
LET'S SEE HERE! A COURT JESTER, A BANK ROBBER, AND... WHO ARE YOU SUPPOSED TO BE, SON?
I'M MISTER MONEYBAGS! FROM MONOPOLY!
OH.
I HATE THAT GAME.
PIFF!
JUST BECAUSE THE GUY PREFERS YAHTZEE, I END UP WITH A WATERMELON SOUR BALL.
Peirce

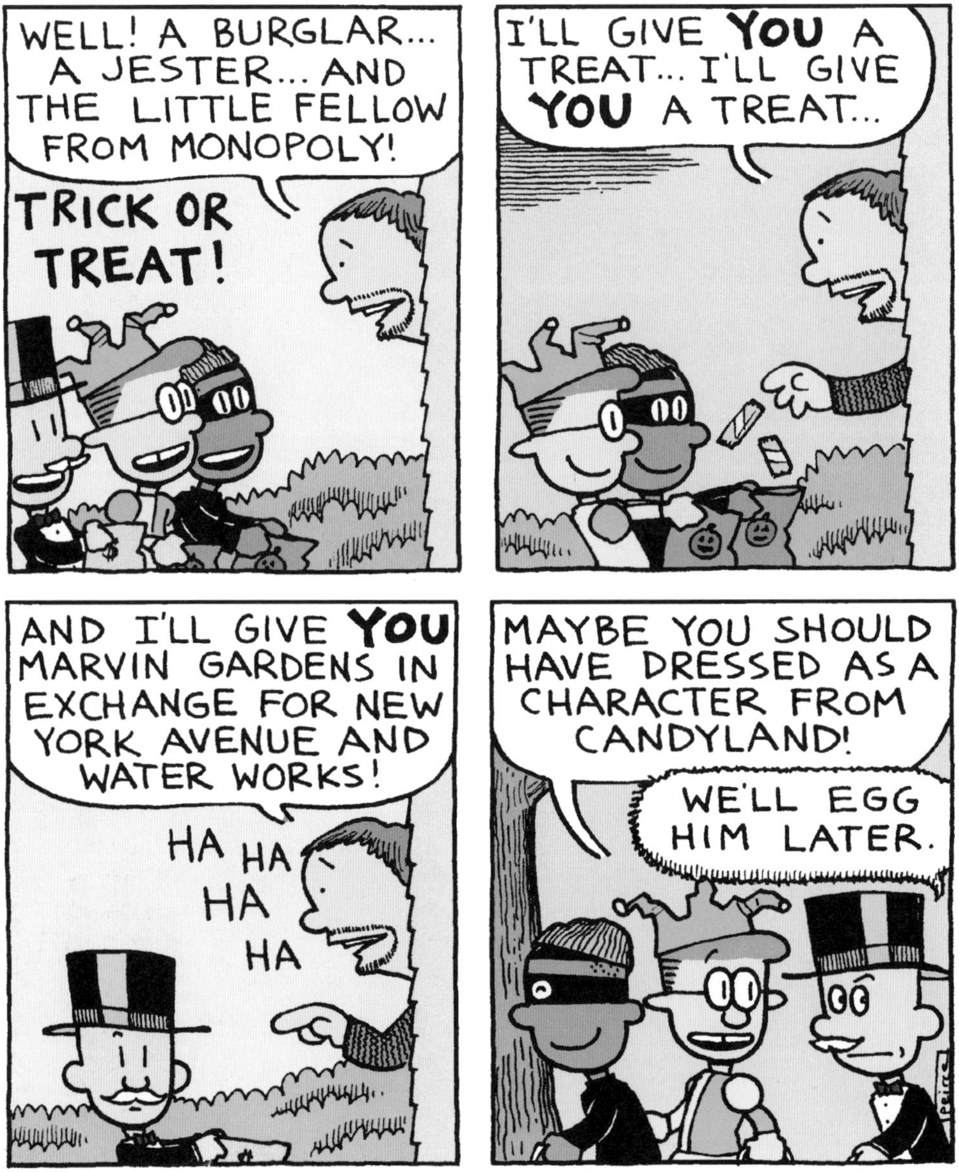

WELL! A BURGLAR... A JESTER... AND THE LITTLE FELLOW FROM MONOPOLY!
TRICK OR TREAT!
I'LL GIVE YOU A TREAT... I'LL GIVE YOU A TREAT...
AND I'LL GIVE YOU MARVIN GARDENS IN EXCHANGE FOR NEW YORK AVENUE AND WATER WORKS!
HA HA HA HA
MAYBE YOU SHOULD HAVE DRESSED AS A CHARACTER FROM CANDYLAND!
WE'LL EGG HIM LATER.

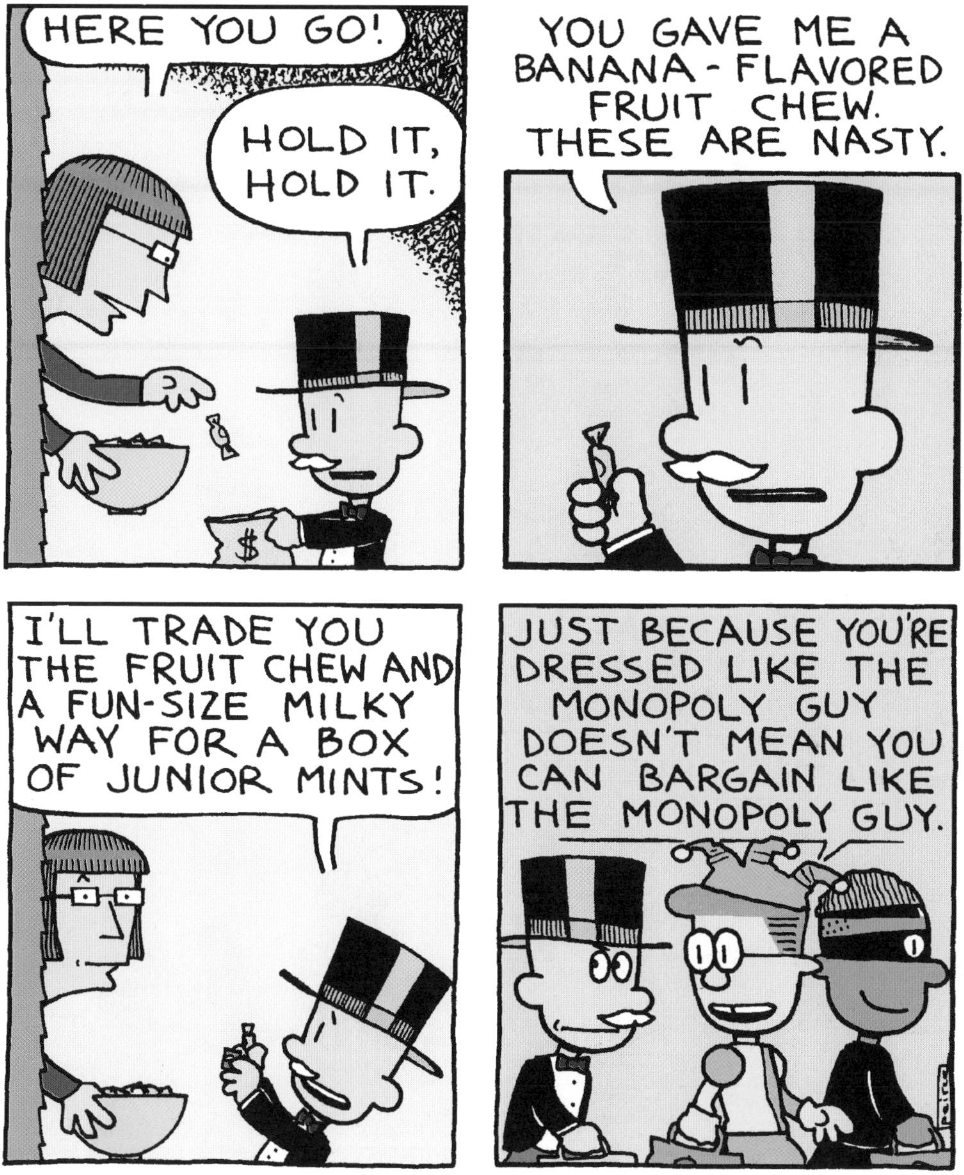
HERE YOU GO!
HOLD IT, HOLD IT.
YOU GAVE ME A BANANA-FLAVORED FRUIT CHEW. THESE ARE NASTY.
I'LL TRADE YOU THE FRUIT CHEW AND A FUN-SIZE MILKY WAY FOR A BOX OF JUNIOR MINTS!
JUST BECAUSE YOU'RE DRESSED LIKE THE MONOPOLY GUY DOESN'T MEAN YOU CAN BARGAIN LIKE THE MONOPOLY GUY.

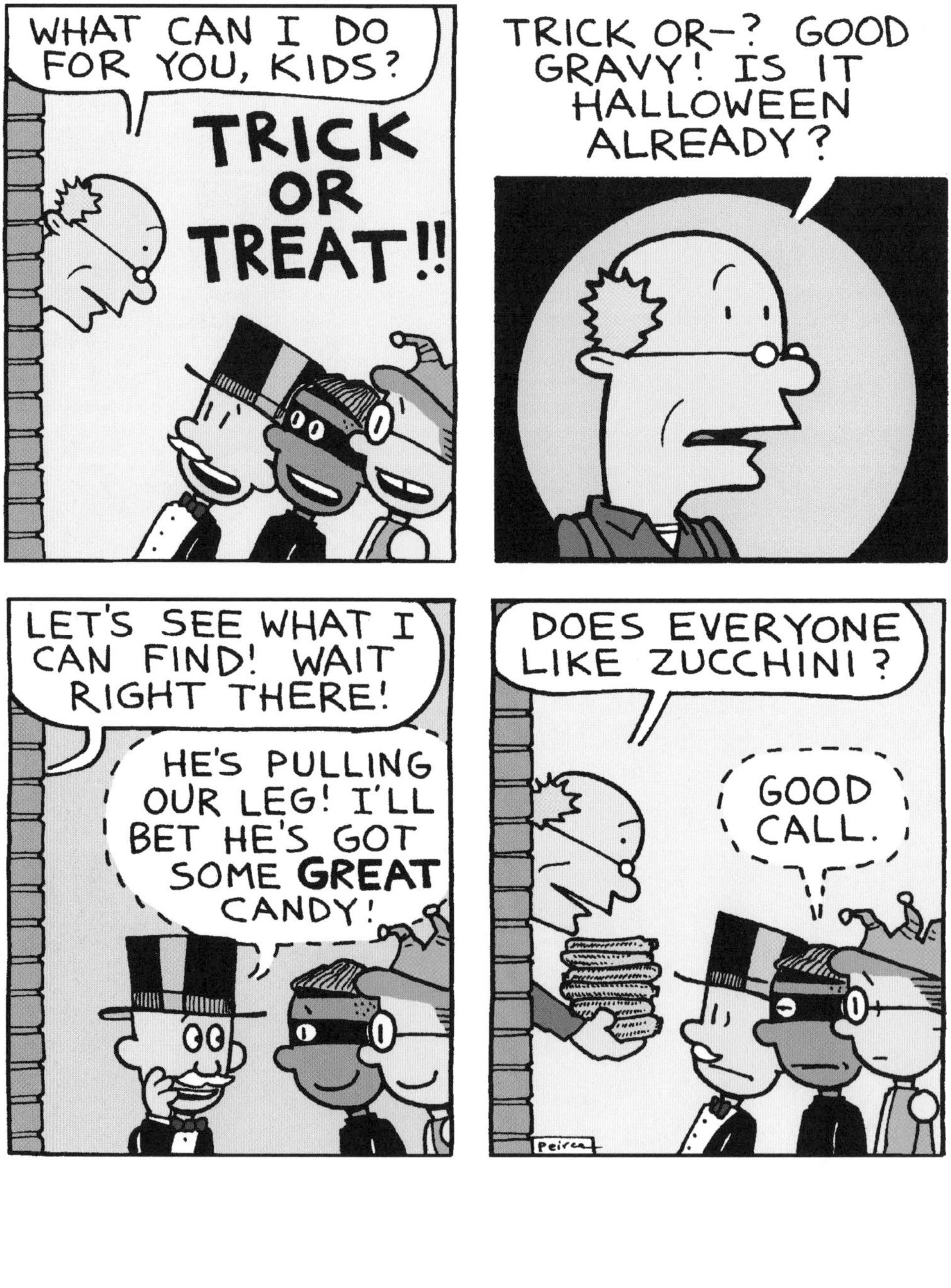
WHAT CAN I DO FOR YOU, KIDS?
TRICK OR TREAT!!
TRICK OR—? GOOD GRAVY! IS IT HALLOWEEN ALREADY?
LET'S SEE WHAT I CAN FIND! WAIT RIGHT THERE!
HE'S PULLING OUR LEG! I'LL BET HE'S GOT SOME GREAT CANDY!
DOES EVERYONE LIKE ZUCCHINI?
GOOD CALL.
Peirce

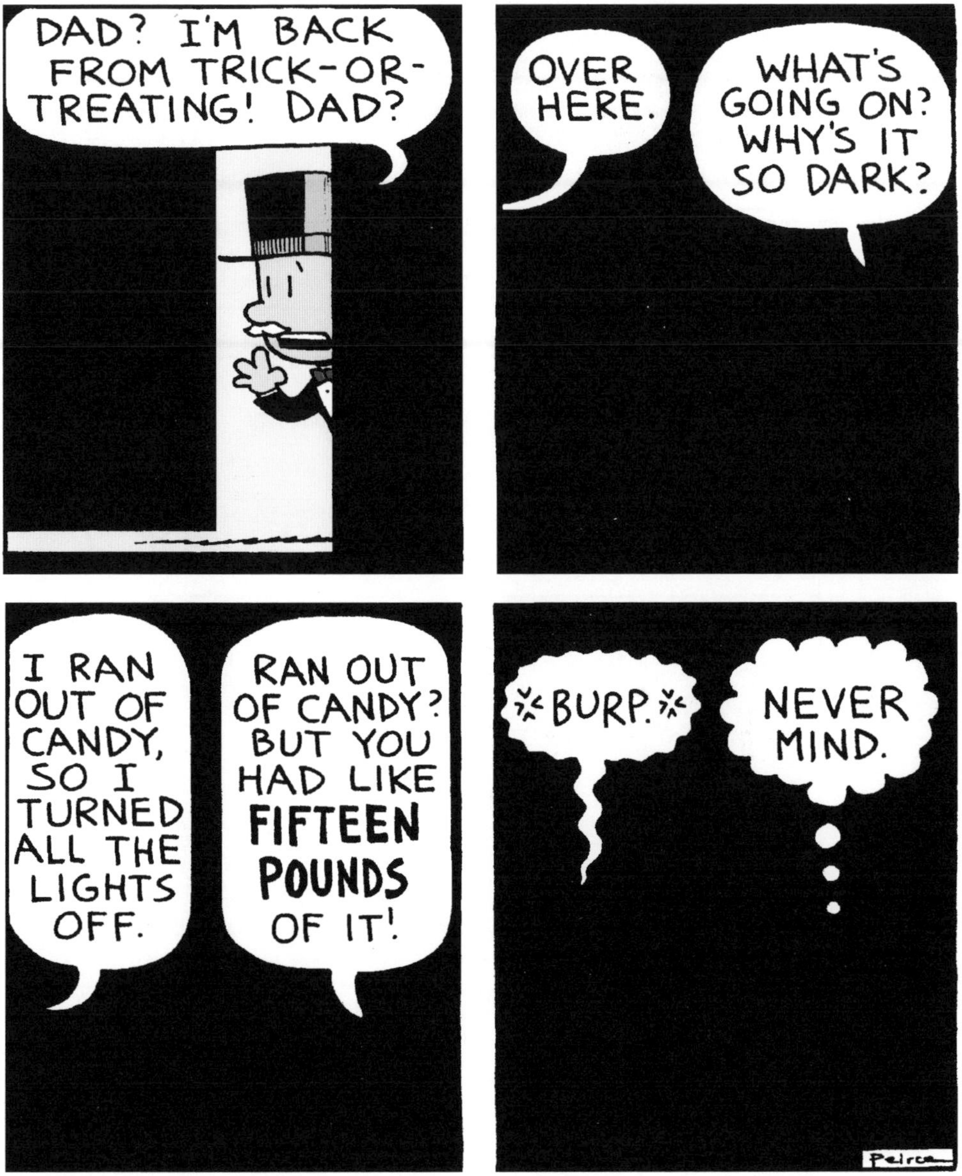
DAD? I'M BACK FROM TRICK-OR-TREATING! DAD?
OVER HERE.
WHAT'S GOING ON? WHY'S IT SO DARK?
I RAN OUT OF CANDY, SO I TURNED ALL THE LIGHTS OFF.
RAN OUT OF CANDY? BUT YOU HAD LIKE FIFTEEN POUNDS OF IT!
BURP.
NEVER MIND.
Peirce

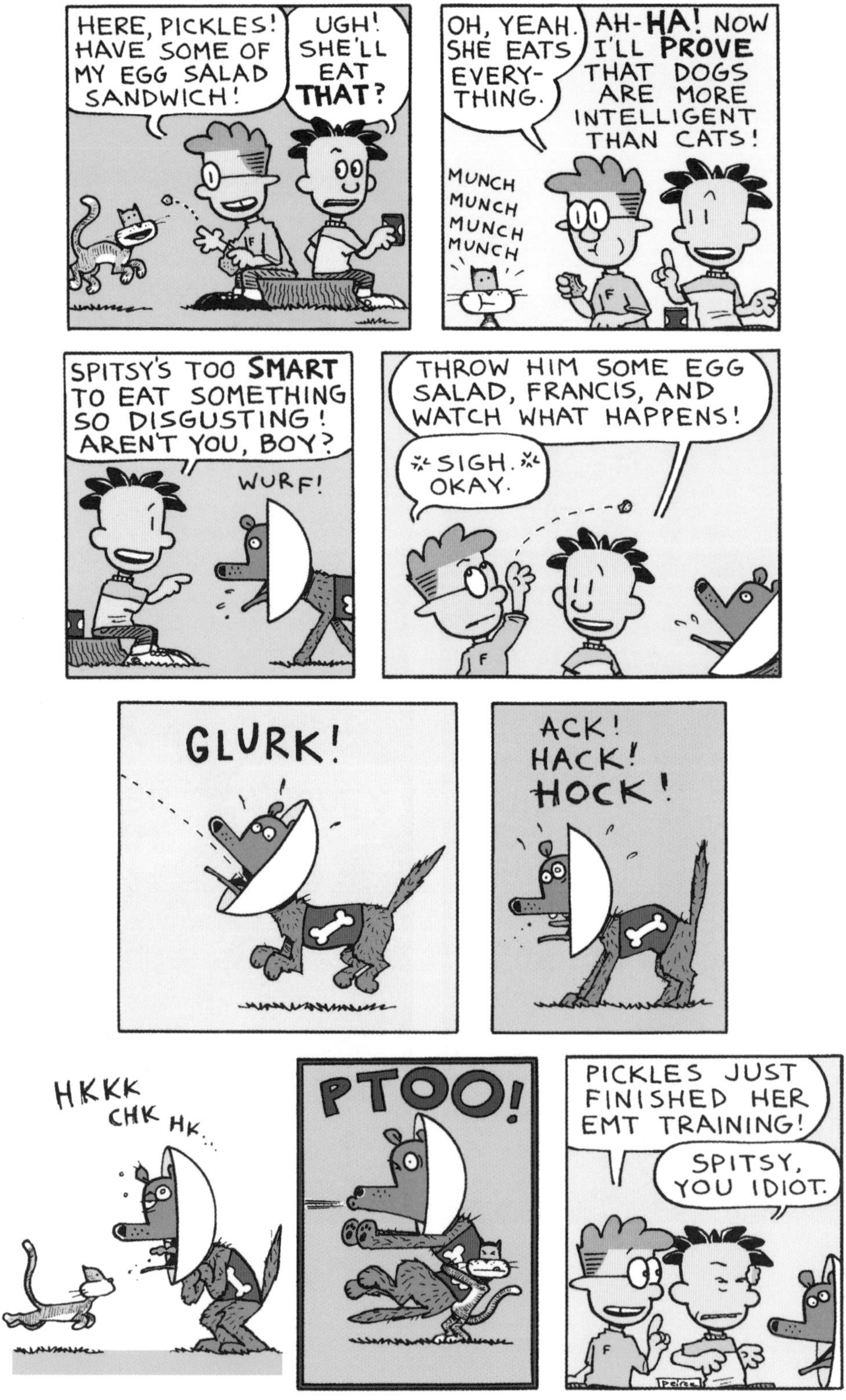

HERE, PICKLES! HAVE SOME OF MY EGG SALAD SANDWICH!
UGH! SHE'LL EAT **THAT**?
OH, YEAH. SHE EATS EVERY-THING.
AH-**HA**! NOW I'LL **PROVE** THAT DOGS ARE MORE INTELLIGENT THAN CATS!
MUNCH MUNCH MUNCH MUNCH
SPITSY'S TOO **SMART** TO EAT SOMETHING SO DISGUSTING! AREN'T YOU, BOY?
WURF!
THROW HIM SOME EGG SALAD, FRANCIS, AND WATCH WHAT HAPPENS!
SIGH. OKAY.
GLURK!
ACK! HACK! HOCK!
HKKK CHK HK...
PTOO!
PICKLES JUST FINISHED HER EMT TRAINING!
SPITSY, YOU IDIOT.

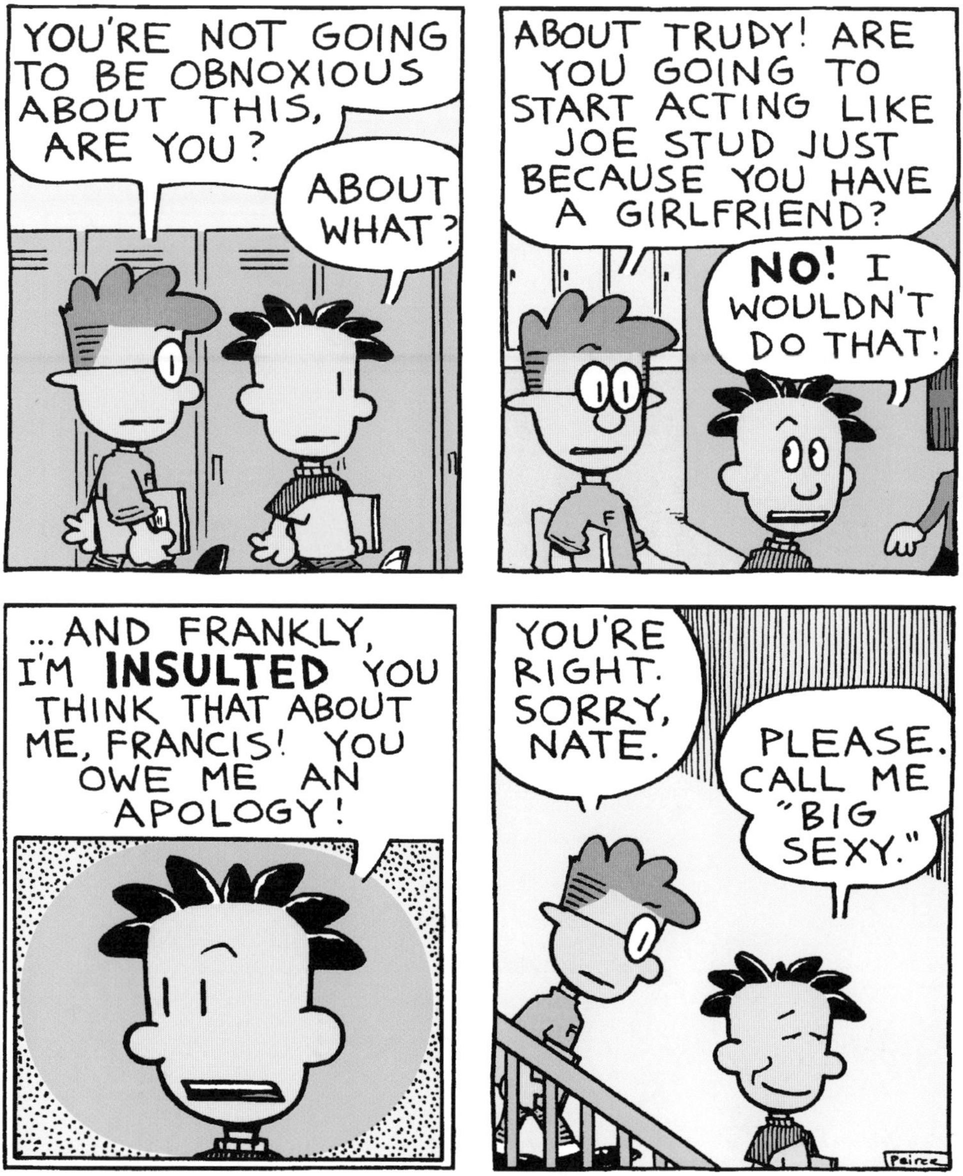

YOU'RE NOT GOING TO BE OBNOXIOUS ABOUT THIS, ARE YOU?
ABOUT WHAT?
ABOUT TRUDY! ARE YOU GOING TO START ACTING LIKE JOE STUD JUST BECAUSE YOU HAVE A GIRLFRIEND?
NO! I WOULDN'T DO THAT!
...AND FRANKLY, I'M INSULTED YOU THINK THAT ABOUT ME, FRANCIS! YOU OWE ME AN APOLOGY!
YOU'RE RIGHT. SORRY, NATE.
PLEASE. CALL ME "BIG SEXY."
Peirce

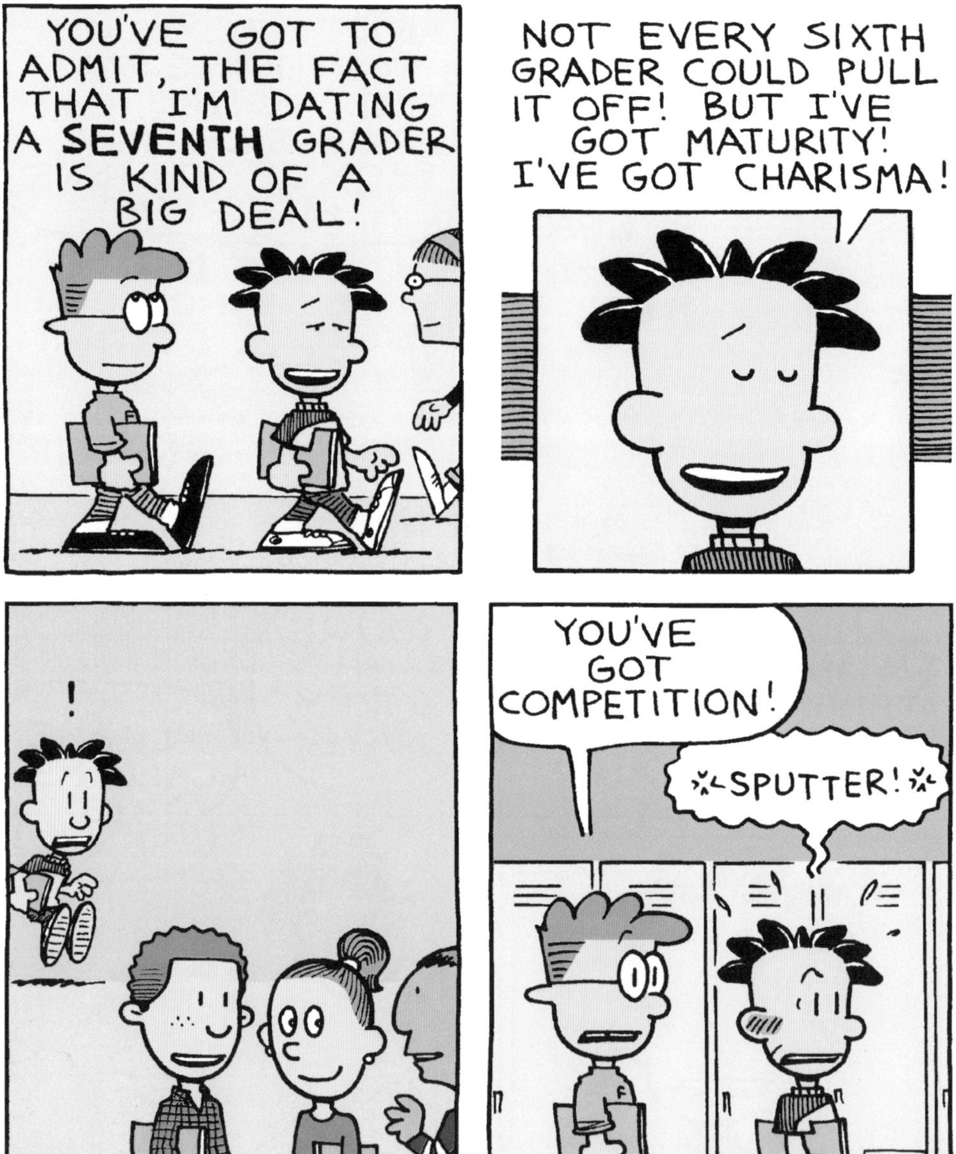
YOU'VE GOT TO ADMIT, THE FACT THAT I'M DATING A SEVENTH GRADER IS KIND OF A BIG DEAL!
NOT EVERY SIXTH GRADER COULD PULL IT OFF! BUT I'VE GOT MATURITY! I'VE GOT CHARISMA!
!
YOU'VE GOT COMPETITION!
SPUTTER!
Peirce

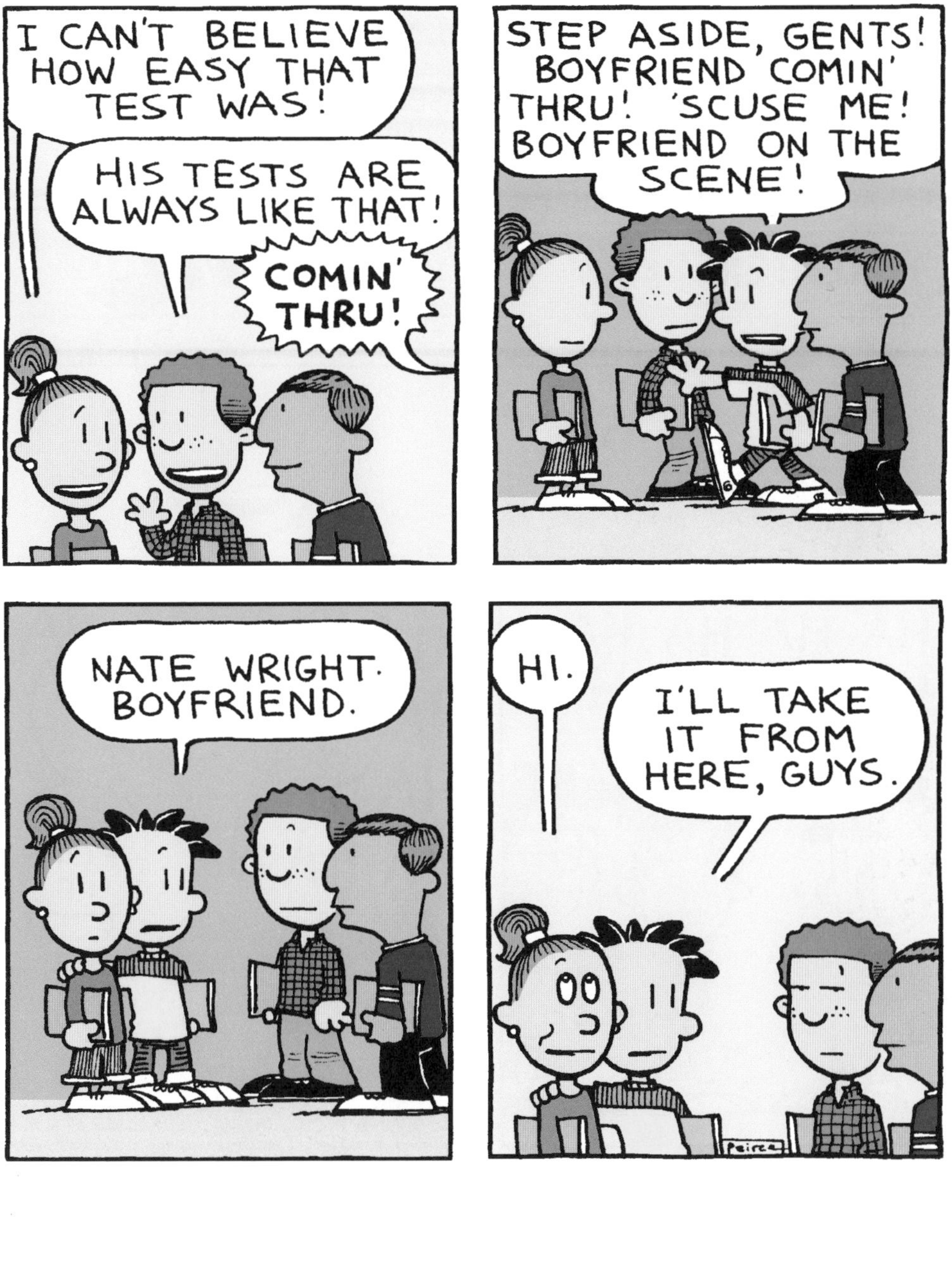
I CAN'T BELIEVE HOW EASY THAT TEST WAS!
HIS TESTS ARE ALWAYS LIKE THAT!
COMIN' THRU!
STEP ASIDE, GENTS! BOYFRIEND COMIN' THRU! 'SCUSE ME! BOYFRIEND ON THE SCENE!
NATE WRIGHT. BOYFRIEND.
HI.
I'LL TAKE IT FROM HERE, GUYS.
Peirce

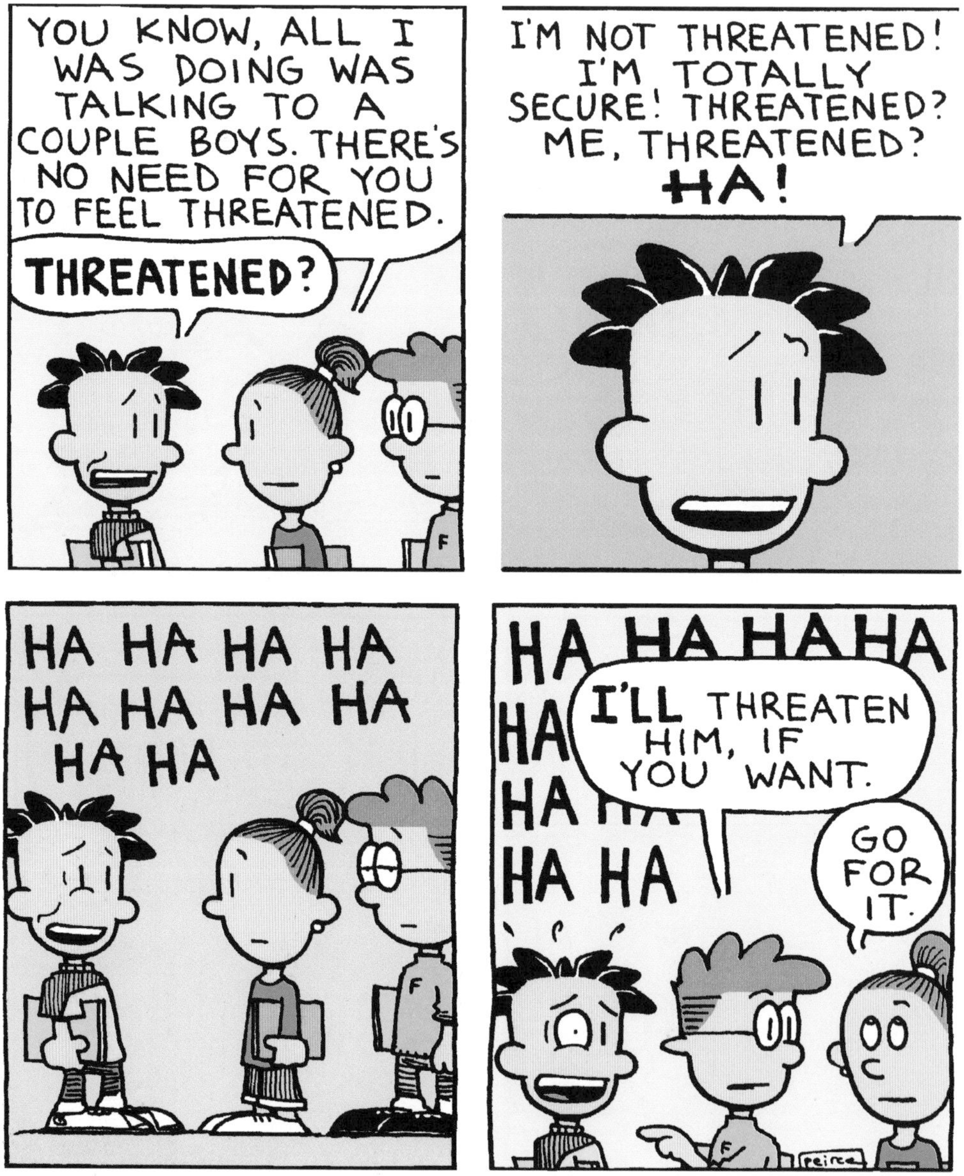
YOU KNOW, ALL I WAS DOING WAS TALKING TO A COUPLE BOYS. THERE'S NO NEED FOR YOU TO FEEL THREATENED.
THREATENED?
I'M NOT THREATENED! I'M TOTALLY SECURE! THREATENED? ME, THREATENED? HA!
HA HA HA HA HA HA HA HA HA HA
HA HA HA HA HA HA HA HA HA HA
I'LL THREATEN HIM, IF YOU WANT.
GO FOR IT.
peirce

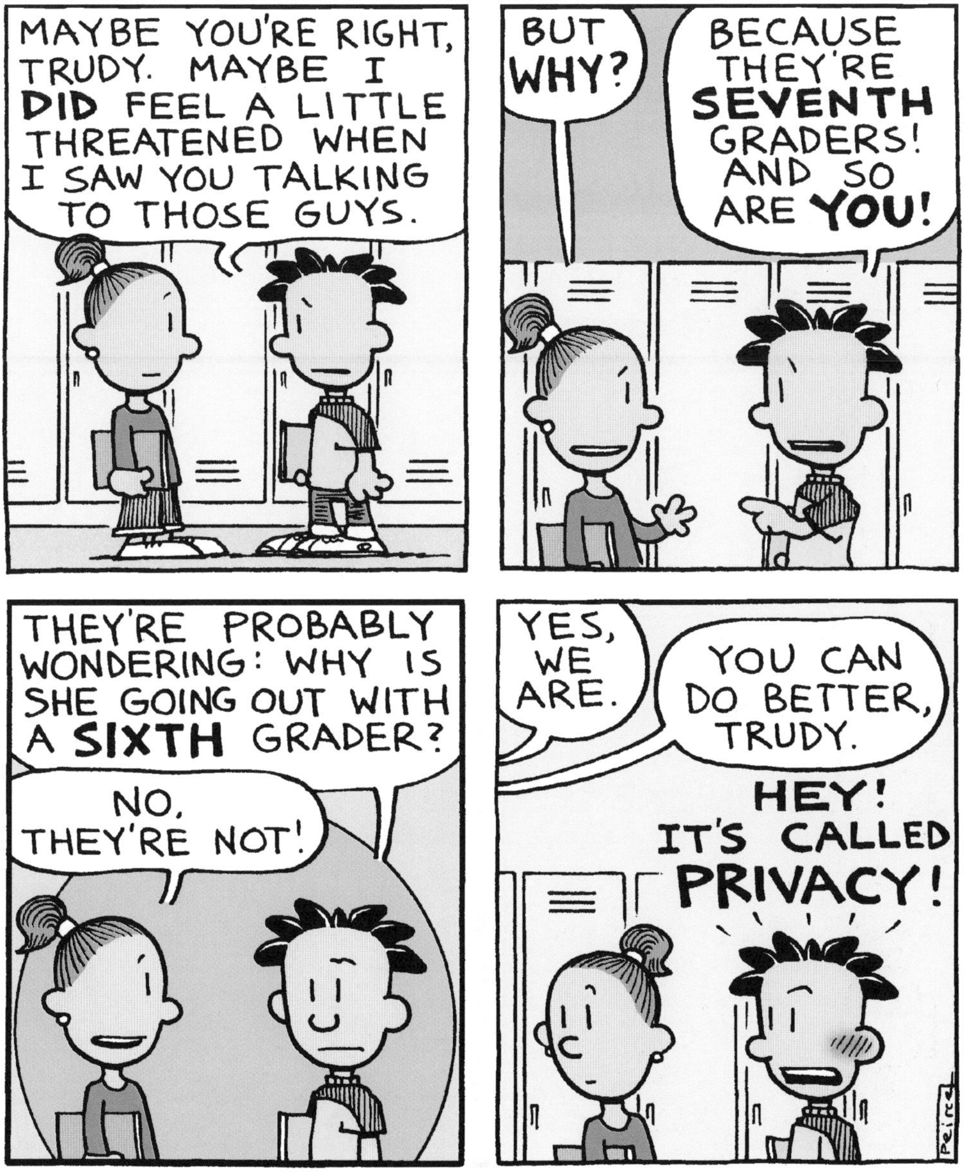
MAYBE YOU'RE RIGHT, TRUDY. MAYBE I **DID** FEEL A LITTLE THREATENED WHEN I SAW YOU TALKING TO THOSE GUYS.
BUT **WHY?**
BECAUSE THEY'RE **SEVENTH** GRADERS! AND SO ARE **YOU!**
THEY'RE PROBABLY WONDERING: WHY IS SHE GOING OUT WITH A **SIXTH** GRADER?
NO, THEY'RE NOT!
YES, WE ARE.
YOU CAN DO BETTER, TRUDY.
HEY! IT'S CALLED PRIVACY!
Peirce

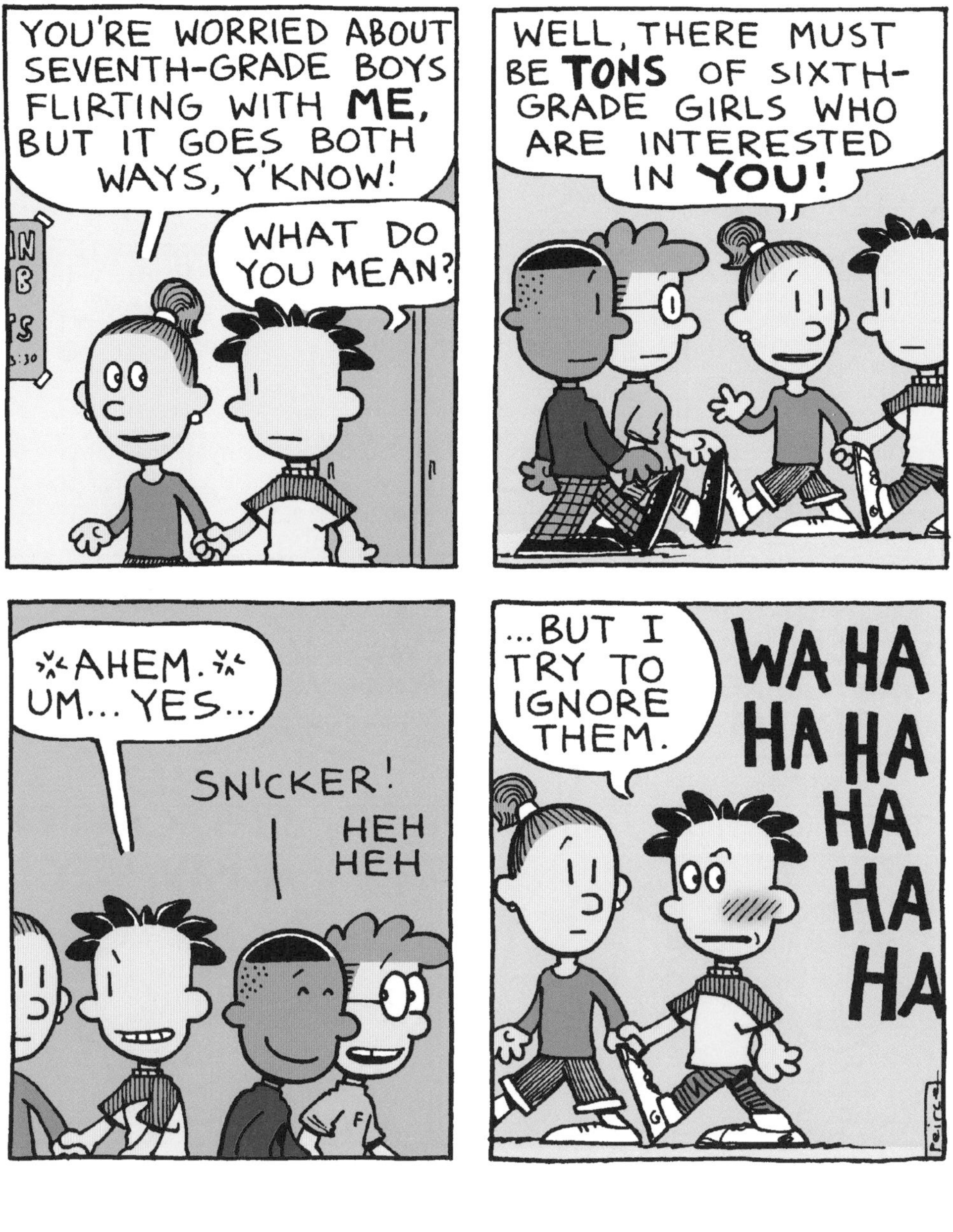
YOU'RE WORRIED ABOUT SEVENTH-GRADE BOYS FLIRTING WITH **ME**, BUT IT GOES BOTH WAYS, Y'KNOW!
WHAT DO YOU MEAN?
WELL, THERE MUST BE **TONS** OF SIXTH-GRADE GIRLS WHO ARE INTERESTED IN **YOU**!
AHEM. UM... YES...
SNICKER!
HEH HEH
...BUT I TRY TO IGNORE THEM.
WA HA HA HA HA HA HA HA

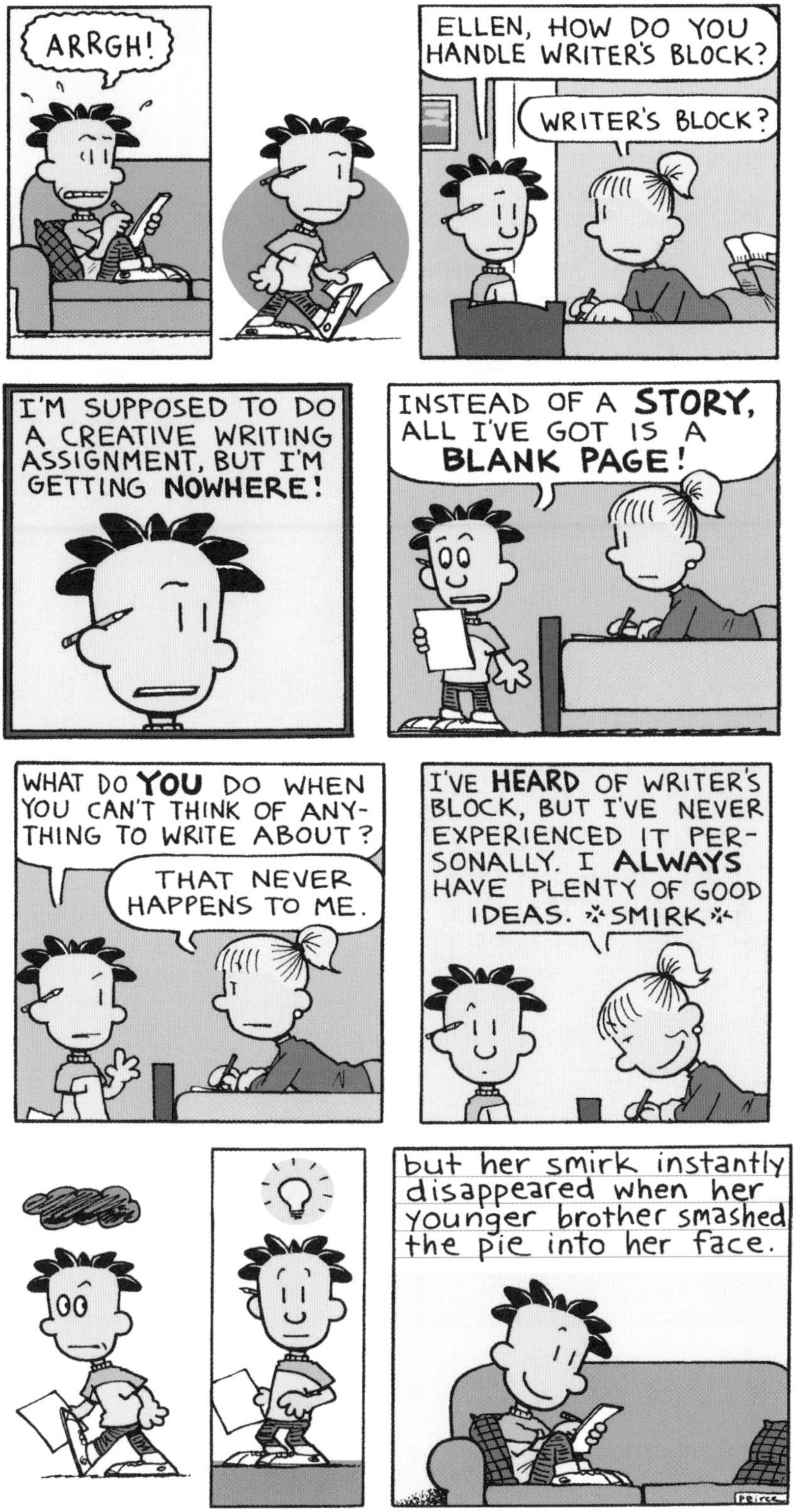
ARRGH!
ELLEN, HOW DO YOU HANDLE WRITER'S BLOCK?
WRITER'S BLOCK?
I'M SUPPOSED TO DO A CREATIVE WRITING ASSIGNMENT, BUT I'M GETTING NOWHERE!
INSTEAD OF A STORY, ALL I'VE GOT IS A BLANK PAGE!
WHAT DO YOU DO WHEN YOU CAN'T THINK OF ANY-THING TO WRITE ABOUT?
THAT NEVER HAPPENS TO ME.
I'VE HEARD OF WRITER'S BLOCK, BUT I'VE NEVER EXPERIENCED IT PER-SONALLY. I ALWAYS HAVE PLENTY OF GOOD IDEAS. *SMIRK*
but her smirk instantly disappeared when her younger brother smashed the pie into her face.
PEIRCE

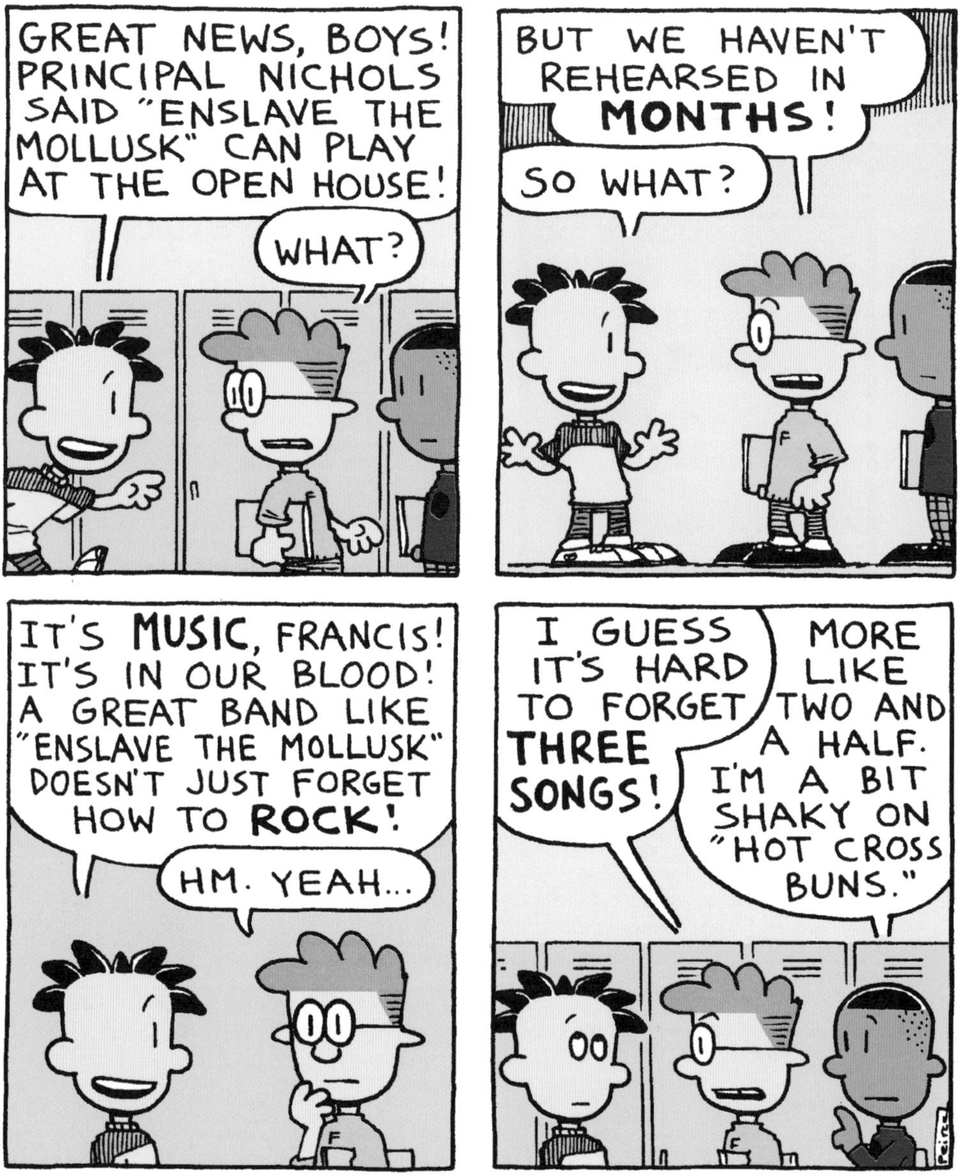
GREAT NEWS, BOYS! PRINCIPAL NICHOLS SAID "ENSLAVE THE MOLLUSK" CAN PLAY AT THE OPEN HOUSE!
WHAT?
BUT WE HAVEN'T REHEARSED IN **MONTHS**!
SO WHAT?
IT'S **MUSIC**, FRANCIS! IT'S IN OUR BLOOD! A GREAT BAND LIKE "ENSLAVE THE MOLLUSK" DOESN'T JUST FORGET HOW TO **ROCK**!
HM. YEAH...
I GUESS IT'S HARD TO FORGET **THREE SONGS**!
MORE LIKE TWO AND A HALF. I'M A BIT SHAKY ON "HOT CROSS BUNS."

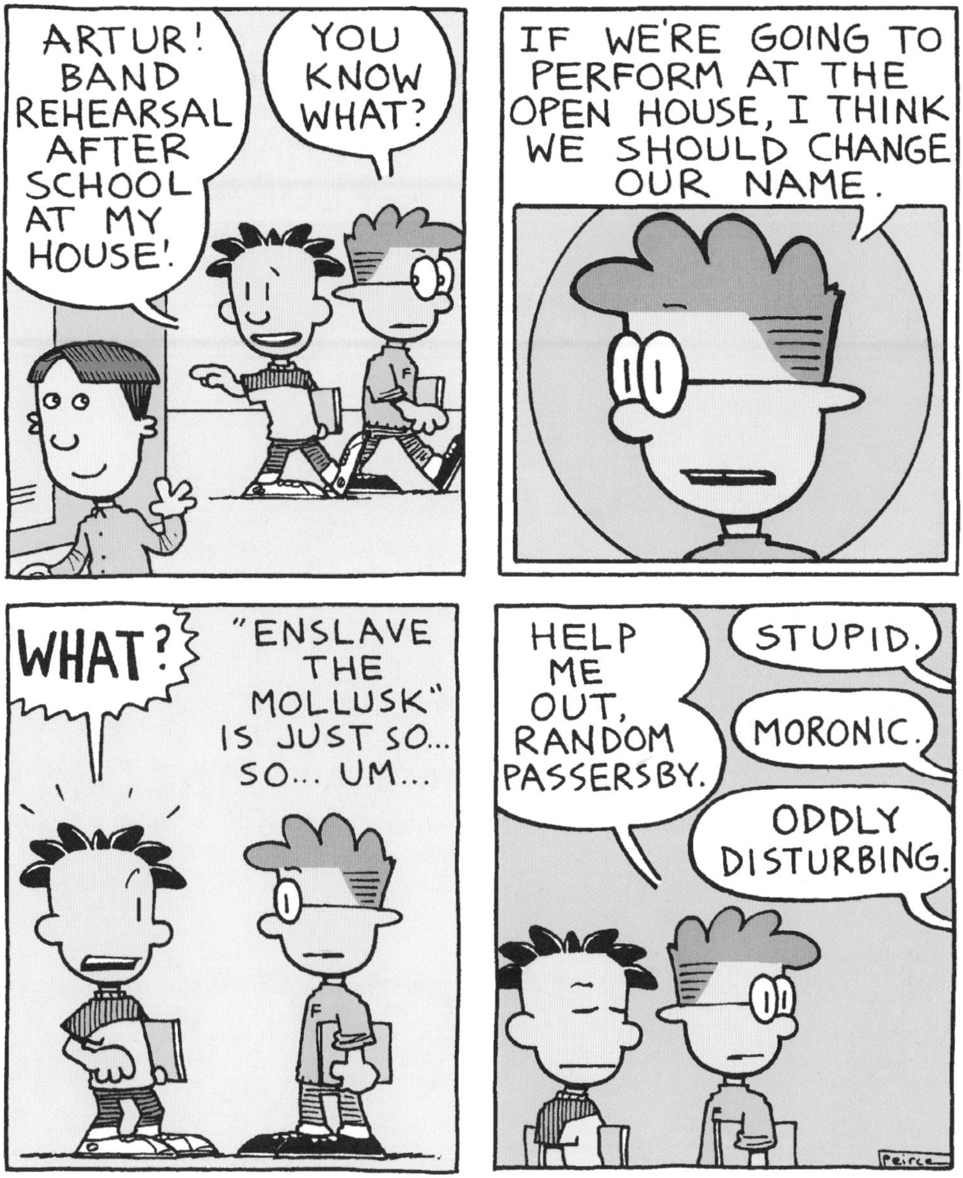
ARTUR! BAND REHEARSAL AFTER SCHOOL AT MY HOUSE!
YOU KNOW WHAT?
IF WE'RE GOING TO PERFORM AT THE OPEN HOUSE, I THINK WE SHOULD CHANGE OUR NAME.
WHAT?
"ENSLAVE THE MOLLUSK" IS JUST SO... SO... UM...
HELP ME OUT, RANDOM PASSERSBY.
STUPID.
MORONIC.
ODDLY DISTURBING.
Peirce

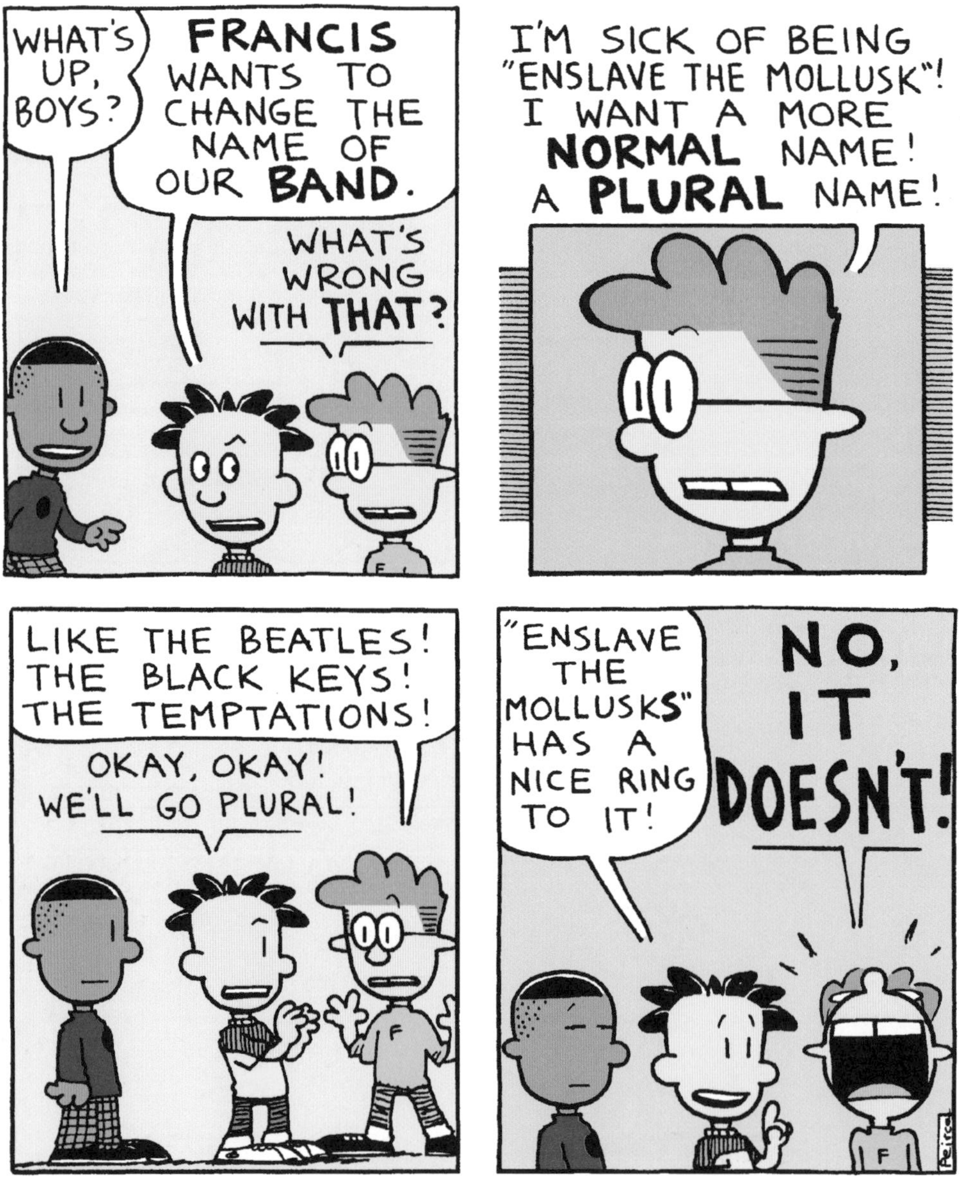
WHAT'S UP, BOYS?
FRANCIS WANTS TO CHANGE THE NAME OF OUR **BAND**.
WHAT'S WRONG WITH **THAT**?
I'M SICK OF BEING "ENSLAVE THE MOLLUSK"! I WANT A MORE **NORMAL** NAME! A **PLURAL** NAME!
LIKE THE BEATLES! THE BLACK KEYS! THE TEMPTATIONS!
OKAY, OKAY! WE'LL GO PLURAL!
"ENSLAVE THE MOLLUSKS" HAS A NICE RING TO IT!
NO, IT DOESN'T!
Peirce

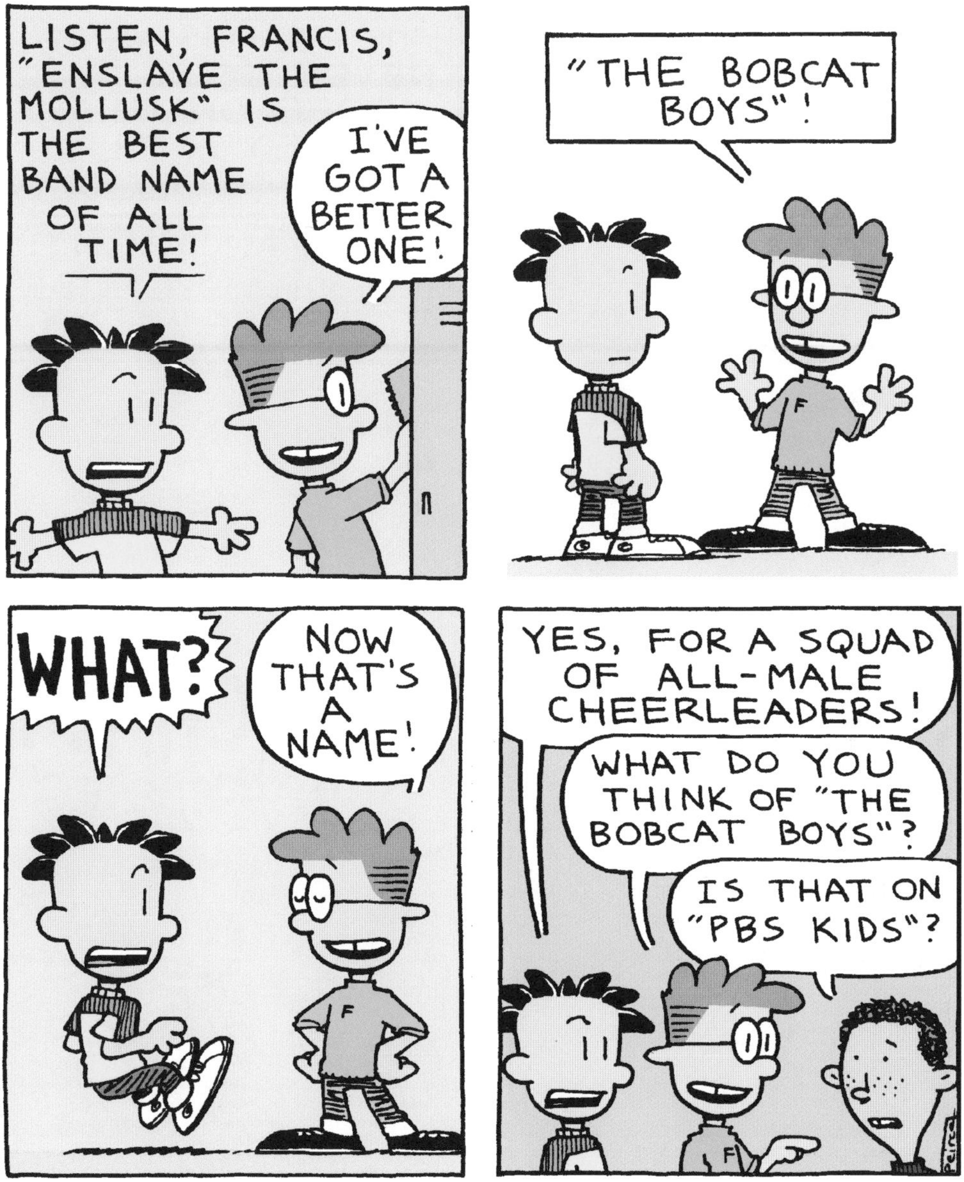
LISTEN, FRANCIS, "ENSLAVE THE MOLLUSK" IS THE BEST BAND NAME OF ALL TIME!
I'VE GOT A BETTER ONE!
"THE BOBCAT BOYS"!
WHAT?
NOW THAT'S A NAME!
YES, FOR A SQUAD OF ALL-MALE CHEERLEADERS!
WHAT DO YOU THINK OF "THE BOBCAT BOYS"?
IS THAT ON "PBS KIDS"?
F
F
F
Peirce

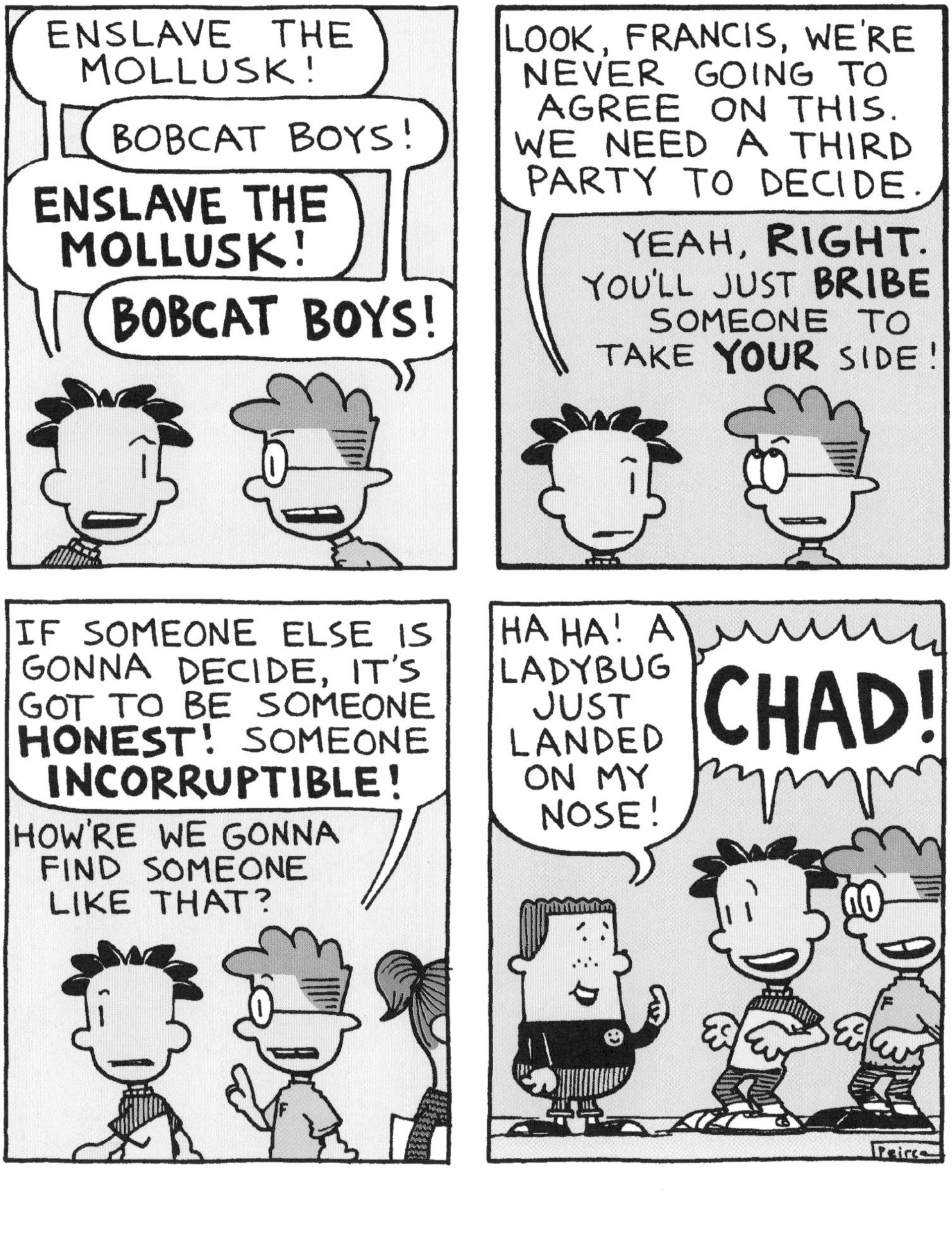
ENSLAVE THE MOLLUSK!
BOBCAT BOYS!
ENSLAVE THE MOLLUSK!
BOBCAT BOYS!
LOOK, FRANCIS, WE'RE NEVER GOING TO AGREE ON THIS. WE NEED A THIRD PARTY TO DECIDE.
YEAH, RIGHT. YOU'LL JUST BRIBE SOMEONE TO TAKE YOUR SIDE!
IF SOMEONE ELSE IS GONNA DECIDE, IT'S GOT TO BE SOMEONE HONEST! SOMEONE INCORRUPTIBLE!
HOW'RE WE GONNA FIND SOMEONE LIKE THAT?
HA HA! A LADYBUG JUST LANDED ON MY NOSE!
CHAD!
Peirce

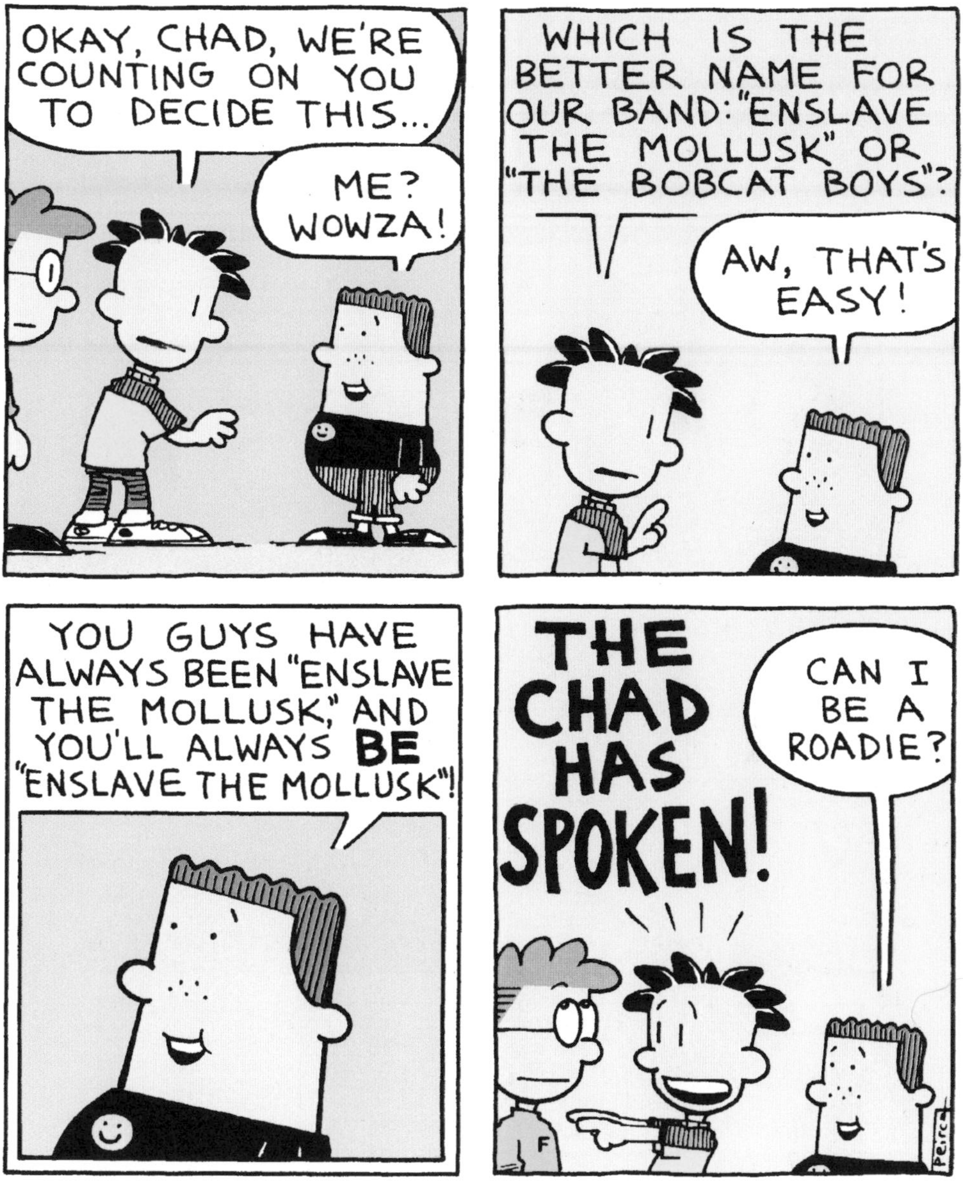

OKAY, CHAD, WE'RE COUNTING ON YOU TO DECIDE THIS...
ME? WOWZA!
WHICH IS THE BETTER NAME FOR OUR BAND: "ENSLAVE THE MOLLUSK" OR "THE BOBCAT BOYS"?
AW, THAT'S EASY!
YOU GUYS HAVE ALWAYS BEEN "ENSLAVE THE MOLLUSK," AND YOU'LL ALWAYS **BE** "ENSLAVE THE MOLLUSK"!
THE CHAD HAS SPOKEN!
CAN I BE A ROADIE?

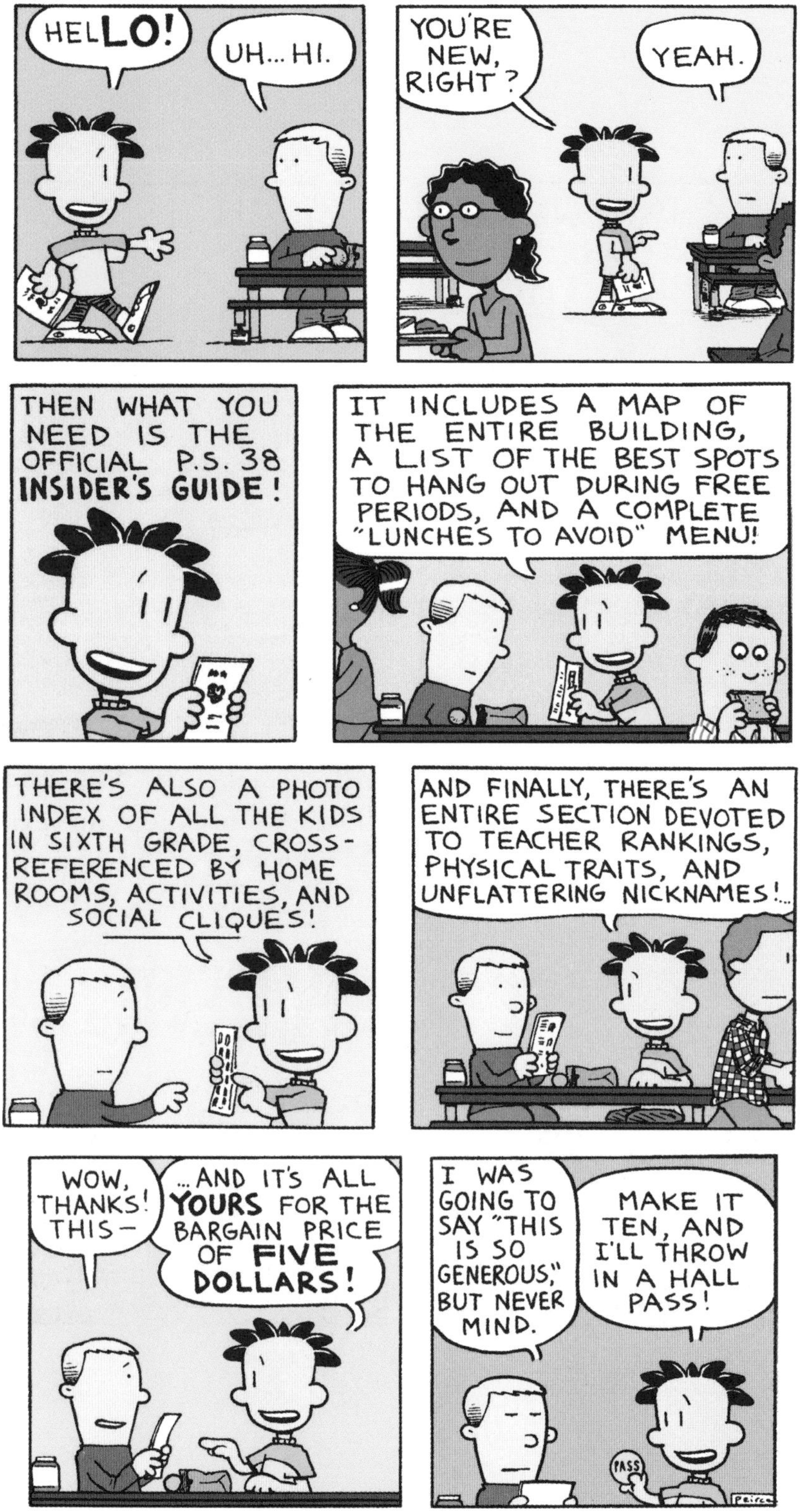
HELLO!
UH... HI.
YOU'RE NEW, RIGHT?
YEAH.
THEN WHAT YOU NEED IS THE OFFICIAL P.S. 38 INSIDER'S GUIDE!
IT INCLUDES A MAP OF THE ENTIRE BUILDING, A LIST OF THE BEST SPOTS TO HANG OUT DURING FREE PERIODS, AND A COMPLETE "LUNCHES TO AVOID" MENU!
THERE'S ALSO A PHOTO INDEX OF ALL THE KIDS IN SIXTH GRADE, CROSS-REFERENCED BY HOME ROOMS, ACTIVITIES, AND SOCIAL CLIQUES!
AND FINALLY, THERE'S AN ENTIRE SECTION DEVOTED TO TEACHER RANKINGS, PHYSICAL TRAITS, AND UNFLATTERING NICKNAMES!...
WOW, THANKS! THIS—
...AND IT'S ALL YOURS FOR THE BARGAIN PRICE OF FIVE DOLLARS!
I WAS GOING TO SAY "THIS IS SO GENEROUS," BUT NEVER MIND.
MAKE IT TEN, AND I'LL THROW IN A HALL PASS!
PASS

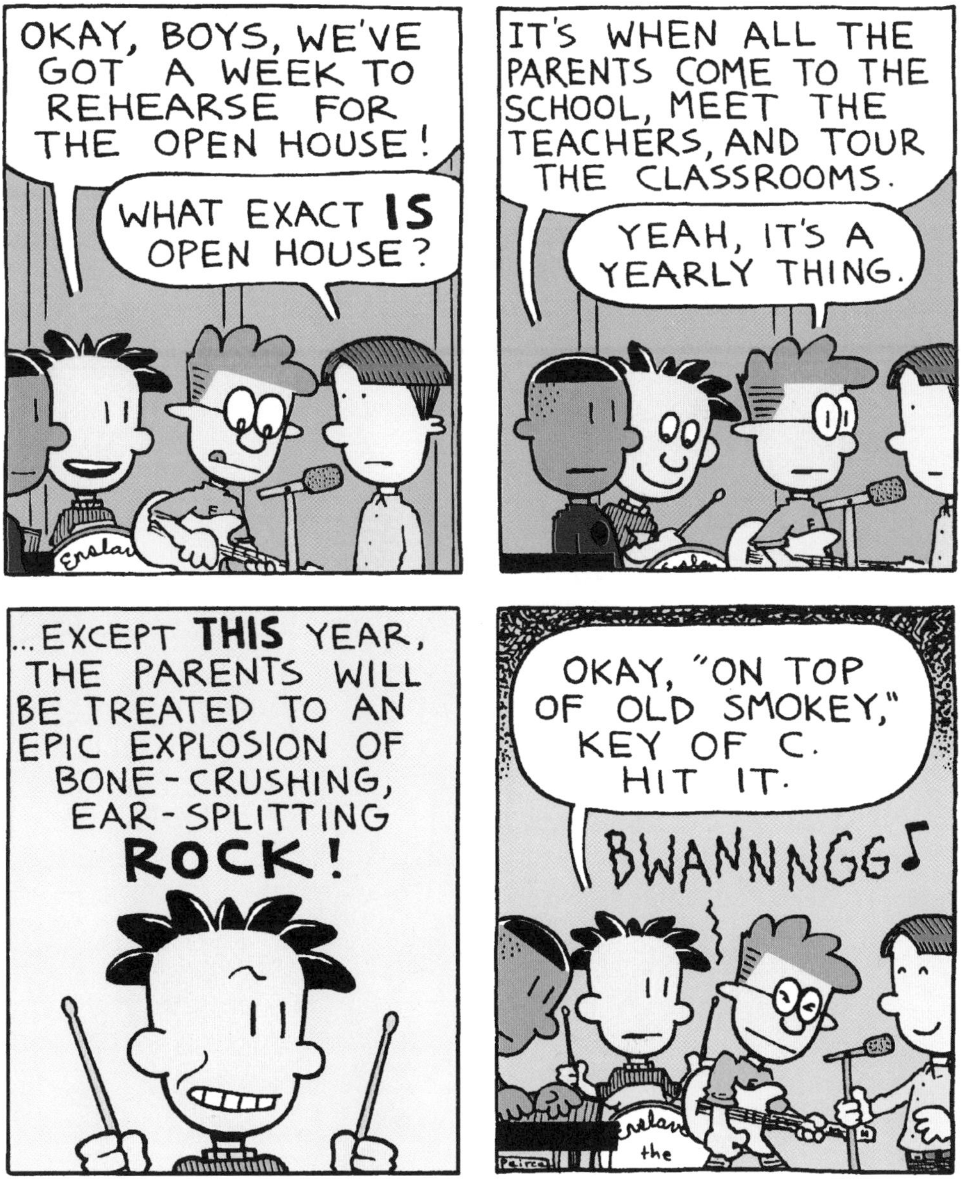
OKAY, BOYS, WE'VE GOT A WEEK TO REHEARSE FOR THE OPEN HOUSE!
WHAT EXACT IS OPEN HOUSE?
IT'S WHEN ALL THE PARENTS COME TO THE SCHOOL, MEET THE TEACHERS, AND TOUR THE CLASSROOMS.
YEAH, IT'S A YEARLY THING.
...EXCEPT THIS YEAR, THE PARENTS WILL BE TREATED TO AN EPIC EXPLOSION OF BONE-CRUSHING, EAR-SPLITTING ROCK!
OKAY, "ON TOP OF OLD SMOKEY," KEY OF C. HIT IT.
BWANNNGG

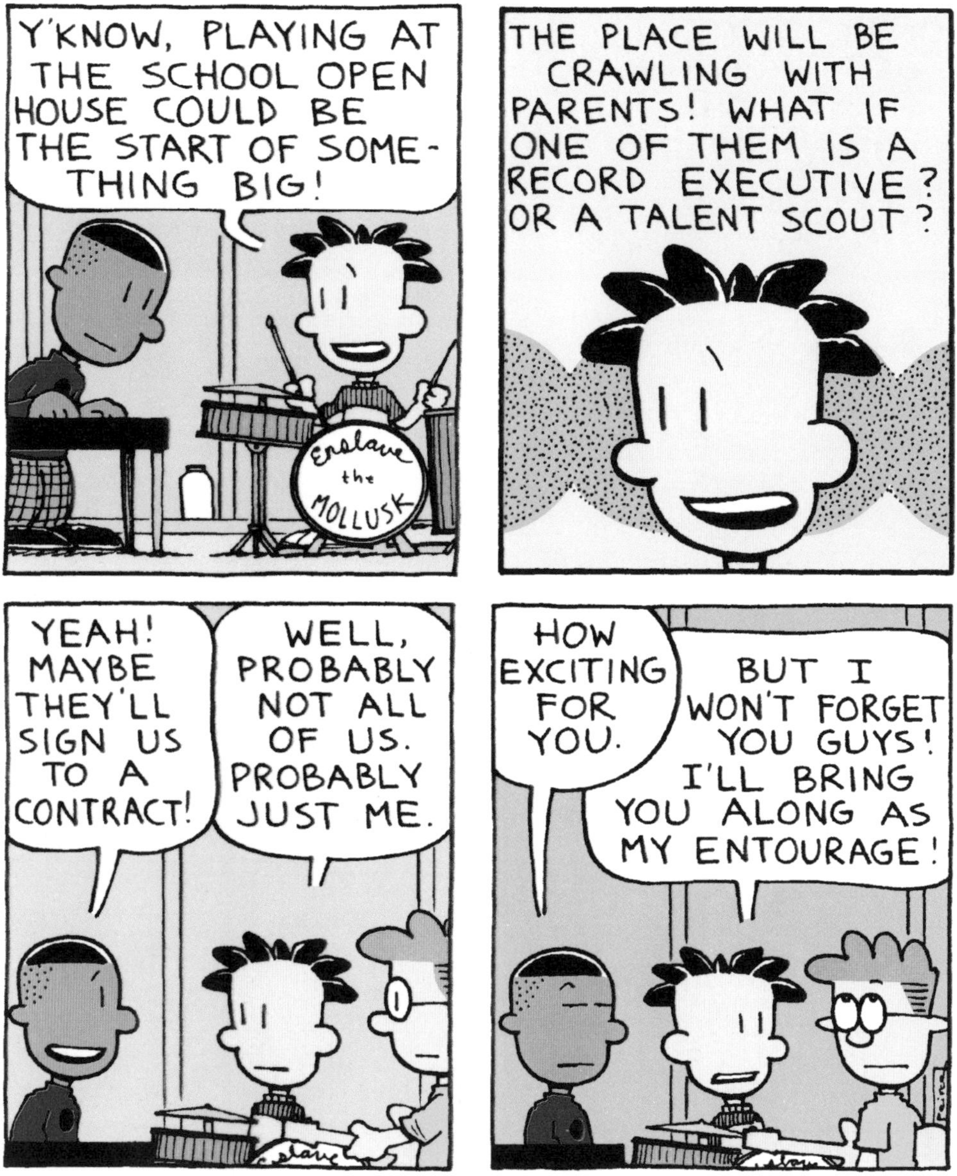
Y'KNOW, PLAYING AT THE SCHOOL OPEN HOUSE COULD BE THE START OF SOME-THING BIG!
Enslave the MOLLUSK
THE PLACE WILL BE CRAWLING WITH PARENTS! WHAT IF ONE OF THEM IS A RECORD EXECUTIVE? OR A TALENT SCOUT?
YEAH! MAYBE THEY'LL SIGN US TO A CONTRACT!
WELL, PROBABLY NOT ALL OF US. PROBABLY JUST ME.
HOW EXCITING FOR YOU.
BUT I WON'T FORGET YOU GUYS! I'LL BRING YOU ALONG AS MY ENTOURAGE!

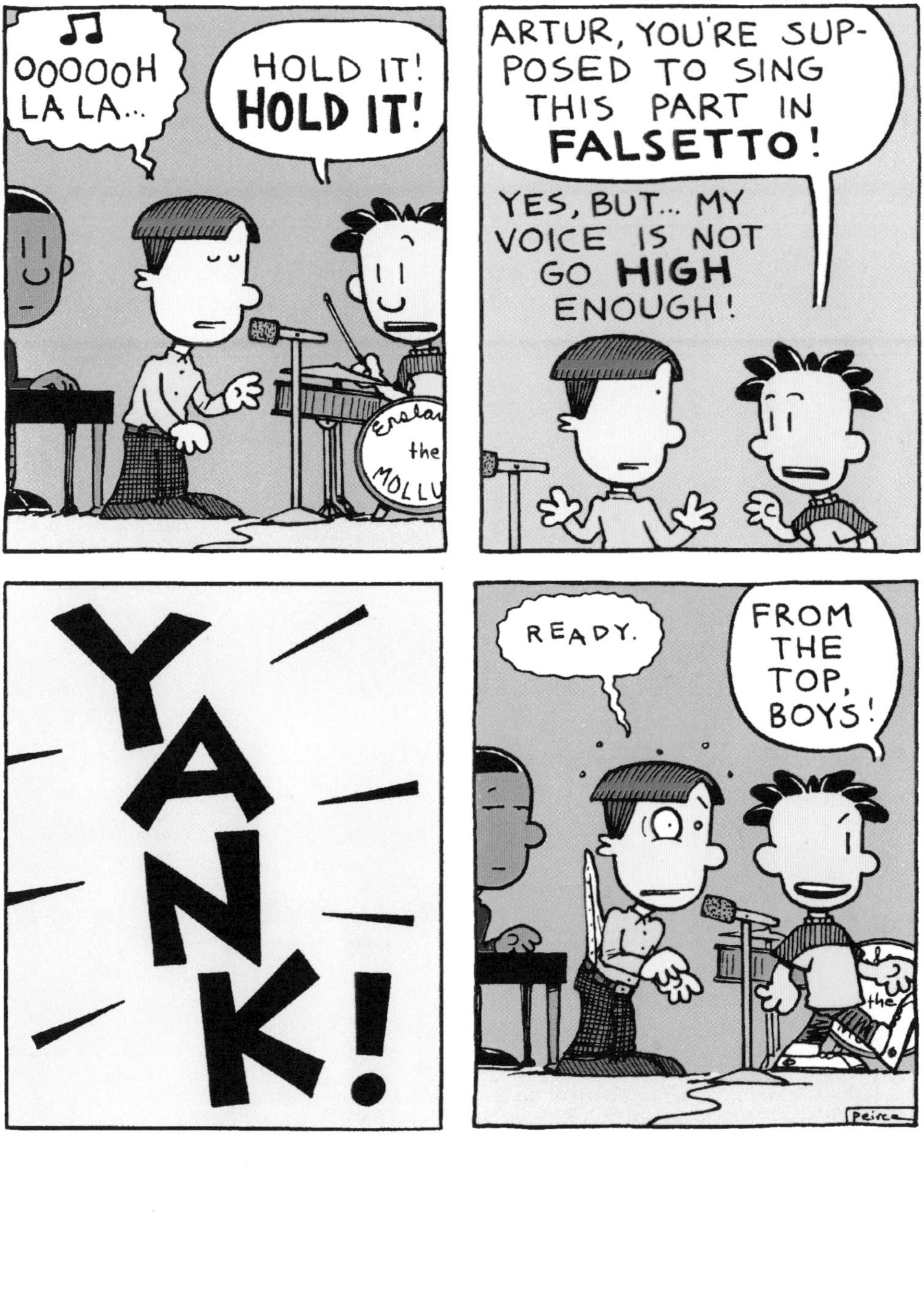
♫ OOOOOH LA LA...
HOLD IT! HOLD IT!
ARTUR, YOU'RE SUP-POSED TO SING THIS PART IN FALSETTO!
YES, BUT... MY VOICE IS NOT GO HIGH ENOUGH!
YANK!
READY.
FROM THE TOP, BOYS!
Peirce

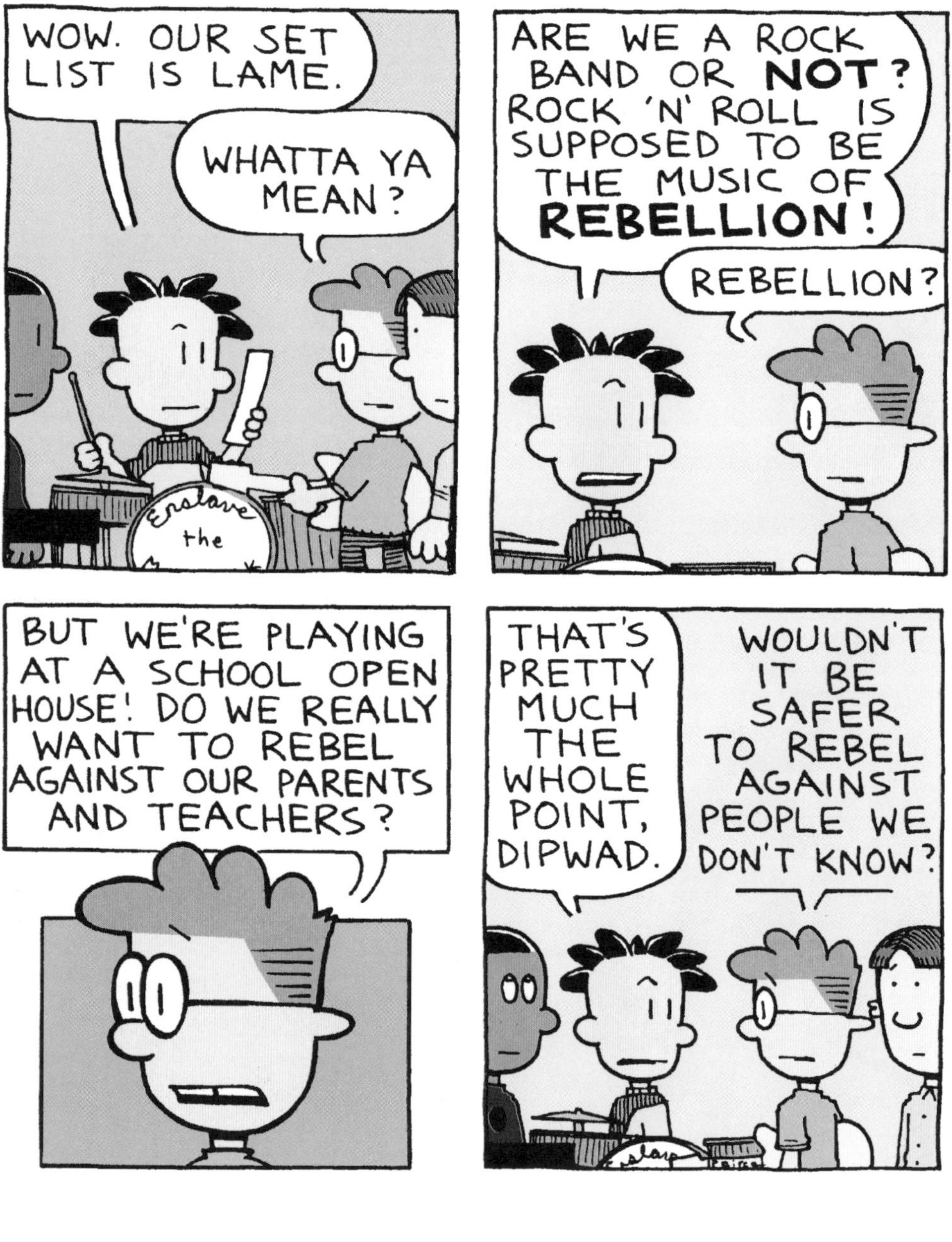
WOW. OUR SET LIST IS LAME.
WHATTA YA MEAN?
Enslave the
ARE WE A ROCK BAND OR **NOT**? ROCK 'N' ROLL IS SUPPOSED TO BE THE MUSIC OF **REBELLION**!
REBELLION?
BUT WE'RE PLAYING AT A SCHOOL OPEN HOUSE! DO WE REALLY WANT TO REBEL AGAINST OUR PARENTS AND TEACHERS?
THAT'S PRETTY MUCH THE WHOLE POINT, DIPWAD.
WOULDN'T IT BE SAFER TO REBEL AGAINST PEOPLE WE DON'T KNOW?

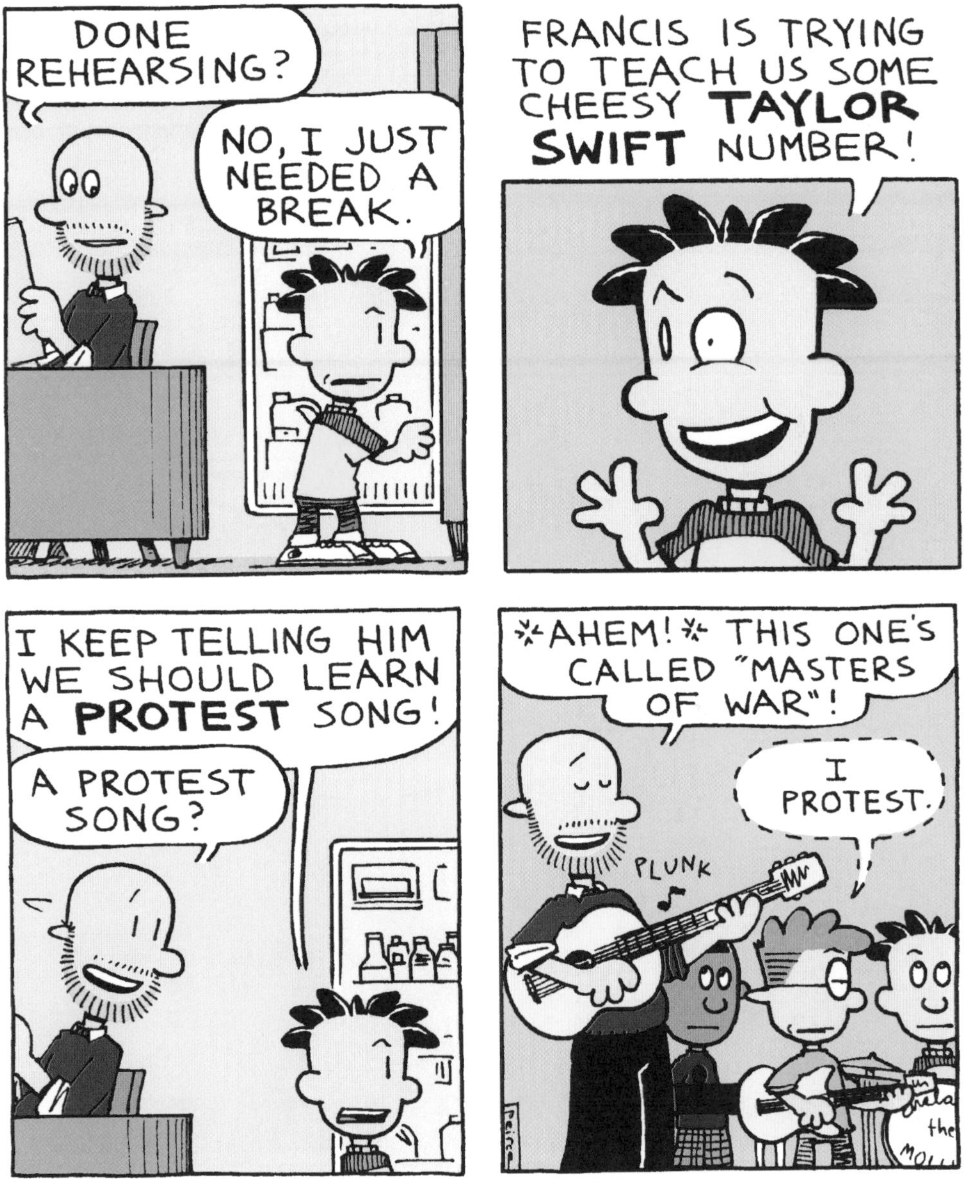
DONE REHEARSING?
NO, I JUST NEEDED A BREAK.
FRANCIS IS TRYING TO TEACH US SOME CHEESY TAYLOR SWIFT NUMBER!
I KEEP TELLING HIM WE SHOULD LEARN A PROTEST SONG!
A PROTEST SONG?
AHEM! THIS ONE'S CALLED "MASTERS OF WAR"!
PLUNK
I PROTEST.

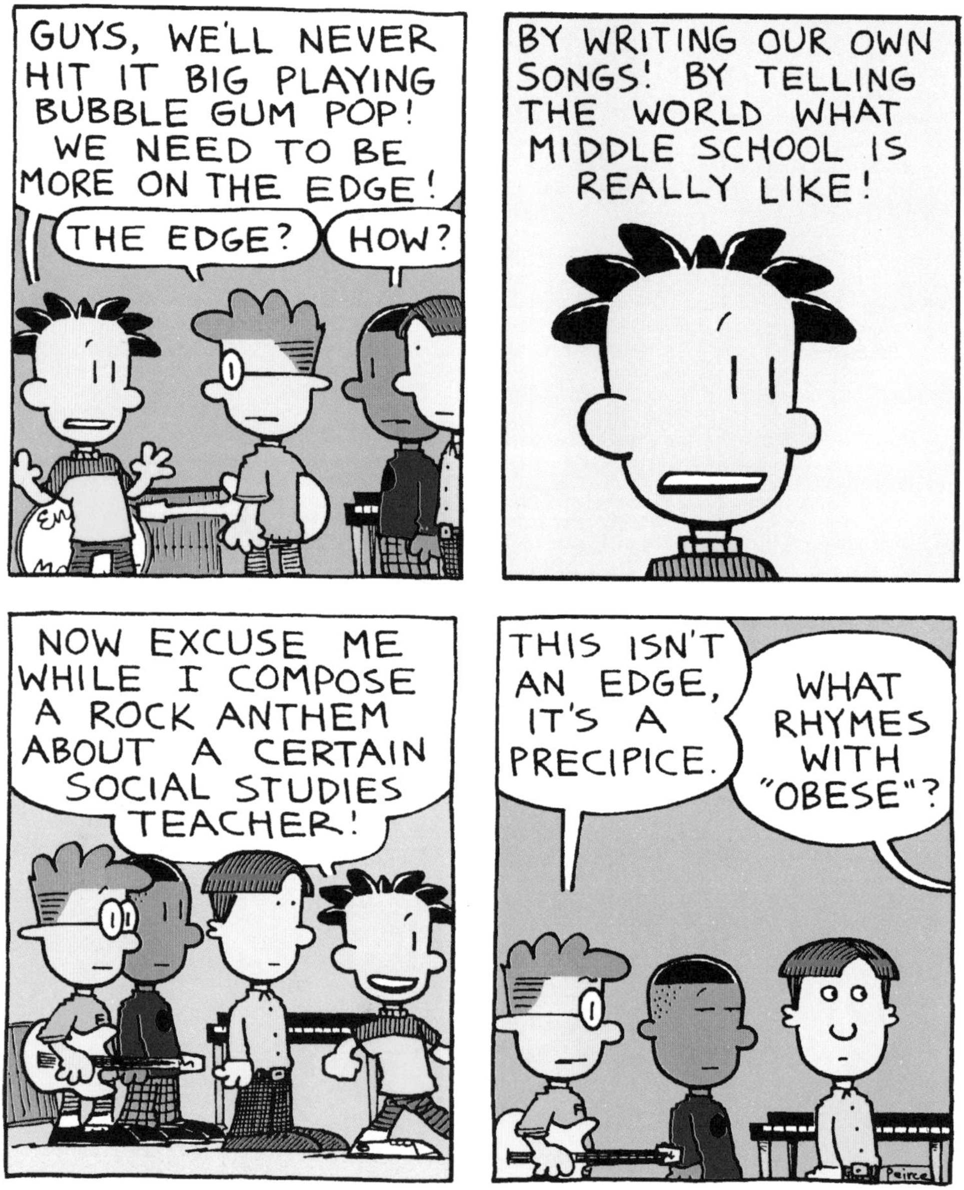
GUYS, WE'LL NEVER HIT IT BIG PLAYING BUBBLE GUM POP! WE NEED TO BE MORE ON THE EDGE!
THE EDGE?
HOW?
BY WRITING OUR OWN SONGS! BY TELLING THE WORLD WHAT MIDDLE SCHOOL IS REALLY LIKE!
NOW EXCUSE ME WHILE I COMPOSE A ROCK ANTHEM ABOUT A CERTAIN SOCIAL STUDIES TEACHER!
THIS ISN'T AN EDGE, IT'S A PRECIPICE.
WHAT RHYMES WITH "OBESE"?
Peirce

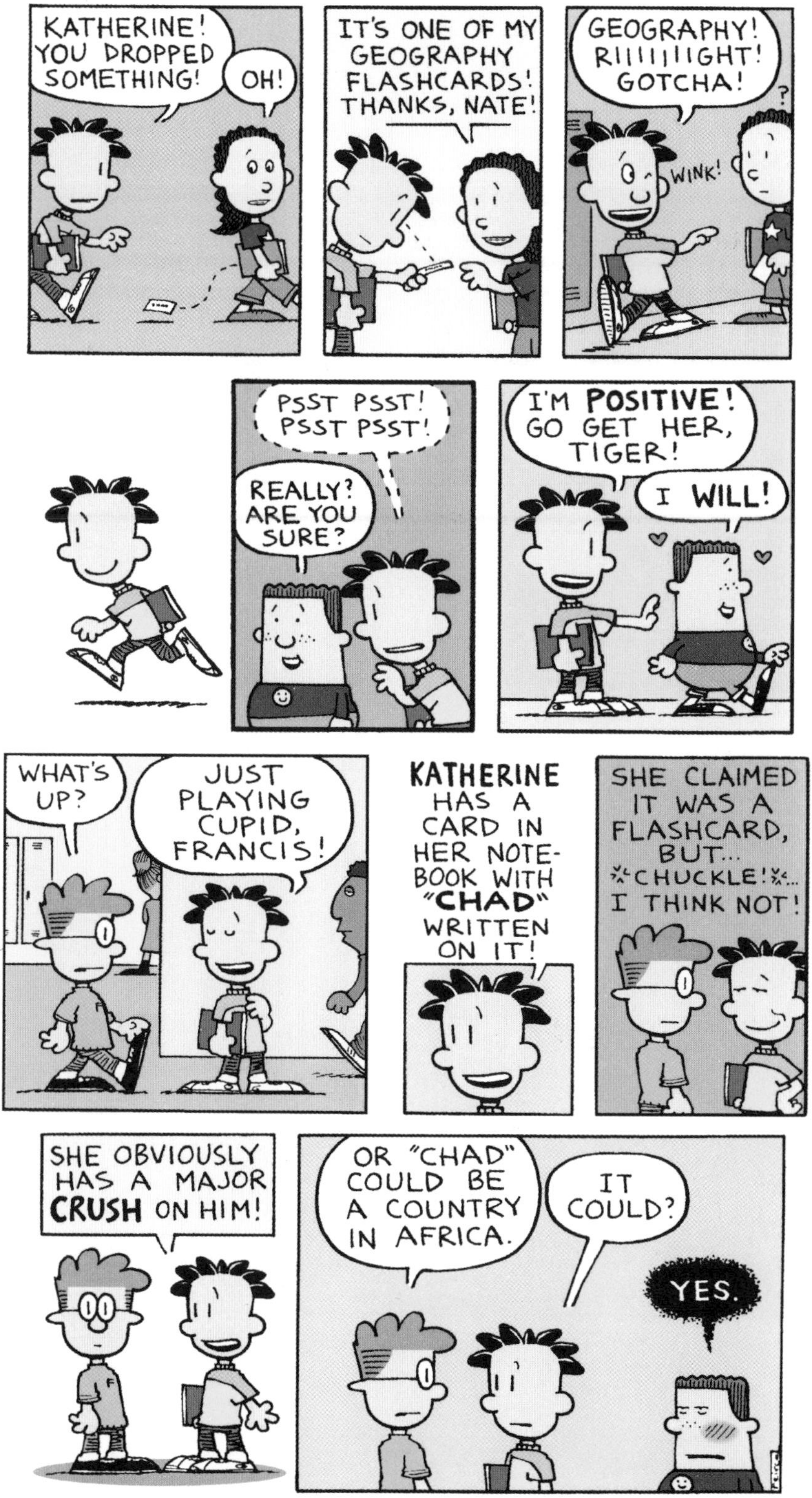
KATHERINE! YOU DROPPED SOMETHING!
OH!
IT'S ONE OF MY GEOGRAPHY FLASHCARDS! THANKS, NATE!
GEOGRAPHY! RIIIIIIIGHT! GOTCHA!
WINK!
?
PSST PSST! PSST PSST!
REALLY? ARE YOU SURE?
I'M POSITIVE! GO GET HER, TIGER!
I WILL!
WHAT'S UP?
JUST PLAYING CUPID, FRANCIS!
KATHERINE HAS A CARD IN HER NOTE-BOOK WITH "CHAD" WRITTEN ON IT!
SHE CLAIMED IT WAS A FLASHCARD, BUT... *CHUCKLE!*... I THINK NOT!
SHE OBVIOUSLY HAS A MAJOR CRUSH ON HIM!
OR "CHAD" COULD BE A COUNTRY IN AFRICA.
IT COULD?
YES.

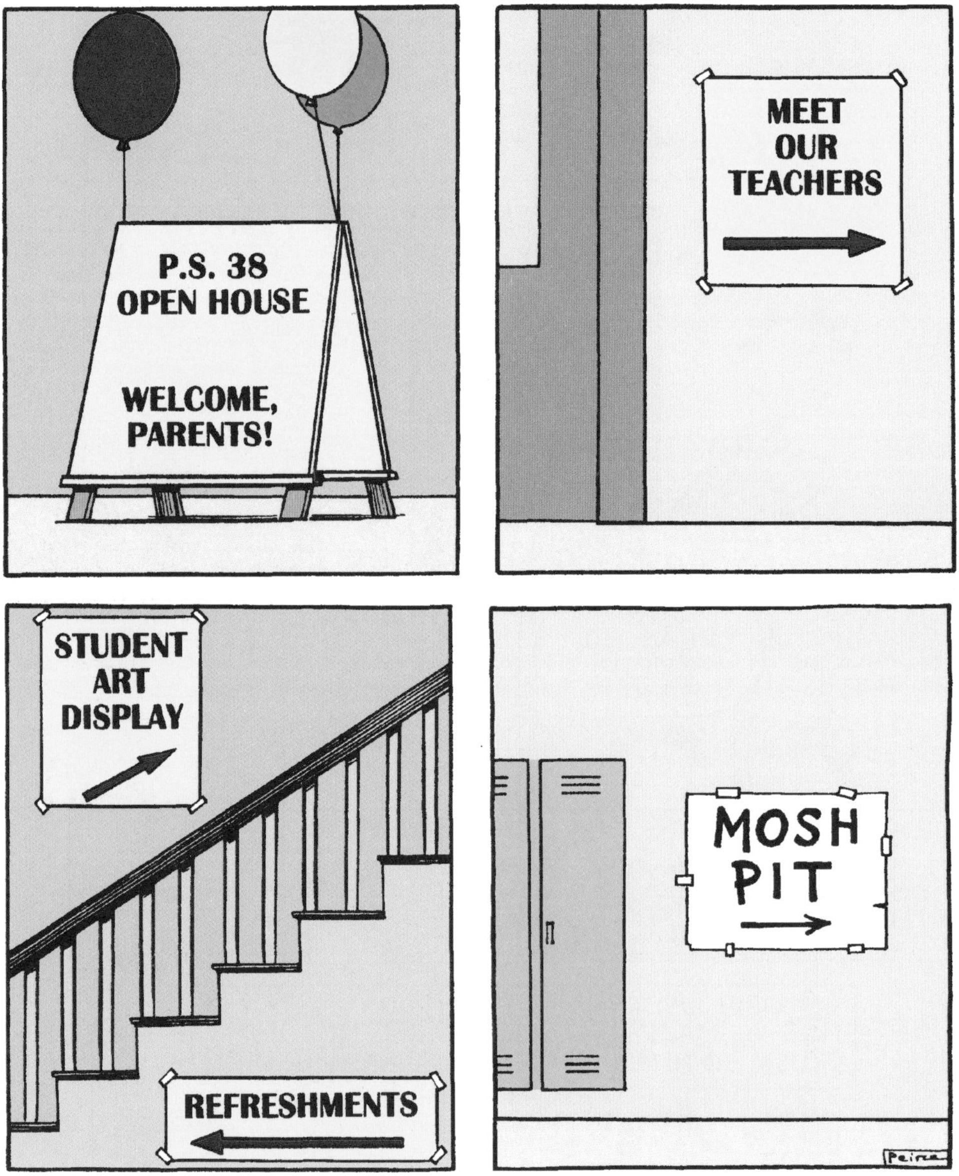
P.S. 38
OPEN HOUSE
WELCOME,
PARENTS!
MEET
OUR
TEACHERS
STUDENT
ART
DISPLAY
REFRESHMENTS
MOSH
PIT
Peirce

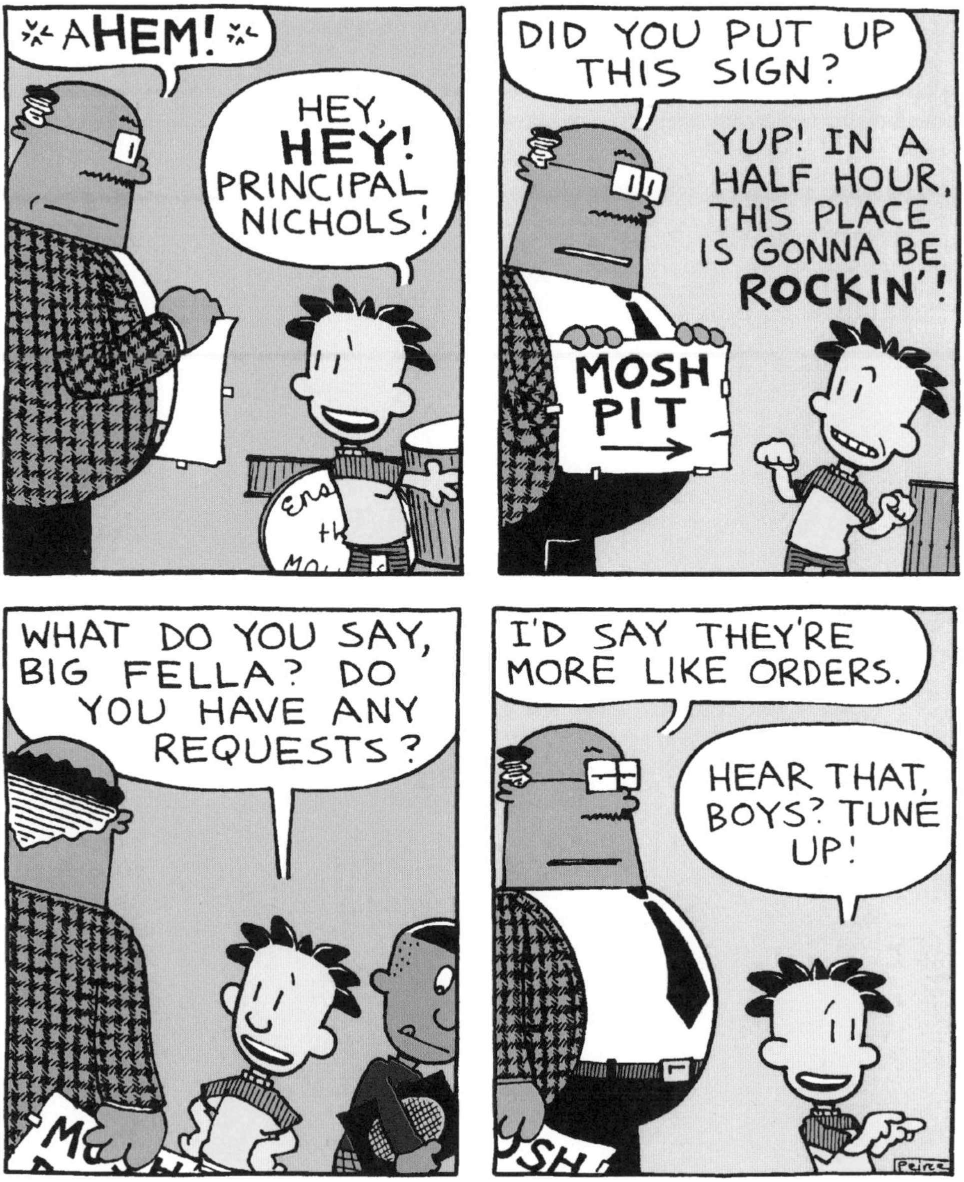
AHEM!
HEY, HEY! PRINCIPAL NICHOLS!
DID YOU PUT UP THIS SIGN?
YUP! IN A HALF HOUR, THIS PLACE IS GONNA BE ROCKIN'!
MOSH PIT
WHAT DO YOU SAY, BIG FELLA? DO YOU HAVE ANY REQUESTS?
I'D SAY THEY'RE MORE LIKE ORDERS.
HEAR THAT, BOYS? TUNE UP!
Peirce

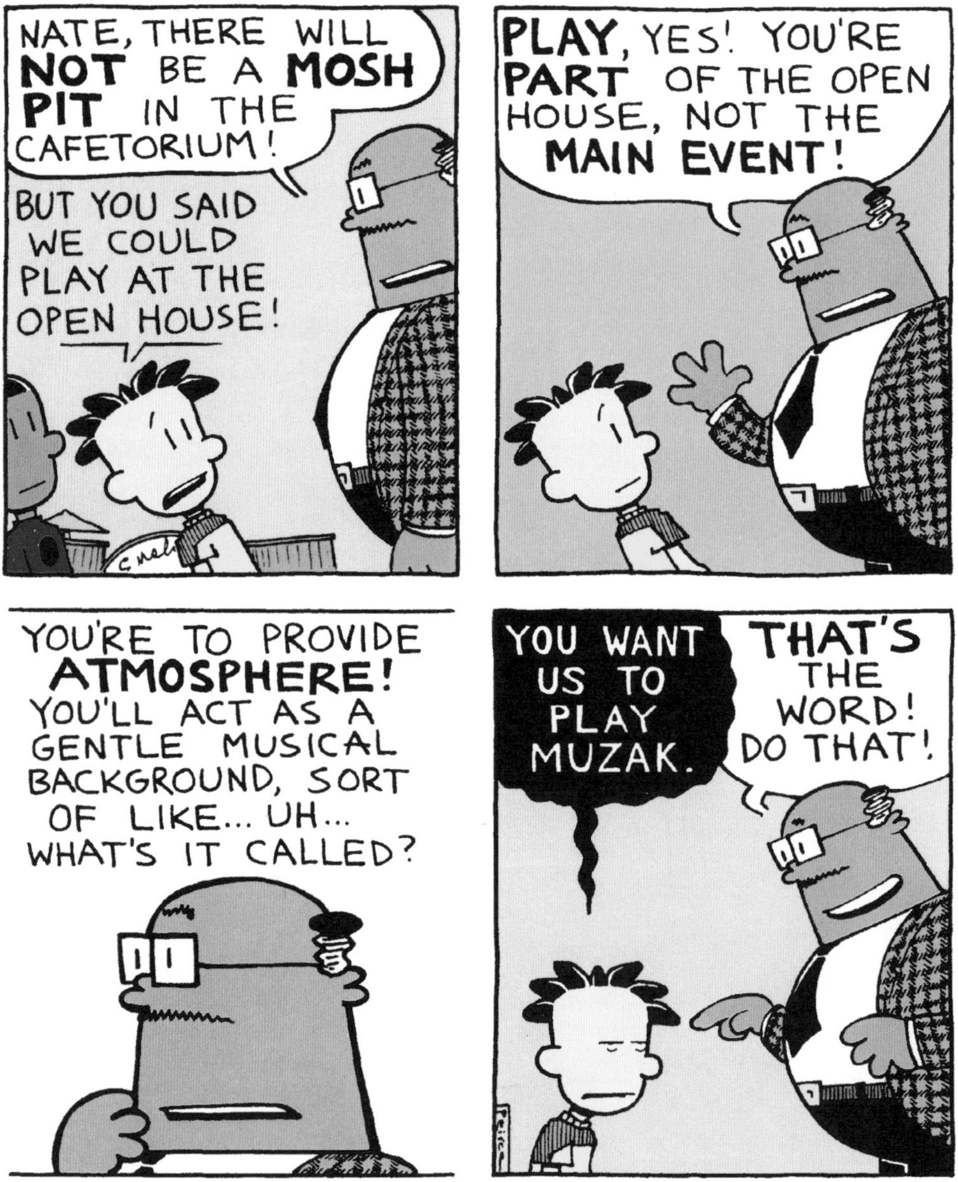
NATE, THERE WILL **NOT** BE A **MOSH PIT** IN THE CAFETORIUM!
BUT YOU SAID WE COULD PLAY AT THE OPEN HOUSE!
PLAY, YES! YOU'RE **PART** OF THE OPEN HOUSE, NOT THE **MAIN EVENT**!
YOU'RE TO PROVIDE **ATMOSPHERE!** YOU'LL ACT AS A GENTLE MUSICAL BACKGROUND, SORT OF LIKE... UH... WHAT'S IT CALLED?
YOU WANT US TO PLAY MUZAK.
THAT'S THE WORD! DO THAT!

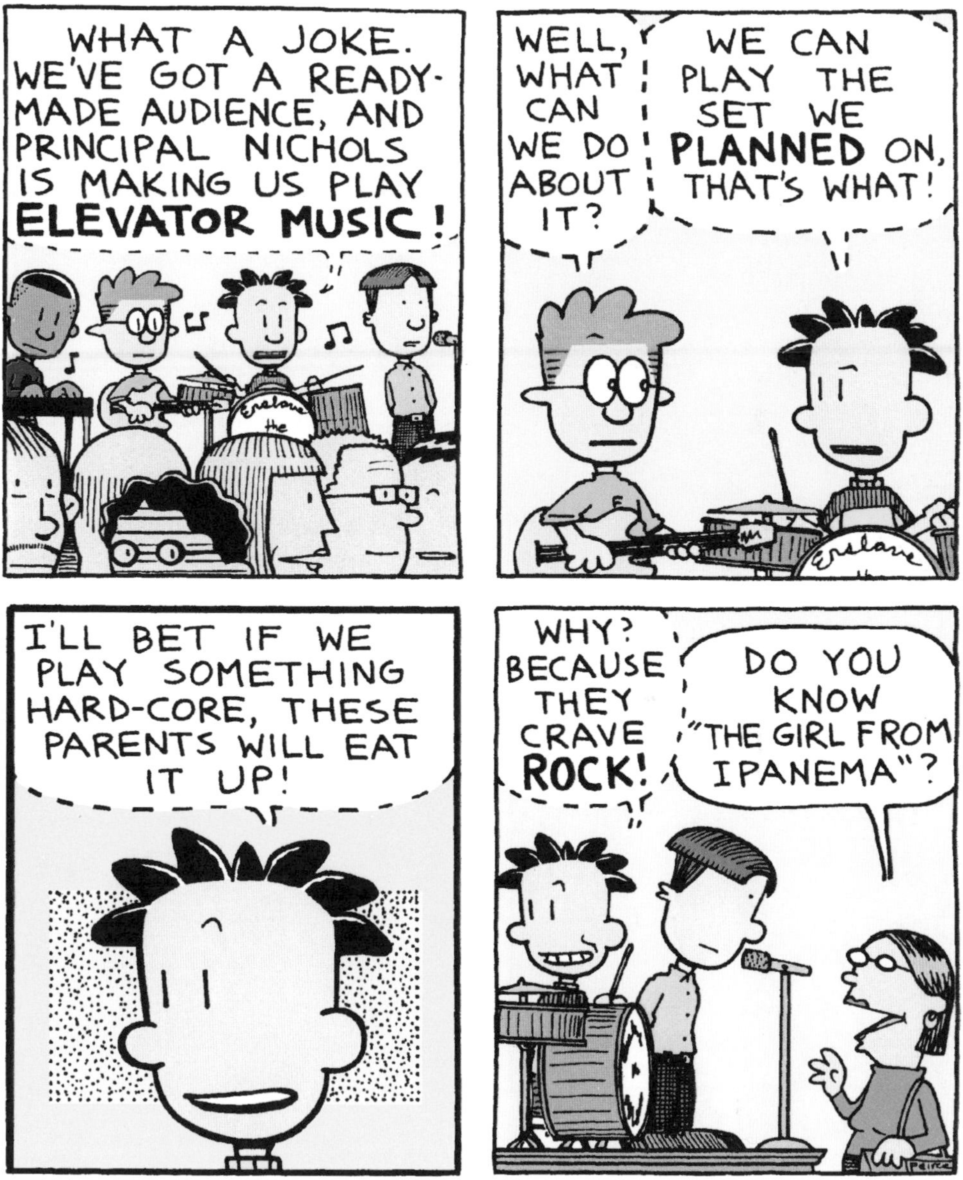
WHAT A JOKE. WE'VE GOT A READY-MADE AUDIENCE, AND PRINCIPAL NICHOLS IS MAKING US PLAY **ELEVATOR MUSIC**!
WELL, WHAT CAN WE DO ABOUT IT?
WE CAN PLAY THE SET WE **PLANNED** ON, THAT'S WHAT!
I'LL BET IF WE PLAY SOMETHING HARD-CORE, THESE PARENTS WILL EAT IT UP!
WHY? BECAUSE THEY CRAVE **ROCK**!
DO YOU KNOW "THE GIRL FROM IPANEMA"?

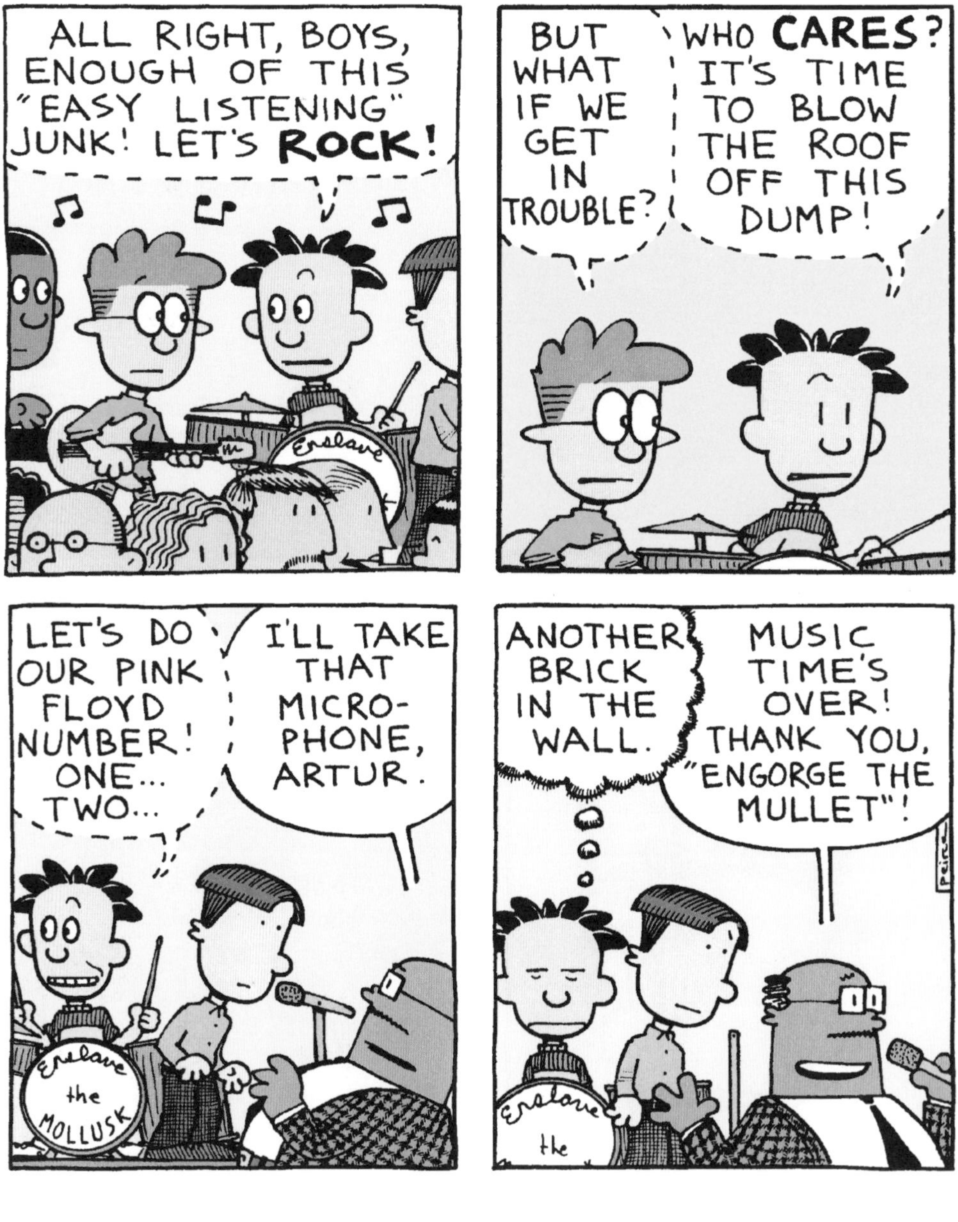
ALL RIGHT, BOYS, ENOUGH OF THIS "EASY LISTENING" JUNK! LET'S **ROCK!**
BUT WHAT IF WE GET IN TROUBLE?
WHO **CARES**? IT'S TIME TO BLOW THE ROOF OFF THIS DUMP!
LET'S DO OUR PINK FLOYD NUMBER! ONE... TWO...
I'LL TAKE THAT MICRO-PHONE, ARTUR.
ANOTHER BRICK IN THE WALL.
MUSIC TIME'S OVER! THANK YOU, "ENGORGE THE MULLET"!
Enslave the MOLLUSK
Peirce

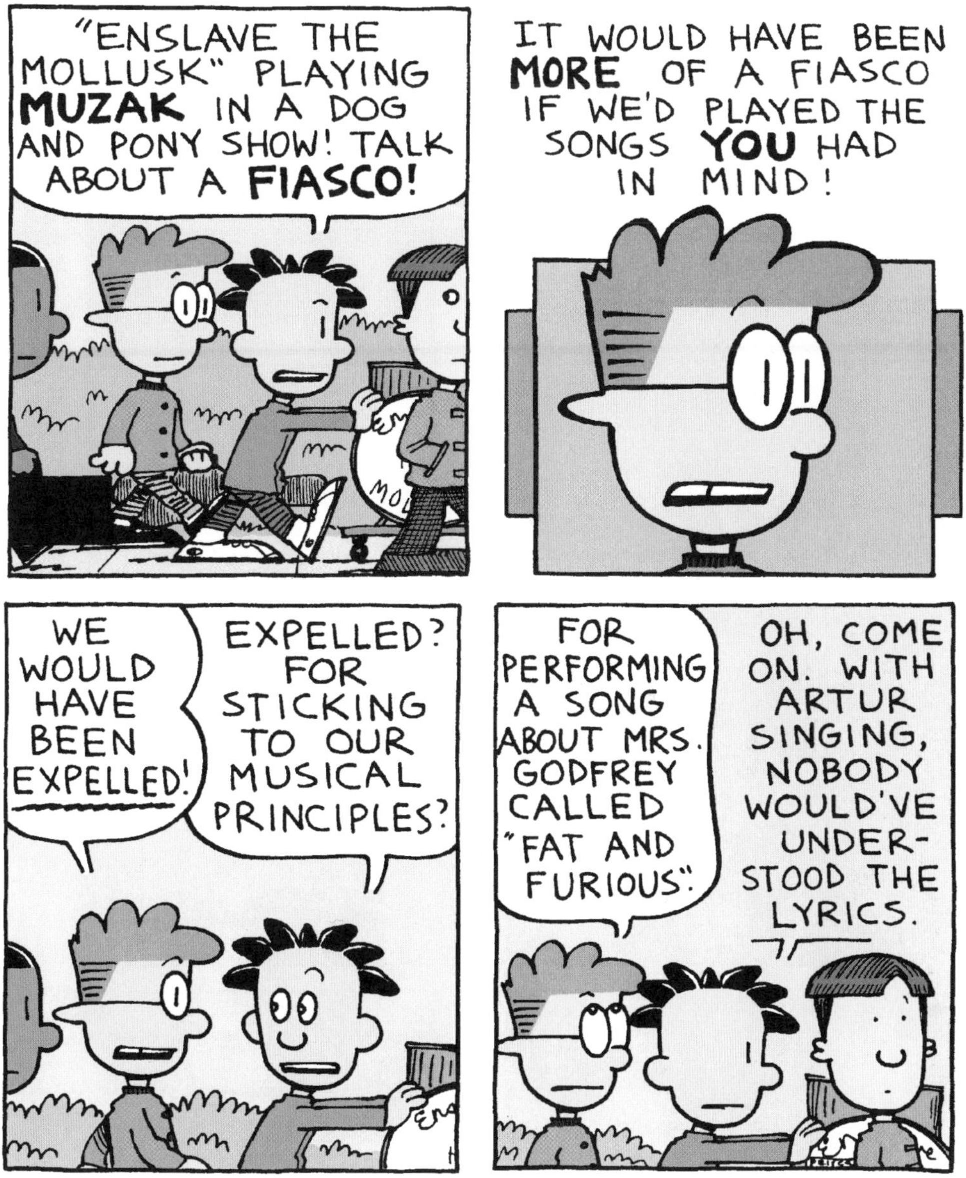
"ENSLAVE THE MOLLUSK" PLAYING **MUZAK** IN A DOG AND PONY SHOW! TALK ABOUT A **FIASCO!**
IT WOULD HAVE BEEN **MORE** OF A FIASCO IF WE'D PLAYED THE SONGS **YOU** HAD IN MIND!
WE WOULD HAVE BEEN EXPELLED!
EXPELLED? FOR STICKING TO OUR MUSICAL PRINCIPLES?
FOR PERFORMING A SONG ABOUT MRS. GODFREY CALLED "FAT AND FURIOUS".
OH, COME ON. WITH ARTUR SINGING, NOBODY WOULD'VE UNDER-STOOD THE LYRICS.

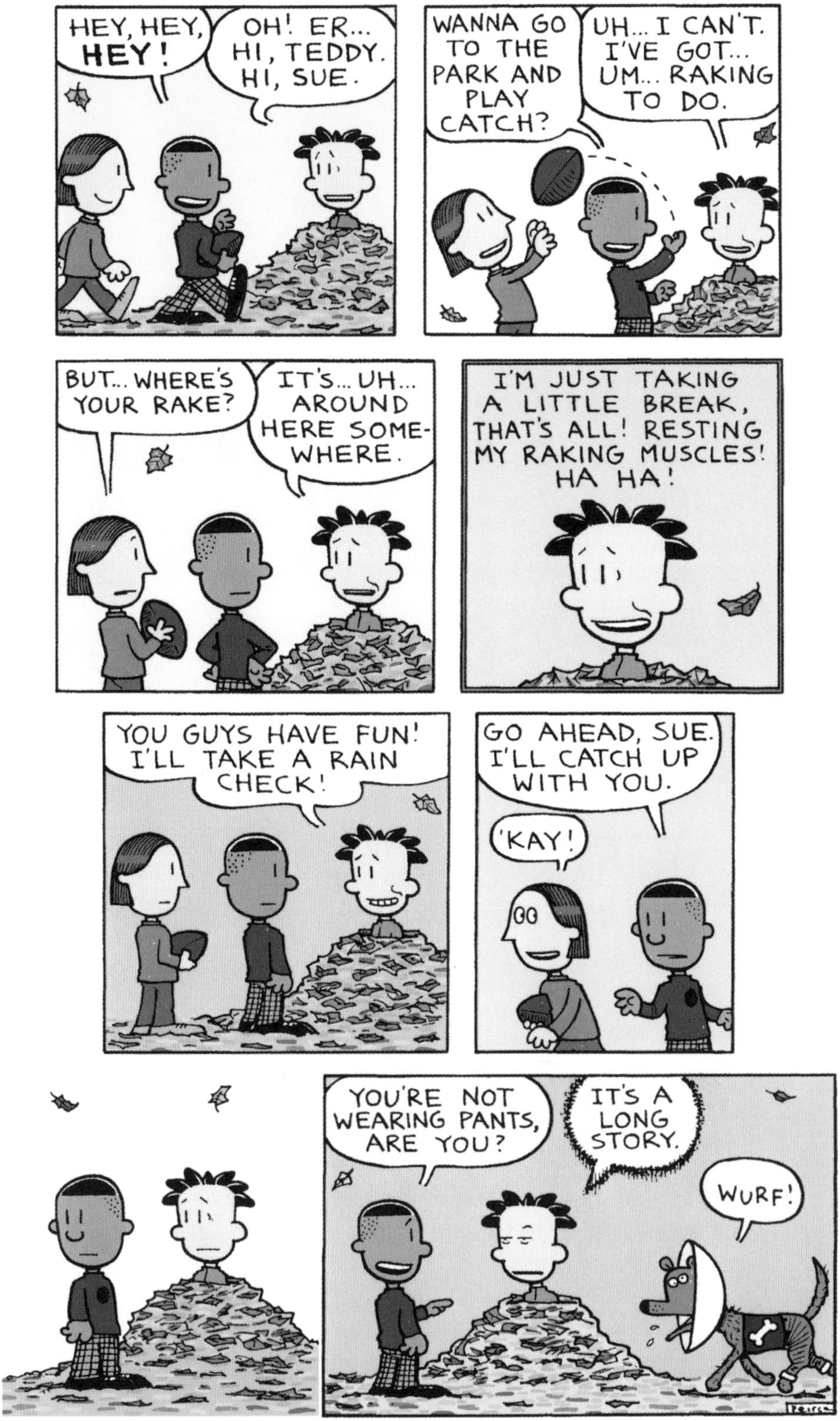
HEY, HEY, HEY!
OH! ER... HI, TEDDY. HI, SUE.
WANNA GO TO THE PARK AND PLAY CATCH?
UH... I CAN'T. I'VE GOT... UM... RAKING TO DO.
BUT... WHERE'S YOUR RAKE?
IT'S... UH... AROUND HERE SOME-WHERE.
I'M JUST TAKING A LITTLE BREAK, THAT'S ALL! RESTING MY RAKING MUSCLES! HA HA!
YOU GUYS HAVE FUN! I'LL TAKE A RAIN CHECK!
GO AHEAD, SUE. I'LL CATCH UP WITH YOU.
'KAY!
YOU'RE NOT WEARING PANTS, ARE YOU?
IT'S A LONG STORY.
WURF!

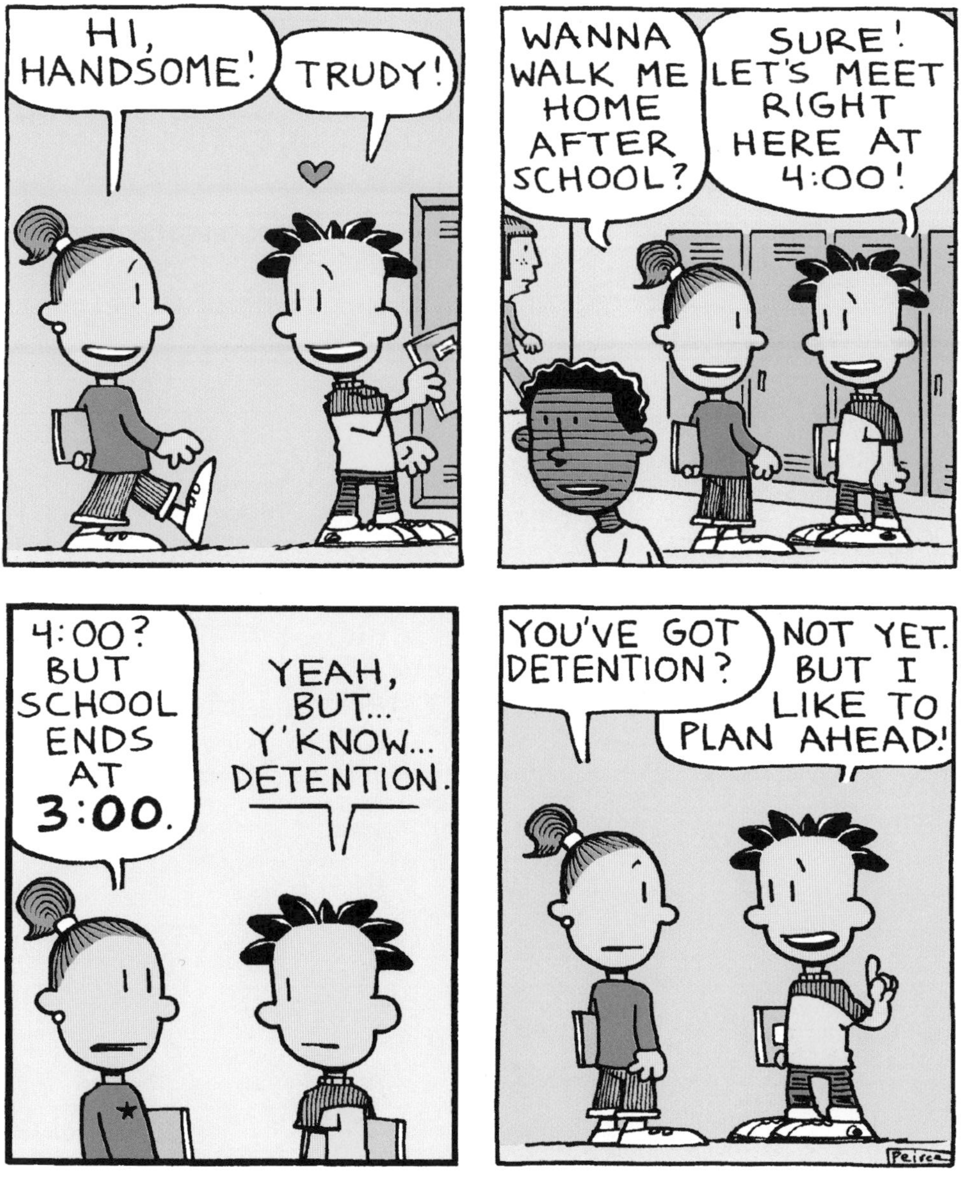
HI, HANDSOME!
TRUDY!
WANNA WALK ME HOME AFTER SCHOOL?
SURE! LET'S MEET RIGHT HERE AT 4:00!
4:00? BUT SCHOOL ENDS AT 3:00.
YEAH, BUT... Y'KNOW... DETENTION.
YOU'VE GOT DETENTION?
NOT YET. BUT I LIKE TO PLAN AHEAD!
Peirce

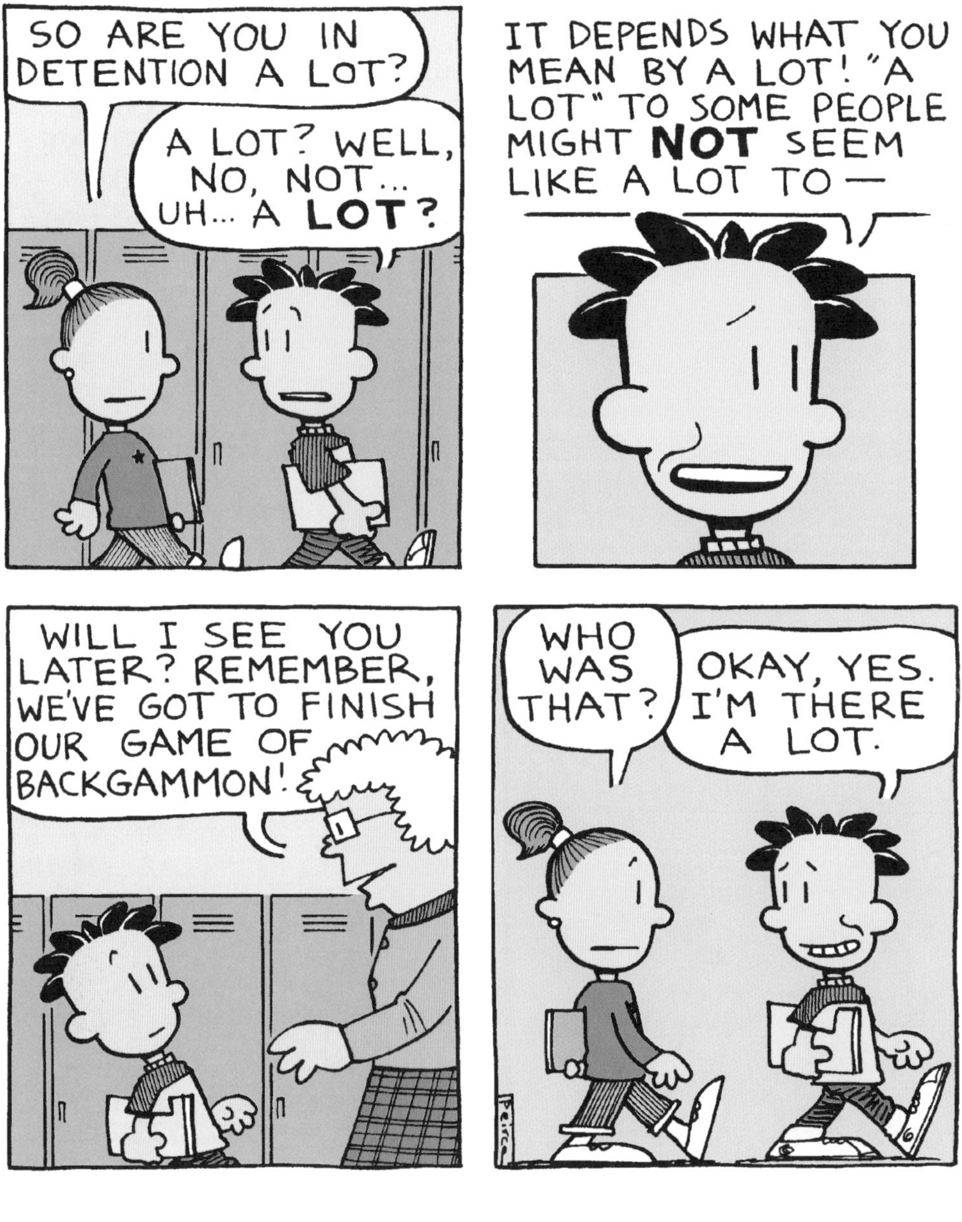
SO ARE YOU IN DETENTION A LOT?
A LOT? WELL, NO, NOT... UH... A **LOT**?
IT DEPENDS WHAT YOU MEAN BY A LOT! "A LOT" TO SOME PEOPLE MIGHT **NOT** SEEM LIKE A LOT TO—
WILL I SEE YOU LATER? REMEMBER, WE'VE GOT TO FINISH OUR GAME OF BACKGAMMON!
WHO WAS THAT?
OKAY, YES. I'M THERE A LOT.

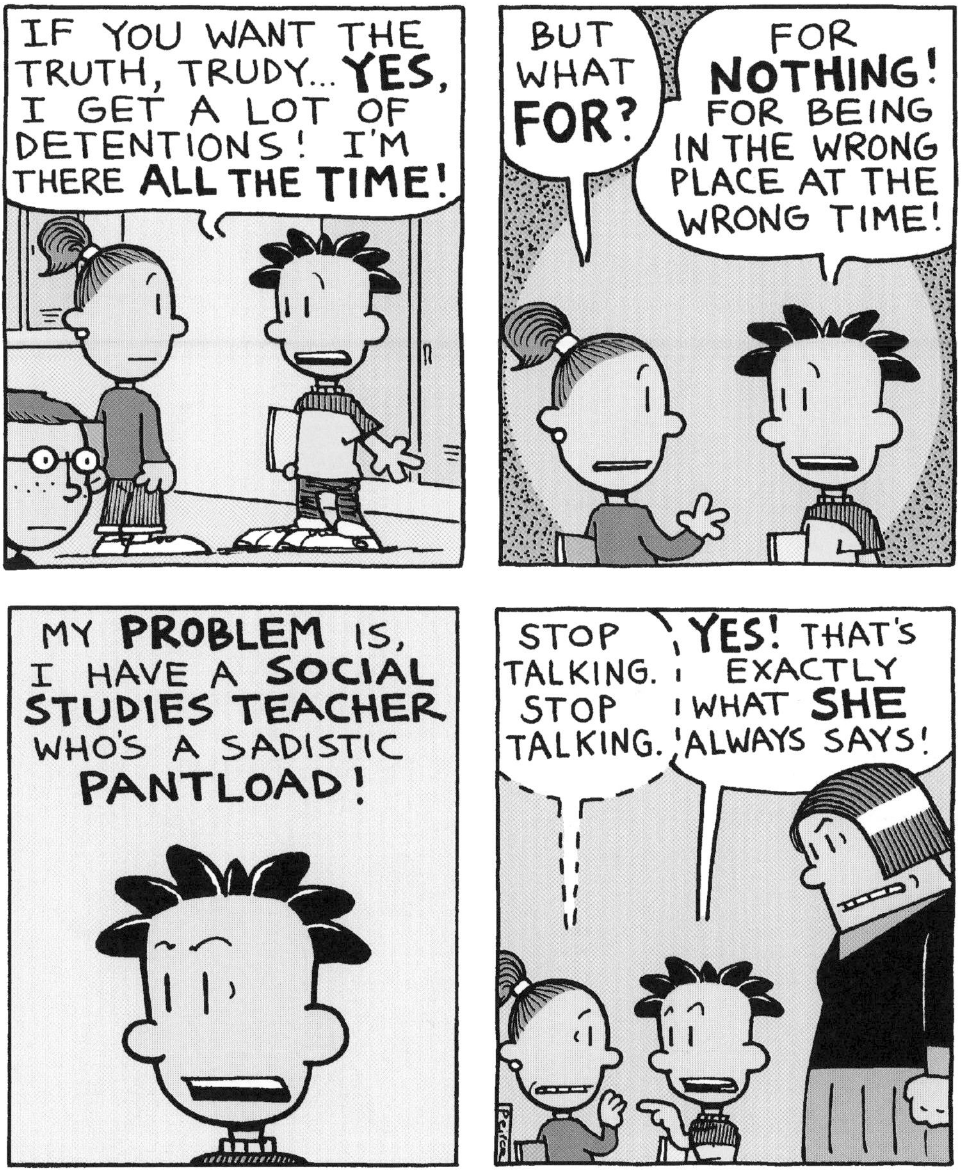
IF YOU WANT THE TRUTH, TRUDY... YES, I GET A LOT OF DETENTIONS! I'M THERE ALL THE TIME!
BUT WHAT FOR?
FOR NOTHING! FOR BEING IN THE WRONG PLACE AT THE WRONG TIME!
MY PROBLEM IS, I HAVE A SOCIAL STUDIES TEACHER WHO'S A SADISTIC PANTLOAD!
STOP TALKING. STOP TALKING. STOP TALKING.
YES! THAT'S EXACTLY WHAT SHE ALWAYS SAYS!

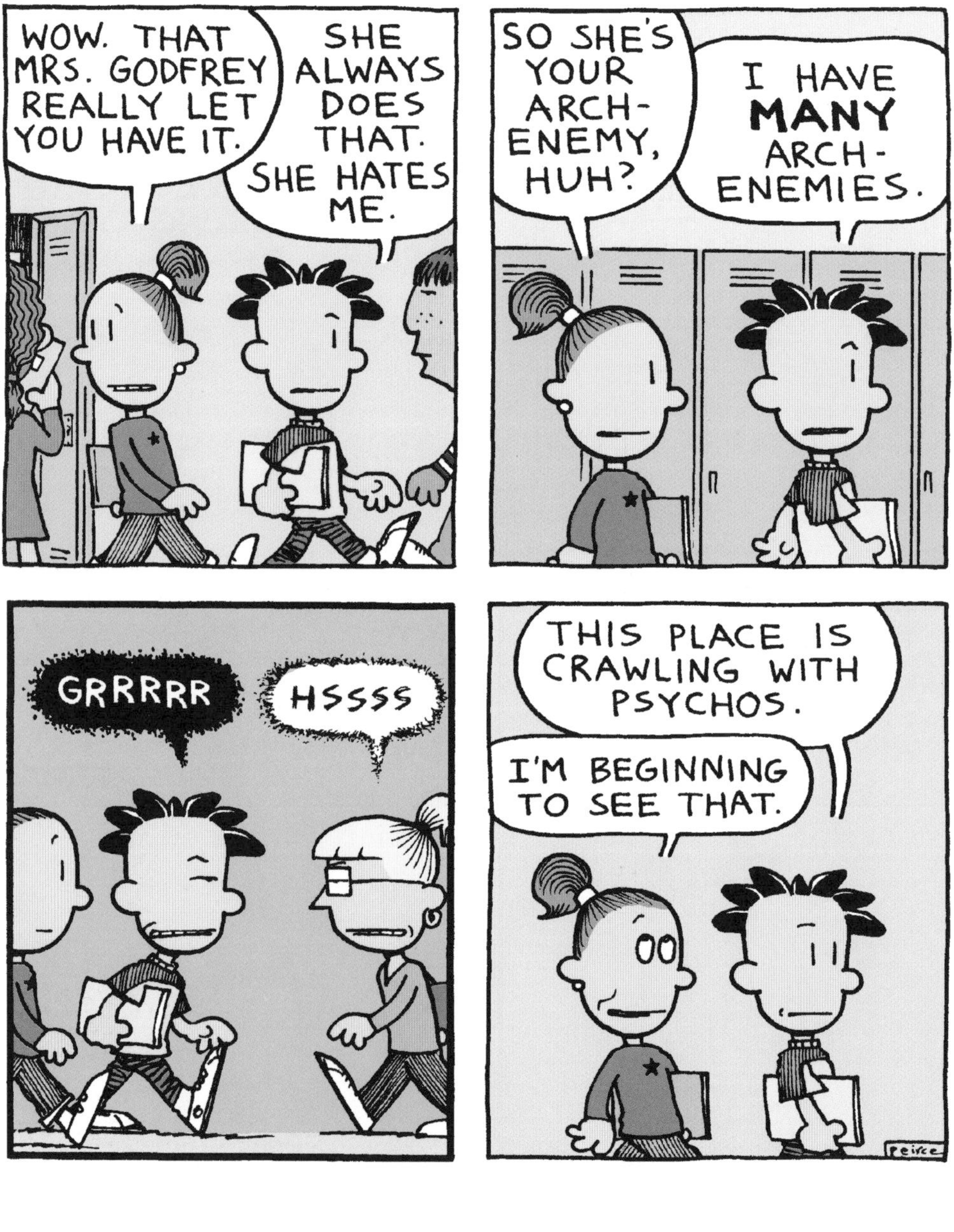
WOW. THAT MRS. GODFREY REALLY LET YOU HAVE IT.
SHE ALWAYS DOES THAT. SHE HATES ME.
SO SHE'S YOUR ARCH-ENEMY, HUH?
I HAVE **MANY** ARCH-ENEMIES.
GRRRRR
HSSSS
THIS PLACE IS CRAWLING WITH PSYCHOS.
I'M BEGINNING TO SEE THAT.
peirce

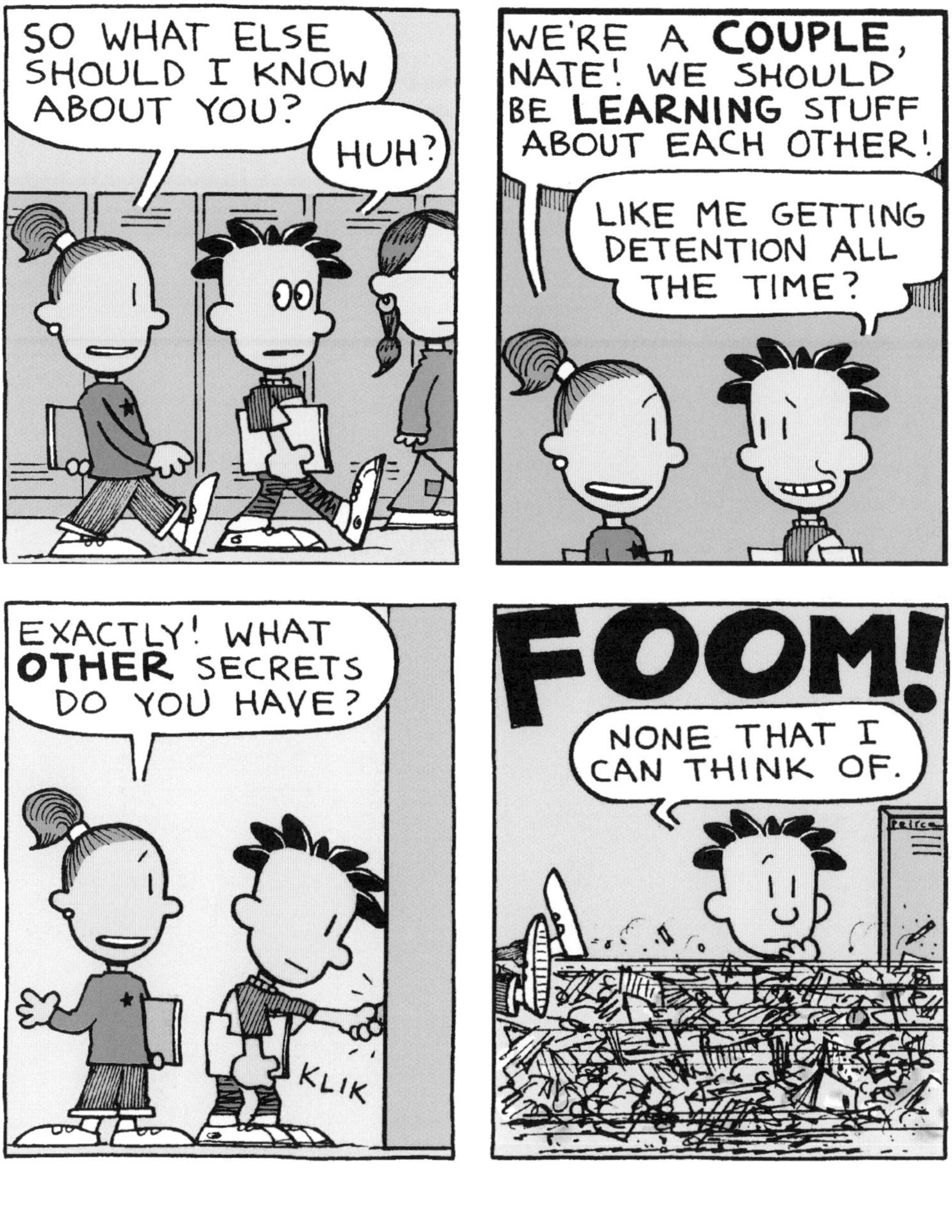
SO WHAT ELSE SHOULD I KNOW ABOUT YOU?
HUH?
WE'RE A **COUPLE**, NATE! WE SHOULD BE **LEARNING** STUFF ABOUT EACH OTHER!
LIKE ME GETTING DETENTION ALL THE TIME?
EXACTLY! WHAT **OTHER** SECRETS DO YOU HAVE?
KLIK
FOOM!
NONE THAT I CAN THINK OF.

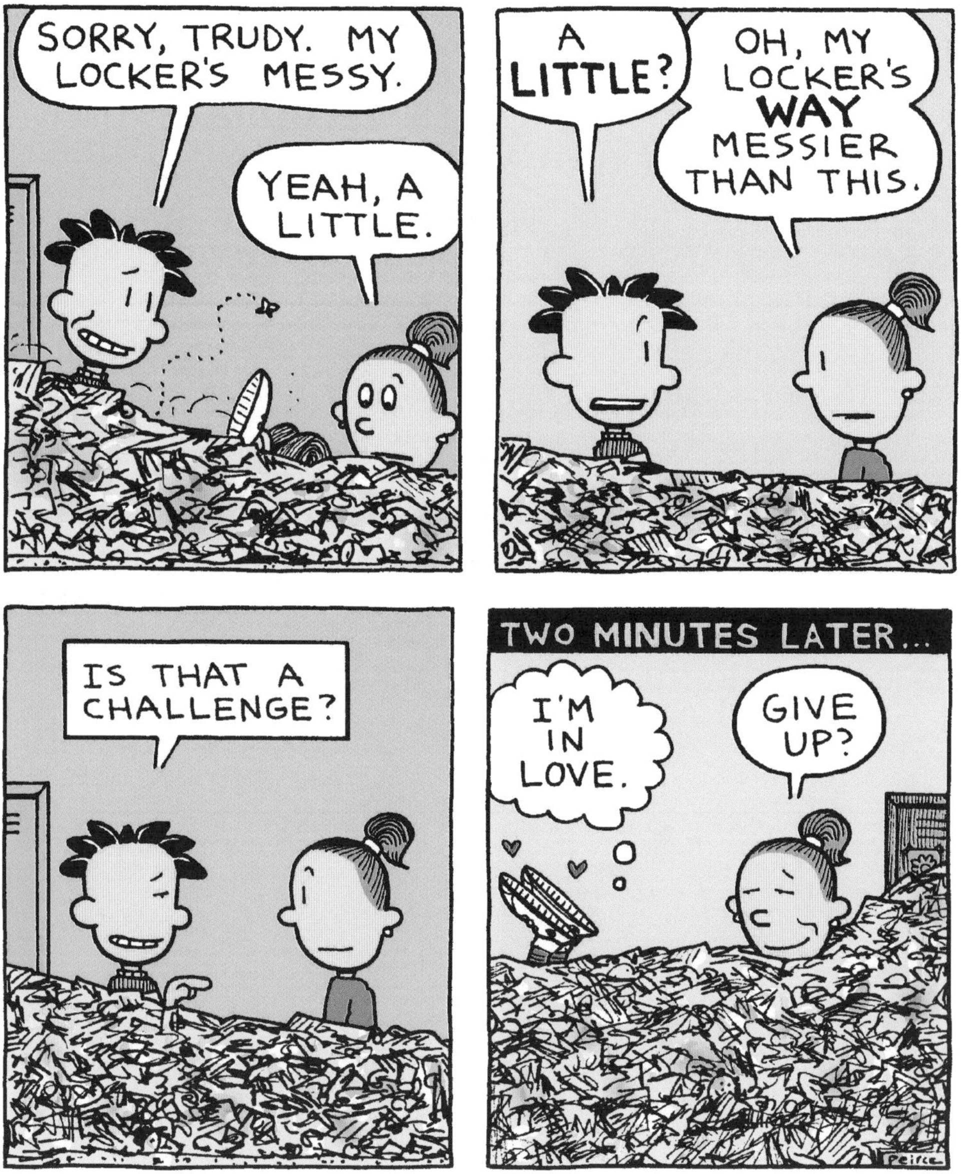
SORRY, TRUDY. MY LOCKER'S MESSY.
YEAH, A LITTLE.
A **LITTLE**?
OH, MY LOCKER'S **WAY** MESSIER THAN THIS.
IS THAT A CHALLENGE?
TWO MINUTES LATER...
I'M IN LOVE.
GIVE UP?
Peirce

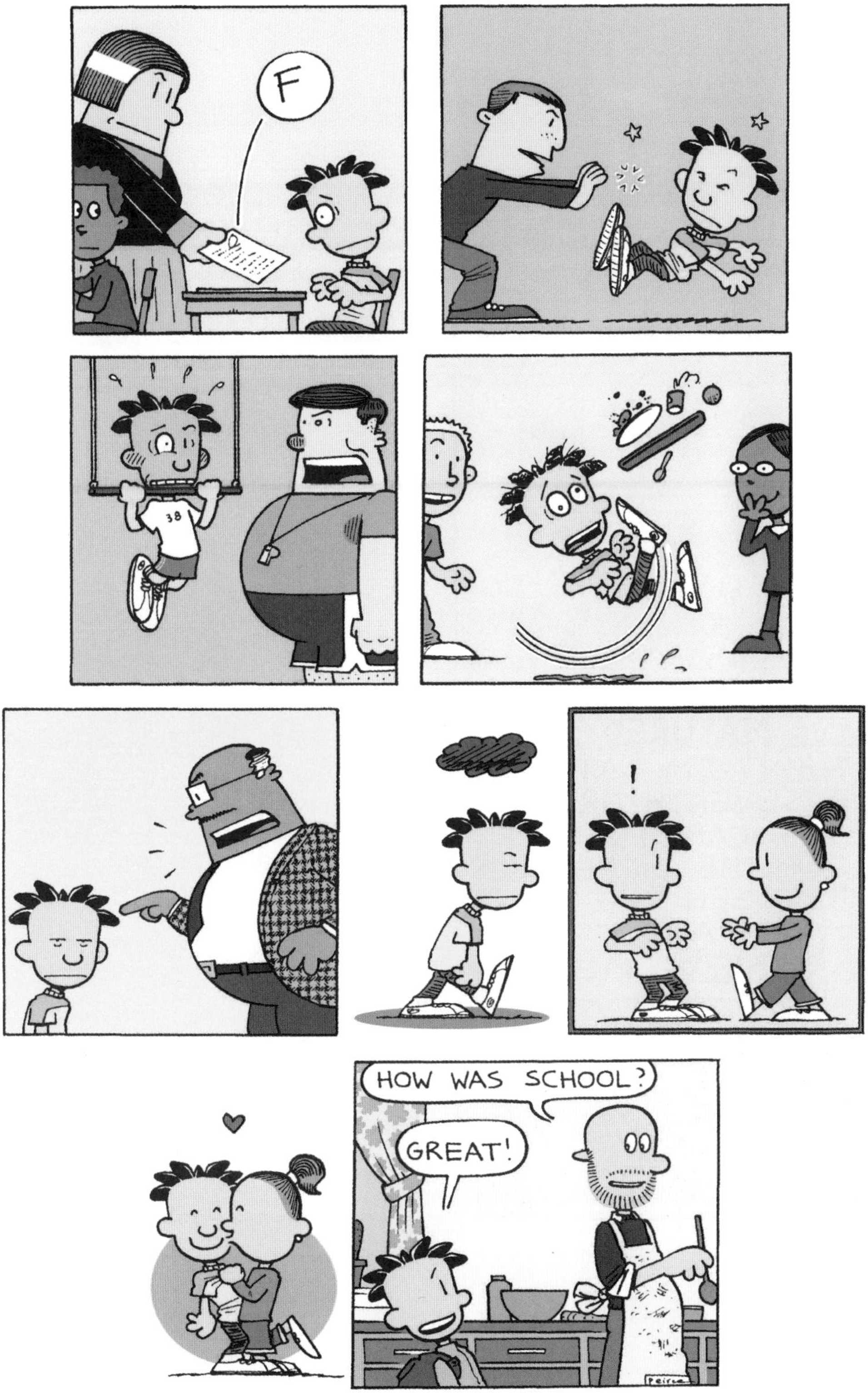
F
!
HOW WAS SCHOOL?
GREAT!

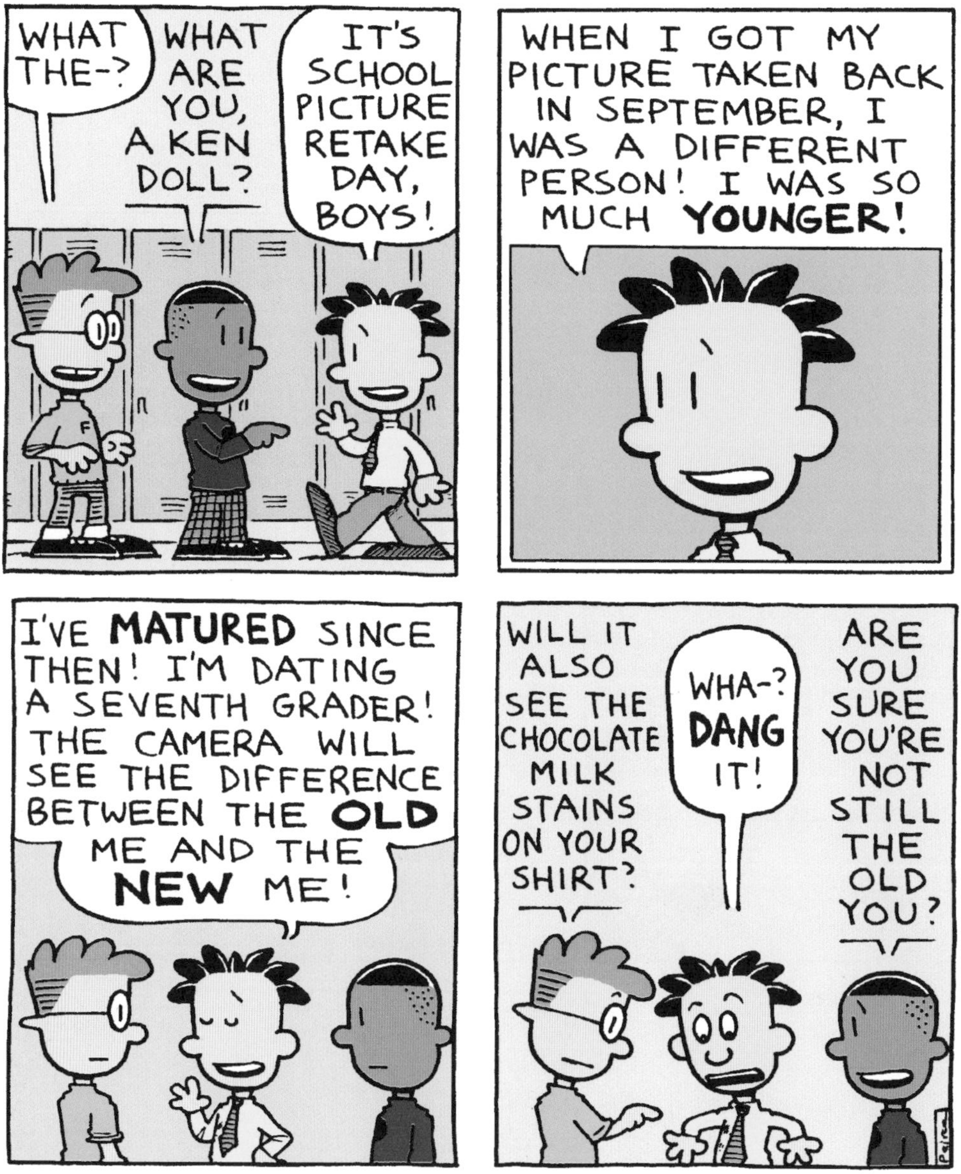
WHAT THE-?
WHAT ARE YOU, A KEN DOLL?
IT'S SCHOOL PICTURE RETAKE DAY, BOYS!
WHEN I GOT MY PICTURE TAKEN BACK IN SEPTEMBER, I WAS A DIFFERENT PERSON! I WAS SO MUCH YOUNGER!
I'VE MATURED SINCE THEN! I'M DATING A SEVENTH GRADER! THE CAMERA WILL SEE THE DIFFERENCE BETWEEN THE OLD ME AND THE NEW ME!
WILL IT ALSO SEE THE CHOCOLATE MILK STAINS ON YOUR SHIRT?
WHA-? DANG IT!
ARE YOU SURE YOU'RE NOT STILL THE OLD YOU?

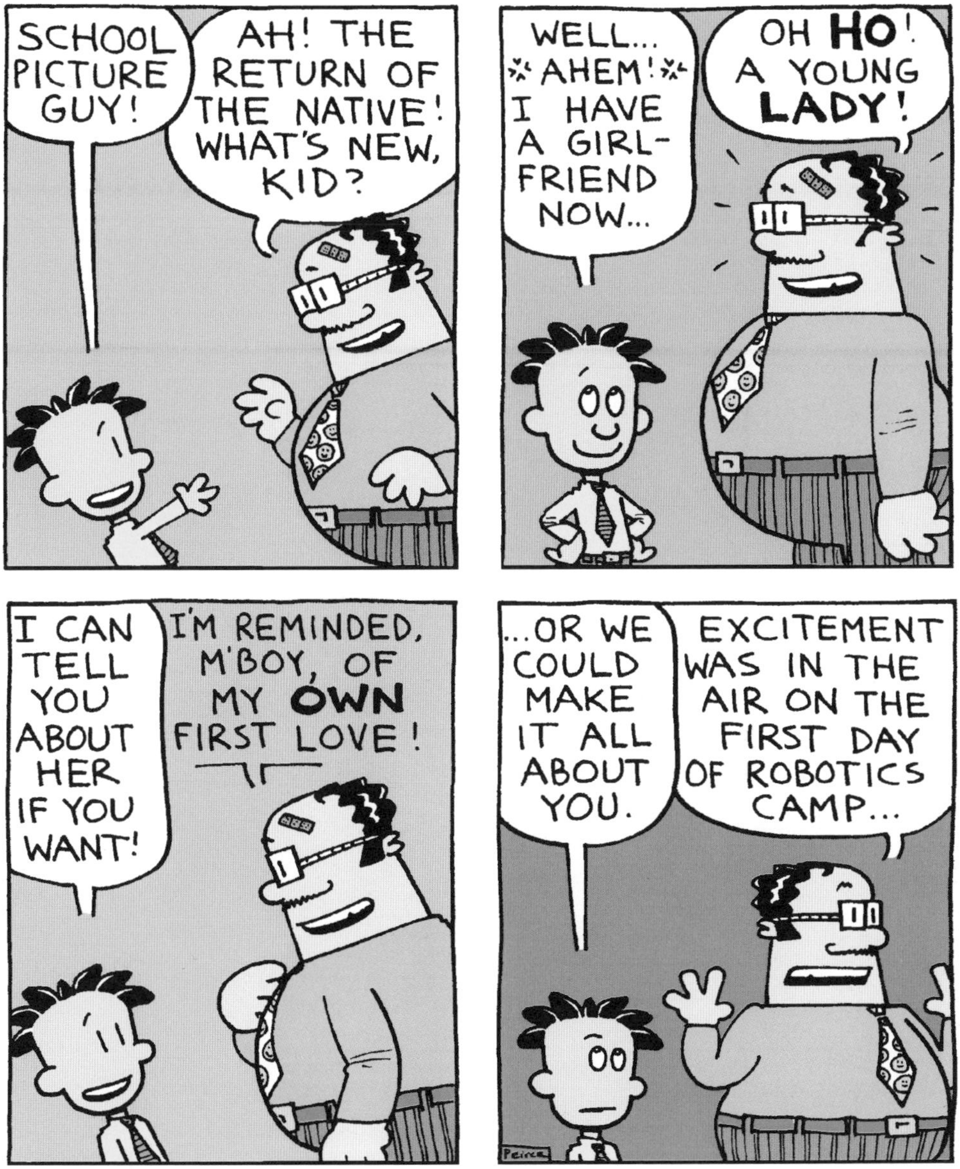
SCHOOL PICTURE GUY!
AH! THE RETURN OF THE NATIVE! WHAT'S NEW, KID?
WELL... *AHEM!* I HAVE A GIRL-FRIEND NOW...
OH **HO**! A YOUNG **LADY**!
I CAN TELL YOU ABOUT HER IF YOU WANT!
I'M REMINDED, M'BOY, OF MY **OWN** FIRST LOVE!
...OR WE COULD MAKE IT ALL ABOUT YOU.
EXCITEMENT WAS IN THE AIR ON THE FIRST DAY OF ROBOTICS CAMP...
Peirce

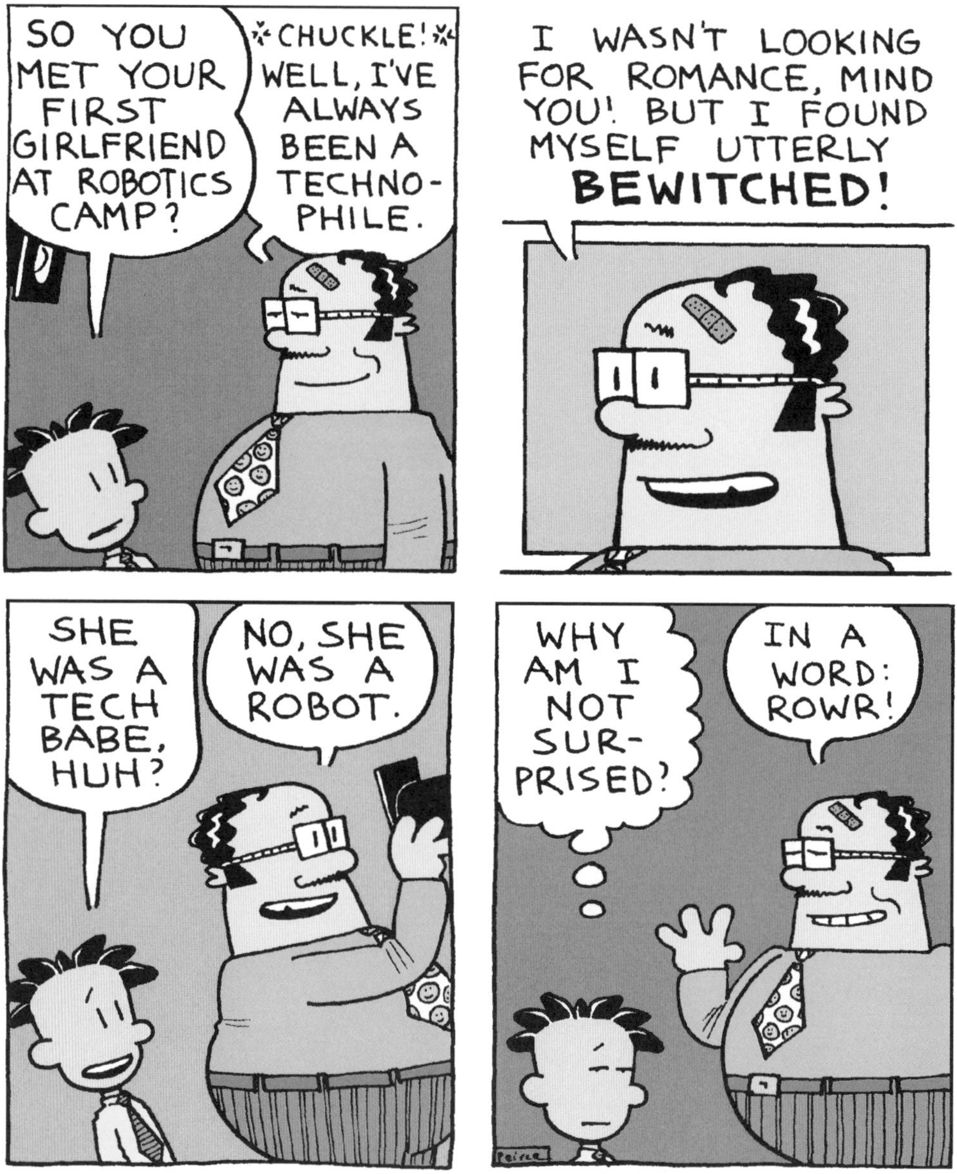
SO YOU MET YOUR FIRST GIRLFRIEND AT ROBOTICS CAMP?
CHUCKLE! WELL, I'VE ALWAYS BEEN A TECHNO-PHILE.
I WASN'T LOOKING FOR ROMANCE, MIND YOU! BUT I FOUND MYSELF UTTERLY **BEWITCHED!**
SHE WAS A TECH BABE, HUH?
NO, SHE WAS A ROBOT.
WHY AM I NOT SUR-PRISED?
IN A WORD: ROWR!
Peirce

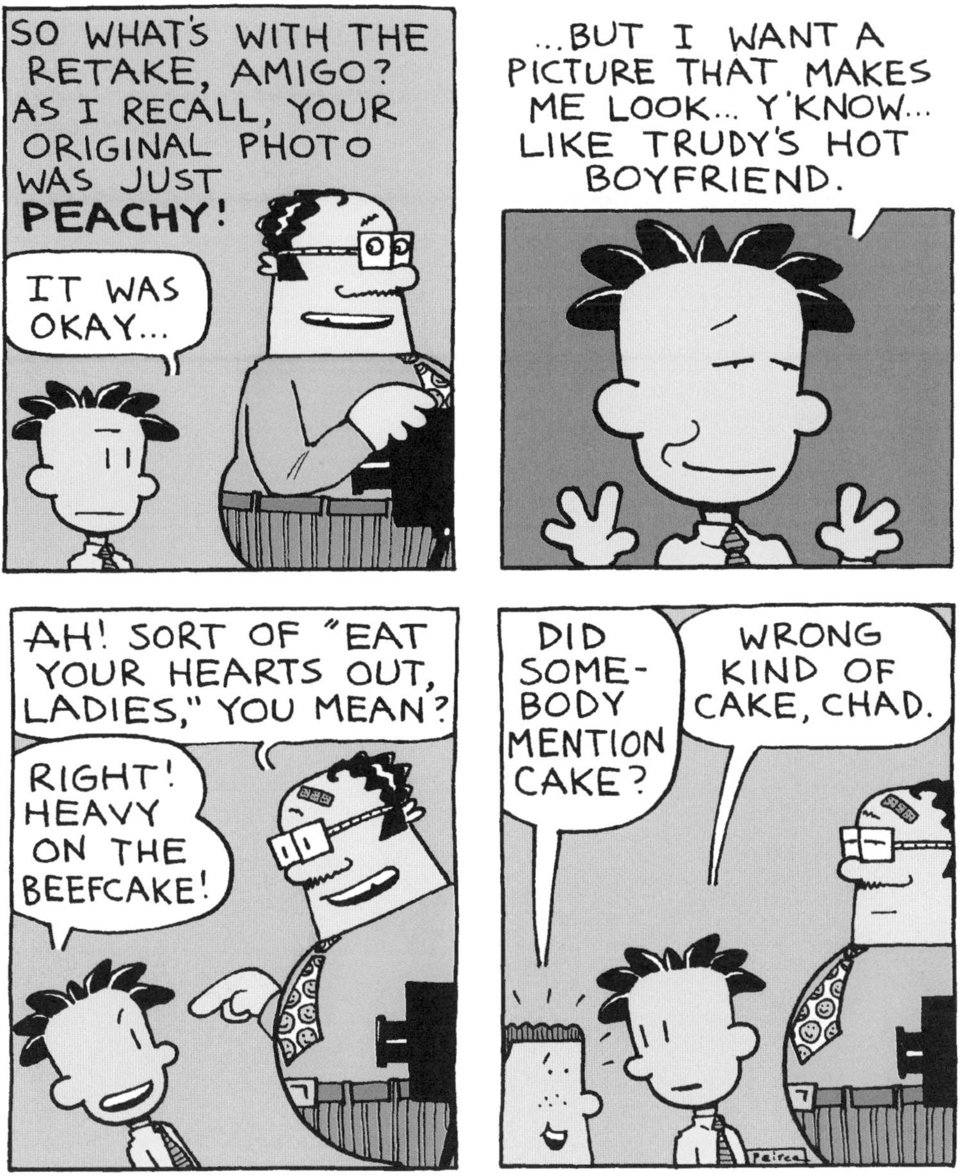
SO WHAT'S WITH THE RETAKE, AMIGO? AS I RECALL, YOUR ORIGINAL PHOTO WAS JUST **PEACHY**!
IT WAS OKAY...
...BUT I WANT A PICTURE THAT MAKES ME LOOK... Y'KNOW... LIKE TRUDY'S HOT BOYFRIEND.
AH! SORT OF "EAT YOUR HEARTS OUT, LADIES," YOU MEAN?
RIGHT! HEAVY ON THE BEEFCAKE!
DID SOMEBODY MENTION CAKE?
WRONG KIND OF CAKE, CHAD.
Peirce

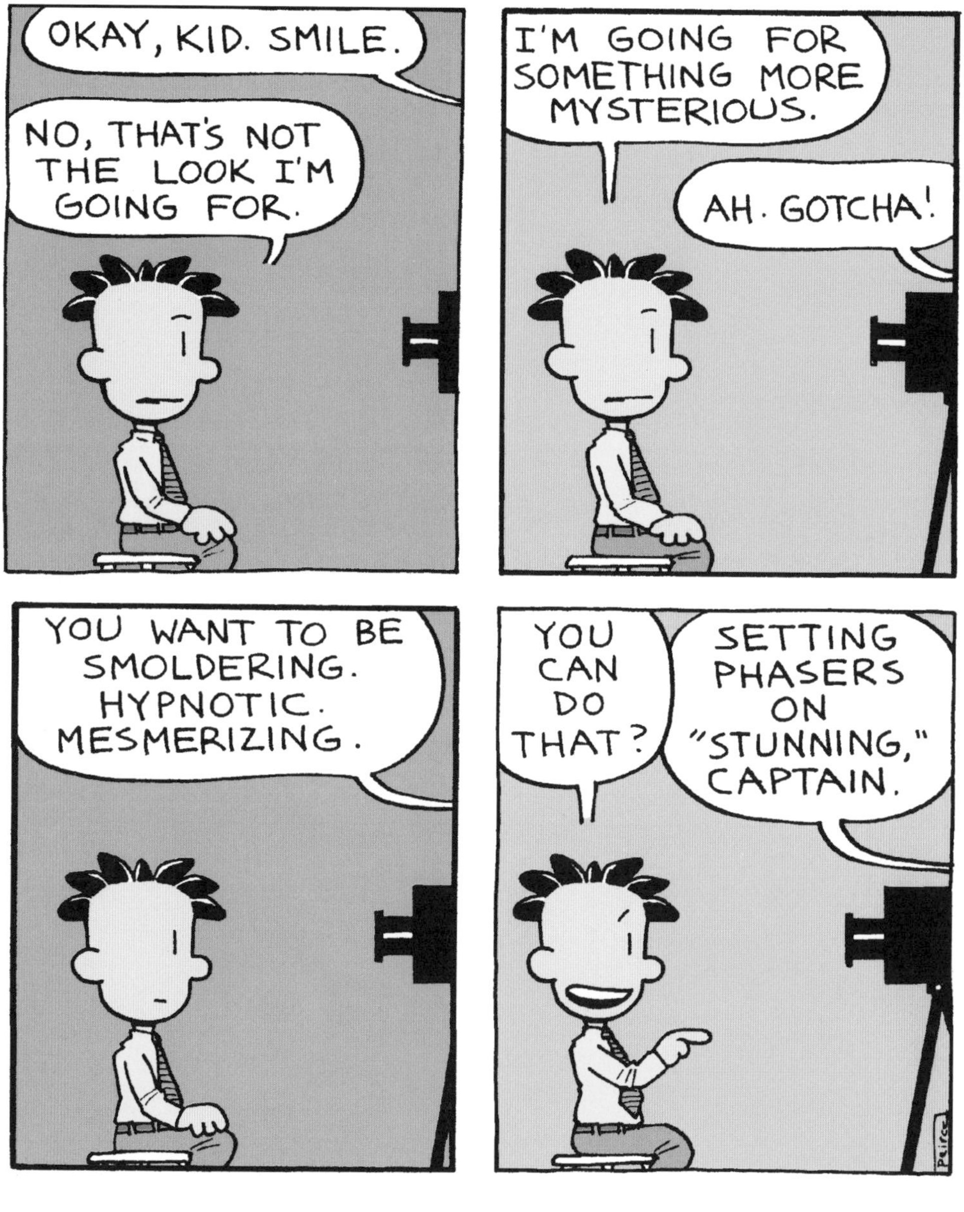
OKAY, KID. SMILE.
NO, THAT'S NOT THE LOOK I'M GOING FOR.
I'M GOING FOR SOMETHING MORE MYSTERIOUS.
AH. GOTCHA!
YOU WANT TO BE SMOLDERING. HYPNOTIC. MESMERIZING.
YOU CAN DO THAT?
SETTING PHASERS ON "STUNNING," CAPTAIN.
PEIRCE

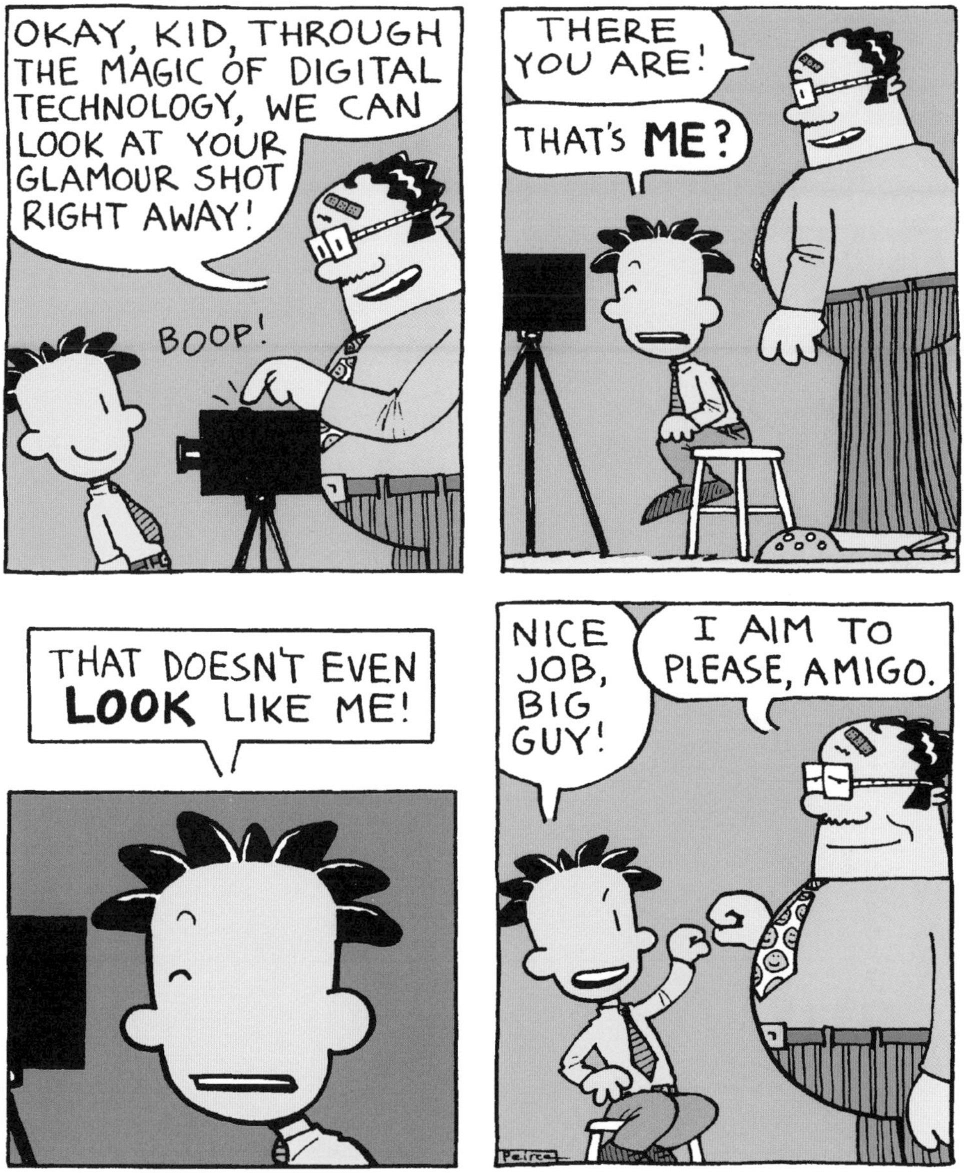
OKAY, KID, THROUGH THE MAGIC OF DIGITAL TECHNOLOGY, WE CAN LOOK AT YOUR GLAMOUR SHOT RIGHT AWAY!
BOOP!
THERE YOU ARE!
THAT'S **ME**?
THAT DOESN'T EVEN **LOOK** LIKE ME!
NICE JOB, BIG GUY!
I AIM TO PLEASE, AMIGO.
Peirce

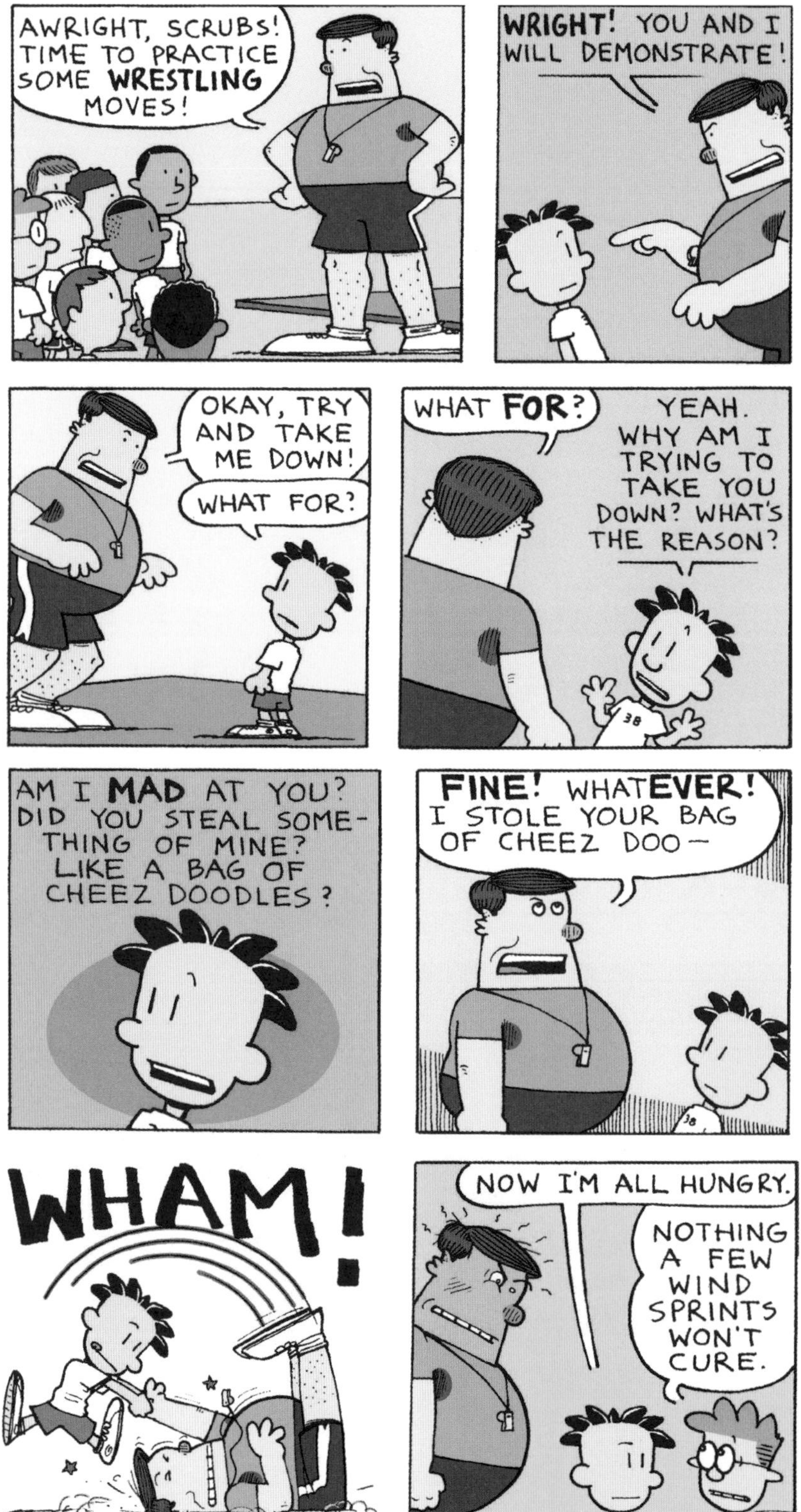
AWRIGHT, SCRUBS! TIME TO PRACTICE SOME **WRESTLING** MOVES!
WRIGHT! YOU AND I WILL DEMONSTRATE!
OKAY, TRY AND TAKE ME DOWN!
WHAT FOR?
WHAT **FOR**?
YEAH. WHY AM I TRYING TO TAKE YOU DOWN? WHAT'S THE REASON?
AM I **MAD** AT YOU? DID YOU STEAL SOME-THING OF MINE? LIKE A BAG OF CHEEZ DOODLES?
FINE! WHAT**EVER!** I STOLE YOUR BAG OF CHEEZ DOO—
WHAM!
NOW I'M ALL HUNGRY.
NOTHING A FEW WIND SPRINTS WON'T CURE.

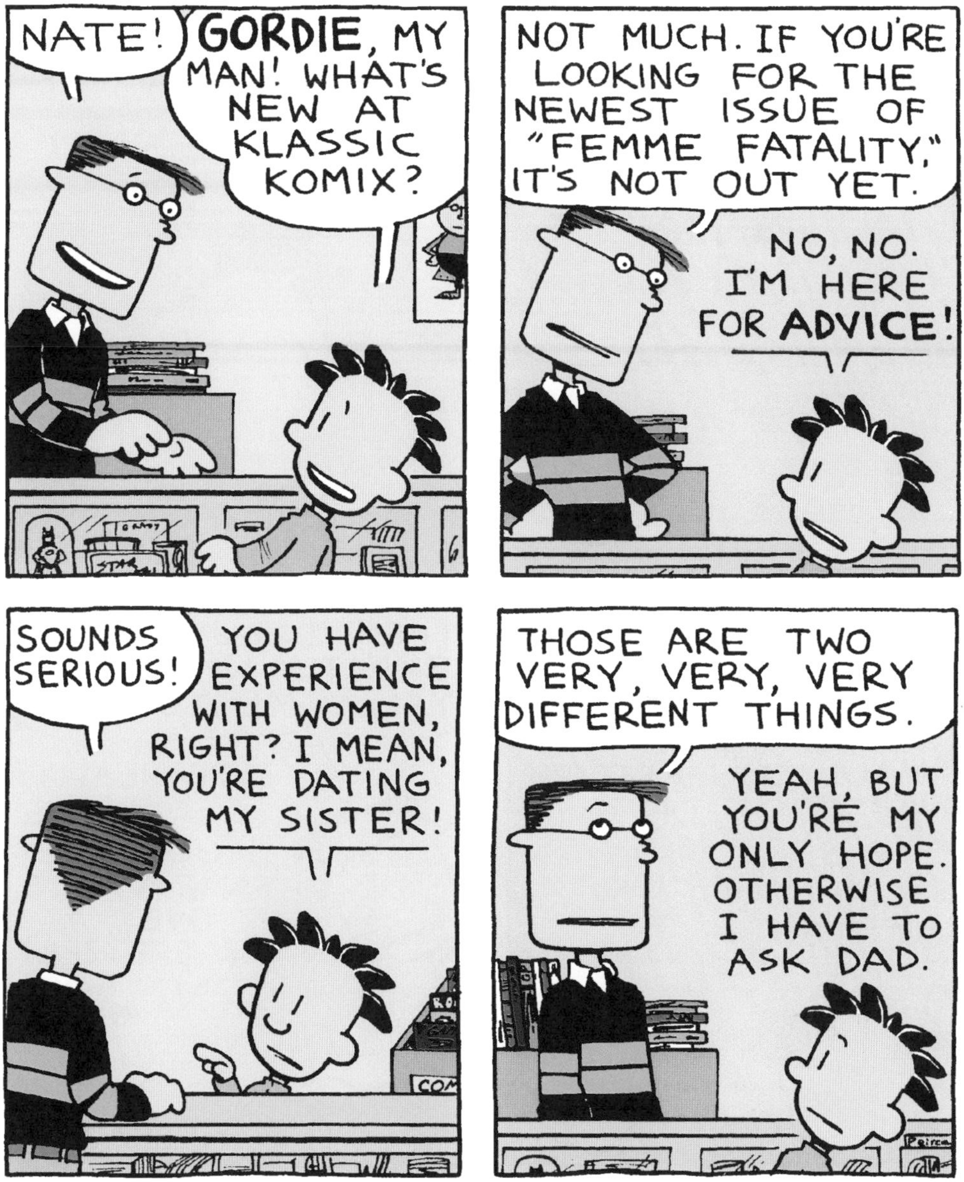
NATE!
GORDIE, MY MAN! WHAT'S NEW AT KLASSIC KOMIX?
NOT MUCH. IF YOU'RE LOOKING FOR THE NEWEST ISSUE OF "FEMME FATALITY," IT'S NOT OUT YET.
NO, NO. I'M HERE FOR ADVICE!
SOUNDS SERIOUS!
YOU HAVE EXPERIENCE WITH WOMEN, RIGHT? I MEAN, YOU'RE DATING MY SISTER!
THOSE ARE TWO VERY, VERY, VERY DIFFERENT THINGS.
YEAH, BUT YOU'RE MY ONLY HOPE. OTHERWISE I HAVE TO ASK DAD.

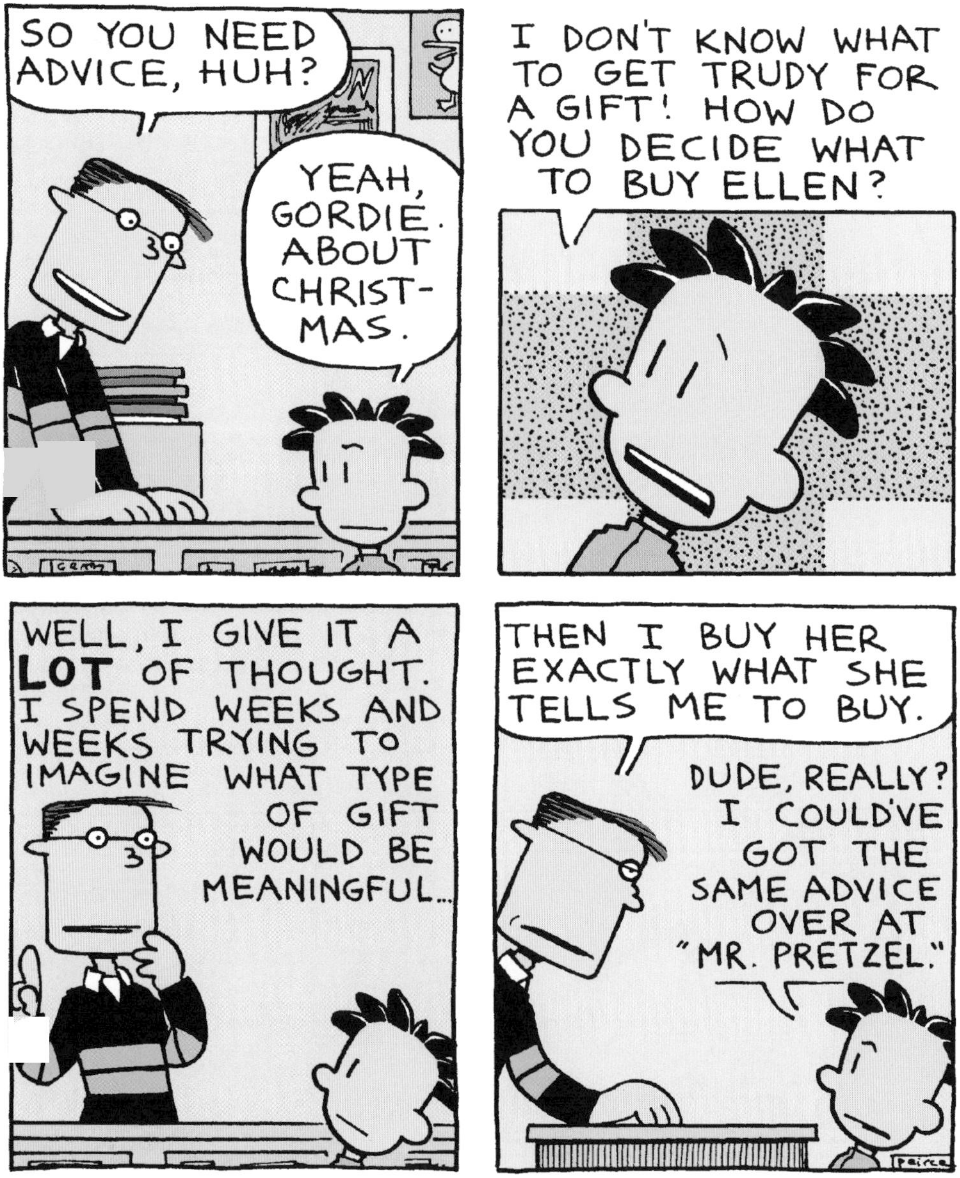
SO YOU NEED ADVICE, HUH?
YEAH, GORDIE. ABOUT CHRIST-MAS.
I DON'T KNOW WHAT TO GET TRUDY FOR A GIFT! HOW DO YOU DECIDE WHAT TO BUY ELLEN?
WELL, I GIVE IT A **LOT** OF THOUGHT. I SPEND WEEKS AND WEEKS TRYING TO IMAGINE WHAT TYPE OF GIFT WOULD BE MEANINGFUL...
THEN I BUY HER EXACTLY WHAT SHE TELLS ME TO BUY.
DUDE, REALLY? I COULD'VE GOT THE SAME ADVICE OVER AT "MR. PRETZEL."

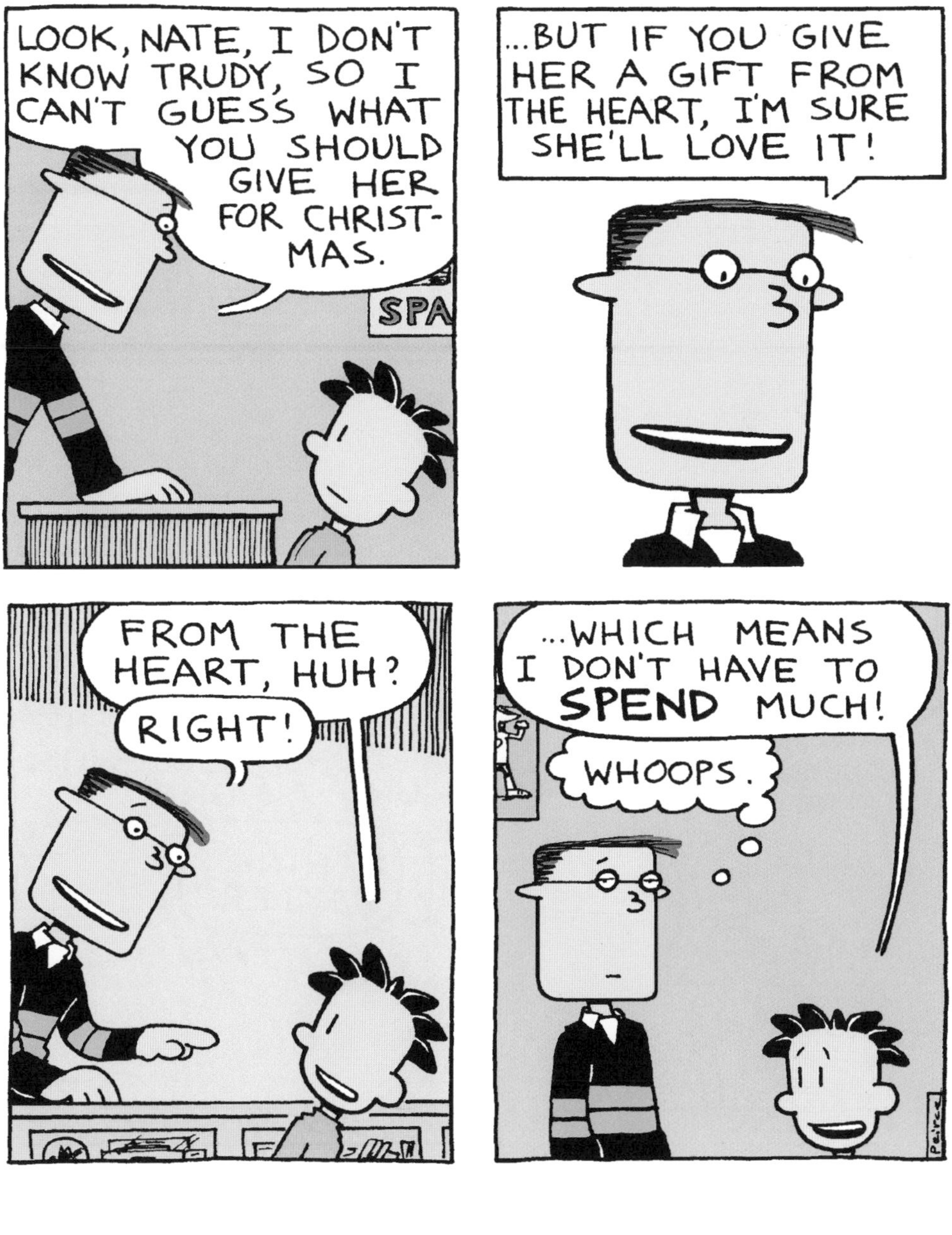
LOOK, NATE, I DON'T KNOW TRUDY, SO I CAN'T GUESS WHAT YOU SHOULD GIVE HER FOR CHRIST-MAS.
SPA
...BUT IF YOU GIVE HER A GIFT FROM THE HEART, I'M SURE SHE'LL LOVE IT!
FROM THE HEART, HUH?
RIGHT!
...WHICH MEANS I DON'T HAVE TO SPEND MUCH!
WHOOPS.
Peirce

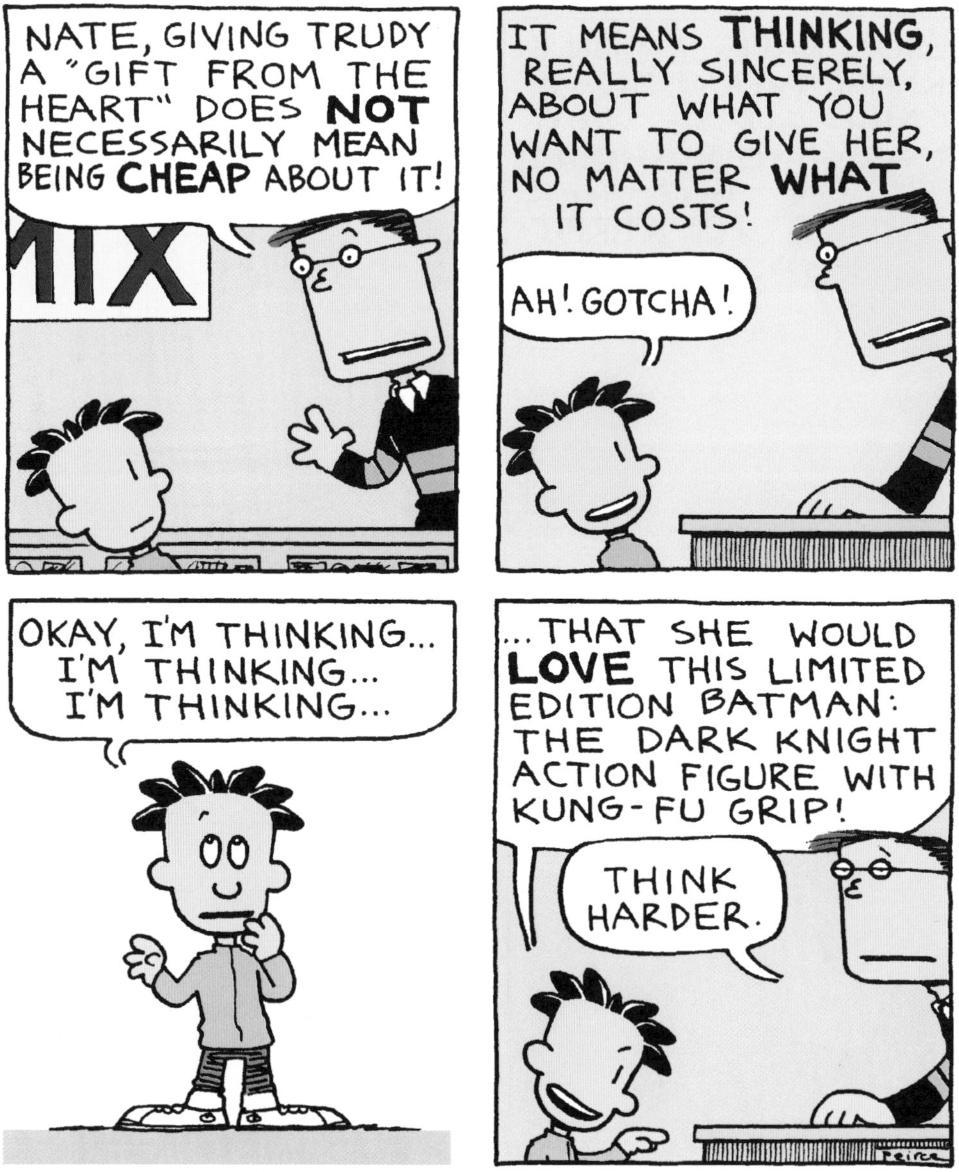
NATE, GIVING TRUDY A "GIFT FROM THE HEART" DOES NOT NECESSARILY MEAN BEING CHEAP ABOUT IT!
MIX
IT MEANS THINKING, REALLY SINCERELY, ABOUT WHAT YOU WANT TO GIVE HER, NO MATTER WHAT IT COSTS!
AH! GOTCHA!
OKAY, I'M THINKING... I'M THINKING... I'M THINKING...
...THAT SHE WOULD LOVE THIS LIMITED EDITION BATMAN: THE DARK KNIGHT ACTION FIGURE WITH KUNG-FU GRIP!
THINK HARDER.

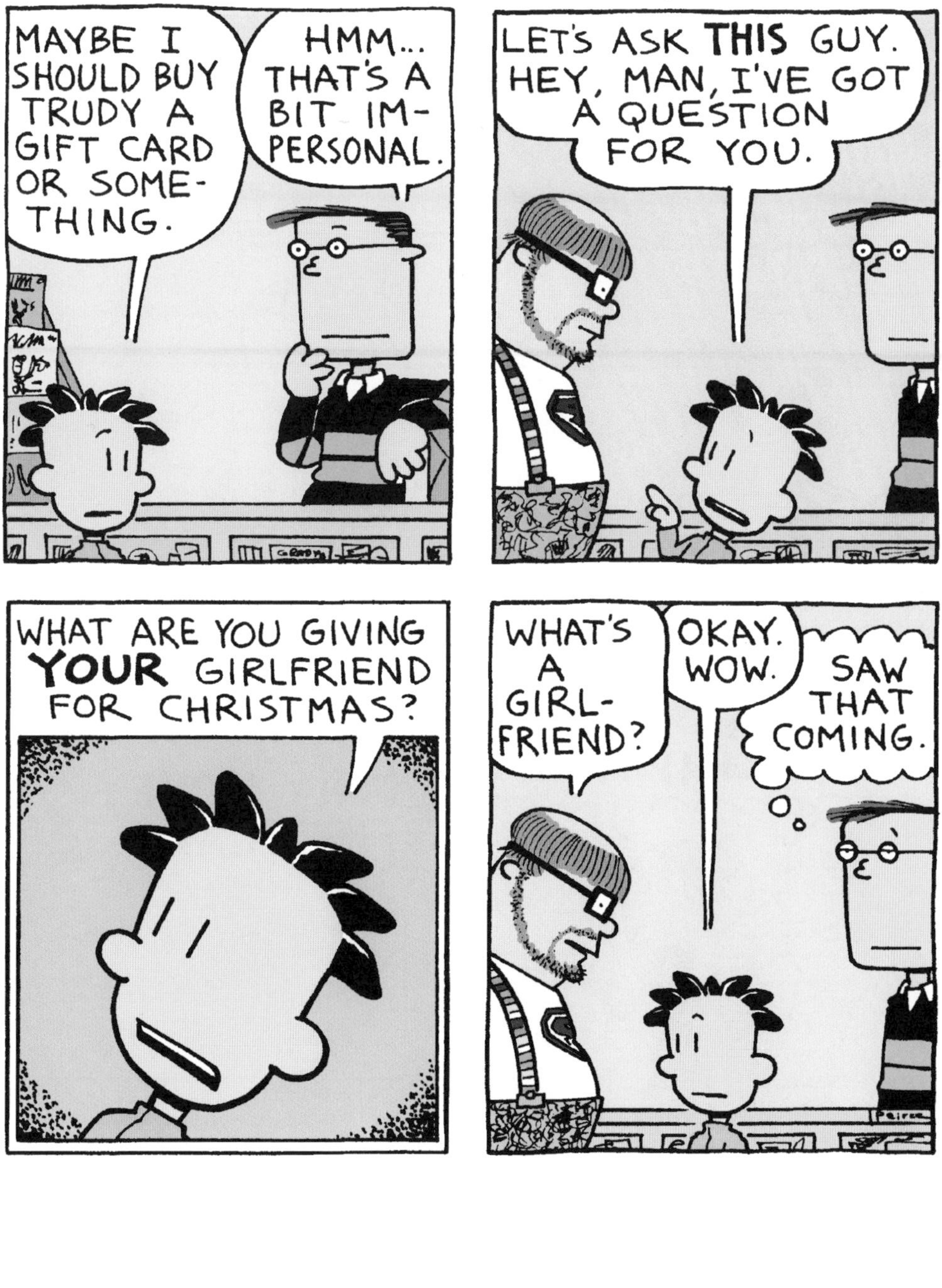
MAYBE I SHOULD BUY TRUDY A GIFT CARD OR SOME-THING.
HMM... THAT'S A BIT IM-PERSONAL.
LET'S ASK **THIS** GUY. HEY, MAN, I'VE GOT A QUESTION FOR YOU.
WHAT ARE YOU GIVING **YOUR** GIRLFRIEND FOR CHRISTMAS?
WHAT'S A GIRL-FRIEND?
OKAY. WOW.
SAW THAT COMING.
Peirce

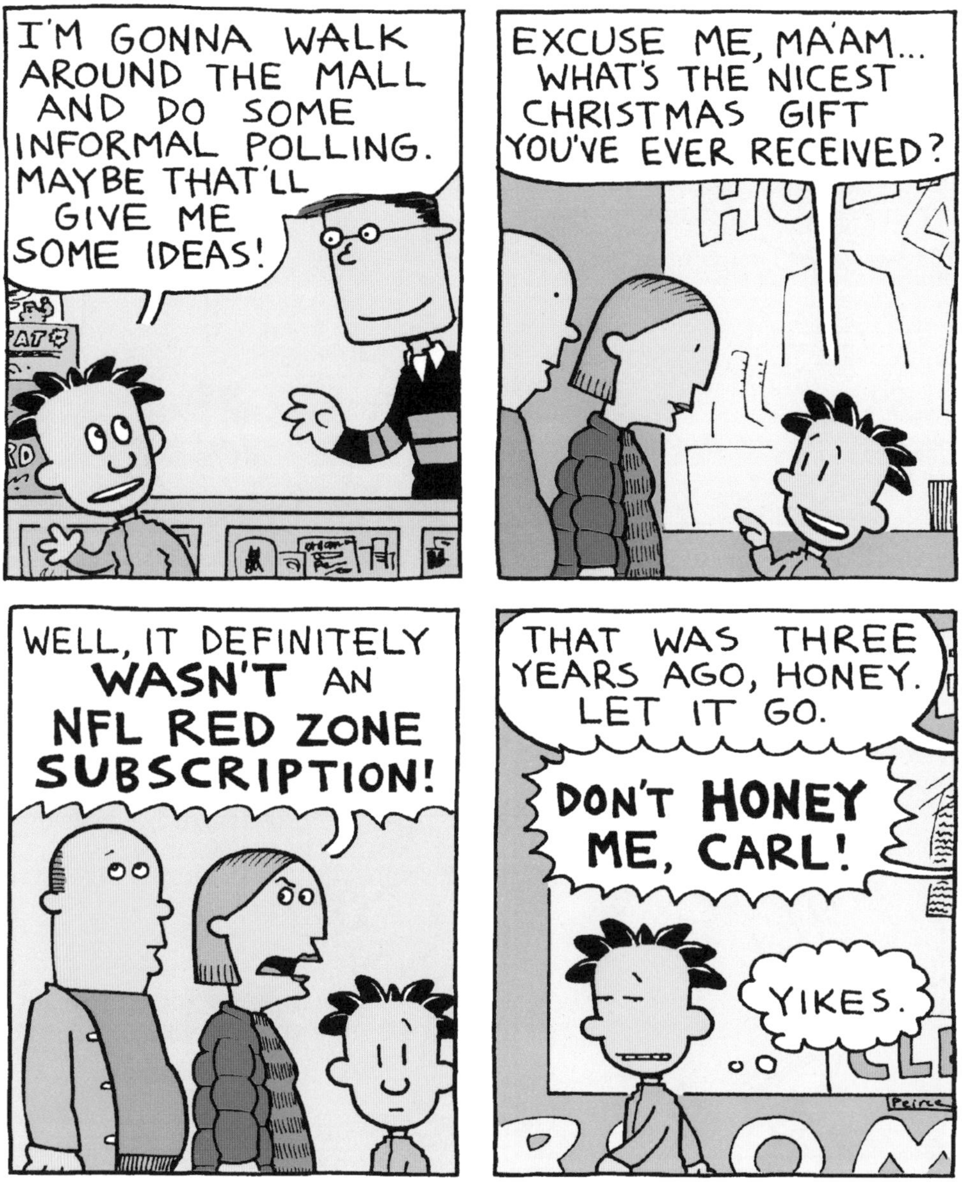
I'M GONNA WALK AROUND THE MALL AND DO SOME INFORMAL POLLING. MAYBE THAT'LL GIVE ME SOME IDEAS!
EXCUSE ME, MA'AM... WHAT'S THE NICEST CHRISTMAS GIFT YOU'VE EVER RECEIVED?
WELL, IT DEFINITELY **WASN'T** AN **NFL RED ZONE SUBSCRIPTION!**
THAT WAS THREE YEARS AGO, HONEY. LET IT GO.
DON'T HONEY ME, CARL!
YIKES.

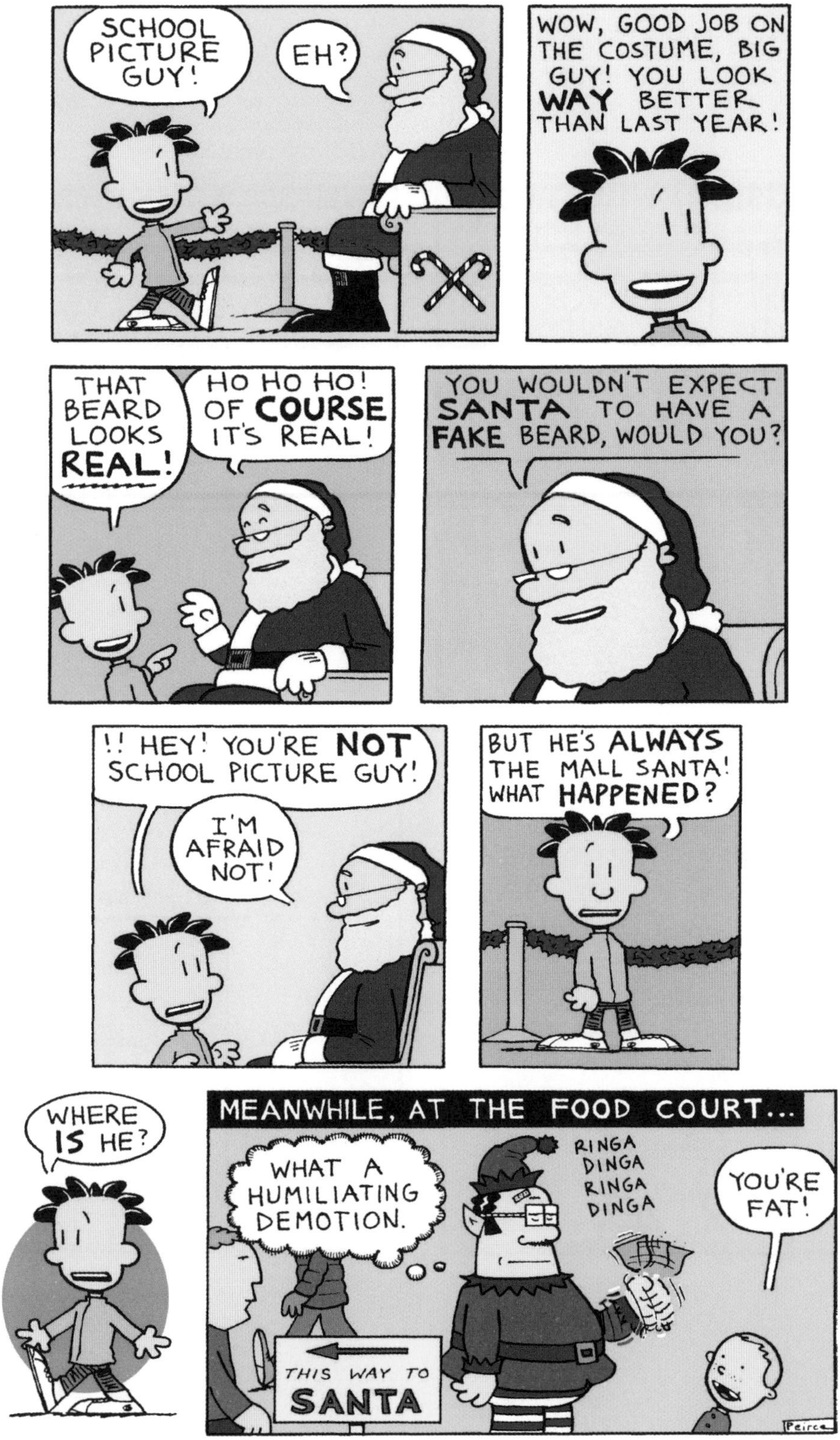
SCHOOL PICTURE GUY!
EH?
WOW, GOOD JOB ON THE COSTUME, BIG GUY! YOU LOOK WAY BETTER THAN LAST YEAR!
THAT BEARD LOOKS REAL!
HO HO HO! OF COURSE IT'S REAL!
YOU WOULDN'T EXPECT SANTA TO HAVE A FAKE BEARD, WOULD YOU?
!! HEY! YOU'RE NOT SCHOOL PICTURE GUY!
I'M AFRAID NOT!
BUT HE'S ALWAYS THE MALL SANTA! WHAT HAPPENED?
WHERE IS HE?
MEANWHILE, AT THE FOOD COURT...
WHAT A HUMILIATING DEMOTION.
RINGA DINGA RINGA DINGA
YOU'RE FAT!
THIS WAY TO SANTA
Peirce

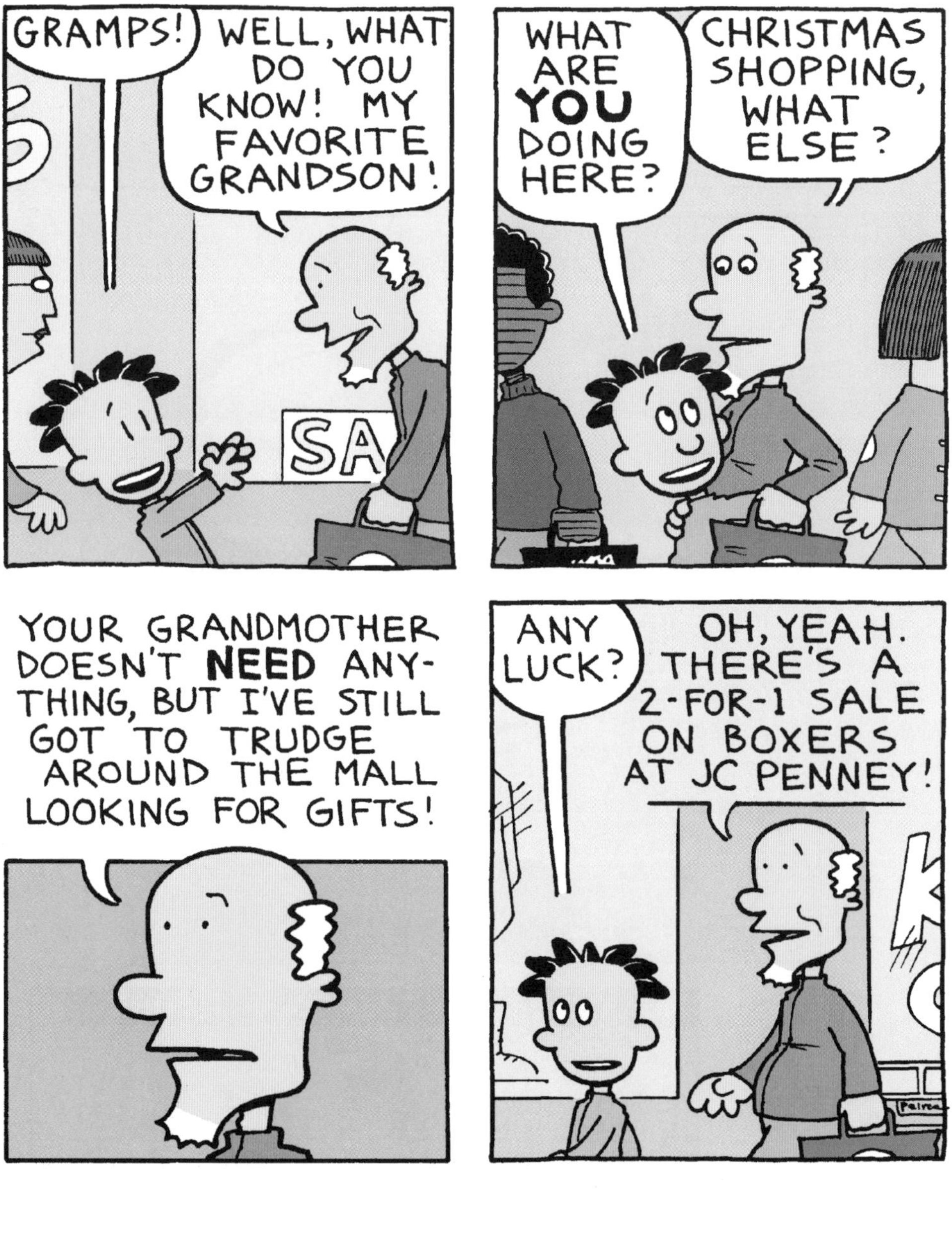
GRAMPS!
WELL, WHAT DO YOU KNOW! MY FAVORITE GRANDSON!
SA
WHAT ARE **YOU** DOING HERE?
CHRISTMAS SHOPPING, WHAT ELSE?
YOUR GRANDMOTHER DOESN'T **NEED** ANYTHING, BUT I'VE STILL GOT TO TRUDGE AROUND THE MALL LOOKING FOR GIFTS!
ANY LUCK?
OH, YEAH. THERE'S A 2-FOR-1 SALE ON BOXERS AT JC PENNEY!

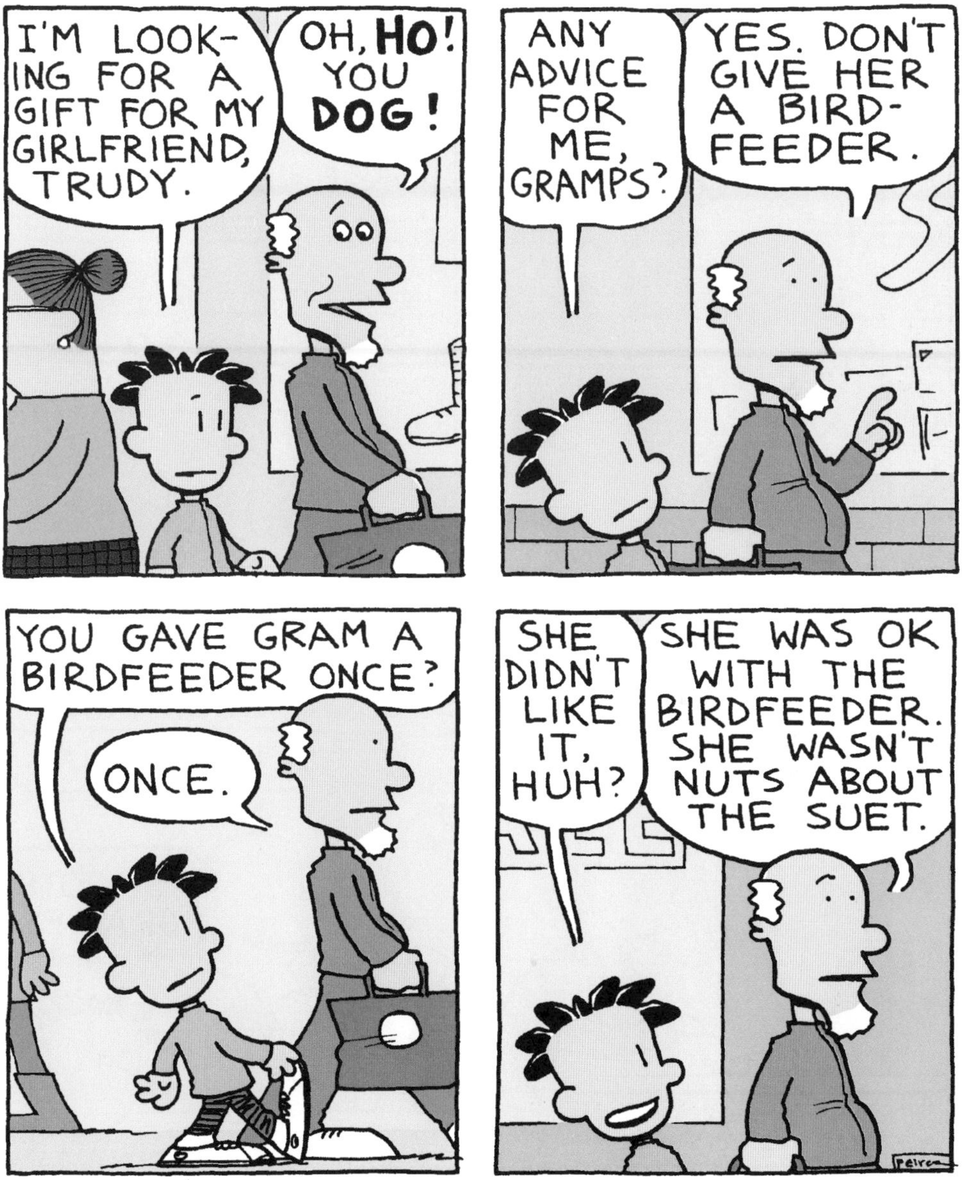
I'M LOOKING FOR A GIFT FOR MY GIRLFRIEND, TRUDY.
OH, **HO**! YOU **DOG**!
ANY ADVICE FOR ME, GRAMPS?
YES. DON'T GIVE HER A BIRDFEEDER.
YOU GAVE GRAM A BIRDFEEDER ONCE?
ONCE.
SHE DIDN'T LIKE IT, HUH?
SHE WAS OK WITH THE BIRDFEEDER. SHE WASN'T NUTS ABOUT THE SUET.

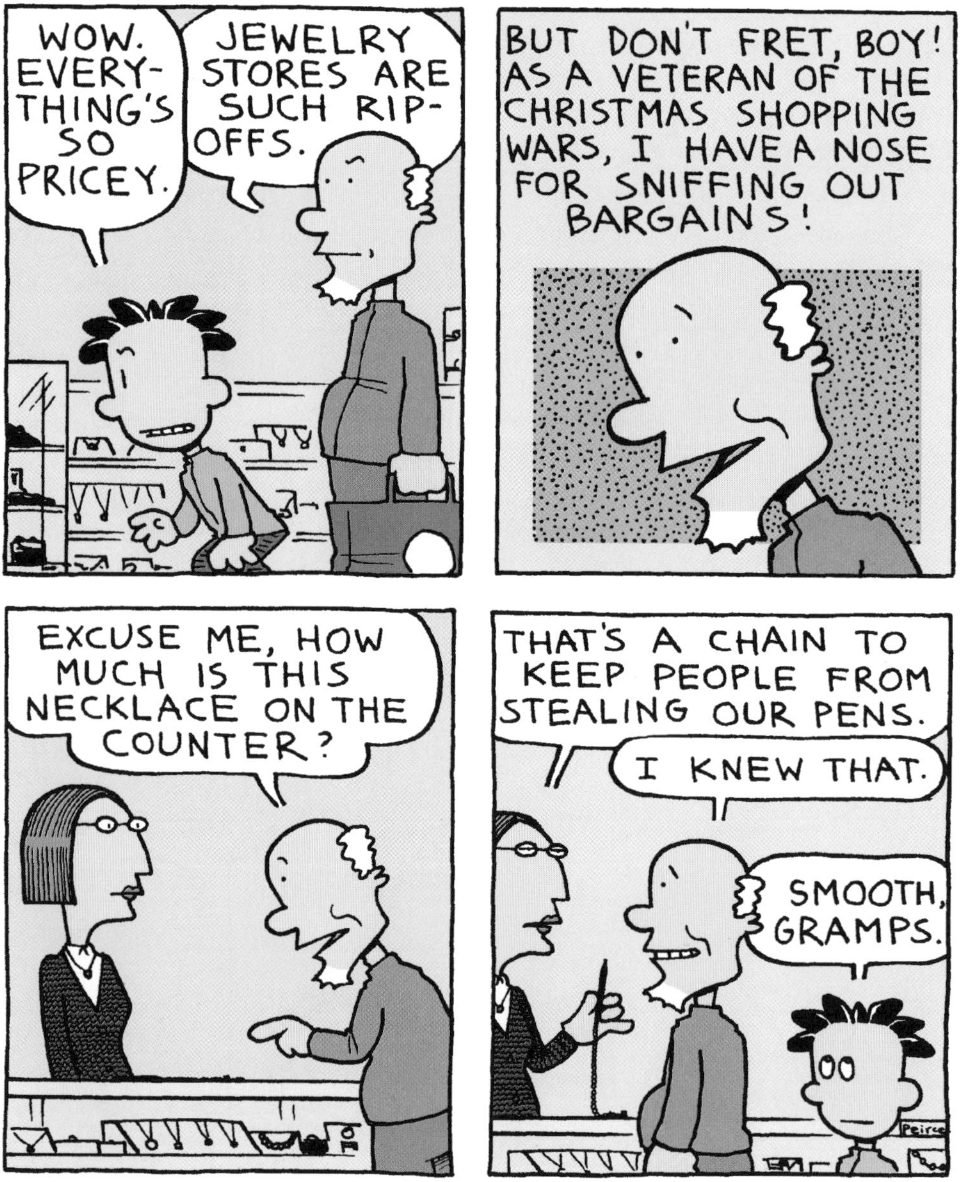
WOW. EVERYTHING'S SO PRICEY.
JEWELRY STORES ARE SUCH RIP-OFFS.
BUT DON'T FRET, BOY! AS A VETERAN OF THE CHRISTMAS SHOPPING WARS, I HAVE A NOSE FOR SNIFFING OUT BARGAINS!
EXCUSE ME, HOW MUCH IS THIS NECKLACE ON THE COUNTER?
THAT'S A CHAIN TO KEEP PEOPLE FROM STEALING OUR PENS.
I KNEW THAT.
SMOOTH, GRAMPS.
Peirce

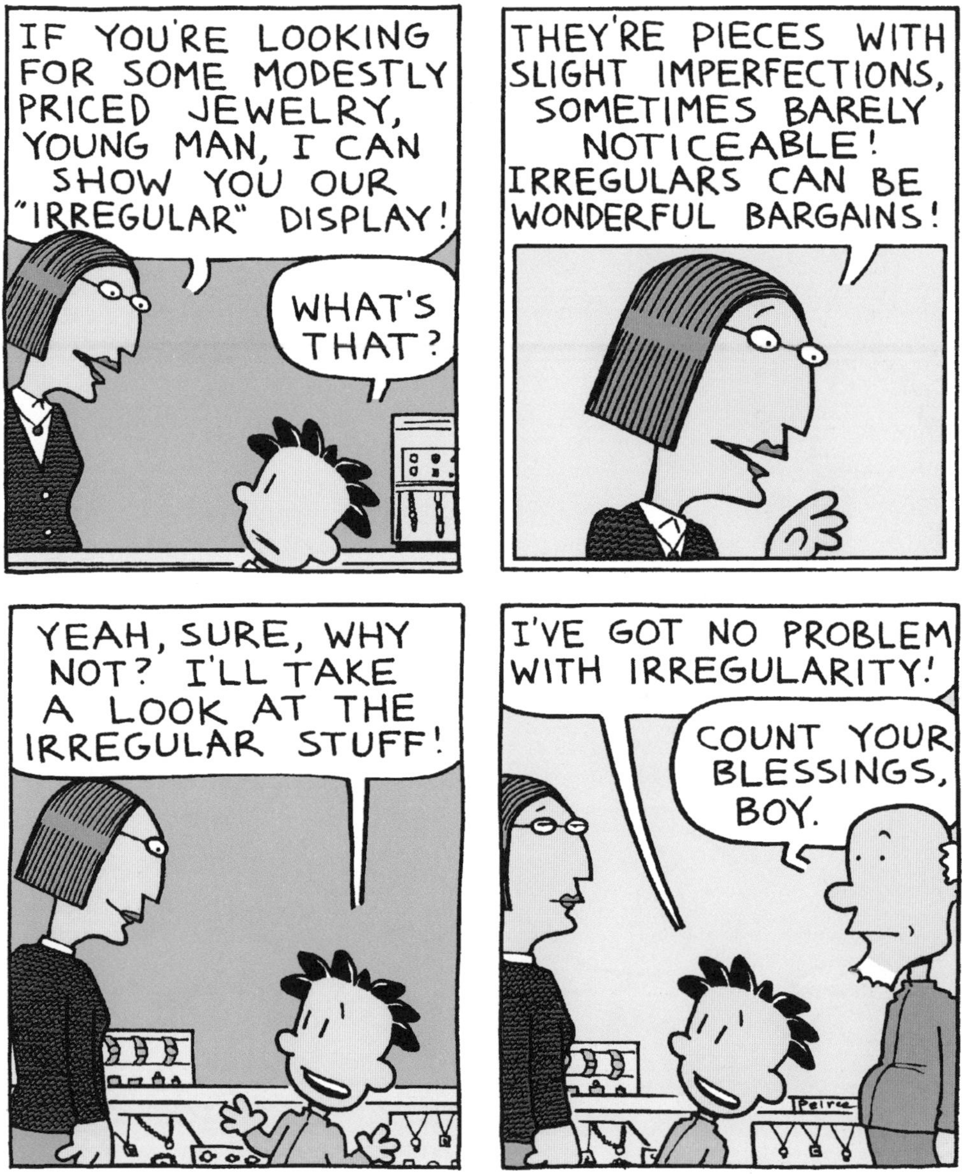
IF YOU'RE LOOKING FOR SOME MODESTLY PRICED JEWELRY, YOUNG MAN, I CAN SHOW YOU OUR "IRREGULAR" DISPLAY!
WHAT'S THAT?
THEY'RE PIECES WITH SLIGHT IMPERFECTIONS, SOMETIMES BARELY NOTICEABLE! IRREGULARS CAN BE WONDERFUL BARGAINS!
YEAH, SURE, WHY NOT? I'LL TAKE A LOOK AT THE IRREGULAR STUFF!
I'VE GOT NO PROBLEM WITH IRREGULARITY!
COUNT YOUR BLESSINGS, BOY.
Peirce

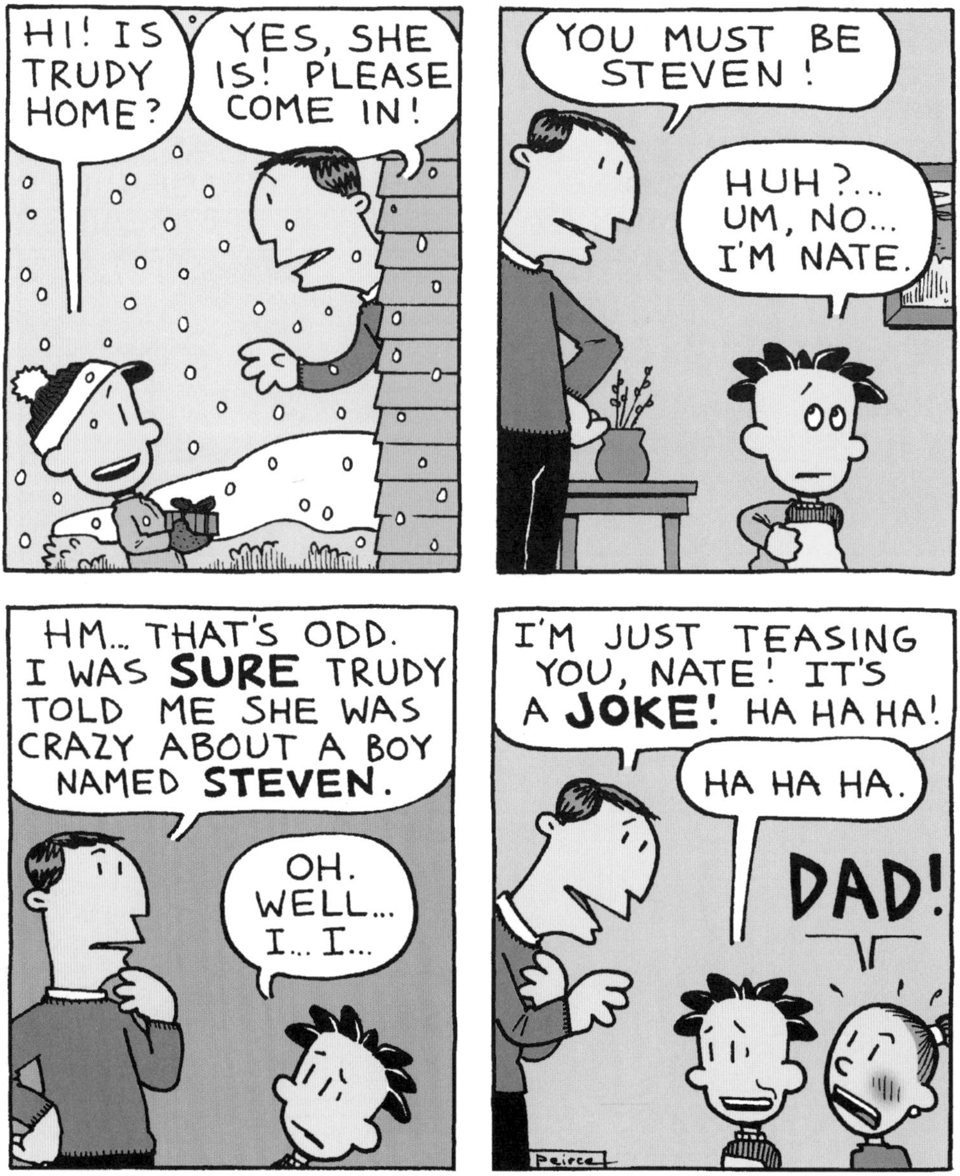
HI! IS TRUDY HOME?
YES, SHE IS! PLEASE COME IN!
YOU MUST BE STEVEN!
HUH?... UM, NO... I'M NATE.
HM... THAT'S ODD. I WAS **SURE** TRUDY TOLD ME SHE WAS CRAZY ABOUT A BOY NAMED **STEVEN**.
OH. WELL... I... I...
I'M JUST TEASING YOU, NATE! IT'S A **JOKE**! HA HA HA!
HA HA HA.
DAD!
Peirce

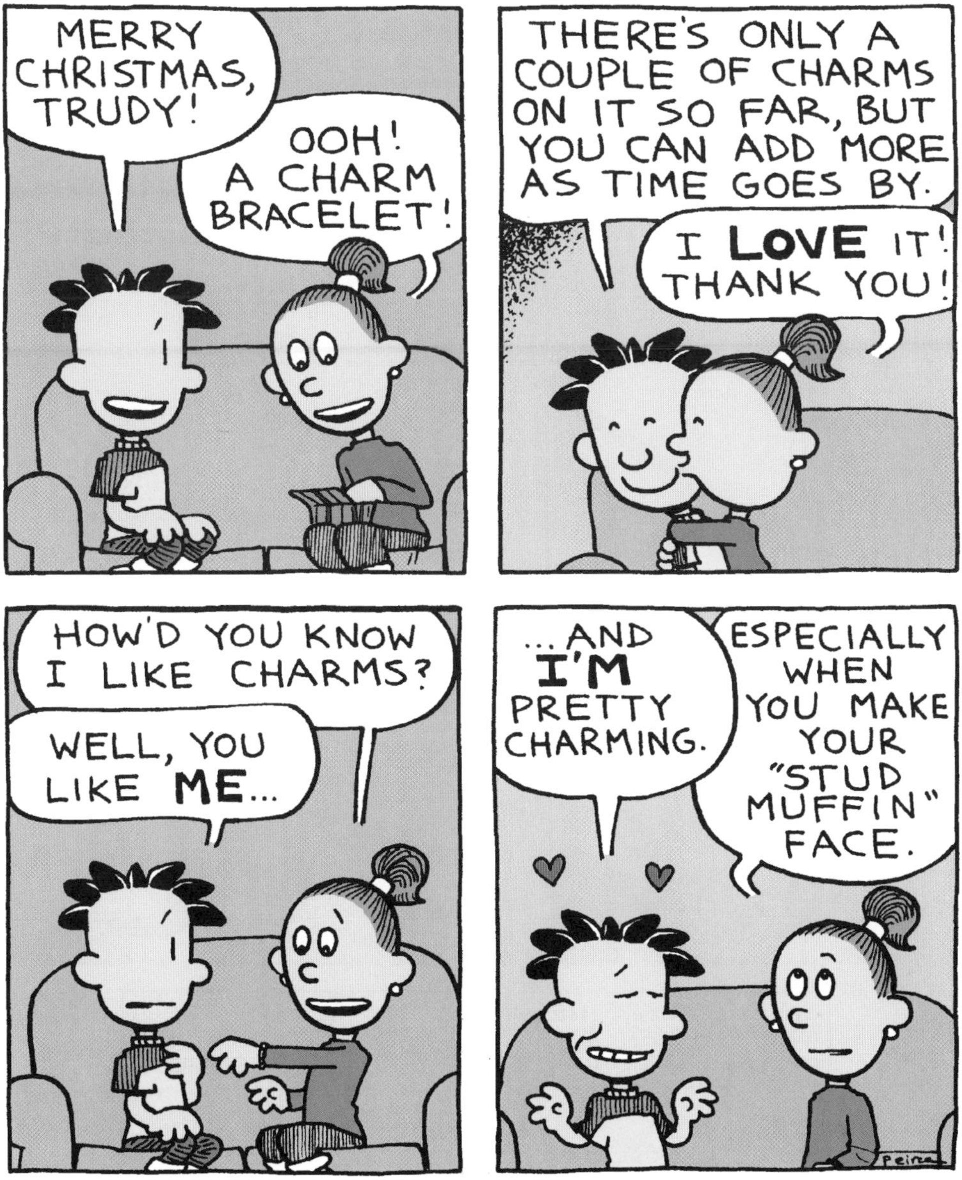
MERRY CHRISTMAS, TRUDY!
OOH! A CHARM BRACELET!
THERE'S ONLY A COUPLE OF CHARMS ON IT SO FAR, BUT YOU CAN ADD MORE AS TIME GOES BY.
I **LOVE** IT! THANK YOU!
HOW'D YOU KNOW I LIKE CHARMS?
WELL, YOU LIKE **ME**...
...AND **I'M** PRETTY CHARMING.
ESPECIALLY WHEN YOU MAKE YOUR "STUD MUFFIN" FACE.
Peirce

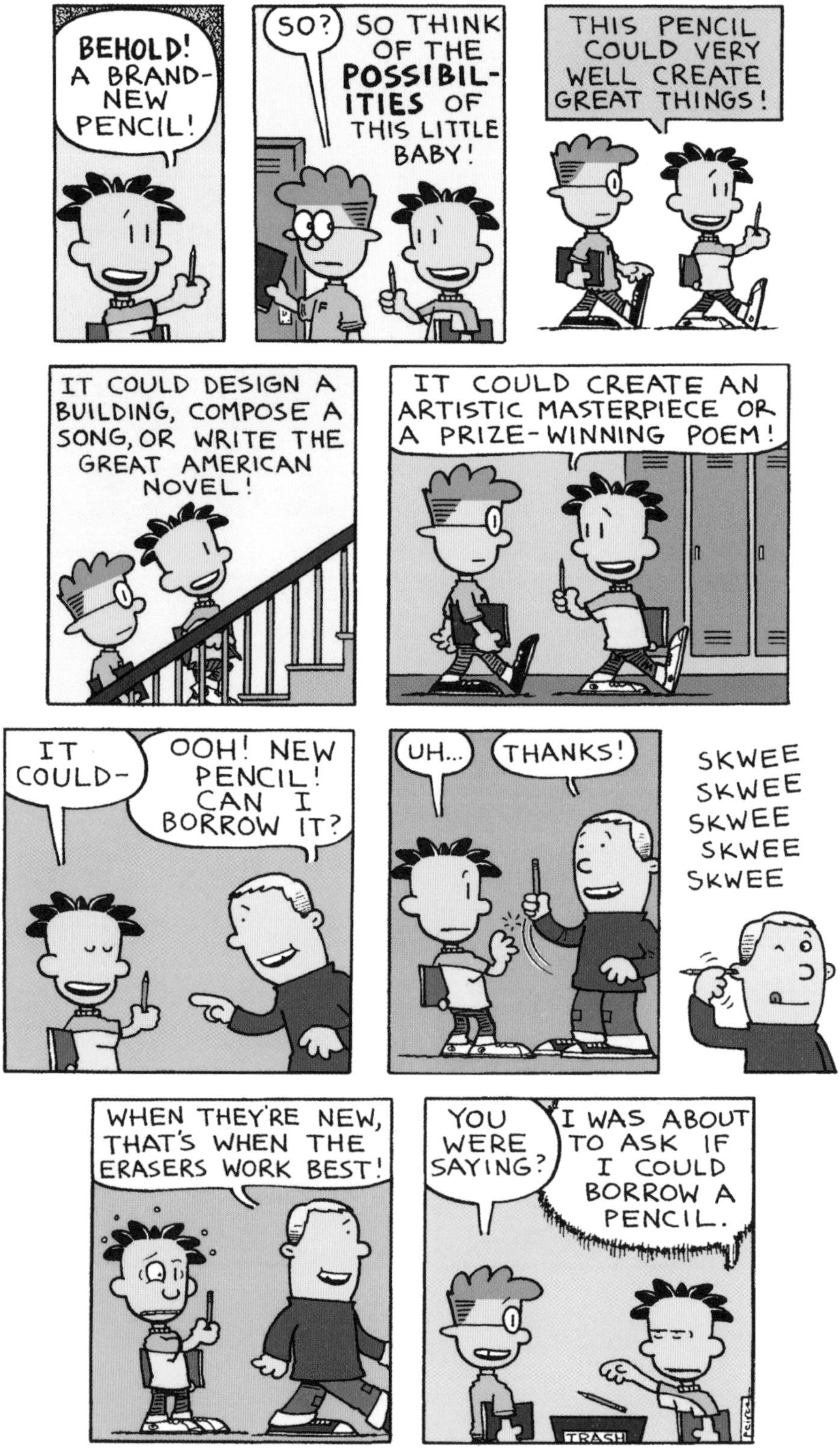
BEHOLD! A BRAND-NEW PENCIL!
SO?
SO THINK OF THE POSSIBILITIES OF THIS LITTLE BABY!
THIS PENCIL COULD VERY WELL CREATE GREAT THINGS!
IT COULD DESIGN A BUILDING, COMPOSE A SONG, OR WRITE THE GREAT AMERICAN NOVEL!
IT COULD CREATE AN ARTISTIC MASTERPIECE OR A PRIZE-WINNING POEM!
IT COULD-
OOH! NEW PENCIL! CAN I BORROW IT?
UH...
THANKS!
SKWEE SKWEE SKWEE SKWEE SKWEE
WHEN THEY'RE NEW, THAT'S WHEN THE ERASERS WORK BEST!
YOU WERE SAYING?
I WAS ABOUT TO ASK IF I COULD BORROW A PENCIL.
TRASH

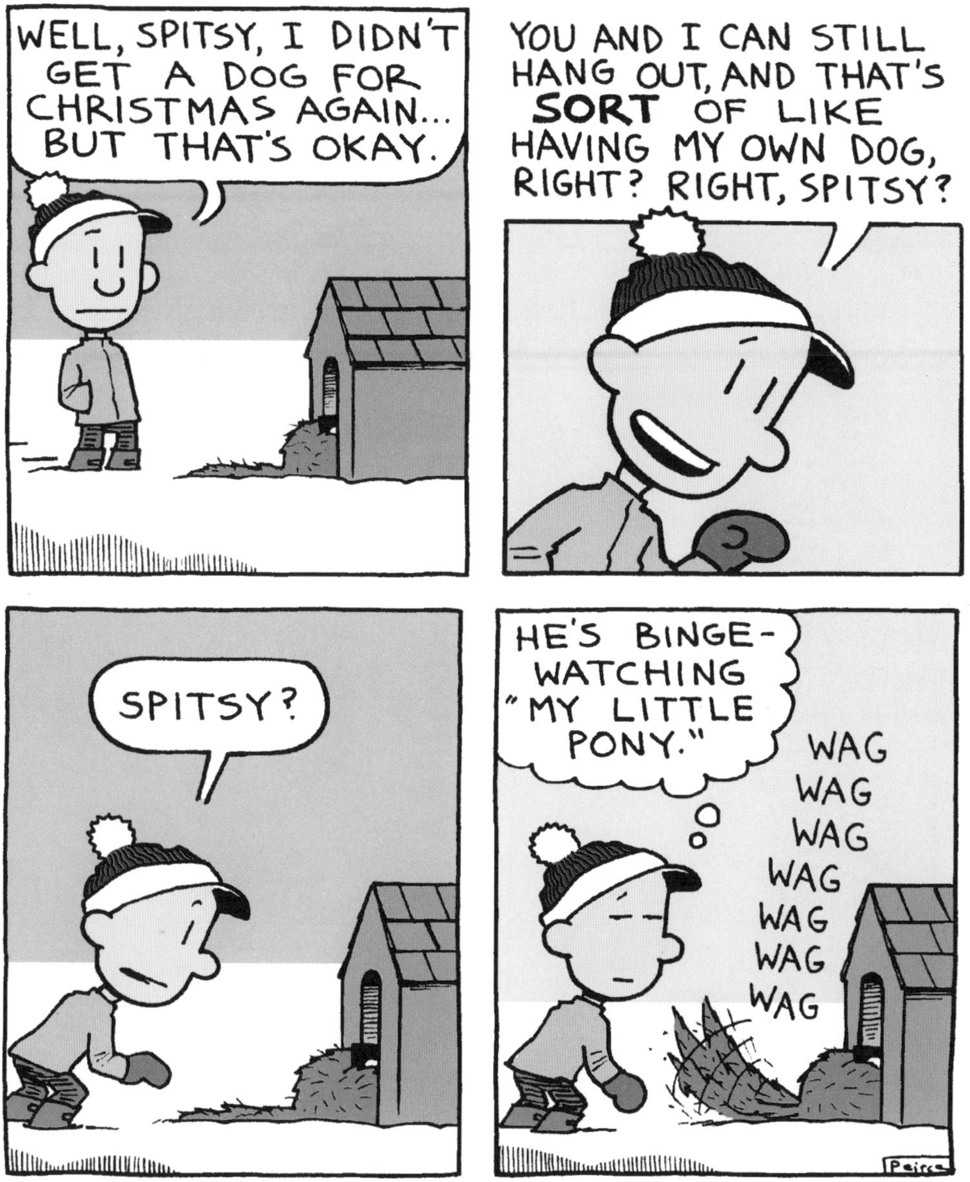
WELL, SPITSY, I DIDN'T GET A DOG FOR CHRISTMAS AGAIN... BUT THAT'S OKAY.
YOU AND I CAN STILL HANG OUT, AND THAT'S **SORT** OF LIKE HAVING MY OWN DOG, RIGHT? RIGHT, SPITSY?
SPITSY?
HE'S BINGE-WATCHING "MY LITTLE PONY."
WAG WAG WAG WAG WAG WAG WAG
Peirce

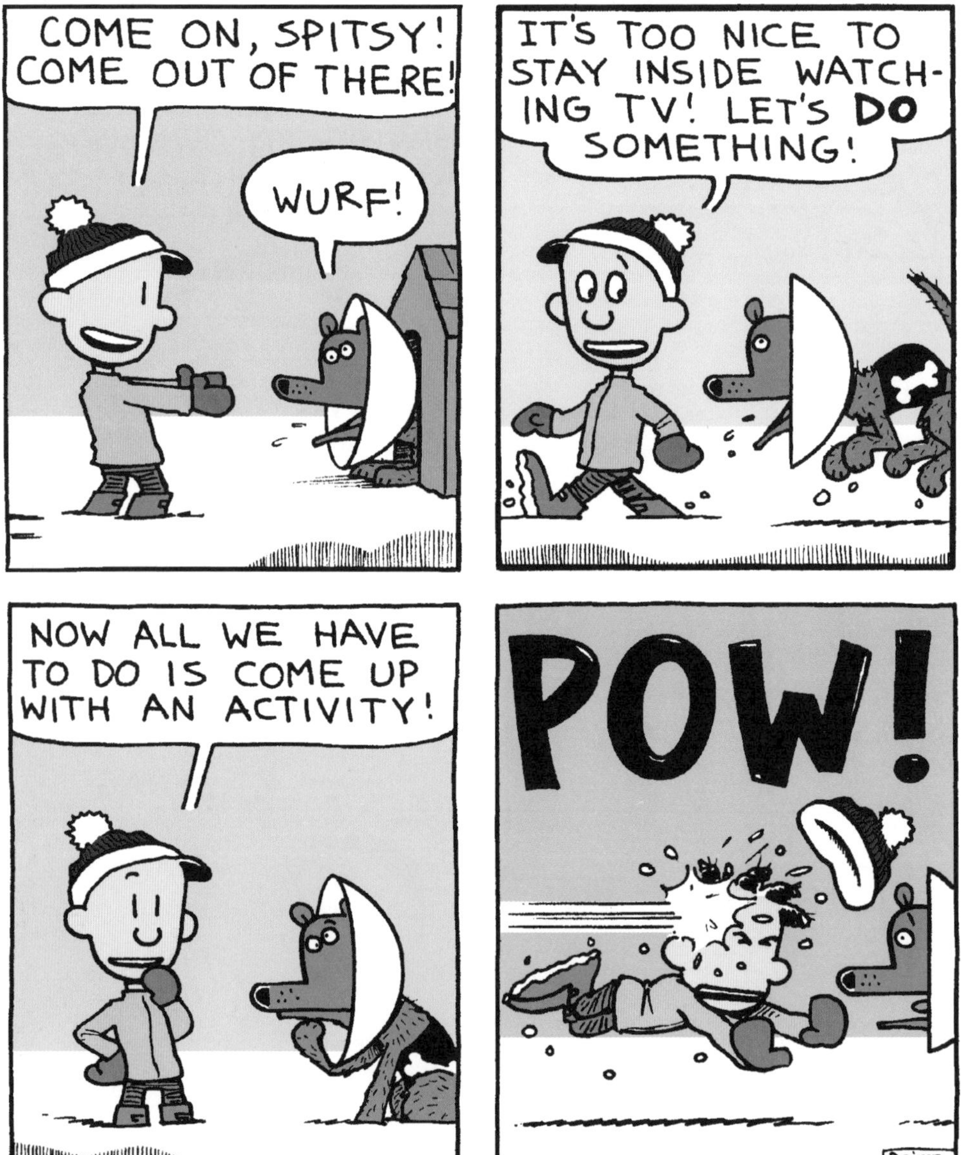
COME ON, SPITSY! COME OUT OF THERE!
WURF!
IT'S TOO NICE TO STAY INSIDE WATCHING TV! LET'S **DO** SOMETHING!
NOW ALL WE HAVE TO DO IS COME UP WITH AN ACTIVITY!
POW!
Peirce

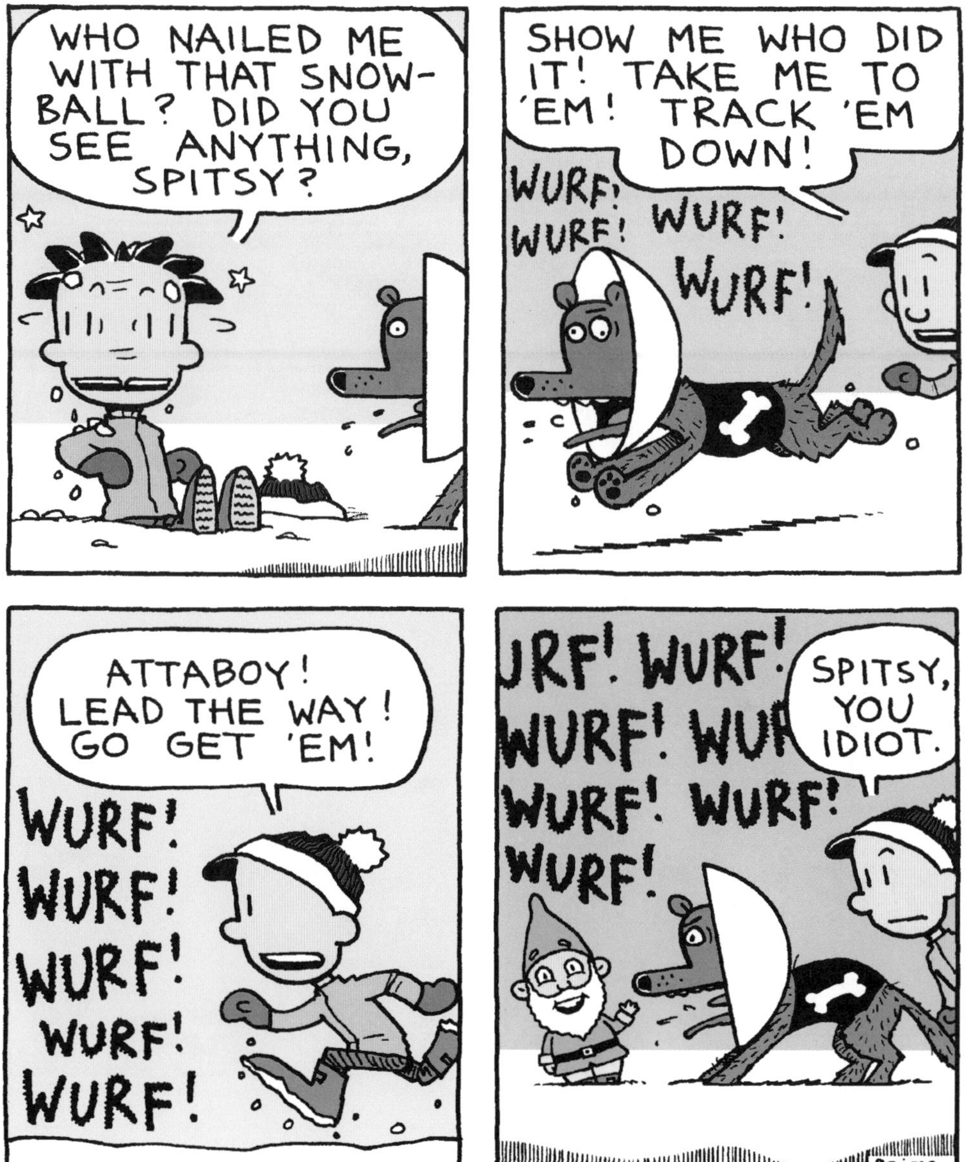
WHO NAILED ME WITH THAT SNOW-BALL? DID YOU SEE ANYTHING, SPITSY?
SHOW ME WHO DID IT! TAKE ME TO 'EM! TRACK 'EM DOWN!
WURF! WURF! WURF! WURF!
ATTABOY! LEAD THE WAY! GO GET 'EM!
WURF! WURF! WURF! WURF! WURF!
RF! WURF! WURF! WUR WURF! WURF! WURF!
SPITSY, YOU IDIOT.
Peirce

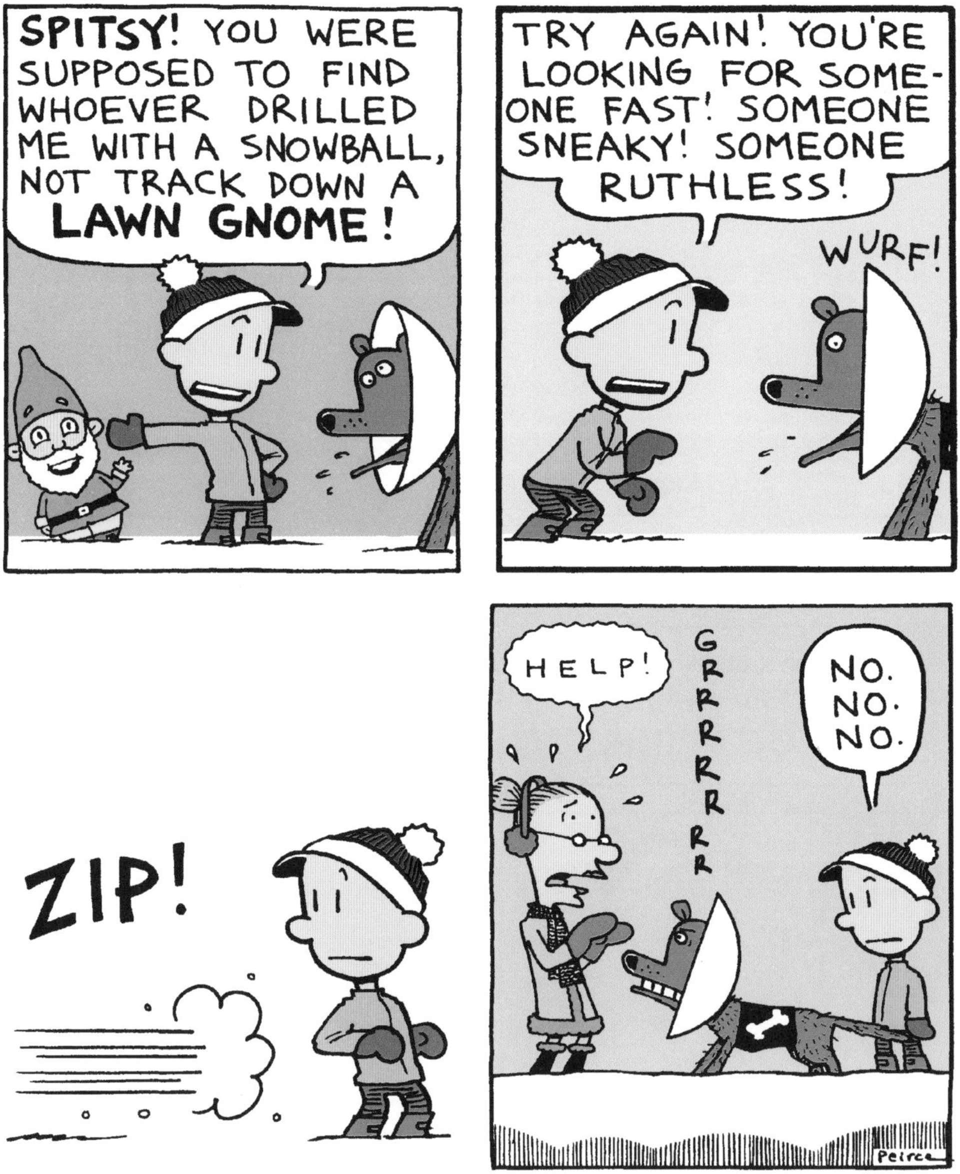
SPITSY! YOU WERE SUPPOSED TO FIND WHOEVER DRILLED ME WITH A SNOWBALL, NOT TRACK DOWN A LAWN GNOME!
TRY AGAIN! YOU'RE LOOKING FOR SOMEONE FAST! SOMEONE SNEAKY! SOMEONE RUTHLESS!
WURF!
ZIP!
HELP!
GRRRRRRRR
NO. NO. NO.
Peirce

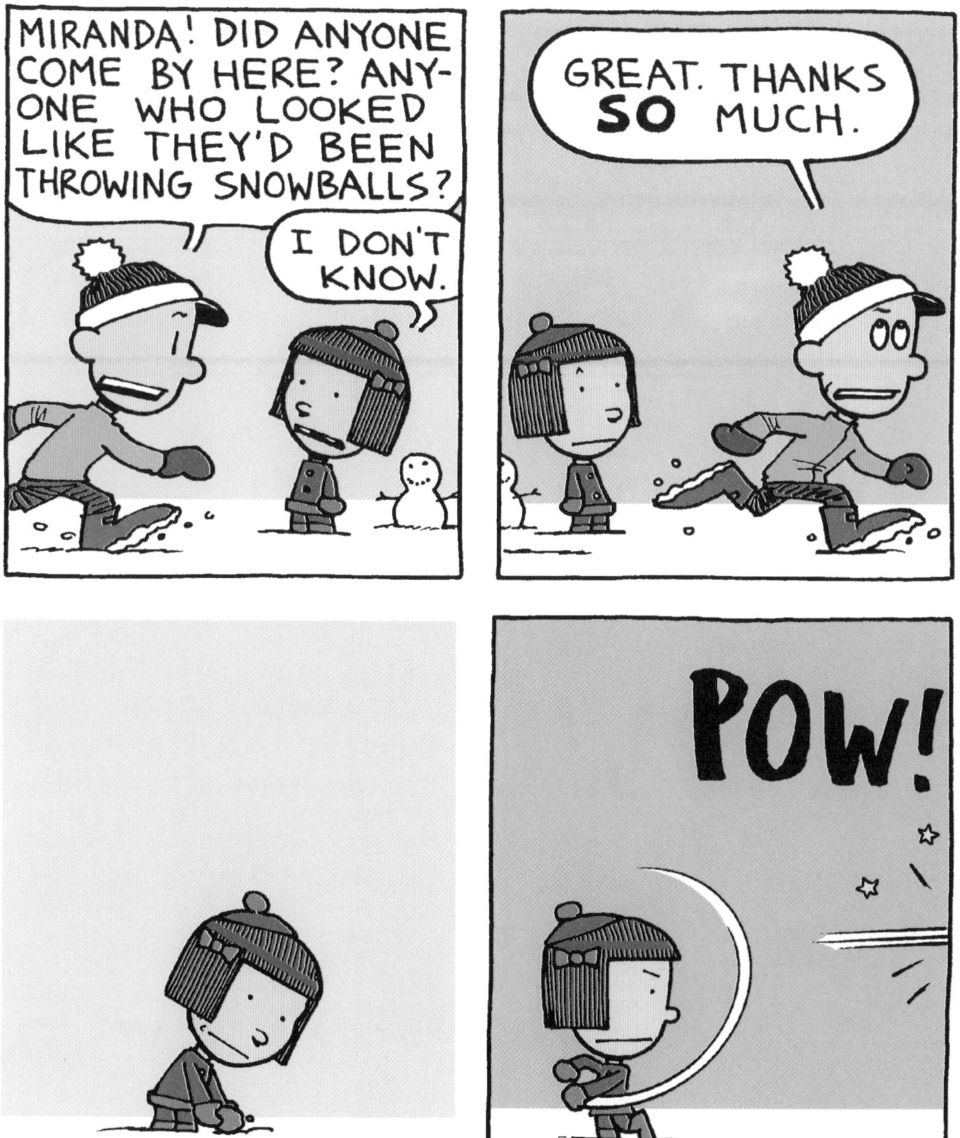
MIRANDA! DID ANYONE COME BY HERE? ANY-ONE WHO LOOKED LIKE THEY'D BEEN THROWING SNOWBALLS?
I DON'T KNOW.
GREAT. THANKS **SO** MUCH.
POW!
Peirce

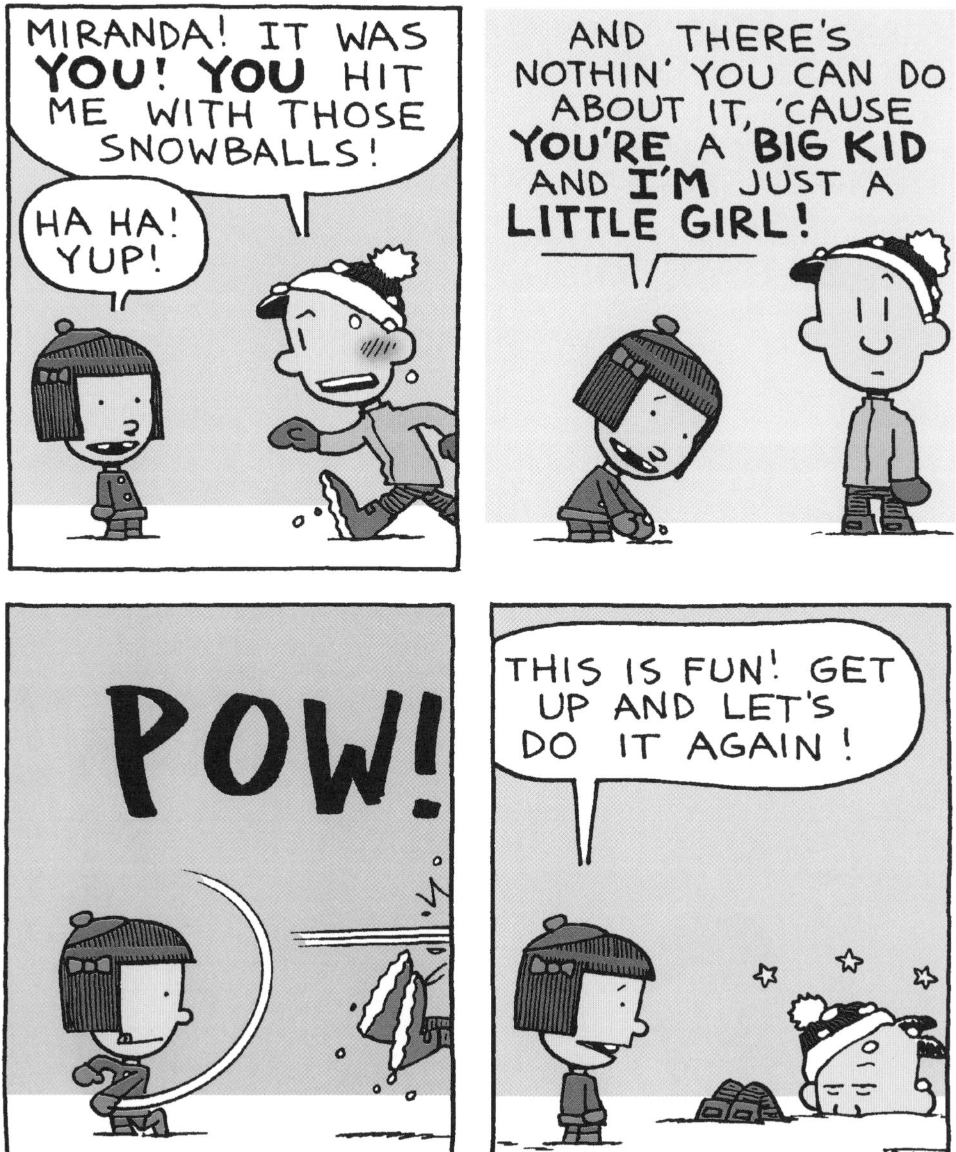
MIRANDA! IT WAS **YOU**! **YOU** HIT ME WITH THOSE SNOWBALLS!
HA HA! YUP!
AND THERE'S NOTHIN' YOU CAN DO ABOUT IT, 'CAUSE **YOU'RE** A **BIG KID** AND **I'M** JUST A **LITTLE GIRL**!
POW!
THIS IS FUN! GET UP AND LET'S DO IT AGAIN!
Peirce

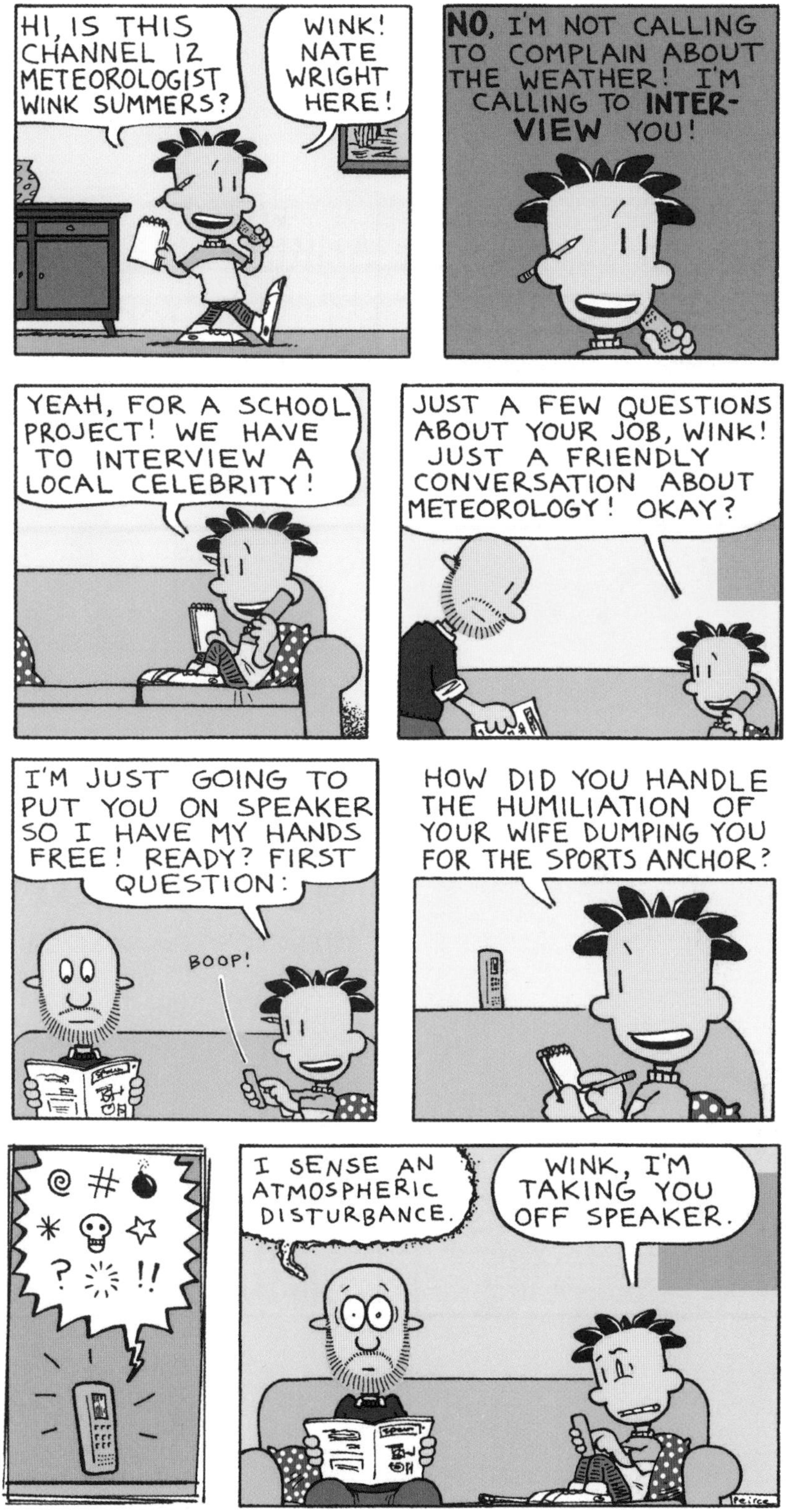
HI, IS THIS CHANNEL 12 METEOROLOGIST WINK SUMMERS?
WINK! NATE WRIGHT HERE!
NO, I'M NOT CALLING TO COMPLAIN ABOUT THE WEATHER! I'M CALLING TO INTERVIEW YOU!
YEAH, FOR A SCHOOL PROJECT! WE HAVE TO INTERVIEW A LOCAL CELEBRITY!
JUST A FEW QUESTIONS ABOUT YOUR JOB, WINK! JUST A FRIENDLY CONVERSATION ABOUT METEOROLOGY! OKAY?
I'M JUST GOING TO PUT YOU ON SPEAKER SO I HAVE MY HANDS FREE! READY? FIRST QUESTION:
BOOP!
HOW DID YOU HANDLE THE HUMILIATION OF YOUR WIFE DUMPING YOU FOR THE SPORTS ANCHOR?
? !!
I SENSE AN ATMOSPHERIC DISTURBANCE.
WINK, I'M TAKING YOU OFF SPEAKER.
Peirce

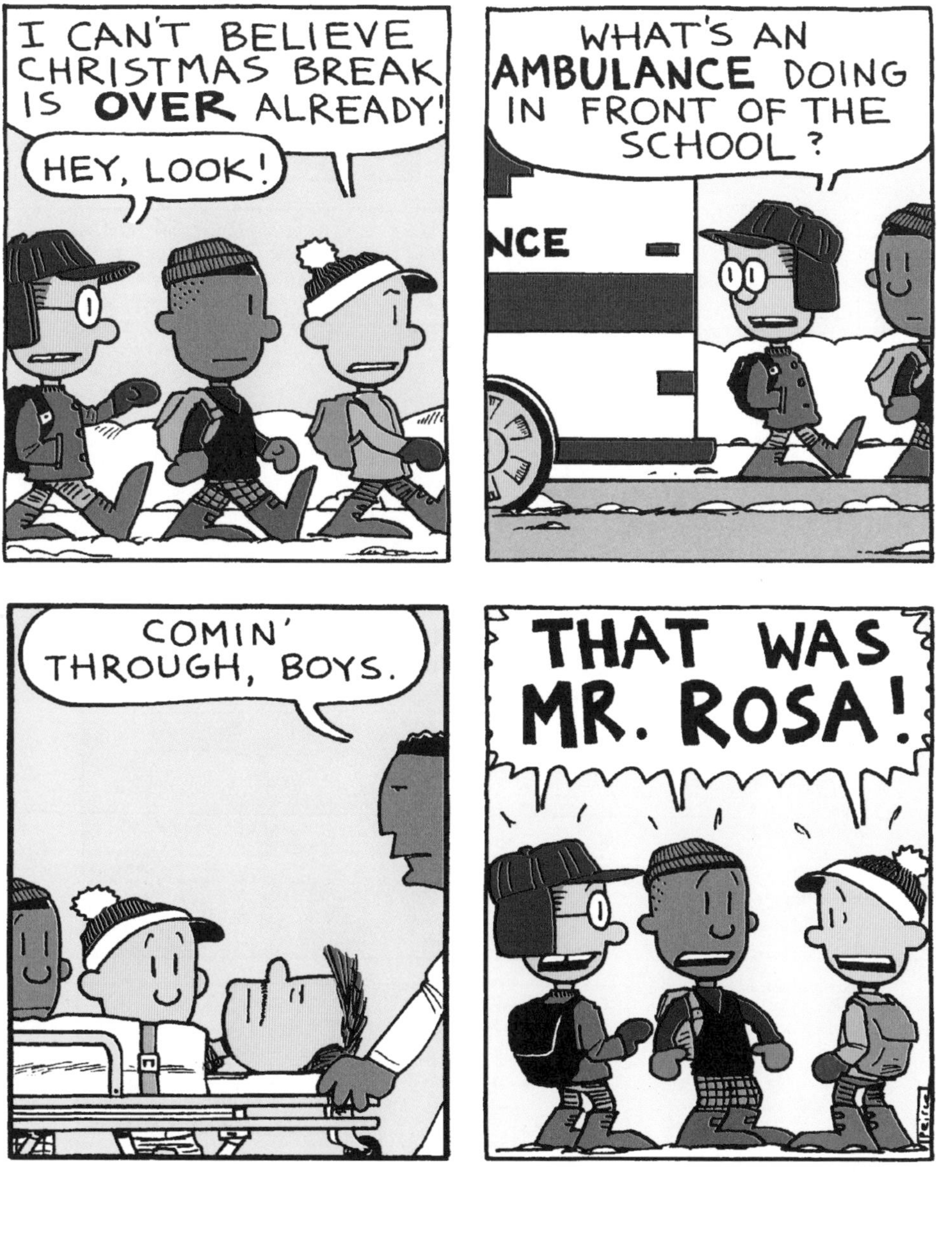
I CAN'T BELIEVE CHRISTMAS BREAK IS **OVER** ALREADY!
HEY, LOOK!
WHAT'S AN **AMBULANCE** DOING IN FRONT OF THE SCHOOL?
NCE
COMIN' THROUGH, BOYS.
THAT WAS MR. ROSA!

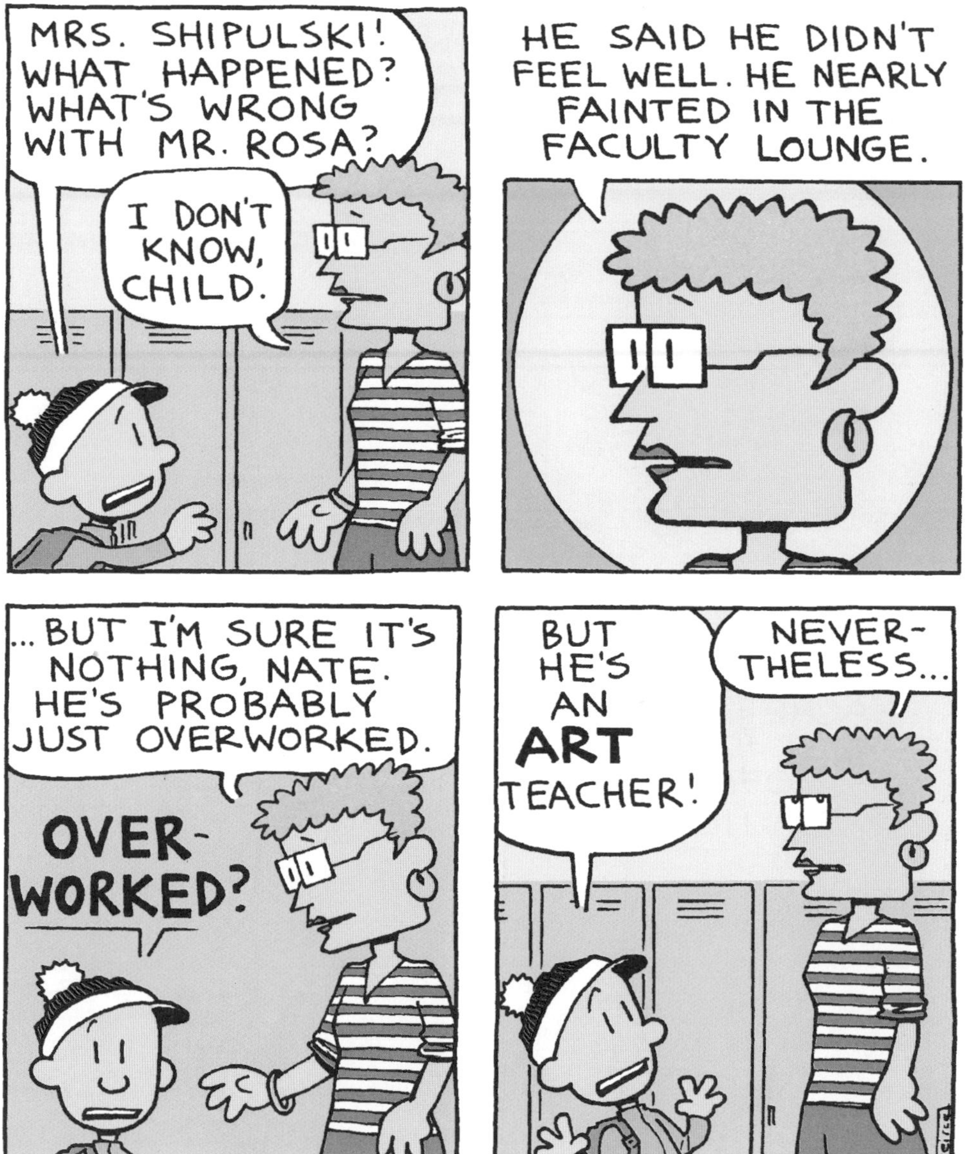
MRS. SHIPULSKI! WHAT HAPPENED? WHAT'S WRONG WITH MR. ROSA?
I DON'T KNOW, CHILD.
HE SAID HE DIDN'T FEEL WELL. HE NEARLY FAINTED IN THE FACULTY LOUNGE.
...BUT I'M SURE IT'S NOTHING, NATE. HE'S PROBABLY JUST OVERWORKED.
OVER-WORKED?
BUT HE'S AN ART TEACHER!
NEVER-THELESS...

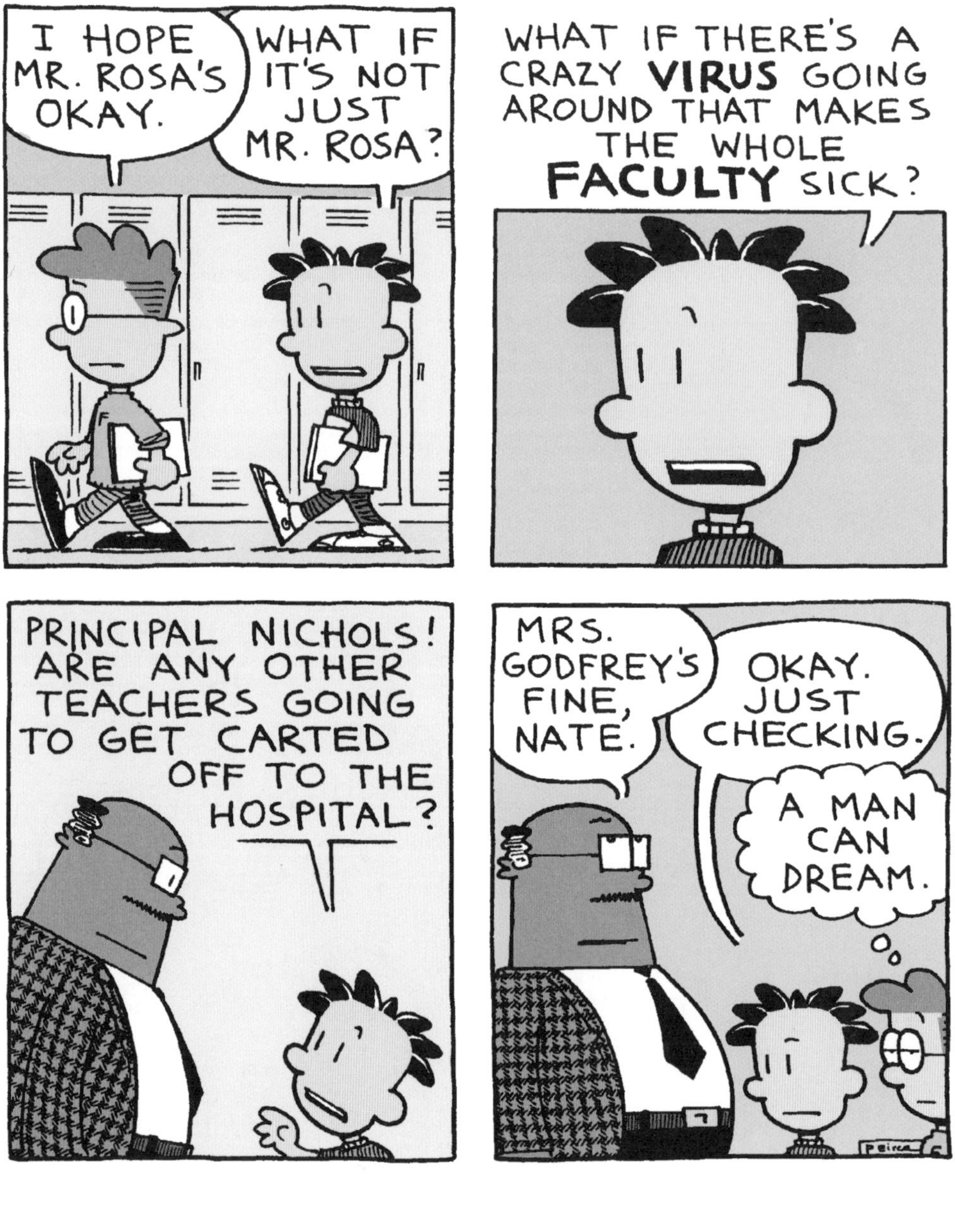
I HOPE MR. ROSA'S OKAY.
WHAT IF IT'S NOT JUST MR. ROSA?
WHAT IF THERE'S A CRAZY **VIRUS** GOING AROUND THAT MAKES THE WHOLE **FACULTY** SICK?
PRINCIPAL NICHOLS! ARE ANY OTHER TEACHERS GOING TO GET CARTED OFF TO THE HOSPITAL?
MRS. GODFREY'S FINE, NATE.
OKAY. JUST CHECKING.
A MAN CAN DREAM.

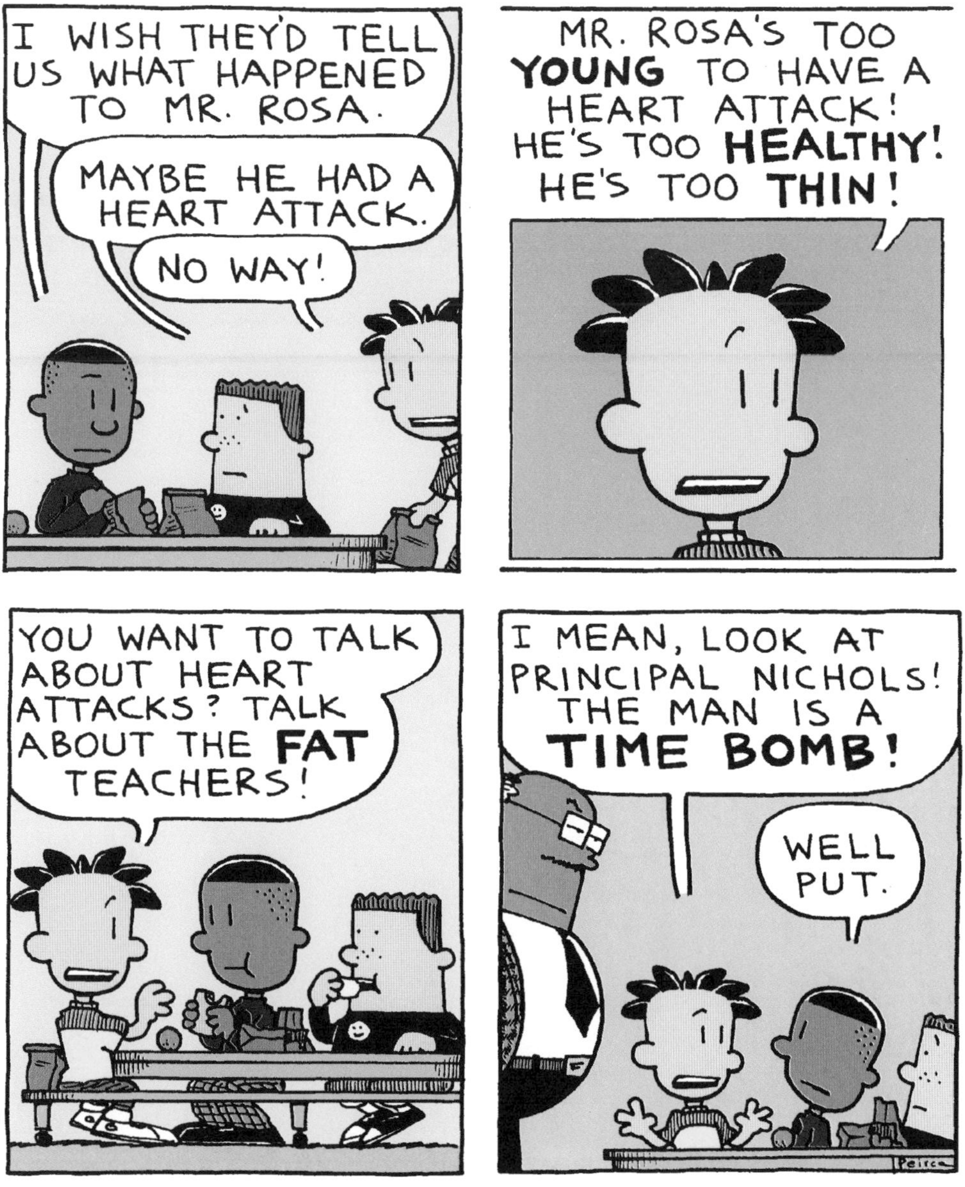
I WISH THEY'D TELL US WHAT HAPPENED TO MR. ROSA.
MAYBE HE HAD A HEART ATTACK.
NO WAY!
MR. ROSA'S TOO **YOUNG** TO HAVE A HEART ATTACK! HE'S TOO **HEALTHY**! HE'S TOO **THIN**!
YOU WANT TO TALK ABOUT HEART ATTACKS? TALK ABOUT THE **FAT** TEACHERS!
I MEAN, LOOK AT PRINCIPAL NICHOLS! THE MAN IS A **TIME BOMB**!
WELL PUT.
Peirce

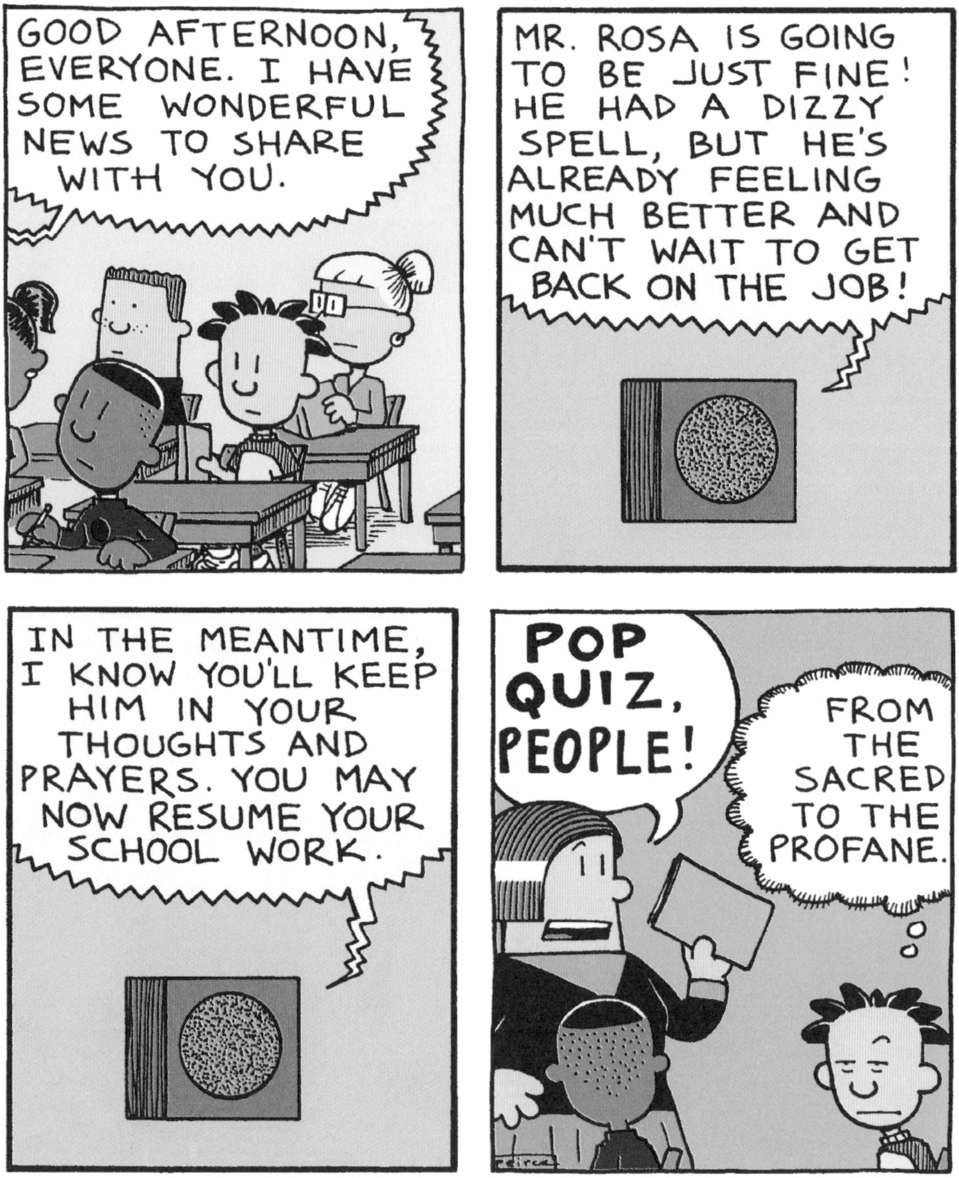
GOOD AFTERNOON, EVERYONE. I HAVE SOME WONDERFUL NEWS TO SHARE WITH YOU.
MR. ROSA IS GOING TO BE JUST FINE! HE HAD A DIZZY SPELL, BUT HE'S ALREADY FEELING MUCH BETTER AND CAN'T WAIT TO GET BACK ON THE JOB!
IN THE MEANTIME, I KNOW YOU'LL KEEP HIM IN YOUR THOUGHTS AND PRAYERS. YOU MAY NOW RESUME YOUR SCHOOL WORK.
POP QUIZ, PEOPLE!
FROM THE SACRED TO THE PROFANE.
peirce

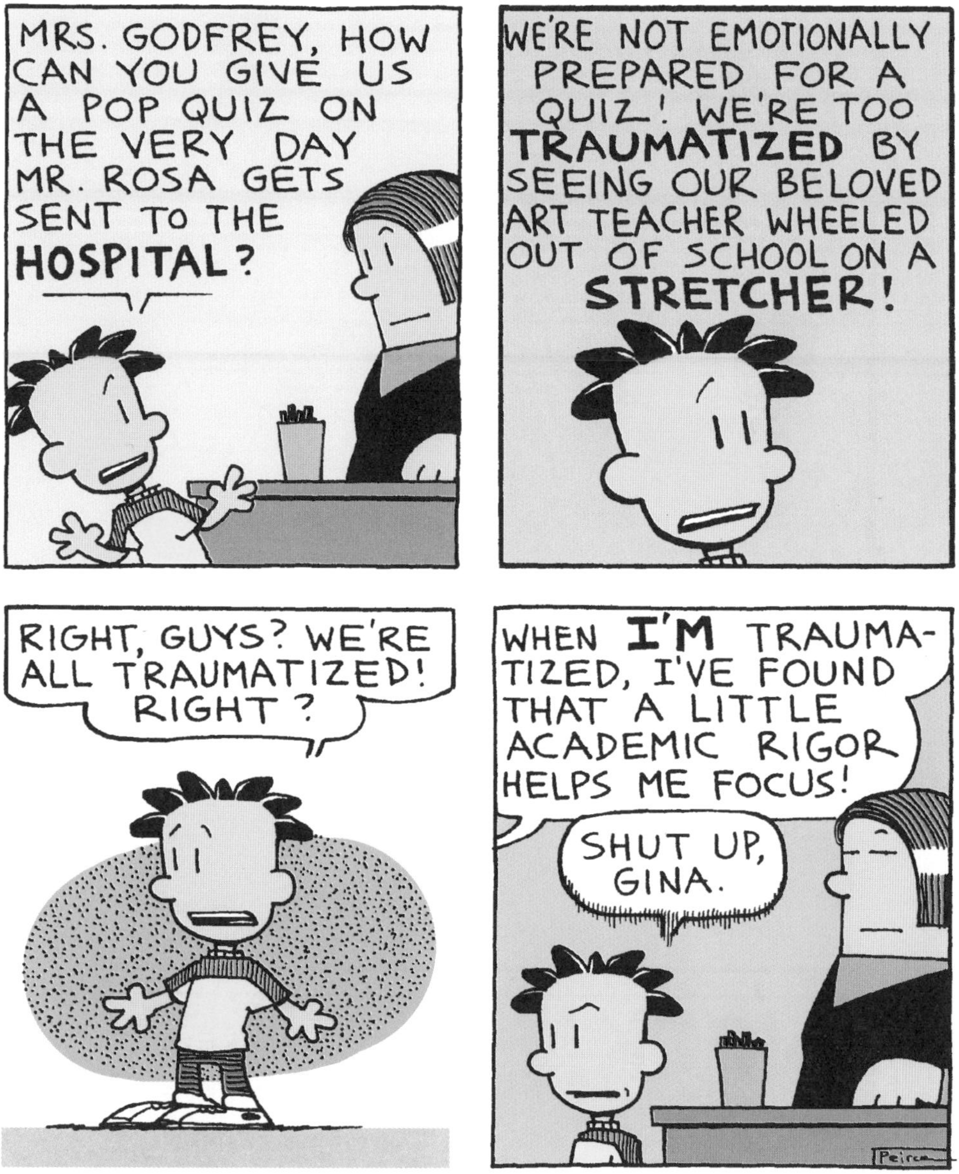
MRS. GODFREY, HOW CAN YOU GIVE US A POP QUIZ ON THE VERY DAY MR. ROSA GETS SENT TO THE **HOSPITAL**?
WE'RE NOT EMOTIONALLY PREPARED FOR A QUIZ! WE'RE TOO **TRAUMATIZED** BY SEEING OUR BELOVED ART TEACHER WHEELED OUT OF SCHOOL ON A **STRETCHER**!
RIGHT, GUYS? WE'RE ALL TRAUMATIZED! RIGHT?
WHEN **I'M** TRAUMATIZED, I'VE FOUND THAT A LITTLE ACADEMIC RIGOR HELPS ME FOCUS!
SHUT UP, GINA.
Peirce

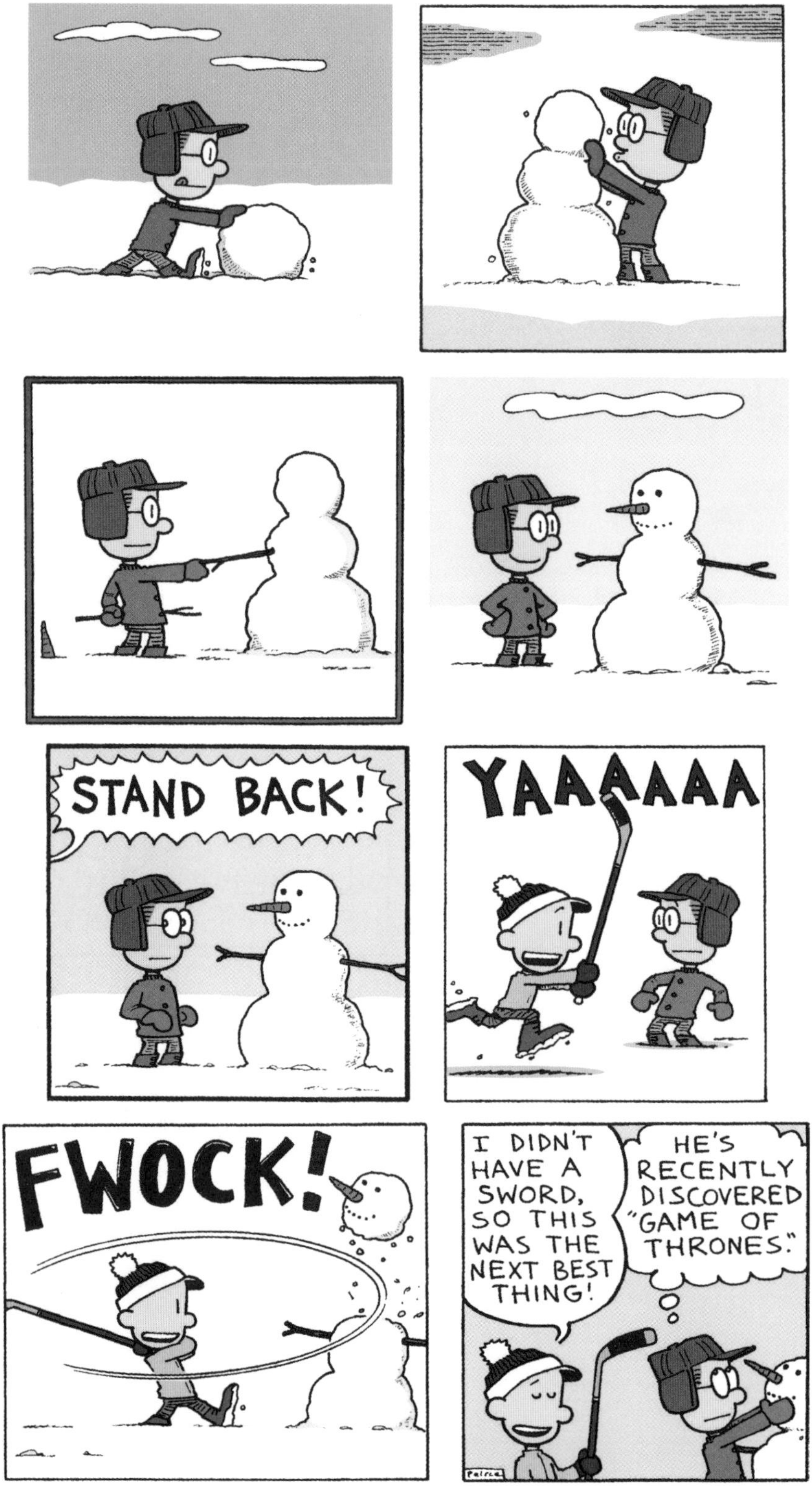
STAND BACK!
YAAAAAA
FWOCK!
I DIDN'T HAVE A SWORD, SO THIS WAS THE NEXT BEST THING!
HE'S RECENTLY DISCOVERED "GAME OF THRONES."
Peirce

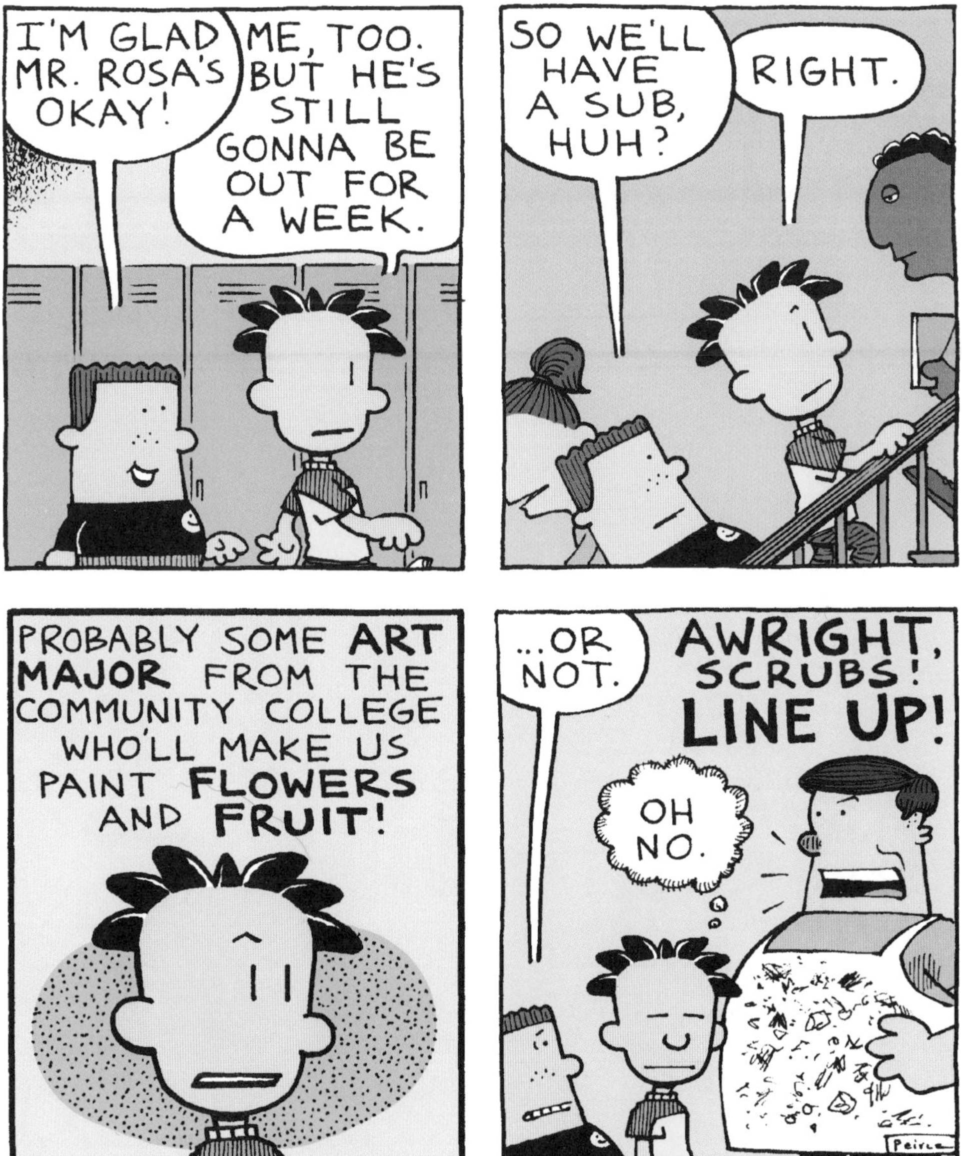
I'M GLAD MR. ROSA'S OKAY!
ME, TOO. BUT HE'S STILL GONNA BE OUT FOR A WEEK.
SO WE'LL HAVE A SUB, HUH?
RIGHT.
PROBABLY SOME ART MAJOR FROM THE COMMUNITY COLLEGE WHO'LL MAKE US PAINT FLOWERS AND FRUIT!
...OR NOT.
AWRIGHT, SCRUBS! LINE UP!
OH NO.
Peirce

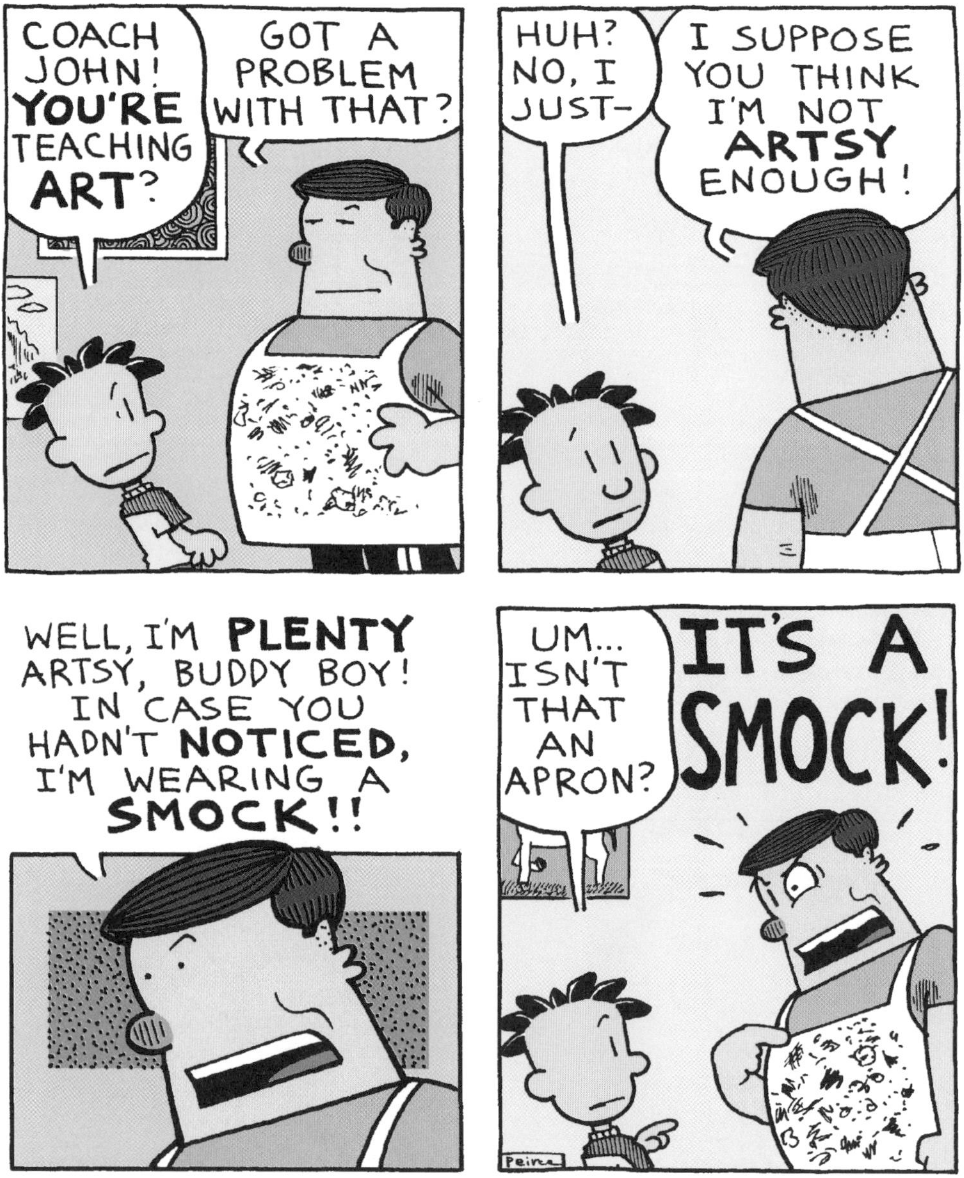

COACH JOHN! **YOU'RE** TEACHING **ART**?
GOT A PROBLEM WITH THAT?
HUH? NO, I JUST-
I SUPPOSE YOU THINK I'M NOT **ARTSY** ENOUGH!
WELL, I'M **PLENTY** ARTSY, BUDDY BOY! IN CASE YOU HADN'T **NOTICED,** I'M WEARING A **SMOCK**!!
UM... ISN'T THAT AN APRON?
IT'S A SMOCK!
Peirce

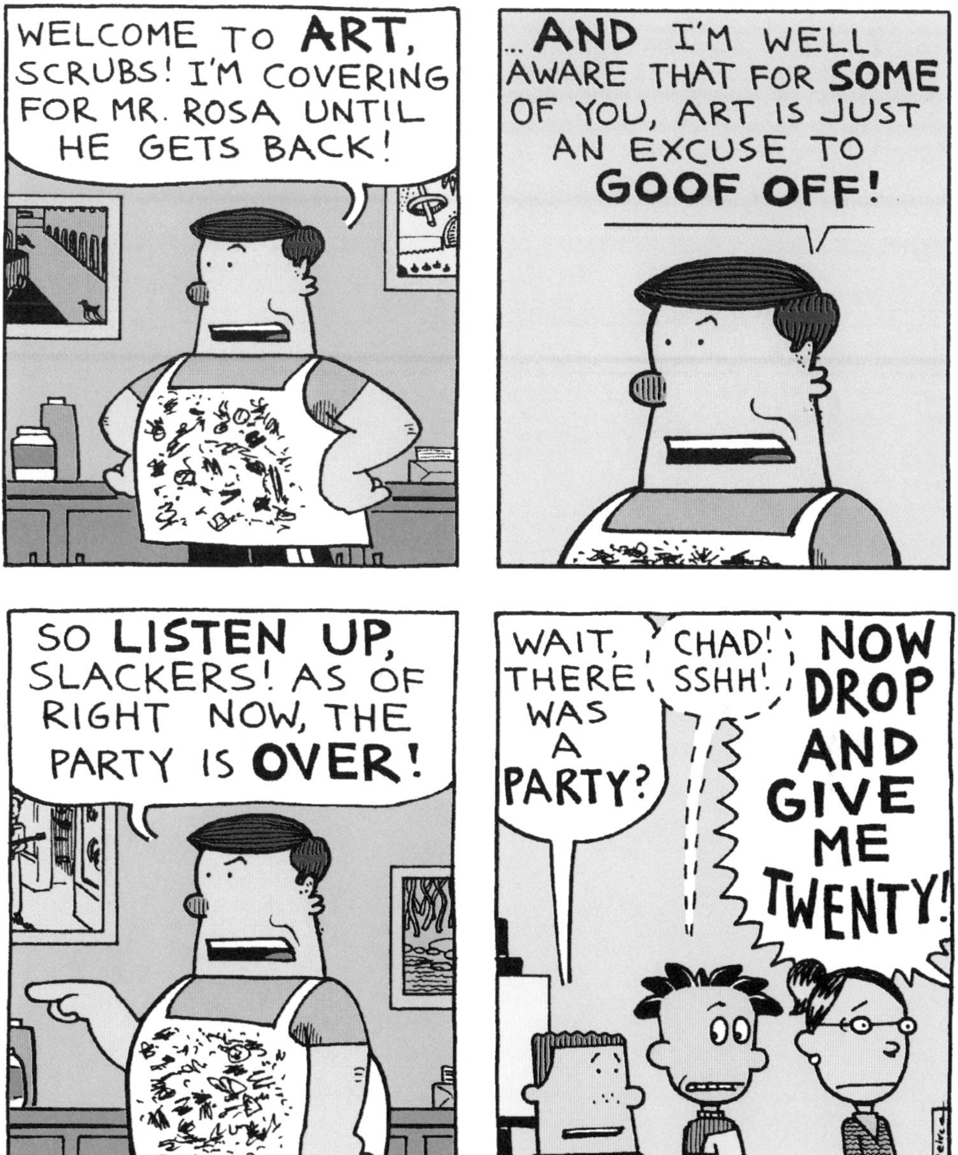
WELCOME TO ART, SCRUBS! I'M COVERING FOR MR. ROSA UNTIL HE GETS BACK!
...AND I'M WELL AWARE THAT FOR SOME OF YOU, ART IS JUST AN EXCUSE TO GOOF OFF!
SO LISTEN UP, SLACKERS! AS OF RIGHT NOW, THE PARTY IS OVER!
WAIT, THERE WAS A PARTY?
CHAD! SSHH!
NOW DROP AND GIVE ME TWENTY!
Peirce

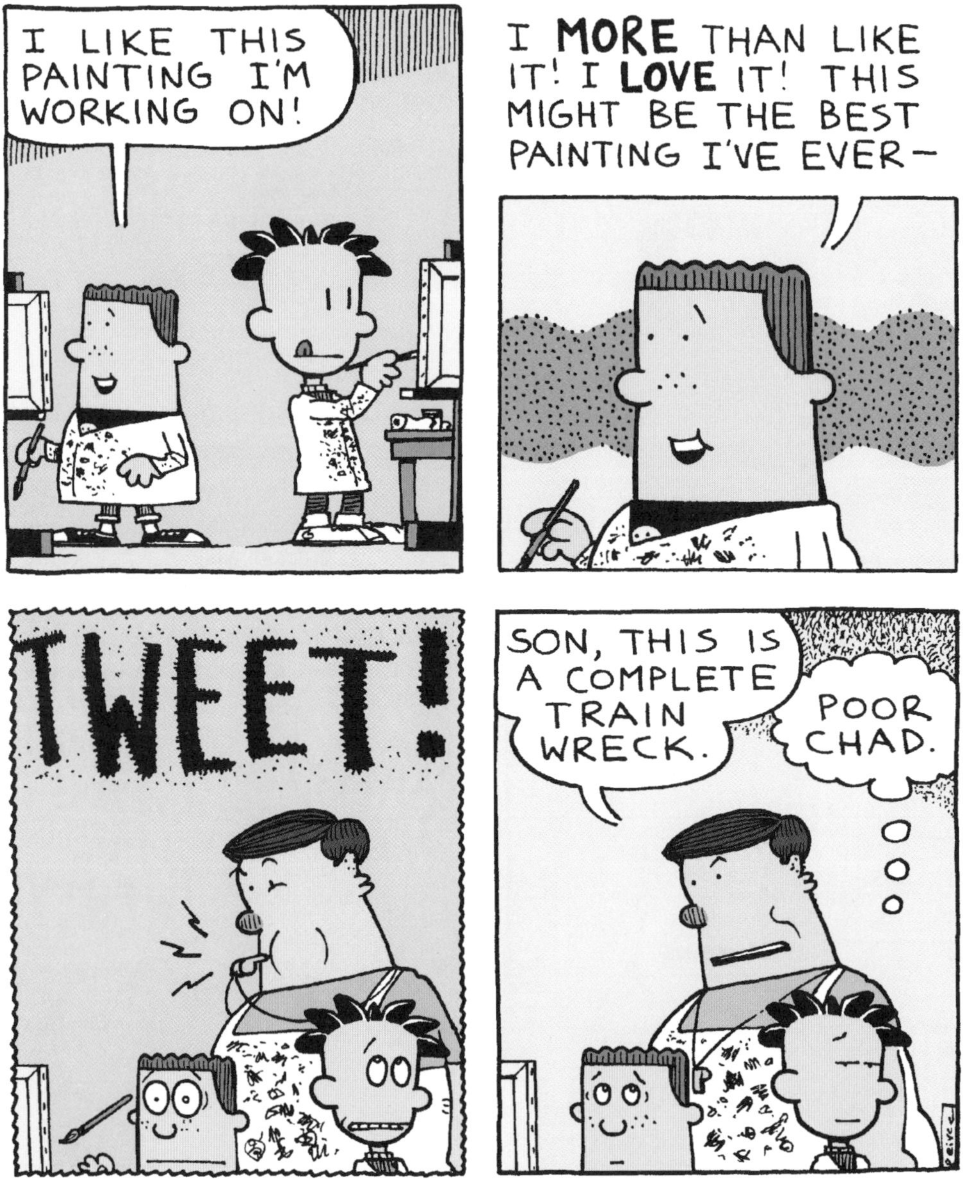
I LIKE THIS PAINTING I'M WORKING ON!
I **MORE** THAN LIKE IT! I **LOVE** IT! THIS MIGHT BE THE BEST PAINTING I'VE EVER—
TWEET!
SON, THIS IS A COMPLETE TRAIN WRECK.
POOR CHAD.

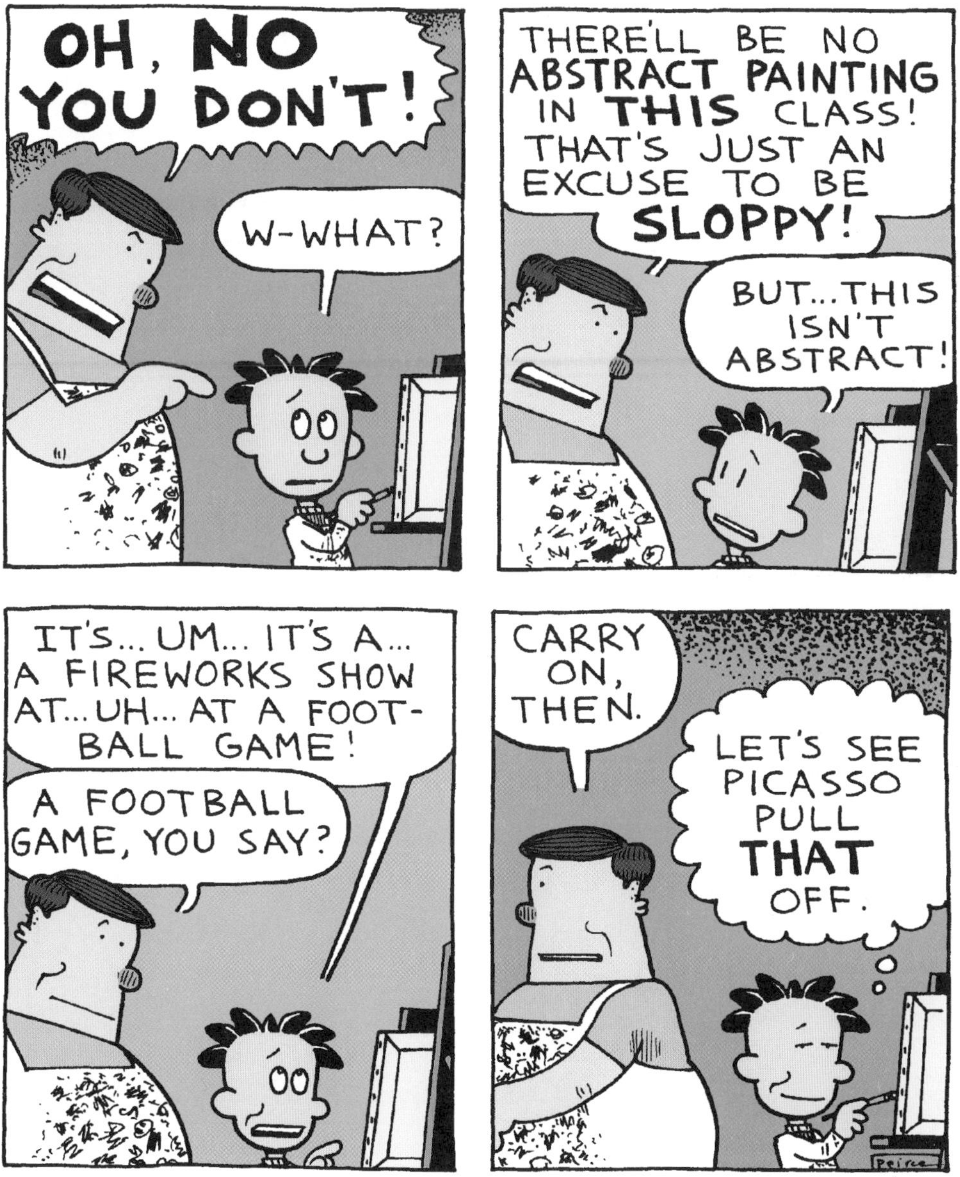
OH, NO YOU DON'T!
W-WHAT?
THERE'LL BE NO ABSTRACT PAINTING IN THIS CLASS! THAT'S JUST AN EXCUSE TO BE SLOPPY!
BUT...THIS ISN'T ABSTRACT!
IT'S... UM... IT'S A... A FIREWORKS SHOW AT...UH... AT A FOOT-BALL GAME!
A FOOTBALL GAME, YOU SAY?
CARRY ON, THEN.
LET'S SEE PICASSO PULL THAT OFF.
Peirce

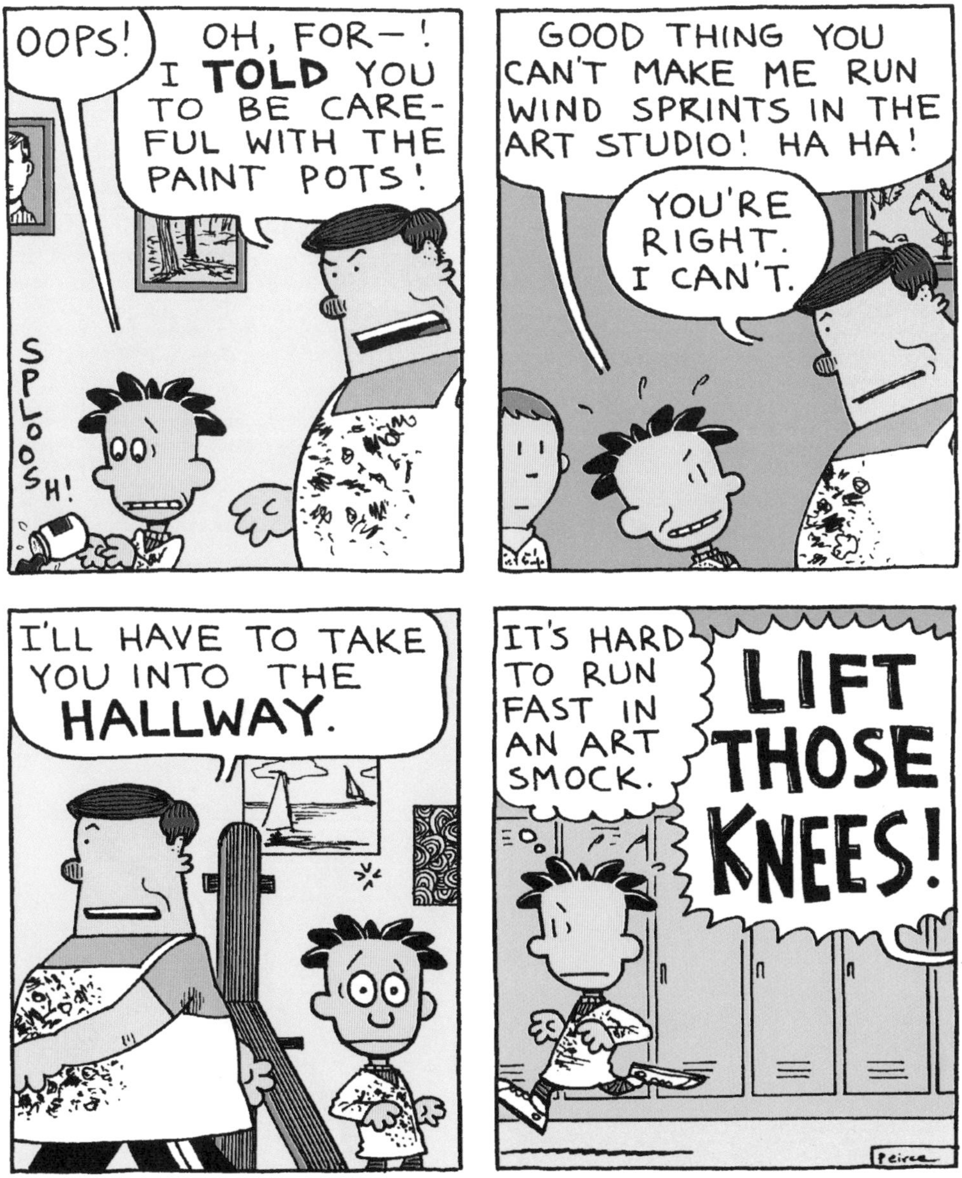
OOPS!
OH, FOR—! I **TOLD** YOU TO BE CARE-FUL WITH THE PAINT POTS!
SPLOOSH!
GOOD THING YOU CAN'T MAKE ME RUN WIND SPRINTS IN THE ART STUDIO! HA HA!
YOU'RE RIGHT. I CAN'T.
I'LL HAVE TO TAKE YOU INTO THE **HALLWAY**.
IT'S HARD TO RUN FAST IN AN ART SMOCK.
LIFT THOSE KNEES!
Peirce

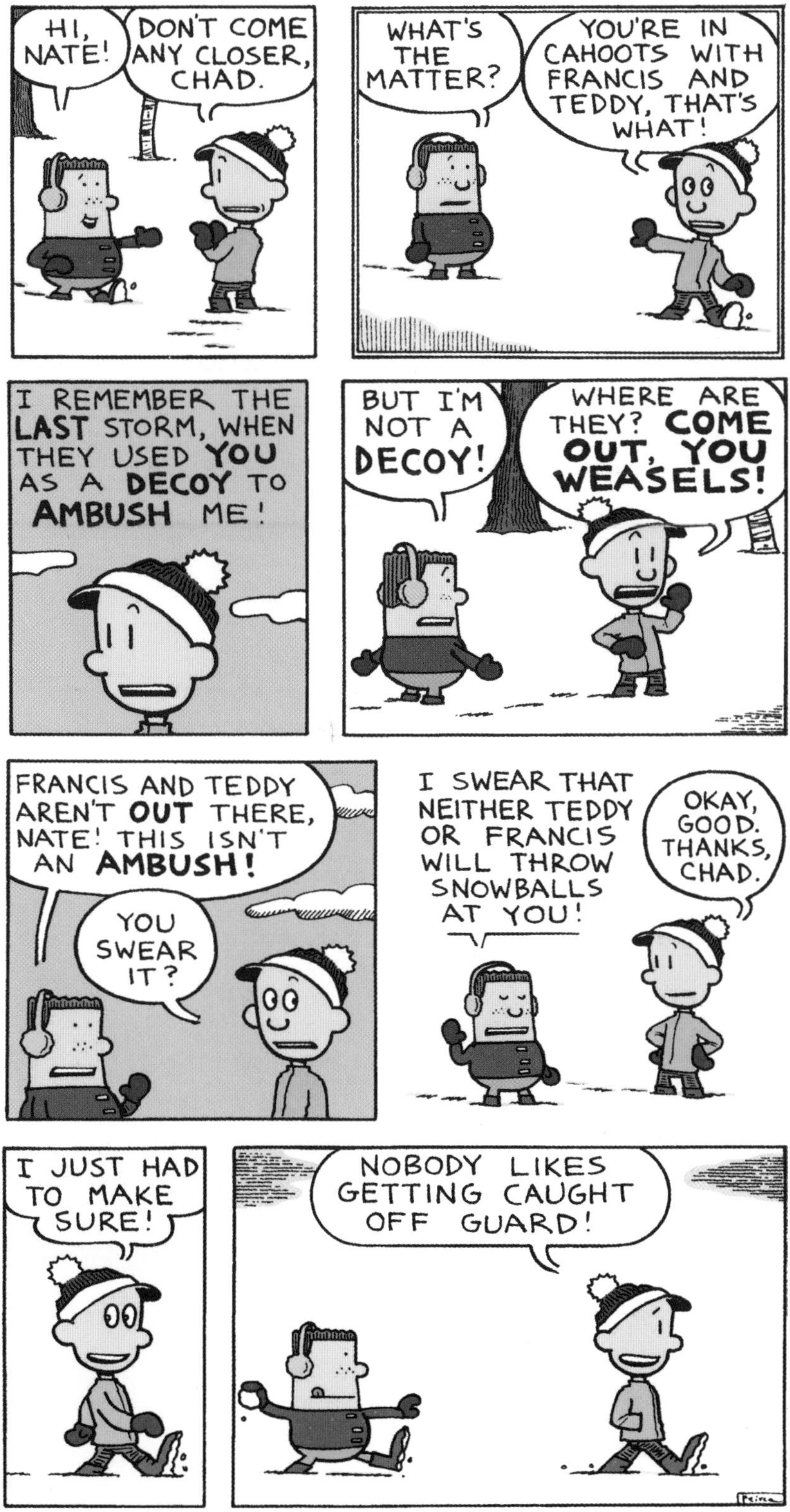
HI, NATE!
DON'T COME ANY CLOSER, CHAD.
WHAT'S THE MATTER?
YOU'RE IN CAHOOTS WITH FRANCIS AND TEDDY, THAT'S WHAT!
I REMEMBER THE LAST STORM, WHEN THEY USED YOU AS A DECOY TO AMBUSH ME!
BUT I'M NOT A DECOY!
WHERE ARE THEY? COME OUT, YOU WEASELS!
FRANCIS AND TEDDY AREN'T OUT THERE, NATE! THIS ISN'T AN AMBUSH!
YOU SWEAR IT?
I SWEAR THAT NEITHER TEDDY OR FRANCIS WILL THROW SNOWBALLS AT YOU!
OKAY, GOOD. THANKS, CHAD.
I JUST HAD TO MAKE SURE!
NOBODY LIKES GETTING CAUGHT OFF GUARD!

The film screened today in Mrs. Godfrey's 6th grade social studies class, *"Abraham Lincoln: From Log Cabin to White House,"* is a festering pimple on the forehead of educational cinema.
TIK TIK TIK
The problems begin in the very first scene, when we meet young Abe as a 9-year-old boy in Kentucky. Abe's mother dies, so of course you're expecting Abe to be totally devastated, right? Duh.
TIK TAK
TIKKA TAKKA
But guess what? The kid playing Abe is a complete stiff. When he "cries" at his mother's bedside, he sounds like a goat passing a kidney stone. I've seen more convincing acting from a plastic lawn gnome.
TAK
TIK
TIK TAK
Then Abe grows up. At this point, the movie really needs a jolt of energy, like a car chase or a kung fu showdown. But no. Instead, Abe reads a lot of books, becomes a lawyer, and gets married. Wow. Exciting.

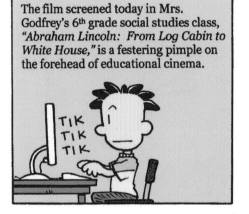

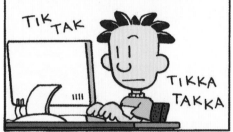

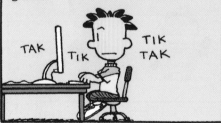

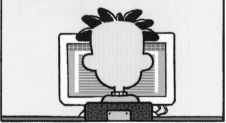

And by the way, the actor playing the grown-up Abe doesn't resemble the real Abraham Lincoln at all. His famous mole appears to be a glob of Silly Putty on his cheek, and his so-called beard looks like a chipmunk taped to his chin.

TIK TIKKA   TAK TAKKA

Somehow, Abe is elected President, and the Civil War begins. Sorry, but the Civil War battle scenes seem SO FAKE. I mean: Hello, if you want authenticity, try using film of REAL Civil War battles. Apparently, that never occurred to the director of this fiasco.

TAK TAK   TIK TIK

And if you're hoping for a happy ending, I have more bad news...

SPOILER ALERT.

MOVIE REVIEWING AIN'T WHAT IT USED TO BE.

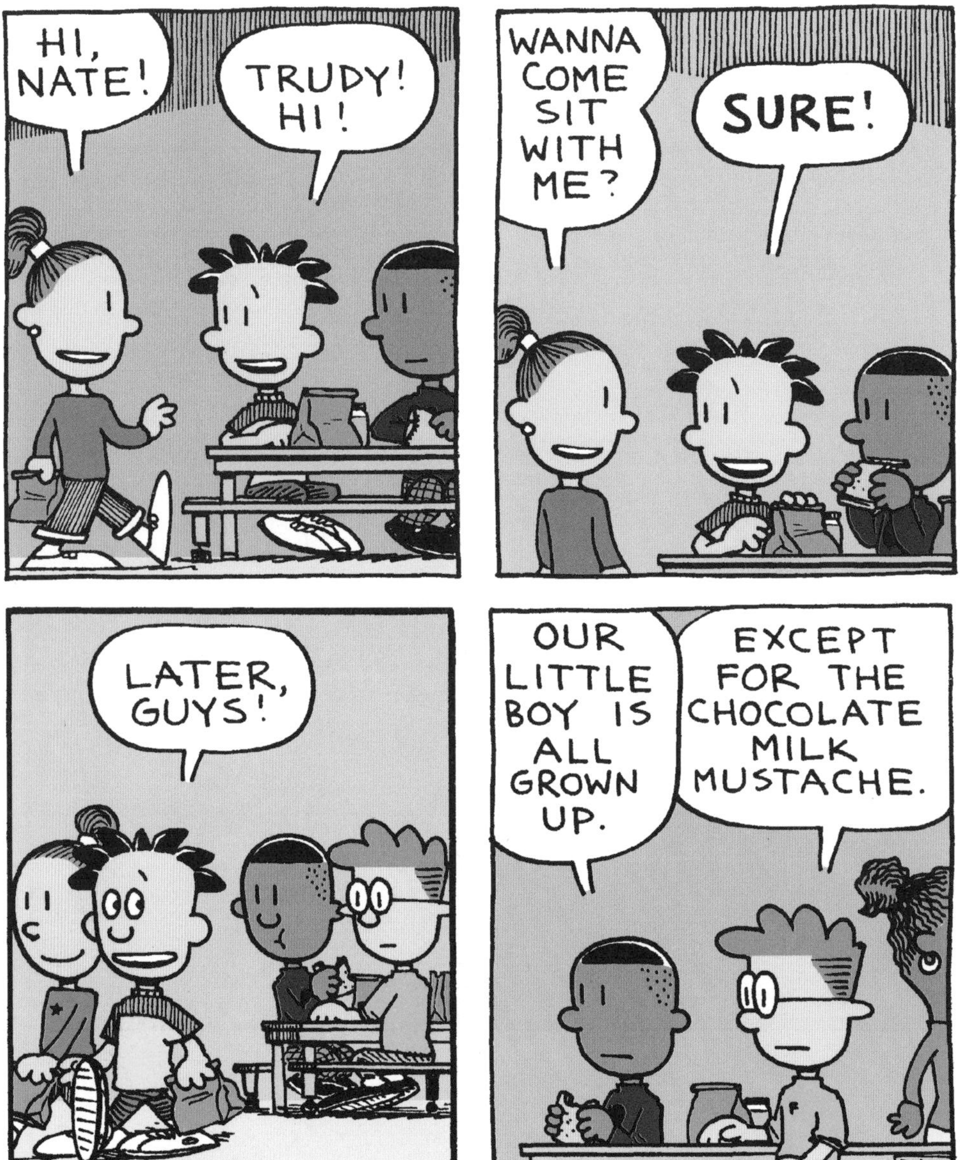
HI, NATE!
TRUDY! HI!
WANNA COME SIT WITH ME?
SURE!
LATER, GUYS!
OUR LITTLE BOY IS ALL GROWN UP.
EXCEPT FOR THE CHOCOLATE MILK MUSTACHE.
Peirce

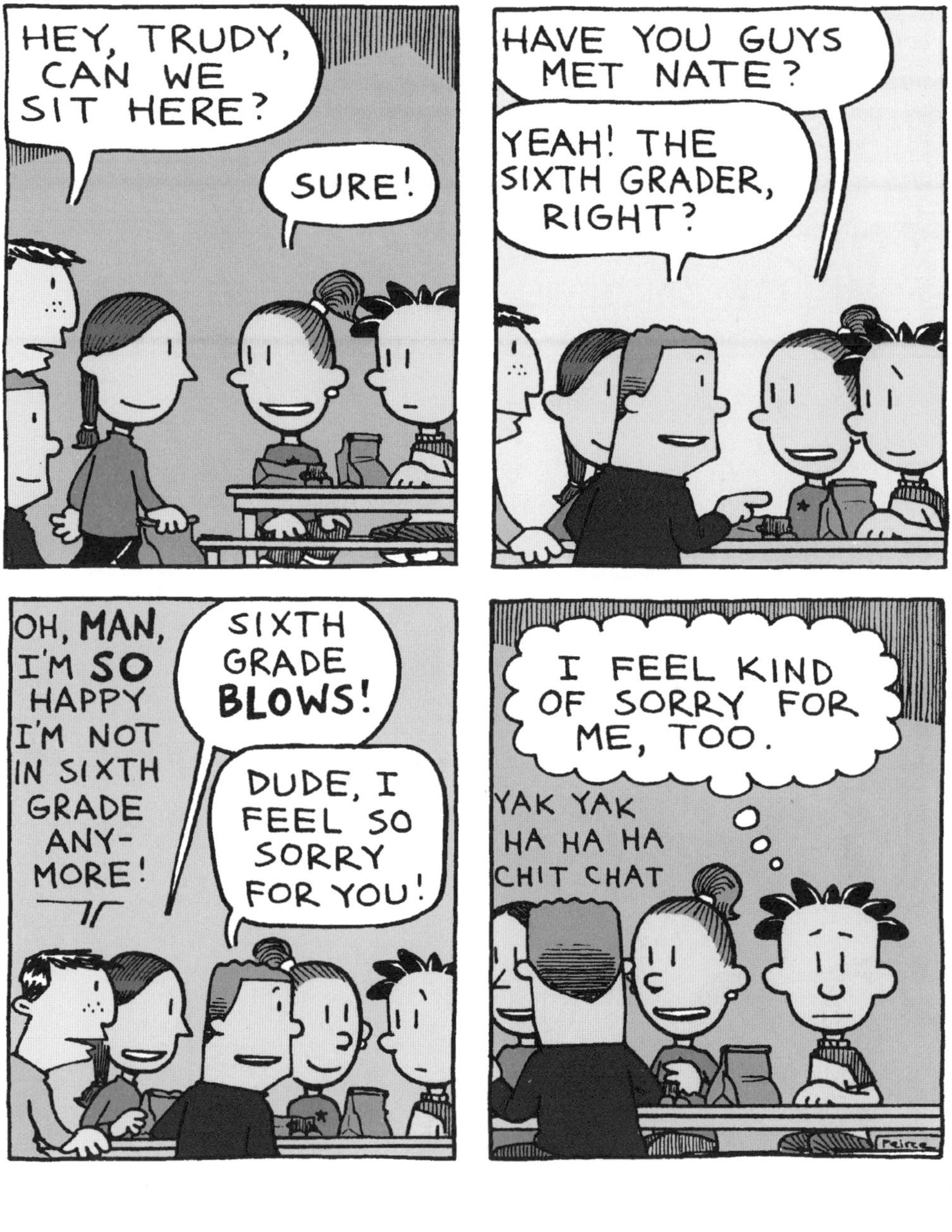
HEY, TRUDY, CAN WE SIT HERE?
SURE!
HAVE YOU GUYS MET NATE?
YEAH! THE SIXTH GRADER, RIGHT?
OH, MAN, I'M SO HAPPY I'M NOT IN SIXTH GRADE ANY-MORE!
SIXTH GRADE BLOWS!
DUDE, I FEEL SO SORRY FOR YOU!
I FEEL KIND OF SORRY FOR ME, TOO.
YAK YAK
HA HA HA
CHIT CHAT

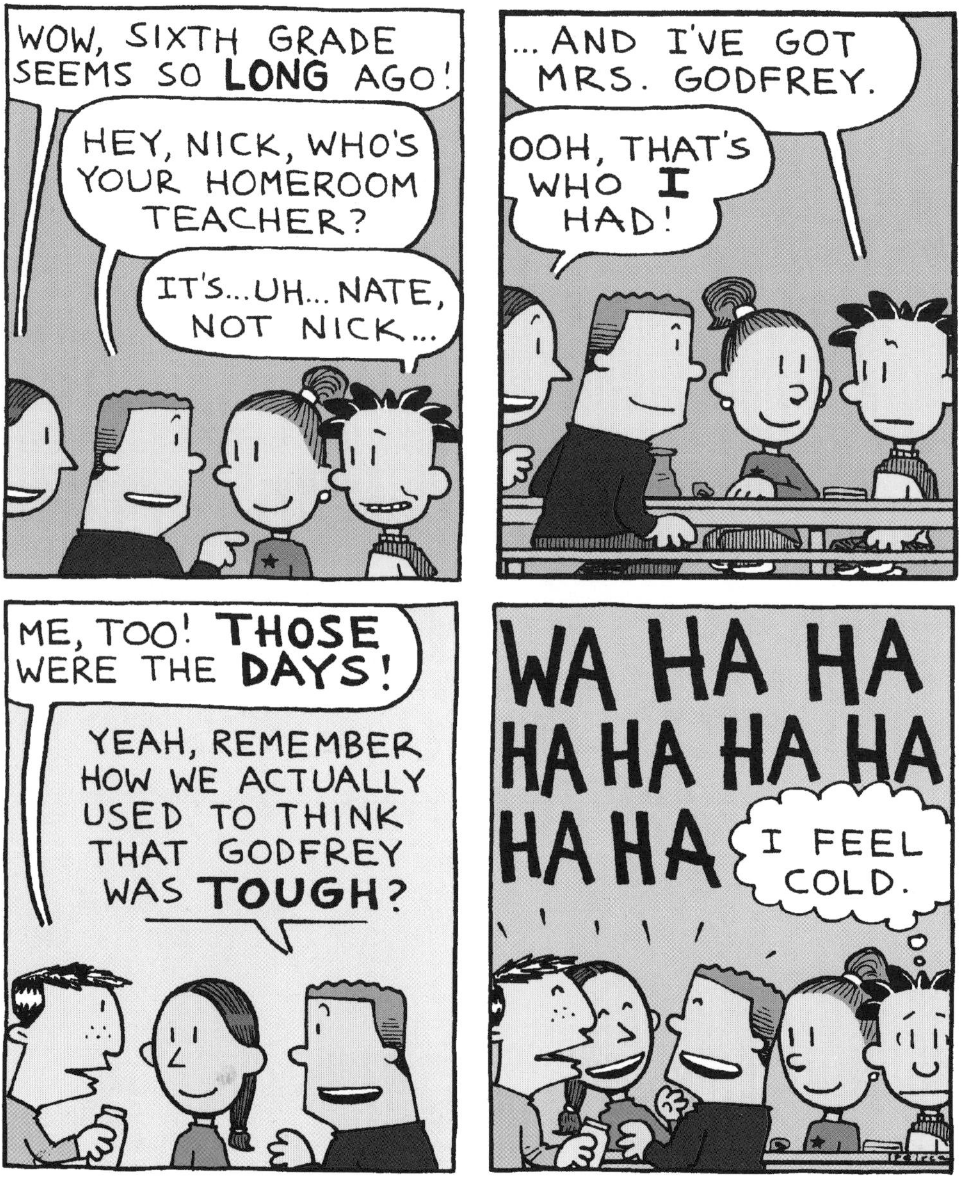
WOW, SIXTH GRADE SEEMS SO **LONG** AGO!
HEY, NICK, WHO'S YOUR HOMEROOM TEACHER?
IT'S...UH...NATE, NOT NICK...
...AND I'VE GOT MRS. GODFREY.
OOH, THAT'S WHO **I** HAD!
ME, TOO! **THOSE** WERE THE **DAYS**!
YEAH, REMEMBER HOW WE ACTUALLY USED TO THINK THAT GODFREY WAS **TOUGH**?
WA HA HA HA HA HA HA HA HA
I FEEL COLD.

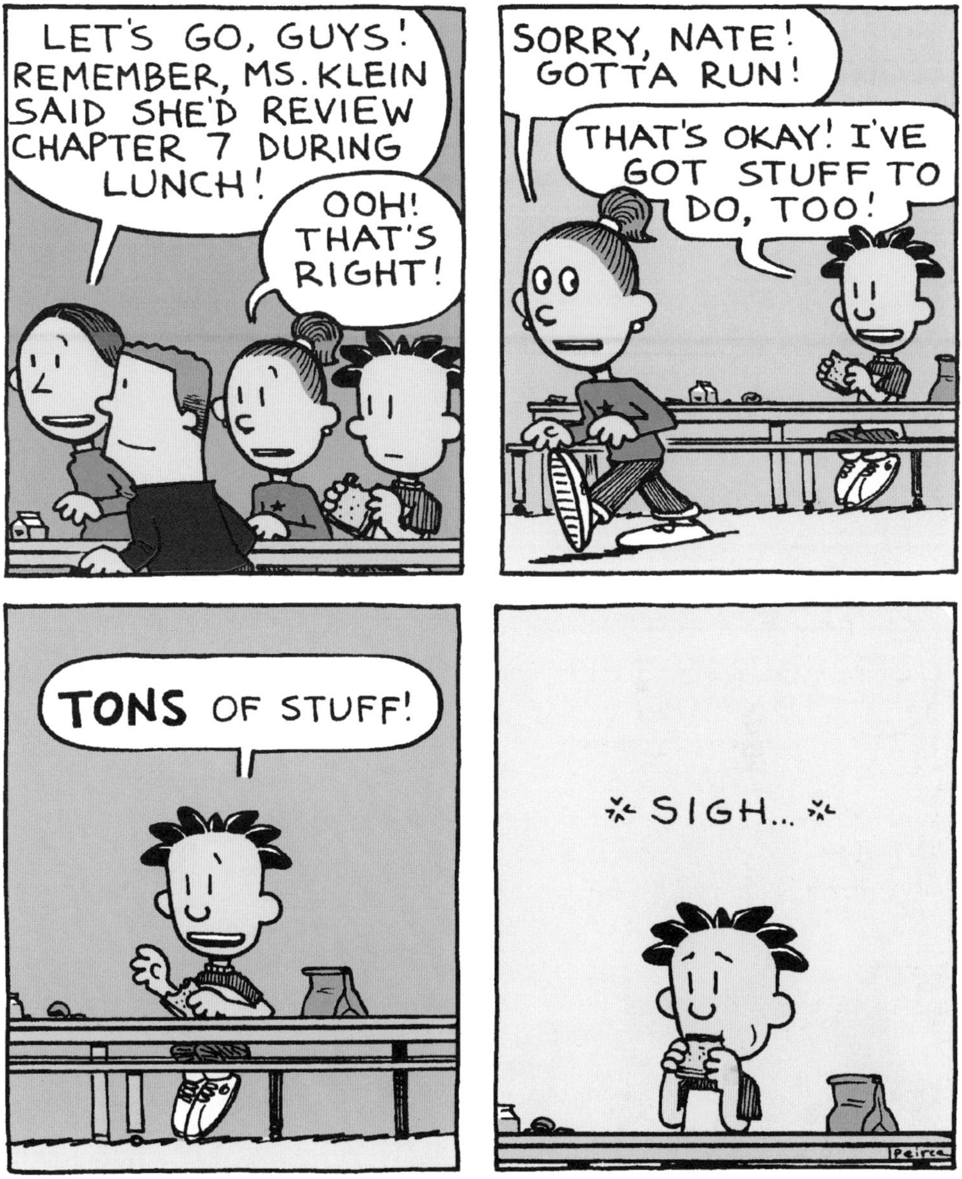
LET'S GO, GUYS! REMEMBER, MS. KLEIN SAID SHE'D REVIEW CHAPTER 7 DURING LUNCH!
OOH! THAT'S RIGHT!
SORRY, NATE! GOTTA RUN!
THAT'S OKAY! I'VE GOT STUFF TO DO, TOO!
TONS OF STUFF!
SIGH...
Peirce

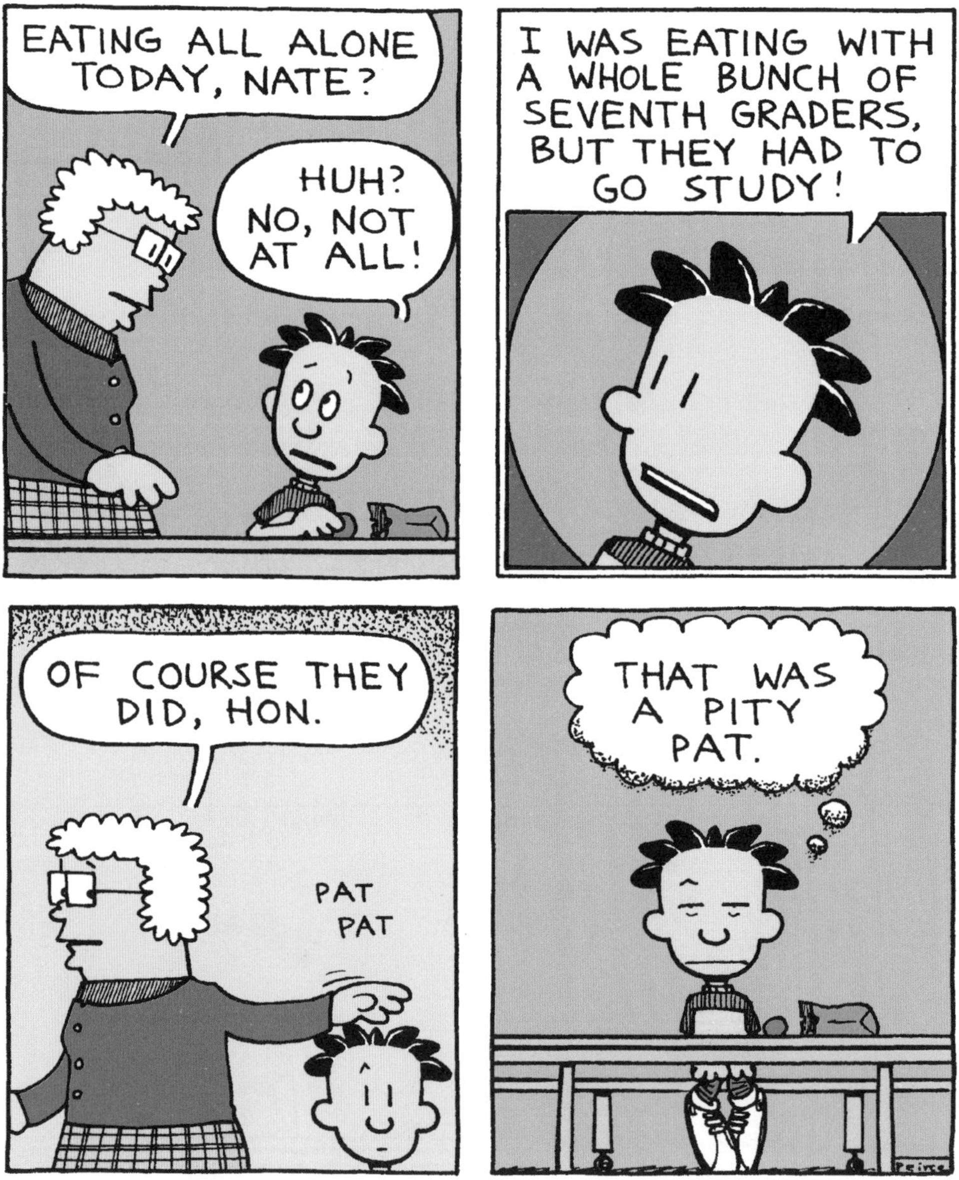
EATING ALL ALONE TODAY, NATE?
HUH? NO, NOT AT ALL!
I WAS EATING WITH A WHOLE BUNCH OF SEVENTH GRADERS, BUT THEY HAD TO GO STUDY!
OF COURSE THEY DID, HON.
PAT PAT
THAT WAS A PITY PAT.
Peirce

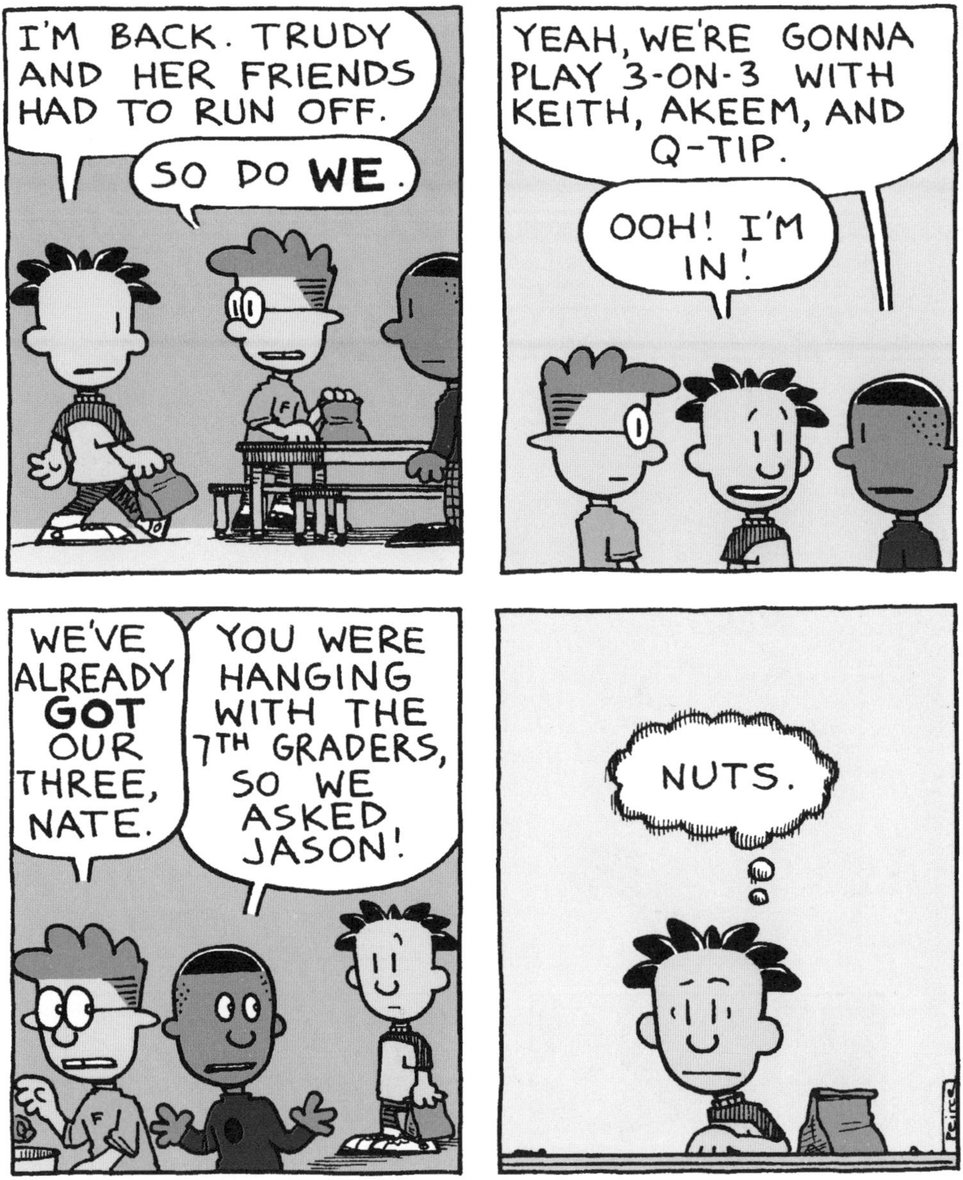
I'M BACK. TRUDY AND HER FRIENDS HAD TO RUN OFF.
SO DO **WE**.
YEAH, WE'RE GONNA PLAY 3-ON-3 WITH KEITH, AKEEM, AND Q-TIP.
OOH! I'M IN!
WE'VE ALREADY **GOT** OUR THREE, NATE.
YOU WERE HANGING WITH THE 7TH GRADERS, SO WE ASKED JASON!
NUTS.
Peirce

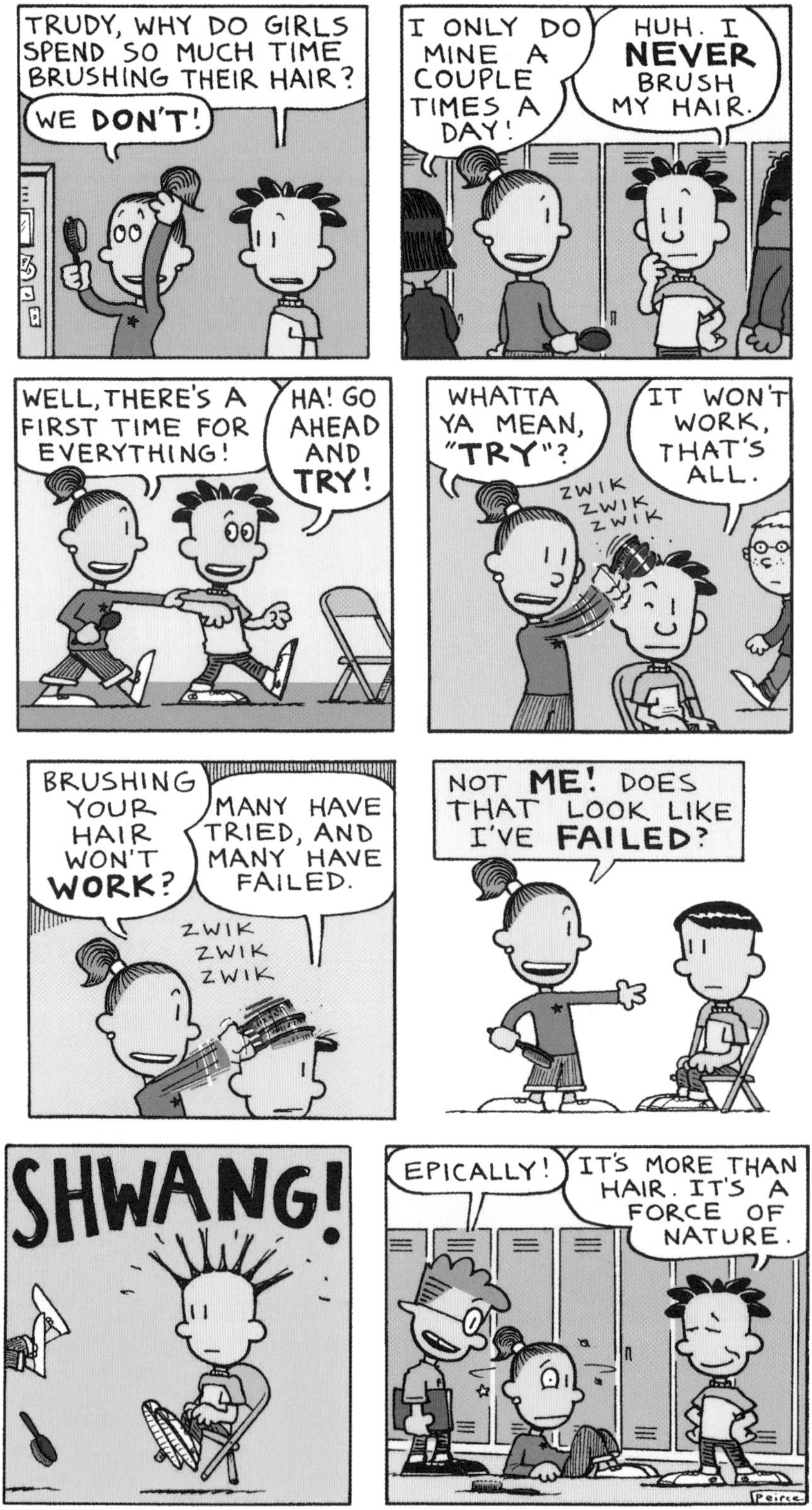
TRUDY, WHY DO GIRLS SPEND SO MUCH TIME BRUSHING THEIR HAIR?
WE DON'T!
I ONLY DO MINE A COUPLE TIMES A DAY!
HUH. I NEVER BRUSH MY HAIR.
WELL, THERE'S A FIRST TIME FOR EVERYTHING!
HA! GO AHEAD AND TRY!
WHATTA YA MEAN, "TRY"?
ZWIK ZWIK ZWIK
IT WON'T WORK, THAT'S ALL.
BRUSHING YOUR HAIR WON'T WORK?
ZWIK ZWIK ZWIK
MANY HAVE TRIED, AND MANY HAVE FAILED.
NOT ME! DOES THAT LOOK LIKE I'VE FAILED?
SHWANG!
EPICALLY!
IT'S MORE THAN HAIR. IT'S A FORCE OF NATURE.
Peirce

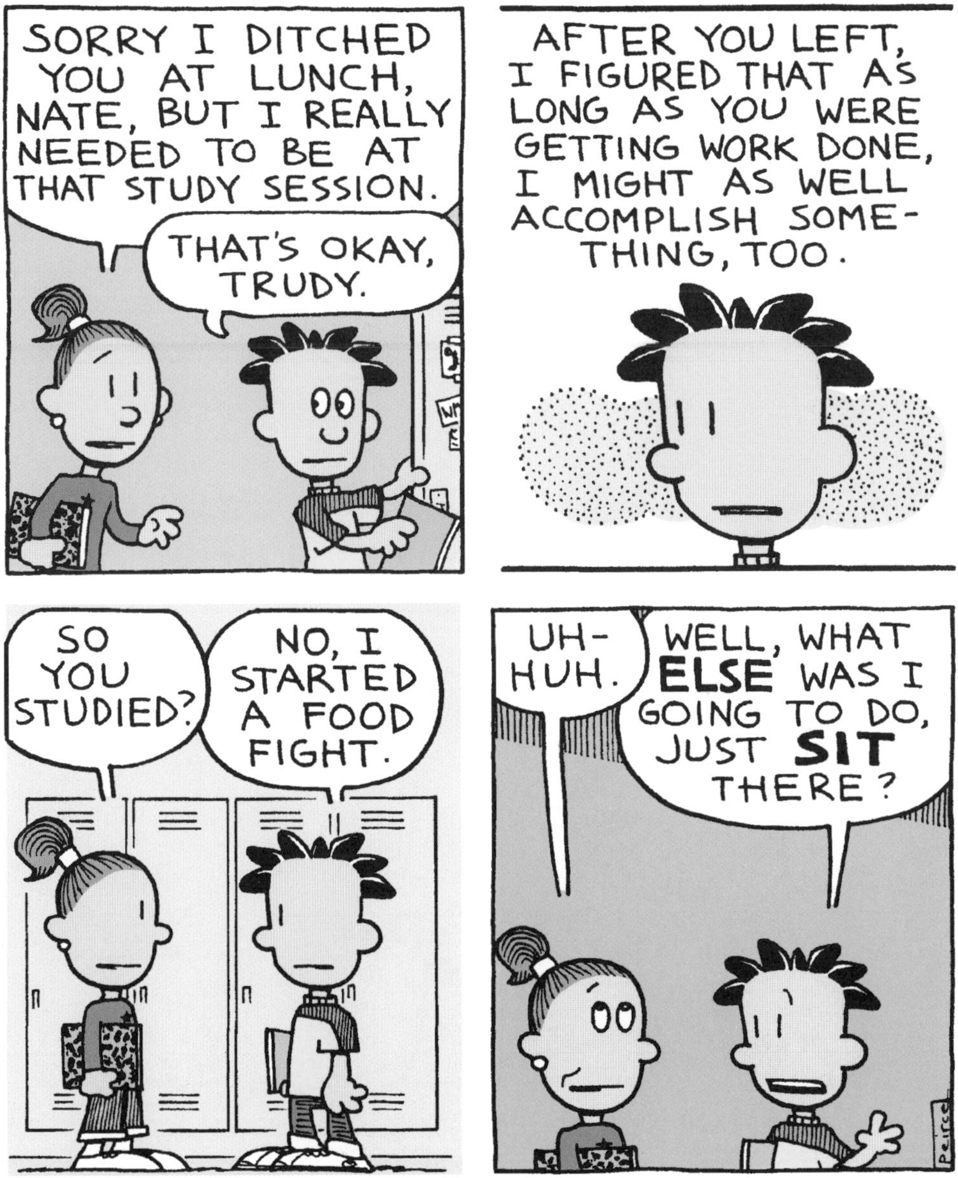
SORRY I DITCHED YOU AT LUNCH, NATE, BUT I REALLY NEEDED TO BE AT THAT STUDY SESSION.
THAT'S OKAY, TRUDY.
AFTER YOU LEFT, I FIGURED THAT AS LONG AS YOU WERE GETTING WORK DONE, I MIGHT AS WELL ACCOMPLISH SOME-THING, TOO.
SO YOU STUDIED?
NO, I STARTED A FOOD FIGHT.
UH-HUH.
WELL, WHAT ELSE WAS I GOING TO DO, JUST SIT THERE?
Peirce

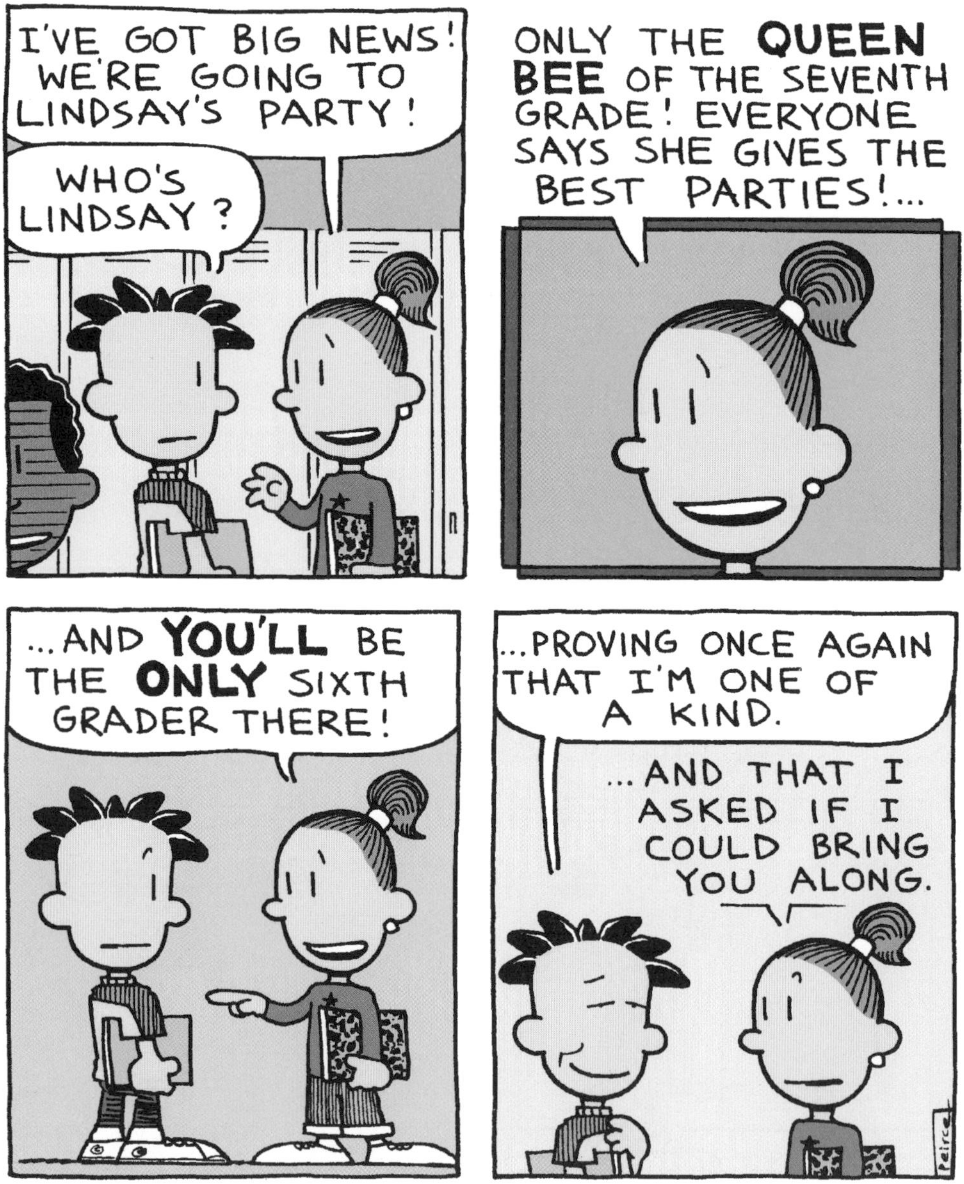
I'VE GOT BIG NEWS! WE'RE GOING TO LINDSAY'S PARTY!
WHO'S LINDSAY?
ONLY THE QUEEN BEE OF THE SEVENTH GRADE! EVERYONE SAYS SHE GIVES THE BEST PARTIES!...
...AND YOU'LL BE THE ONLY SIXTH GRADER THERE!
...PROVING ONCE AGAIN THAT I'M ONE OF A KIND.
...AND THAT I ASKED IF I COULD BRING YOU ALONG.
Peirce

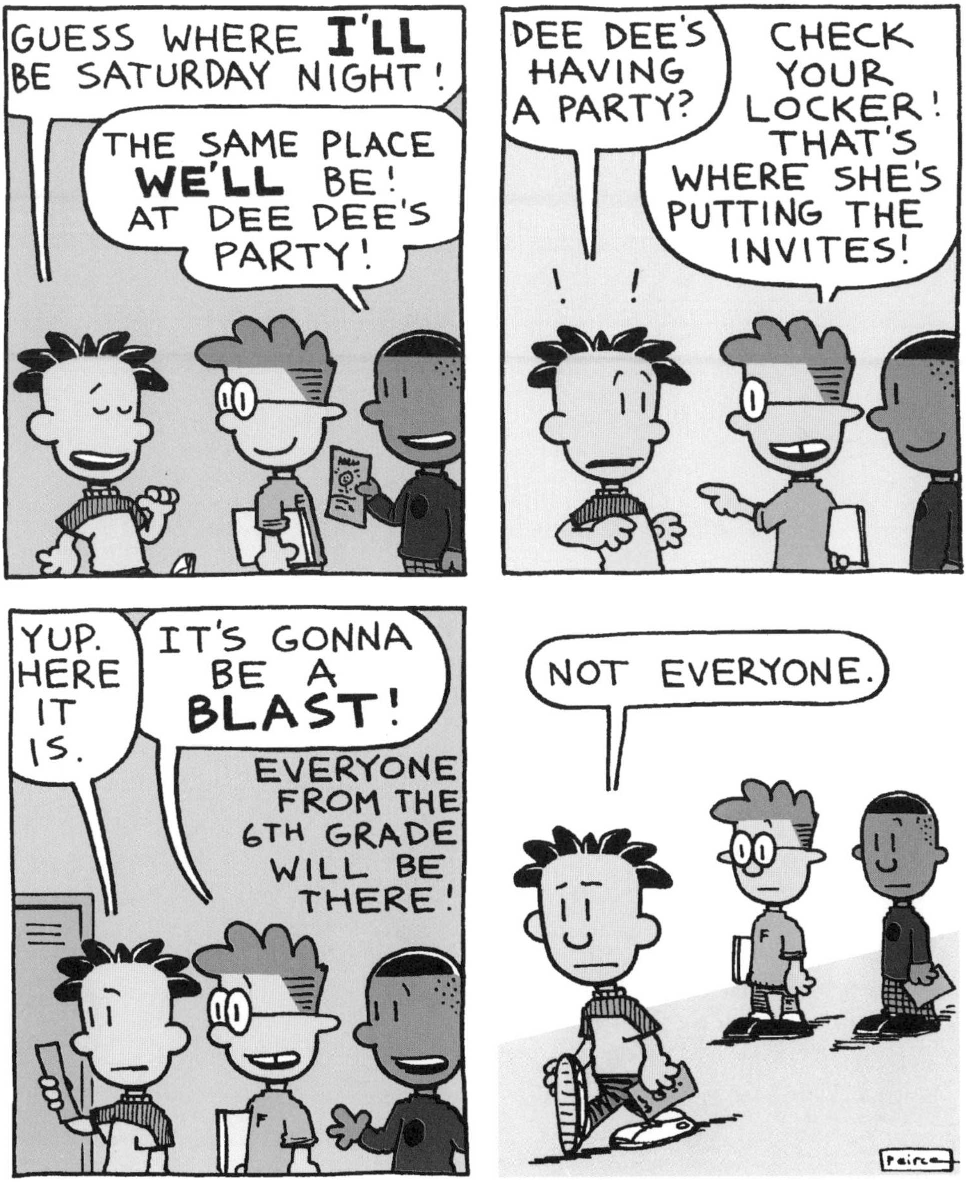
GUESS WHERE I'LL BE SATURDAY NIGHT!
THE SAME PLACE WE'LL BE! AT DEE DEE'S PARTY!
DEE DEE'S HAVING A PARTY?
! !
CHECK YOUR LOCKER! THAT'S WHERE SHE'S PUTTING THE INVITES!
YUP. HERE IT IS.
IT'S GONNA BE A BLAST!
EVERYONE FROM THE 6TH GRADE WILL BE THERE!
NOT EVERYONE.
Peirce

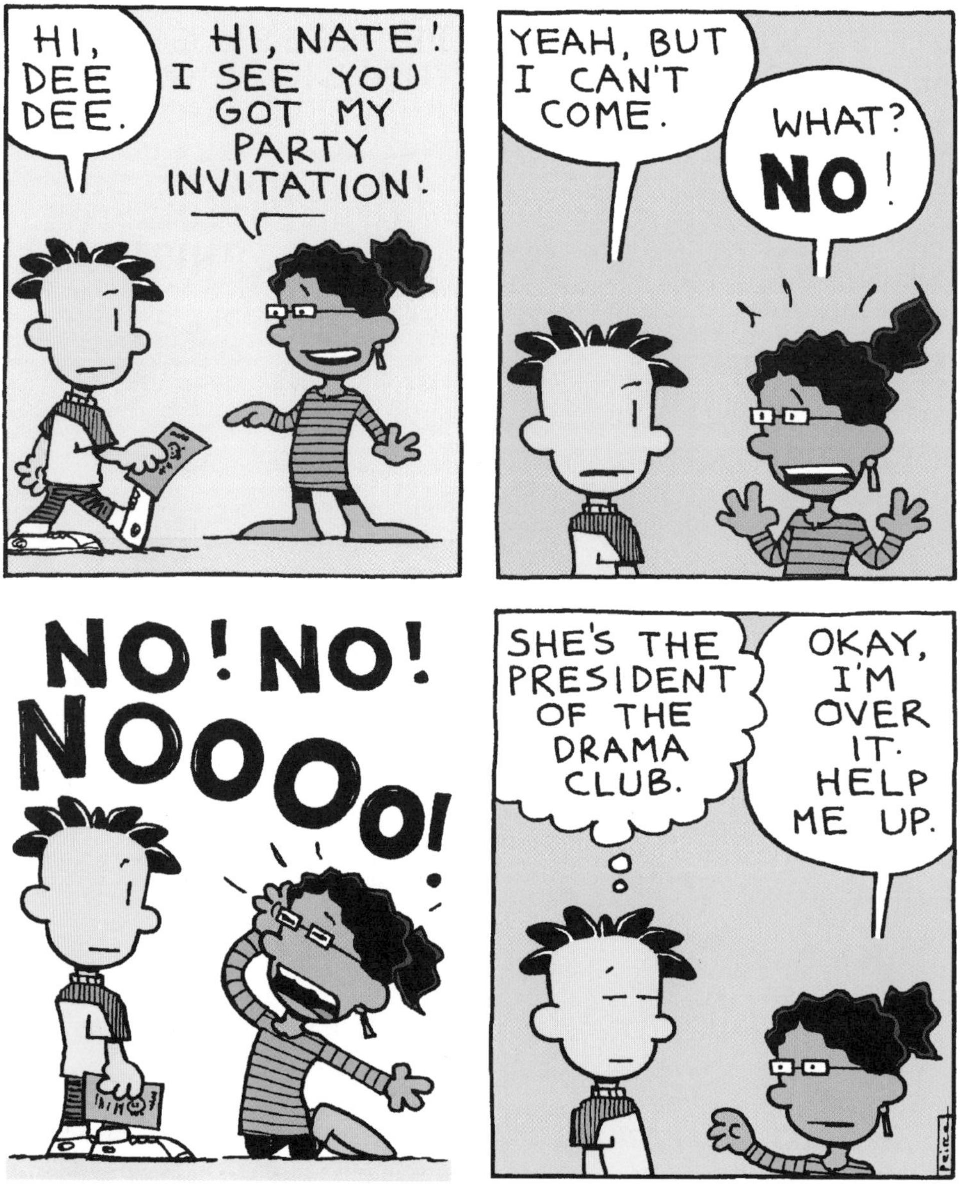

HI, DEE DEE.
HI, NATE! I SEE YOU GOT MY PARTY INVITATION!
YEAH, BUT I CAN'T COME.
WHAT? NO!
NO! NO! NOOOOO!
SHE'S THE PRESIDENT OF THE DRAMA CLUB.
OKAY, I'M OVER IT. HELP ME UP.

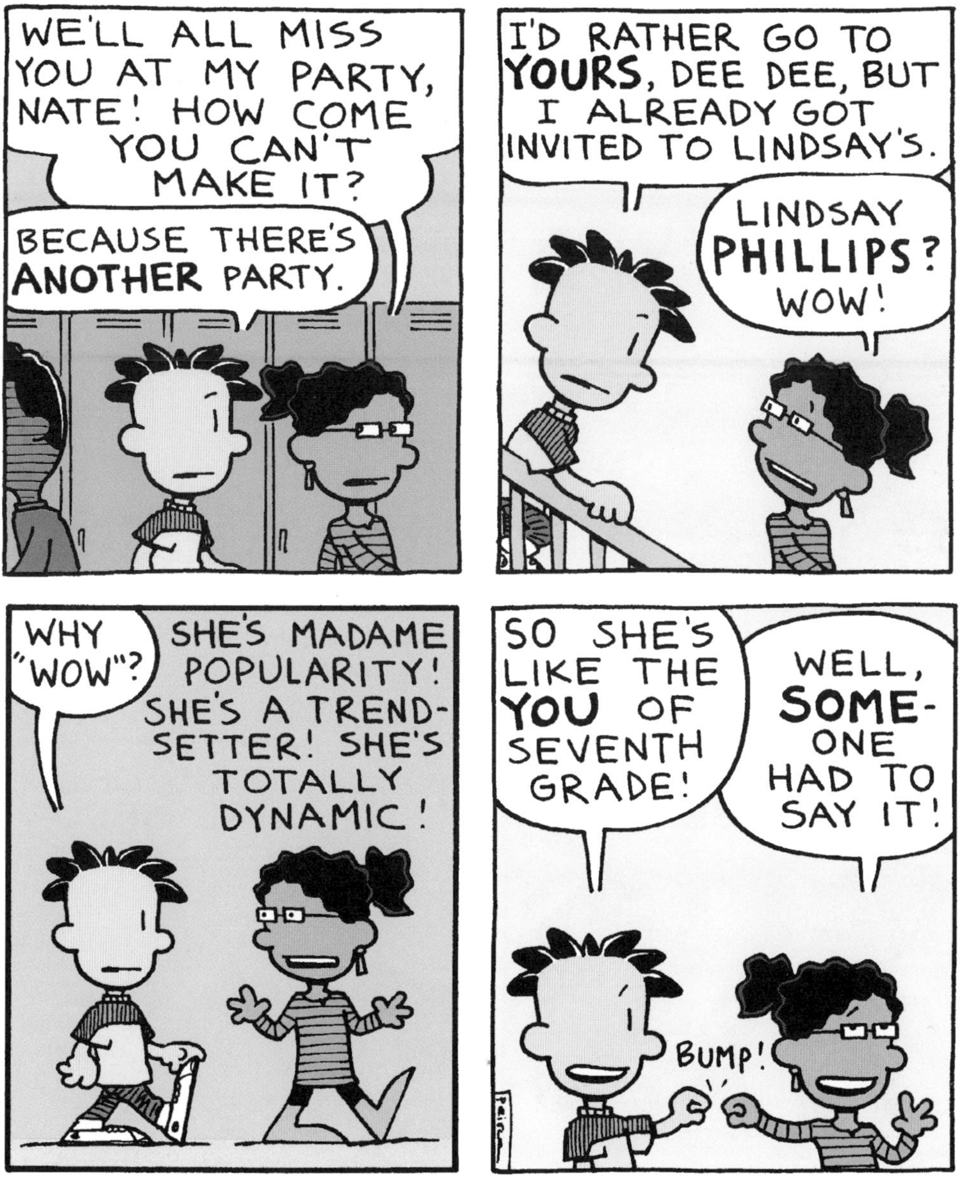
WE'LL ALL MISS YOU AT MY PARTY, NATE! HOW COME YOU CAN'T MAKE IT?
BECAUSE THERE'S **ANOTHER** PARTY.
I'D RATHER GO TO **YOURS**, DEE DEE, BUT I ALREADY GOT INVITED TO LINDSAY'S.
LINDSAY **PHILLIPS**? WOW!
WHY "WOW"?
SHE'S MADAME POPULARITY! SHE'S A TREND-SETTER! SHE'S TOTALLY DYNAMIC!
SO SHE'S LIKE THE **YOU** OF SEVENTH GRADE!
WELL, **SOME**-ONE HAD TO SAY IT!
BUMP!

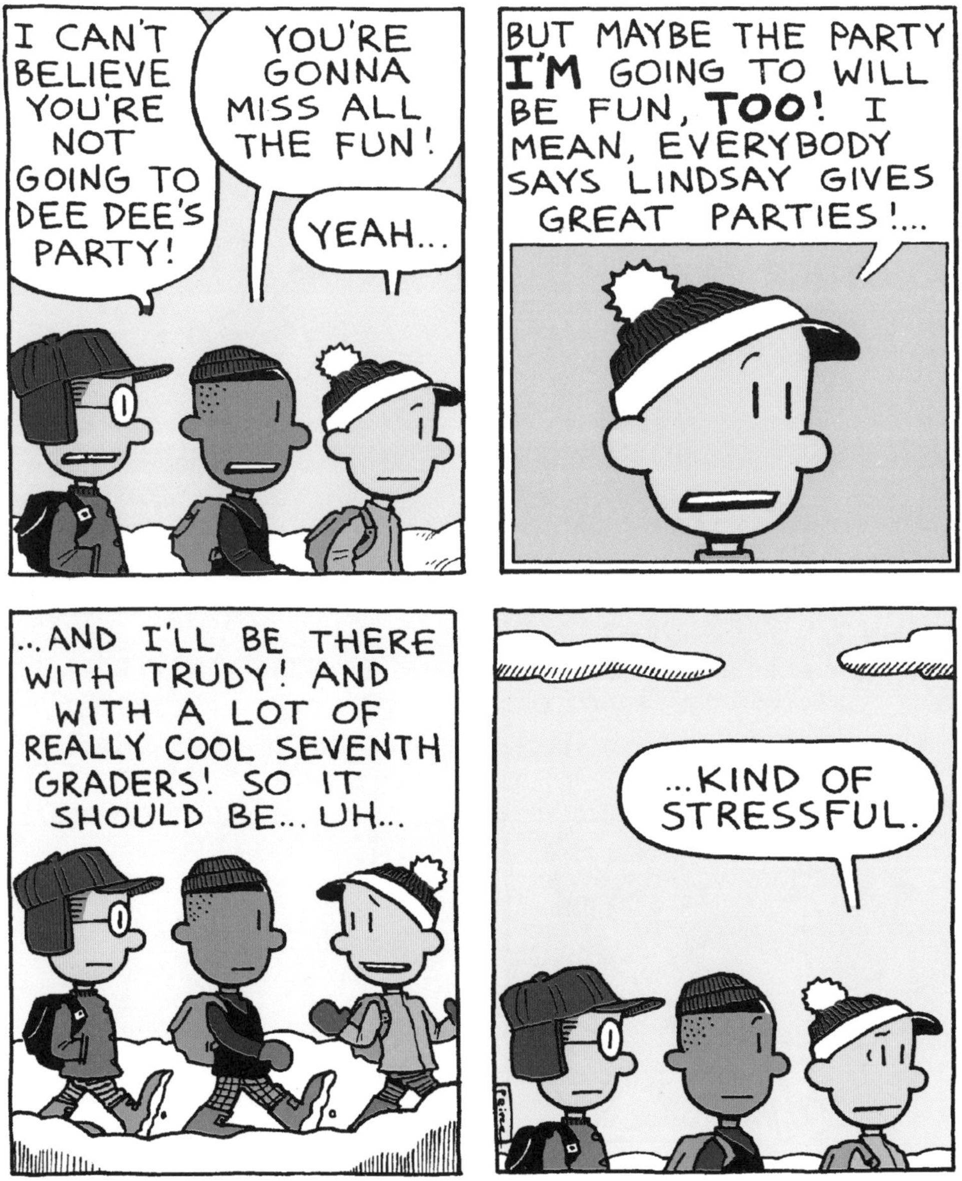
I CAN'T BELIEVE YOU'RE NOT GOING TO DEE DEE'S PARTY!
YOU'RE GONNA MISS ALL THE FUN!
YEAH...
BUT MAYBE THE PARTY I'M GOING TO WILL BE FUN, TOO! I MEAN, EVERYBODY SAYS LINDSAY GIVES GREAT PARTIES!...
...AND I'LL BE THERE WITH TRUDY! AND WITH A LOT OF REALLY COOL SEVENTH GRADERS! SO IT SHOULD BE... UH...
...KIND OF STRESSFUL.

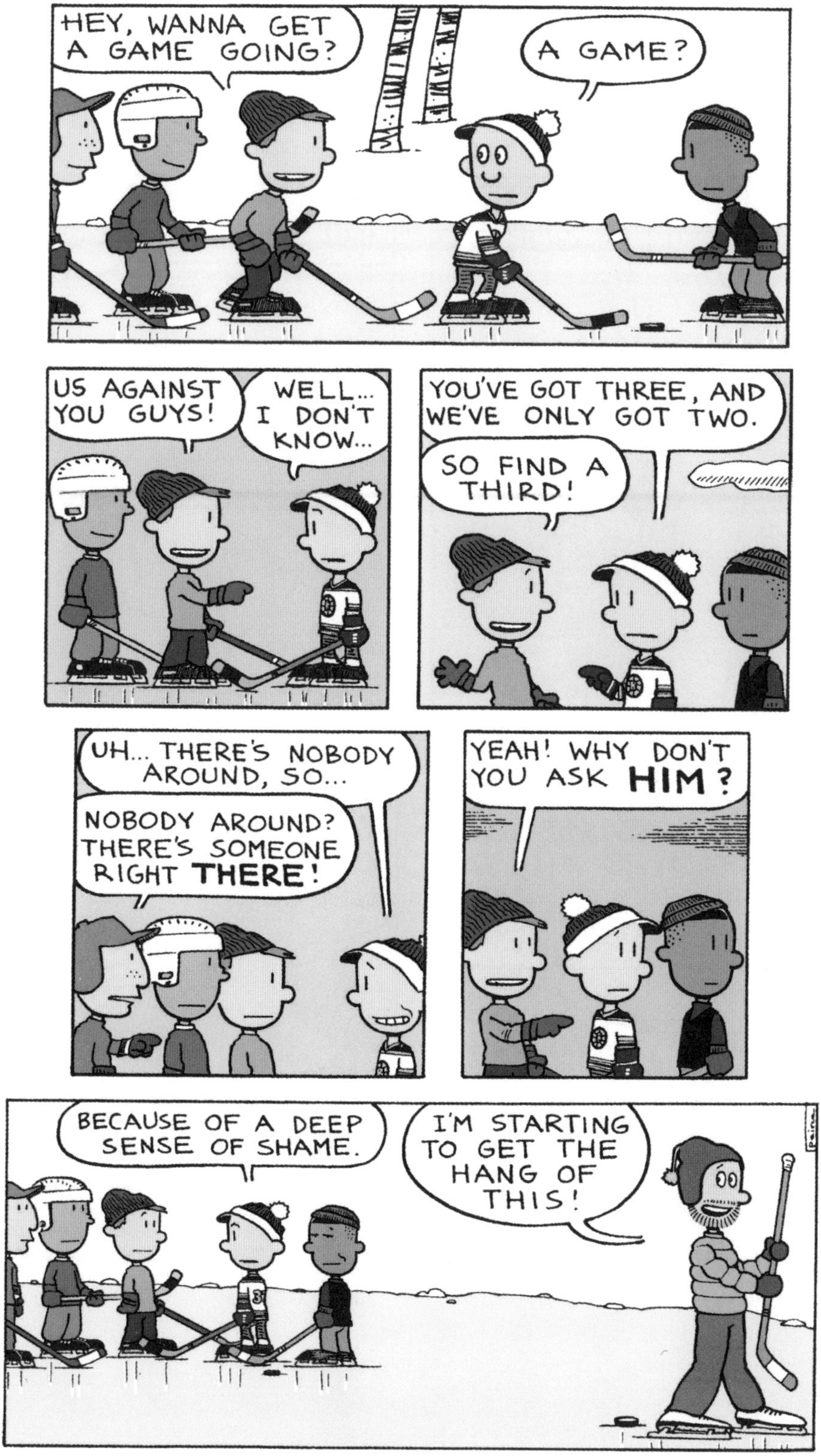
HEY, WANNA GET A GAME GOING?
A GAME?
US AGAINST YOU GUYS!
WELL... I DON'T KNOW...
YOU'VE GOT THREE, AND WE'VE ONLY GOT TWO.
SO FIND A THIRD!
UH... THERE'S NOBODY AROUND, SO...
NOBODY AROUND? THERE'S SOMEONE RIGHT THERE!
YEAH! WHY DON'T YOU ASK HIM?
BECAUSE OF A DEEP SENSE OF SHAME.
I'M STARTING TO GET THE HANG OF THIS!

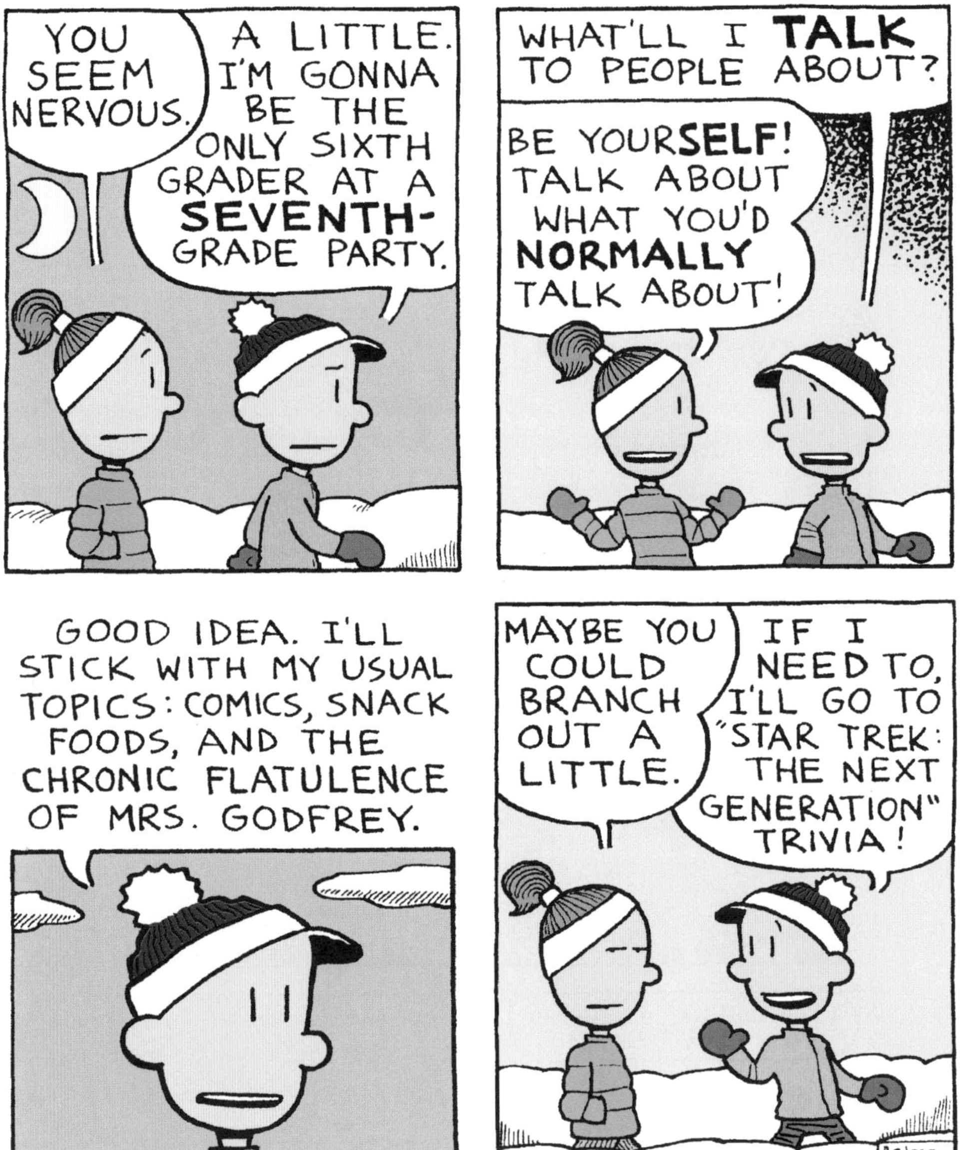
YOU SEEM NERVOUS.
A LITTLE. I'M GONNA BE THE ONLY SIXTH GRADER AT A **SEVENTH-** GRADE PARTY.
WHAT'LL I **TALK** TO PEOPLE ABOUT?
BE YOUR**SELF**! TALK ABOUT WHAT YOU'D **NORMALLY** TALK ABOUT!
GOOD IDEA. I'LL STICK WITH MY USUAL TOPICS: COMICS, SNACK FOODS, AND THE CHRONIC FLATULENCE OF MRS. GODFREY.
MAYBE YOU COULD BRANCH OUT A LITTLE.
IF I NEED TO, I'LL GO TO "STAR TREK: THE NEXT GENERATION" TRIVIA!
Peirce

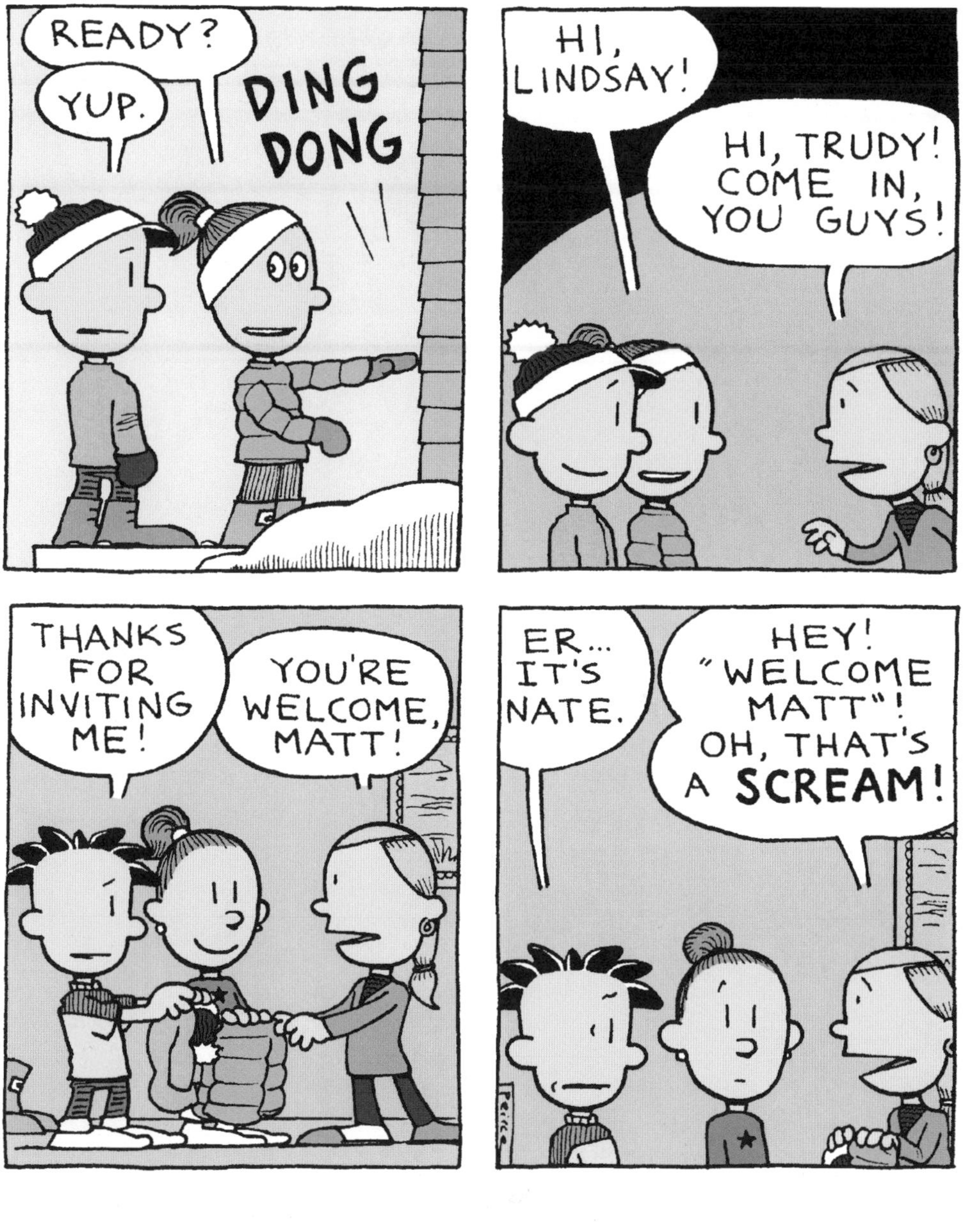
READY?
YUP.
DING DONG
HI, LINDSAY!
HI, TRUDY! COME IN, YOU GUYS!
THANKS FOR INVITING ME!
YOU'RE WELCOME, MATT!
ER... IT'S NATE.
HEY! "WELCOME MATT"! OH, THAT'S A **SCREAM**!
PEIRCE

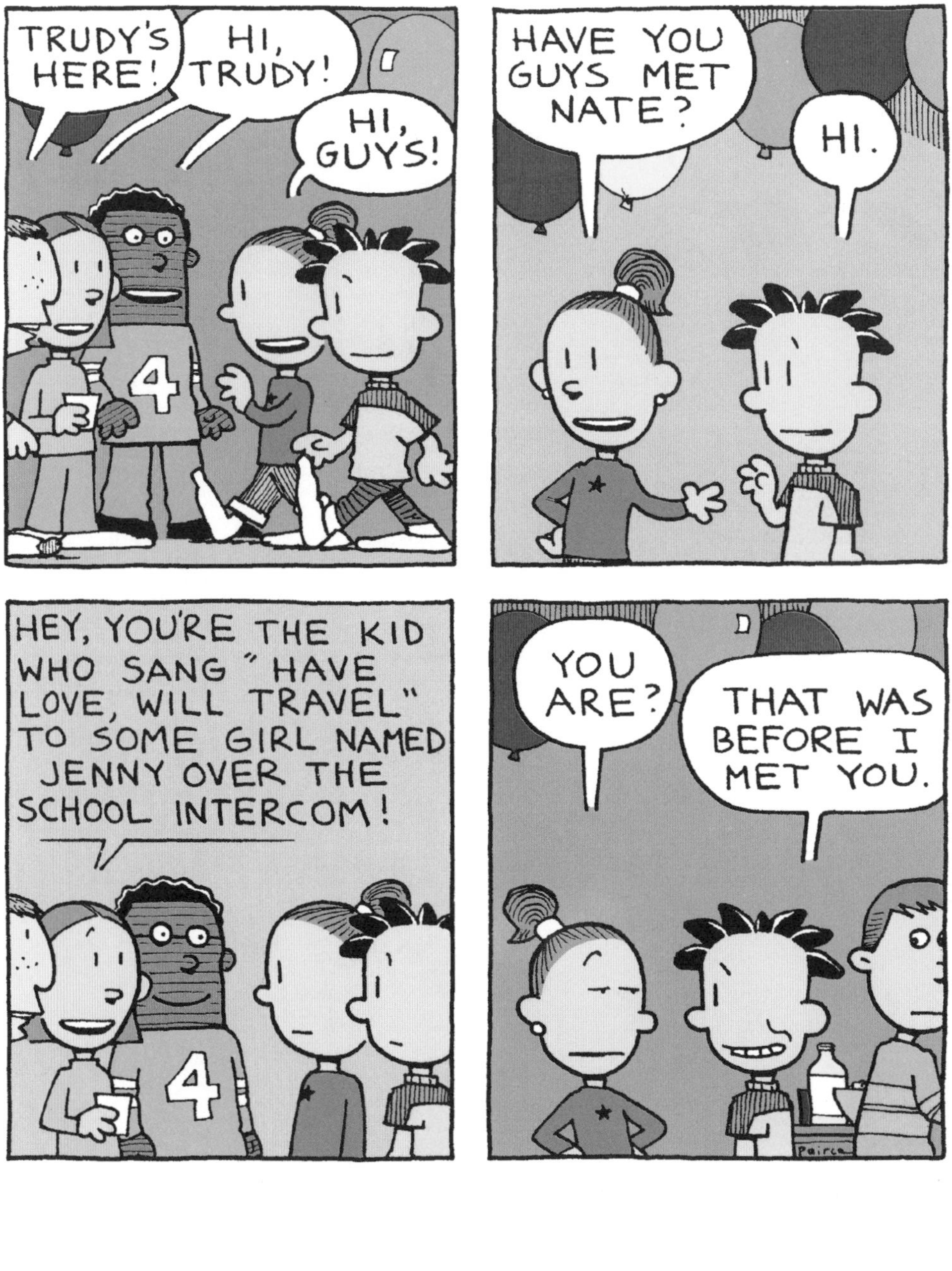
TRUDY'S HERE!
HI, TRUDY!
HI, GUYS!
HAVE YOU GUYS MET NATE?
HI.
HEY, YOU'RE THE KID WHO SANG "HAVE LOVE, WILL TRAVEL" TO SOME GIRL NAMED JENNY OVER THE SCHOOL INTERCOM!
YOU ARE?
THAT WAS BEFORE I MET YOU.

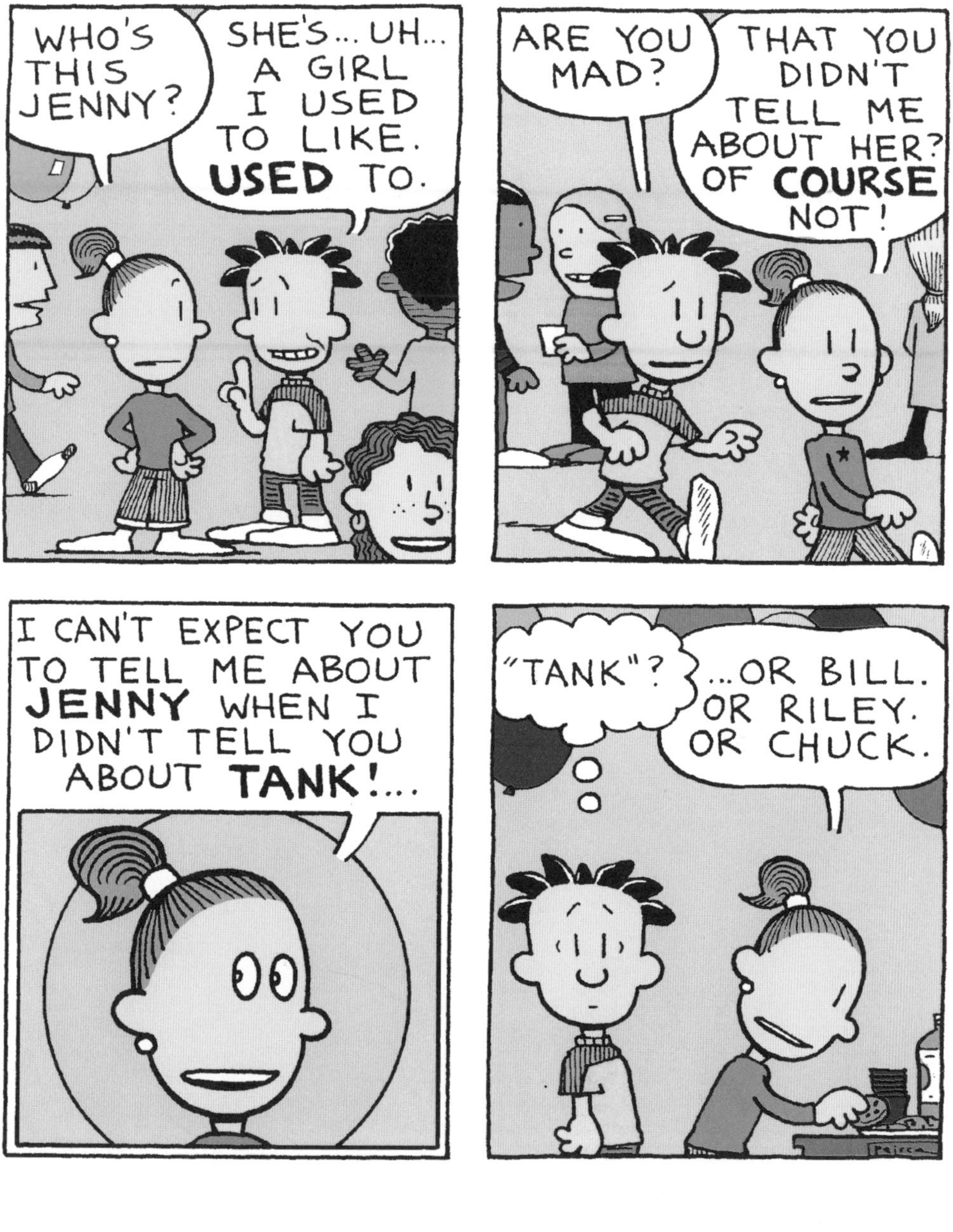
WHO'S THIS JENNY?
SHE'S... UH... A GIRL I USED TO LIKE. **USED** TO.
ARE YOU MAD?
THAT YOU DIDN'T TELL ME ABOUT HER? OF **COURSE** NOT!
I CAN'T EXPECT YOU TO TELL ME ABOUT **JENNY** WHEN I DIDN'T TELL YOU ABOUT **TANK!**...
"TANK"?
...OR BILL. OR RILEY. OR CHUCK.

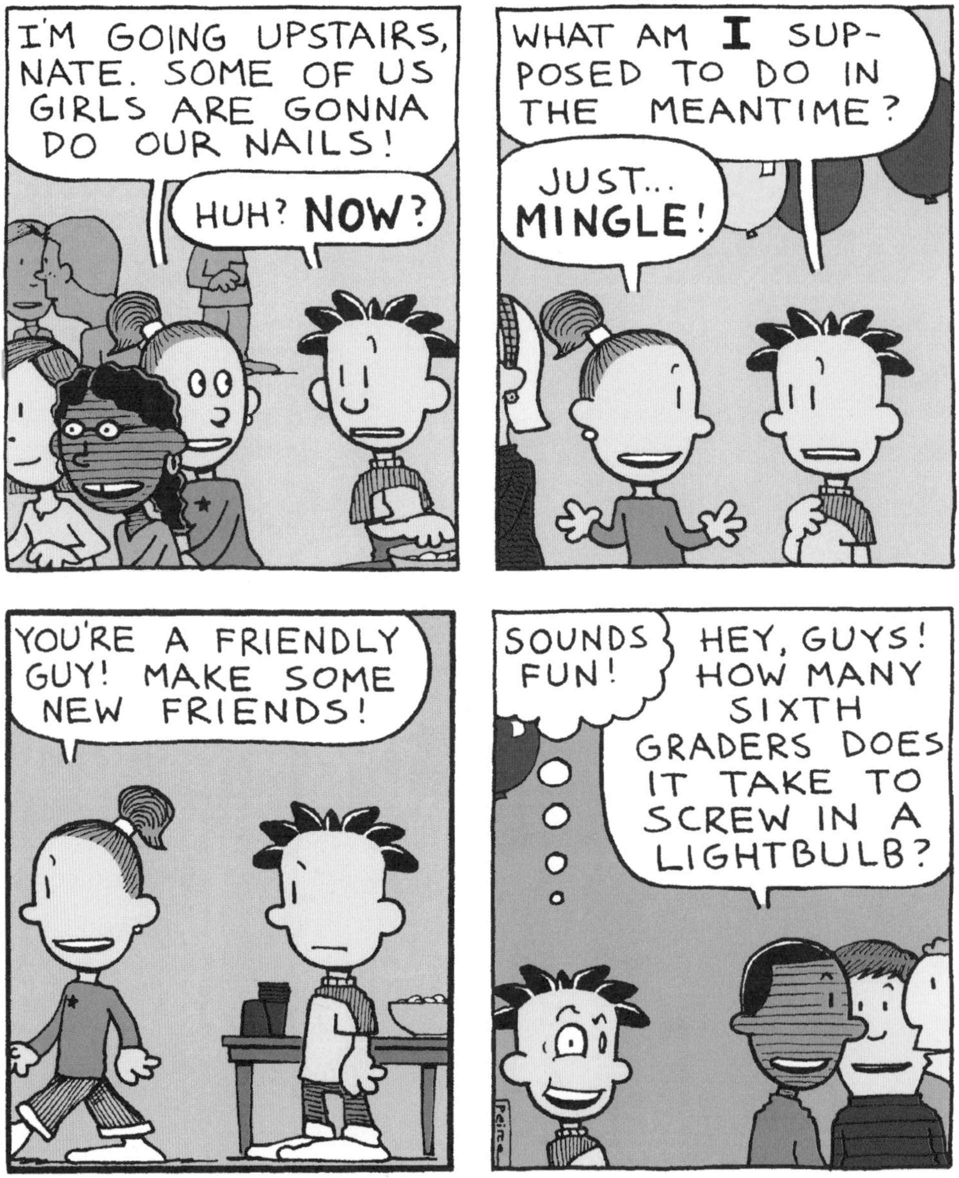
I'M GOING UPSTAIRS, NATE. SOME OF US GIRLS ARE GONNA DO OUR NAILS!
HUH? **NOW**?
WHAT AM **I** SUPPOSED TO DO IN THE MEANTIME?
JUST... **MINGLE**!
YOU'RE A FRIENDLY GUY! MAKE SOME NEW FRIENDS!
SOUNDS FUN!
HEY, GUYS! HOW MANY SIXTH GRADERS DOES IT TAKE TO SCREW IN A LIGHTBULB?

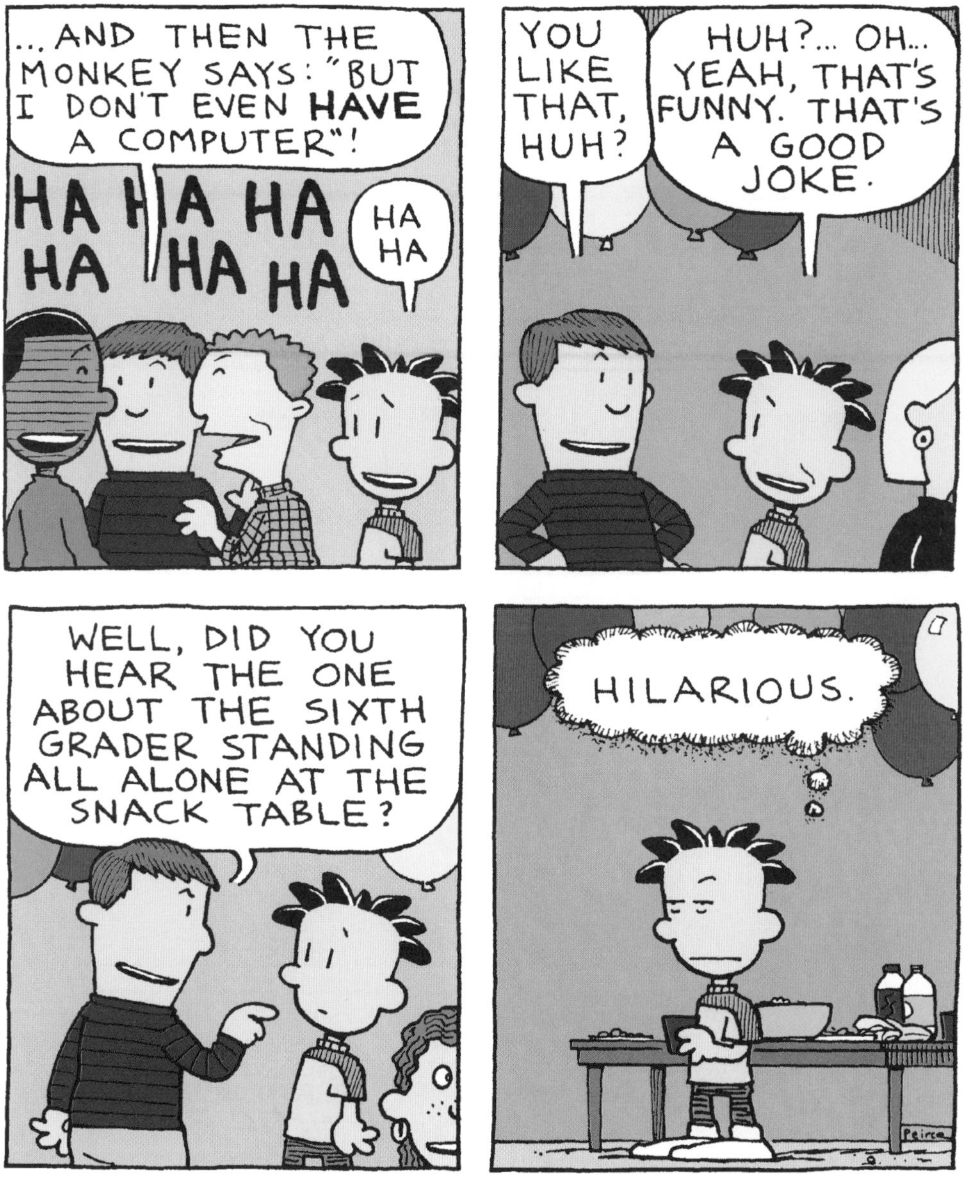
...AND THEN THE MONKEY SAYS: "BUT I DON'T EVEN **HAVE** A COMPUTER"!
HA HA HA HA HA HA HA HA
HA HA
YOU LIKE THAT, HUH?
HUH?... OH... YEAH, THAT'S FUNNY. THAT'S A GOOD JOKE.
WELL, DID YOU HEAR THE ONE ABOUT THE SIXTH GRADER STANDING ALL ALONE AT THE SNACK TABLE?
HILARIOUS.
Peirce

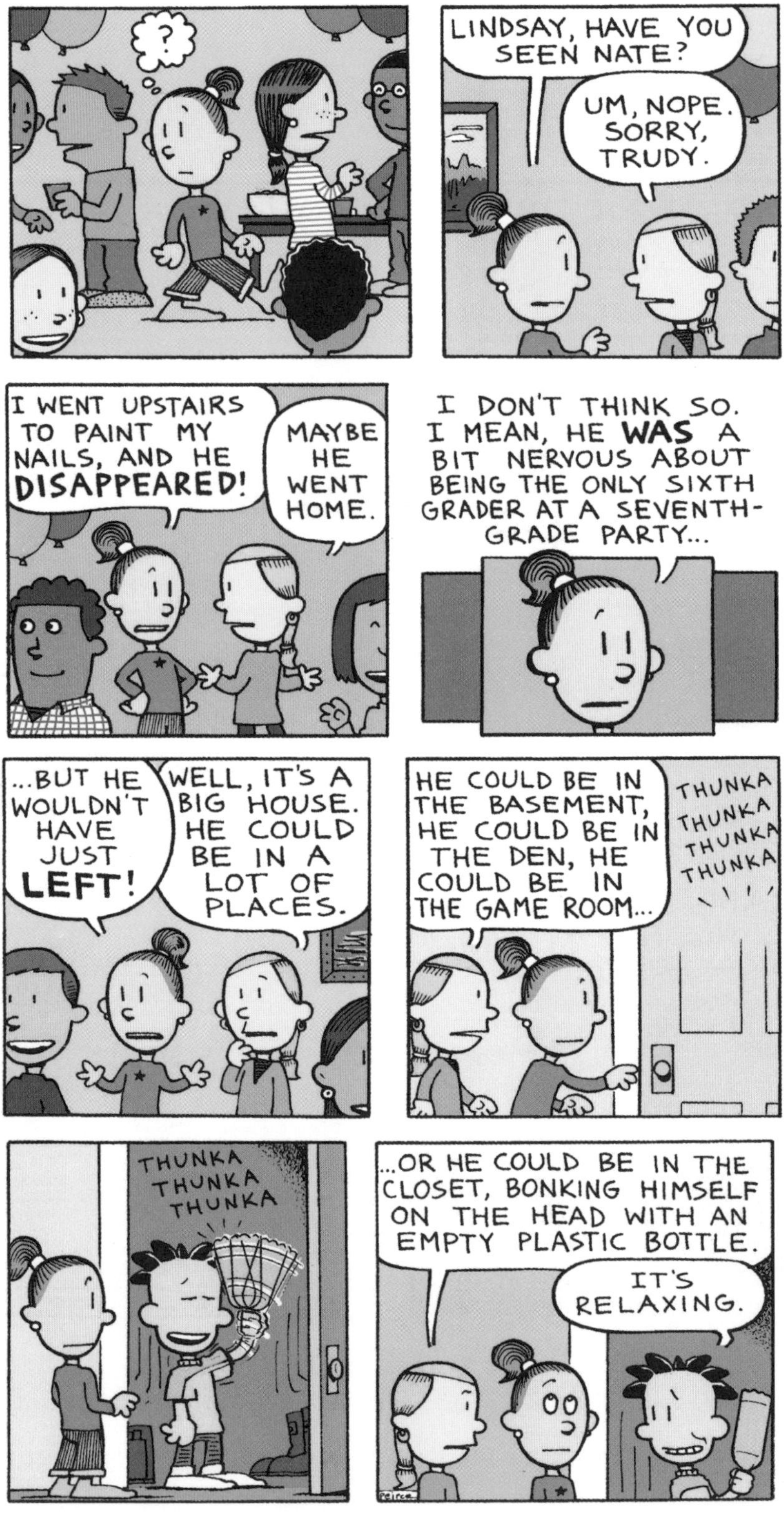
?
LINDSAY, HAVE YOU SEEN NATE?
UM, NOPE. SORRY, TRUDY.
I WENT UPSTAIRS TO PAINT MY NAILS, AND HE **DISAPPEARED**!
MAYBE HE WENT HOME.
I DON'T THINK SO. I MEAN, HE **WAS** A BIT NERVOUS ABOUT BEING THE ONLY SIXTH GRADER AT A SEVENTH-GRADE PARTY...
...BUT HE WOULDN'T HAVE JUST **LEFT**!
WELL, IT'S A BIG HOUSE. HE COULD BE IN A LOT OF PLACES.
HE COULD BE IN THE BASEMENT, HE COULD BE IN THE DEN, HE COULD BE IN THE GAME ROOM...
THUNKA THUNKA THUNKA THUNKA
THUNKA THUNKA THUNKA
...OR HE COULD BE IN THE CLOSET, BONKING HIMSELF ON THE HEAD WITH AN EMPTY PLASTIC BOTTLE.
IT'S RELAXING.

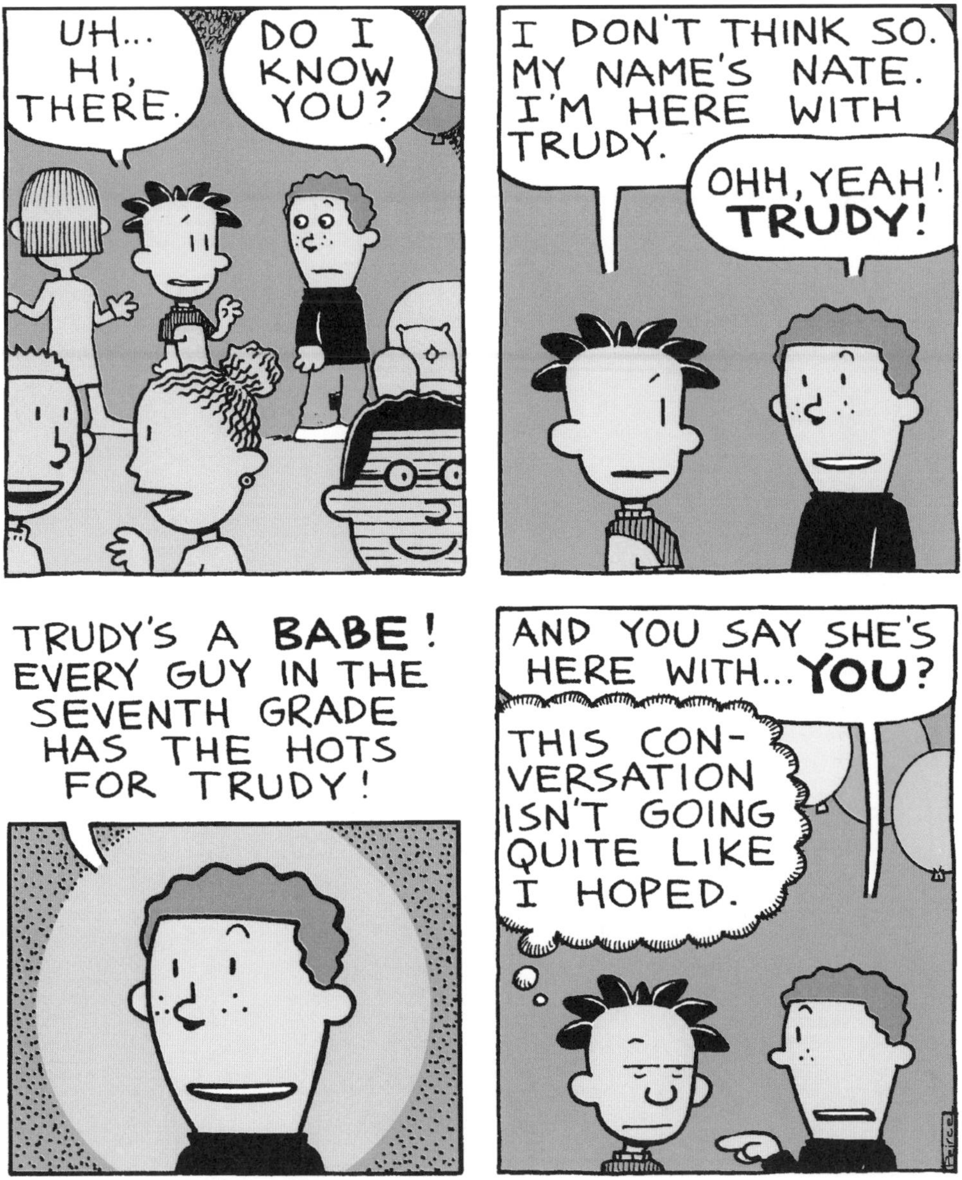
UH... HI, THERE.
DO I KNOW YOU?
I DON'T THINK SO. MY NAME'S NATE. I'M HERE WITH TRUDY.
OHH, YEAH! TRUDY!
TRUDY'S A BABE! EVERY GUY IN THE SEVENTH GRADE HAS THE HOTS FOR TRUDY!
AND YOU SAY SHE'S HERE WITH... YOU?
THIS CONVERSATION ISN'T GOING QUITE LIKE I HOPED.
Peirce

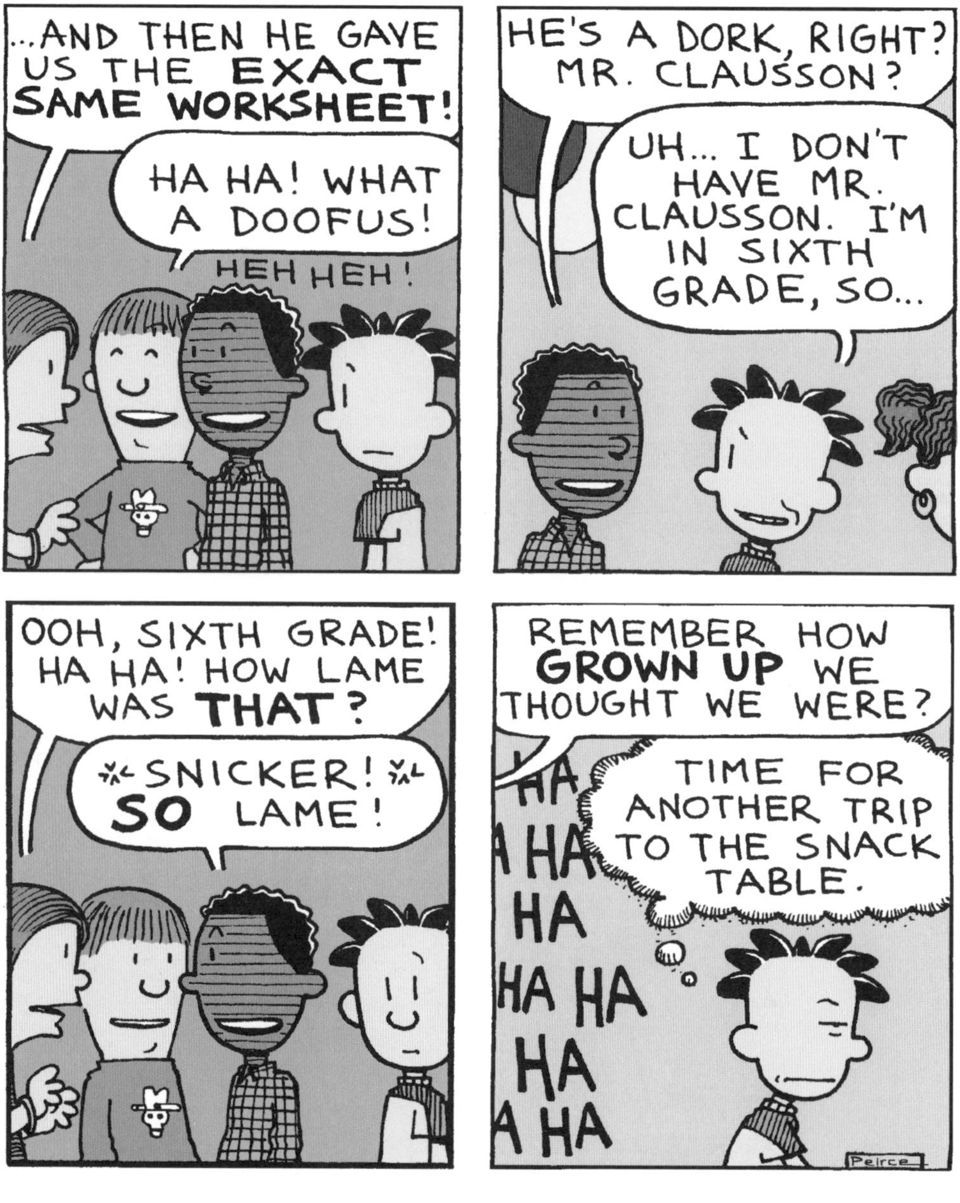

...AND THEN HE GAVE US THE EXACT SAME WORKSHEET!
HA HA! WHAT A DOOFUS!
HEH HEH!
HE'S A DORK, RIGHT? MR. CLAUSSON?
UH... I DON'T HAVE MR. CLAUSSON. I'M IN SIXTH GRADE, SO...
OOH, SIXTH GRADE! HA HA! HOW LAME WAS THAT?
SNICKER! SO LAME!
REMEMBER HOW GROWN UP WE THOUGHT WE WERE?
HA HA HA HA HA HA HA HA HA
TIME FOR ANOTHER TRIP TO THE SNACK TABLE.
Peirce

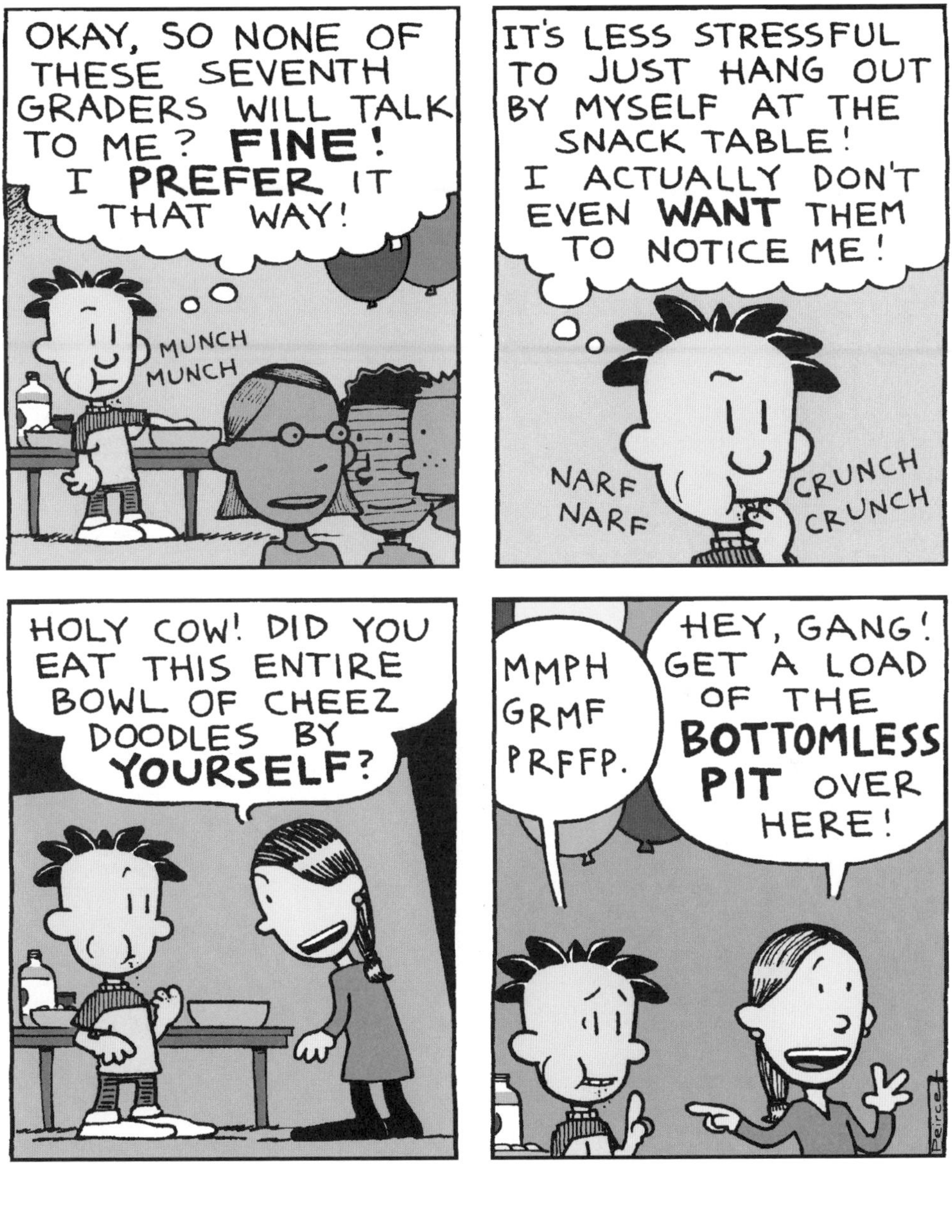
OKAY, SO NONE OF THESE SEVENTH GRADERS WILL TALK TO ME? FINE! I PREFER IT THAT WAY!
MUNCH MUNCH
IT'S LESS STRESSFUL TO JUST HANG OUT BY MYSELF AT THE SNACK TABLE! I ACTUALLY DON'T EVEN WANT THEM TO NOTICE ME!
NARF NARF
CRUNCH CRUNCH
HOLY COW! DID YOU EAT THIS ENTIRE BOWL OF CHEEZ DOODLES BY YOURSELF?
MMPH GRMF PRFFP.
HEY, GANG! GET A LOAD OF THE BOTTOMLESS PIT OVER HERE!
Peirce

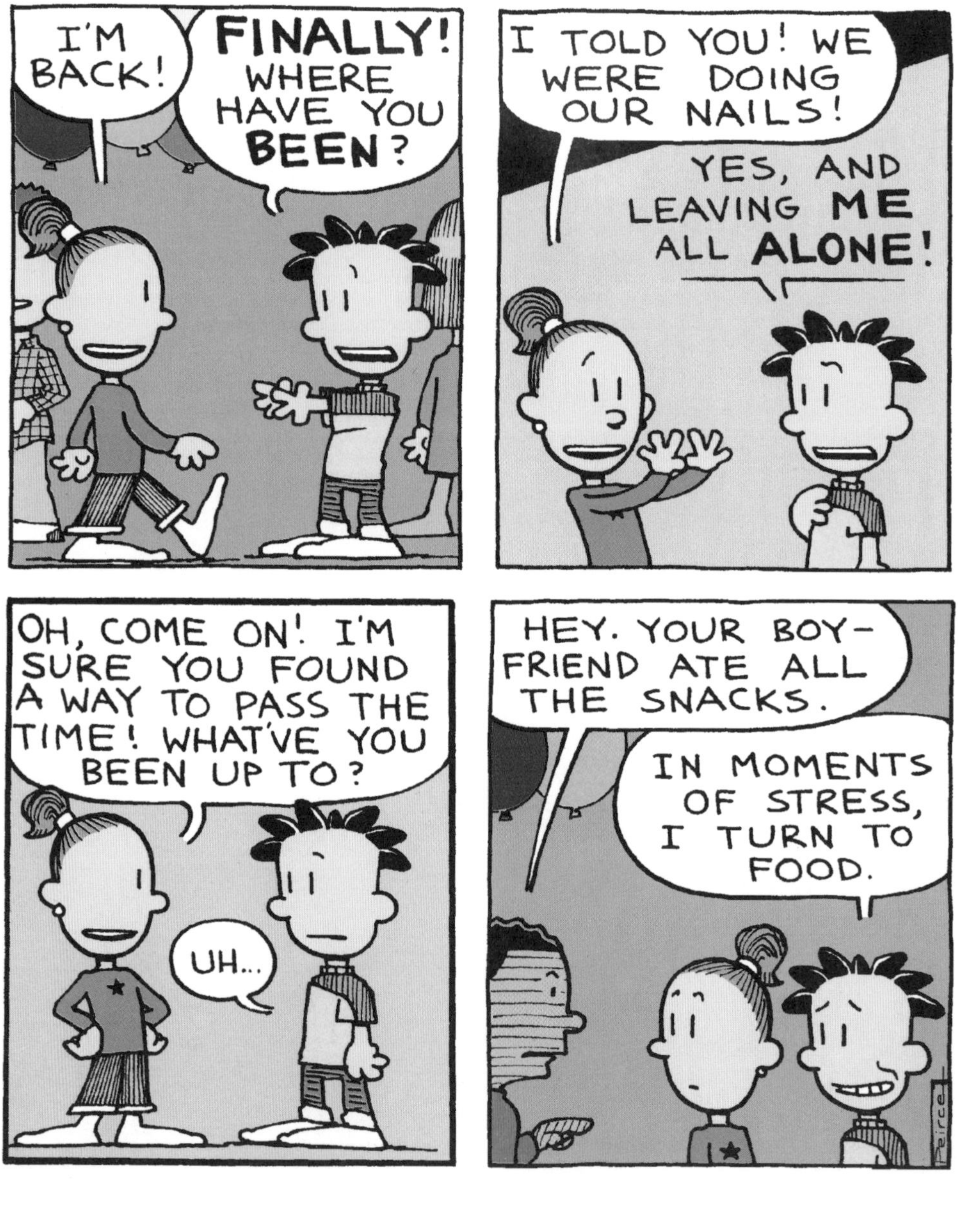
I'M BACK!
FINALLY! WHERE HAVE YOU BEEN?
I TOLD YOU! WE WERE DOING OUR NAILS!
YES, AND LEAVING ME ALL ALONE!
OH, COME ON! I'M SURE YOU FOUND A WAY TO PASS THE TIME! WHAT'VE YOU BEEN UP TO?
UH...
HEY. YOUR BOY-FRIEND ATE ALL THE SNACKS.
IN MOMENTS OF STRESS, I TURN TO FOOD.
Peirce

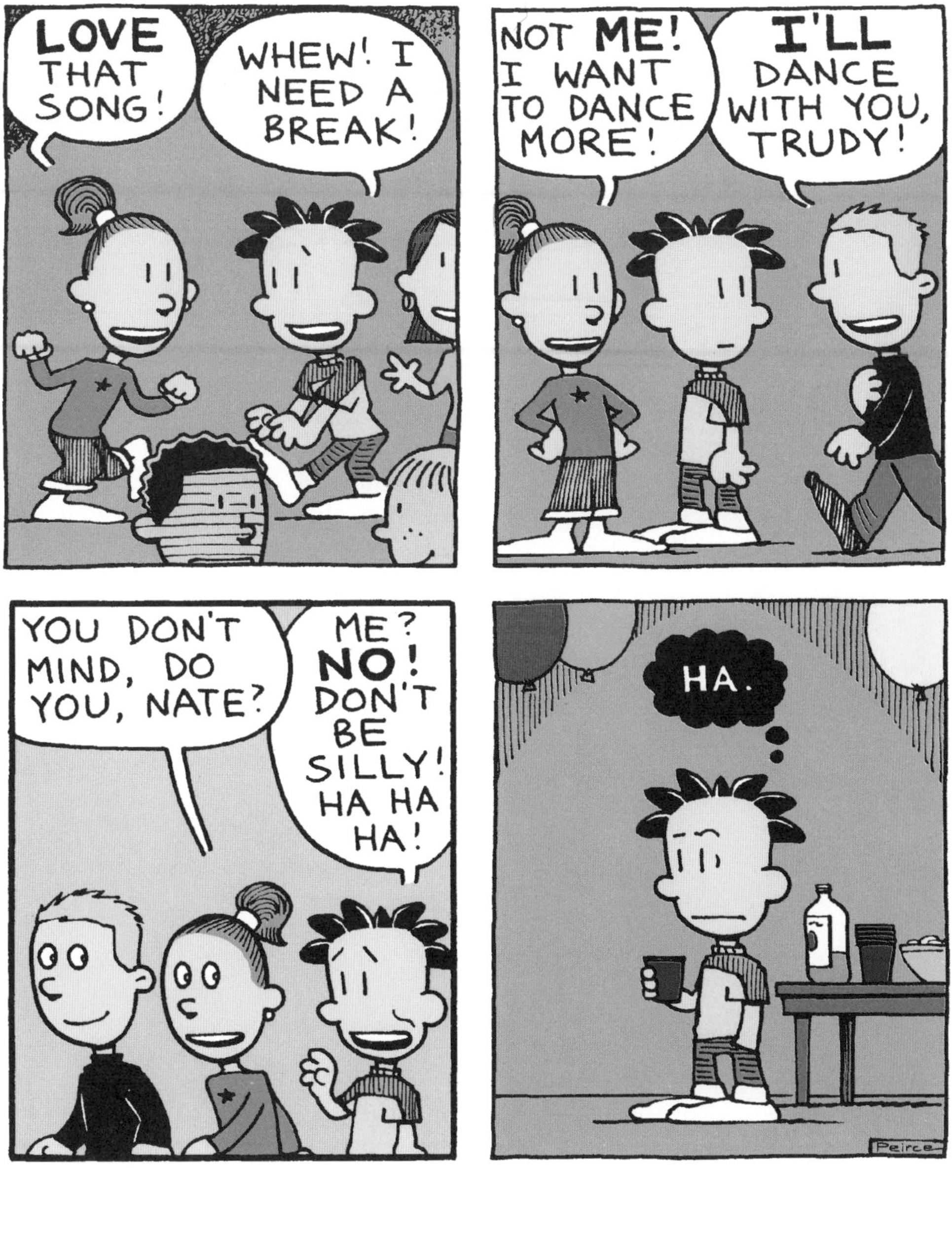
LOVE THAT SONG!
WHEW! I NEED A BREAK!
NOT ME! I WANT TO DANCE MORE!
I'LL DANCE WITH YOU, TRUDY!
YOU DON'T MIND, DO YOU, NATE?
ME? NO! DON'T BE SILLY! HA HA HA!
HA.
Peirce

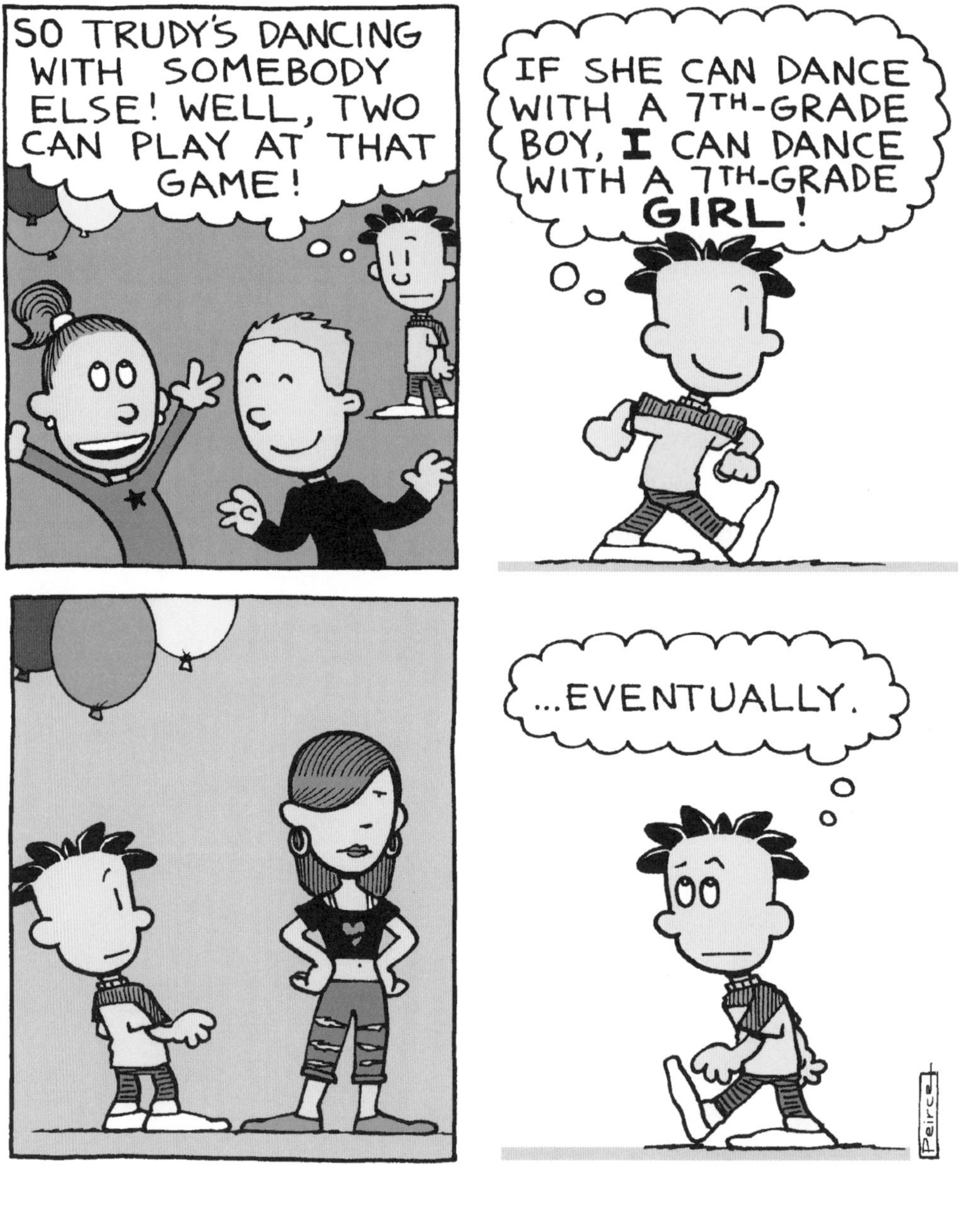
SO TRUDY'S DANCING WITH SOMEBODY ELSE! WELL, TWO CAN PLAY AT THAT GAME!
IF SHE CAN DANCE WITH A 7TH-GRADE BOY, **I** CAN DANCE WITH A 7TH-GRADE **GIRL**!
...EVENTUALLY.
Peirce

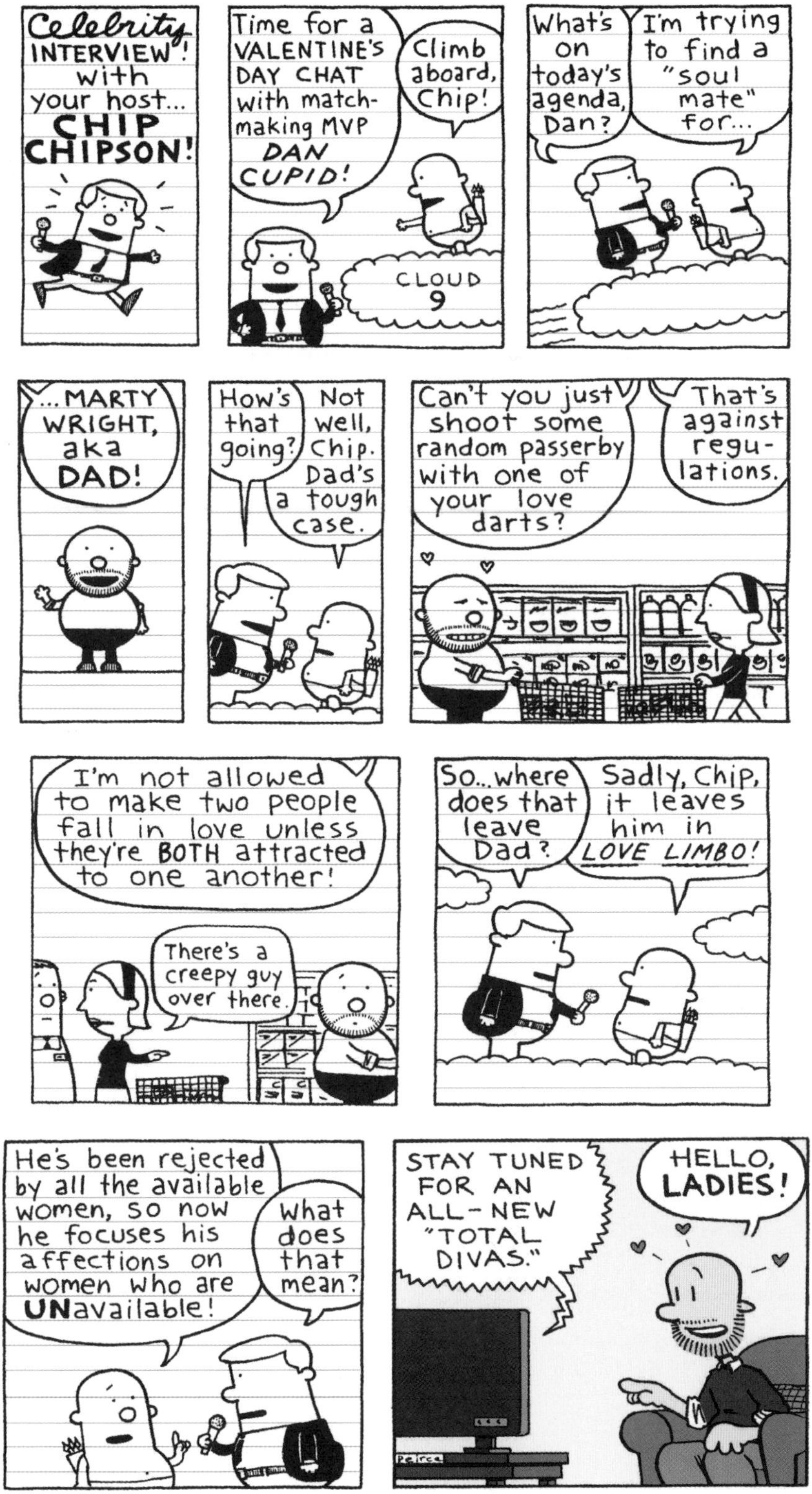
Celebrity INTERVIEW! with your host... CHIP CHIPSON!
Time for a VALENTINE'S DAY CHAT with match-making MVP DAN CUPID!
Climb aboard, Chip!
CLOUD 9
What's on today's agenda, Dan?
I'm trying to find a "soul mate" for...
...MARTY WRIGHT, aka DAD!
How's that going?
Not well, Chip. Dad's a tough case.
Can't you just shoot some random passerby with one of your love darts?
That's against regu-lations.
I'm not allowed to make two people fall in love unless they're BOTH attracted to one another!
There's a creepy guy over there.
So...where does that leave Dad?
Sadly, Chip, it leaves him in LOVE LIMBO!
He's been rejected by all the available women, so now he focuses his affections on women who are UNavailable!
What does that mean?
STAY TUNED FOR AN ALL-NEW "TOTAL DIVAS."
HELLO, LADIES!
Peirce

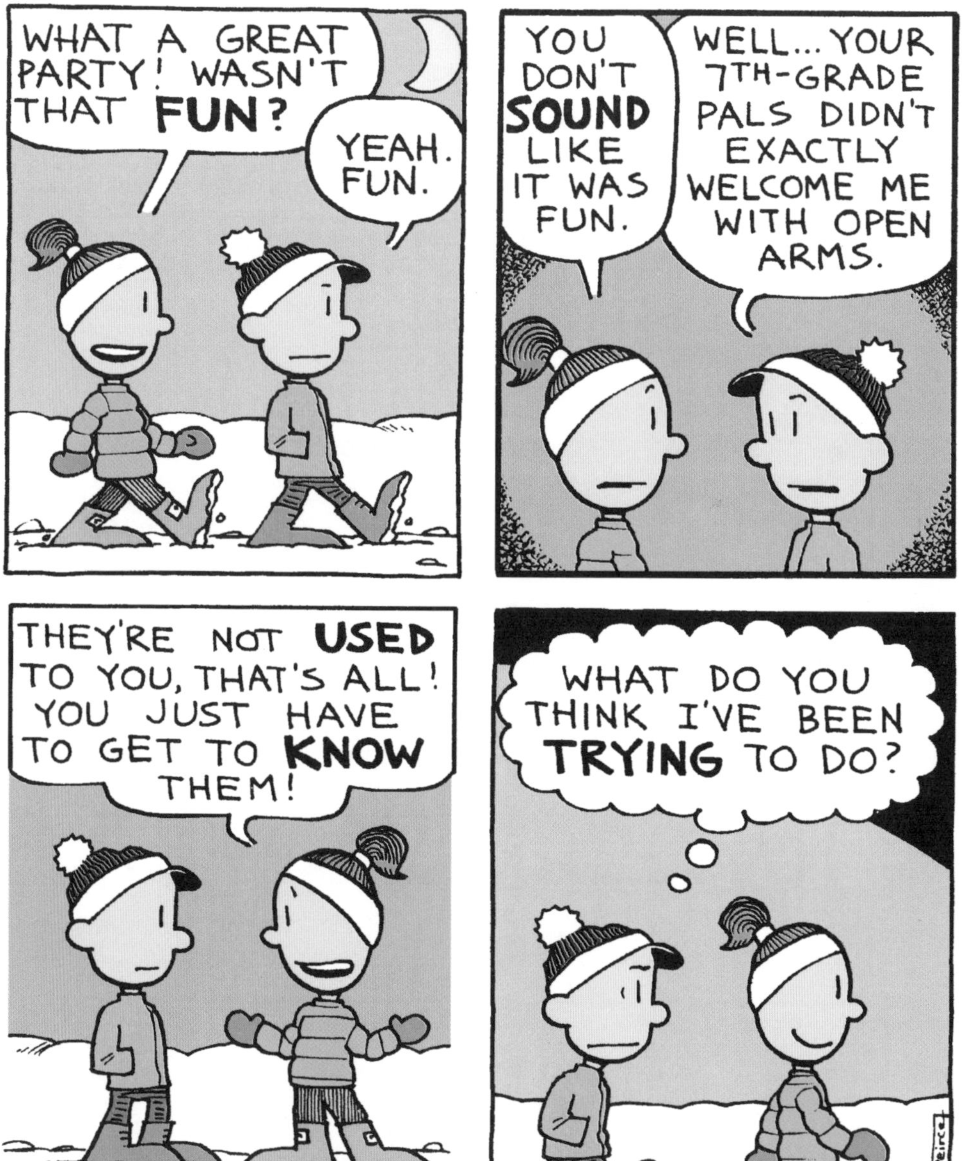
WHAT A GREAT PARTY! WASN'T THAT FUN?
YEAH. FUN.
YOU DON'T SOUND LIKE IT WAS FUN.
WELL... YOUR 7TH-GRADE PALS DIDN'T EXACTLY WELCOME ME WITH OPEN ARMS.
THEY'RE NOT USED TO YOU, THAT'S ALL! YOU JUST HAVE TO GET TO KNOW THEM!
WHAT DO YOU THINK I'VE BEEN TRYING TO DO?
Peirce

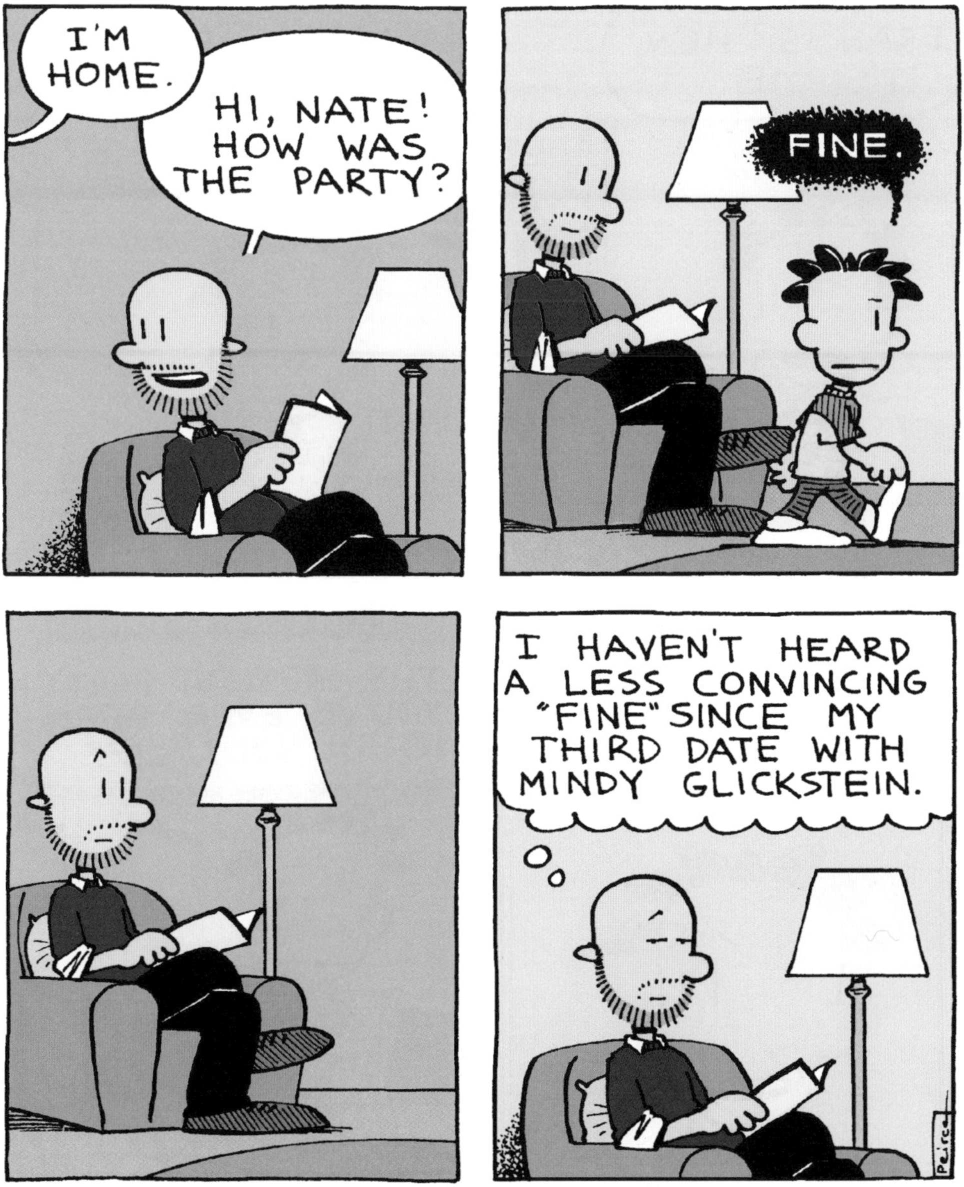
I'M HOME.
HI, NATE! HOW WAS THE PARTY?
FINE.
I HAVEN'T HEARD A LESS CONVINCING "FINE" SINCE MY THIRD DATE WITH MINDY GLICKSTEIN.
Peirce

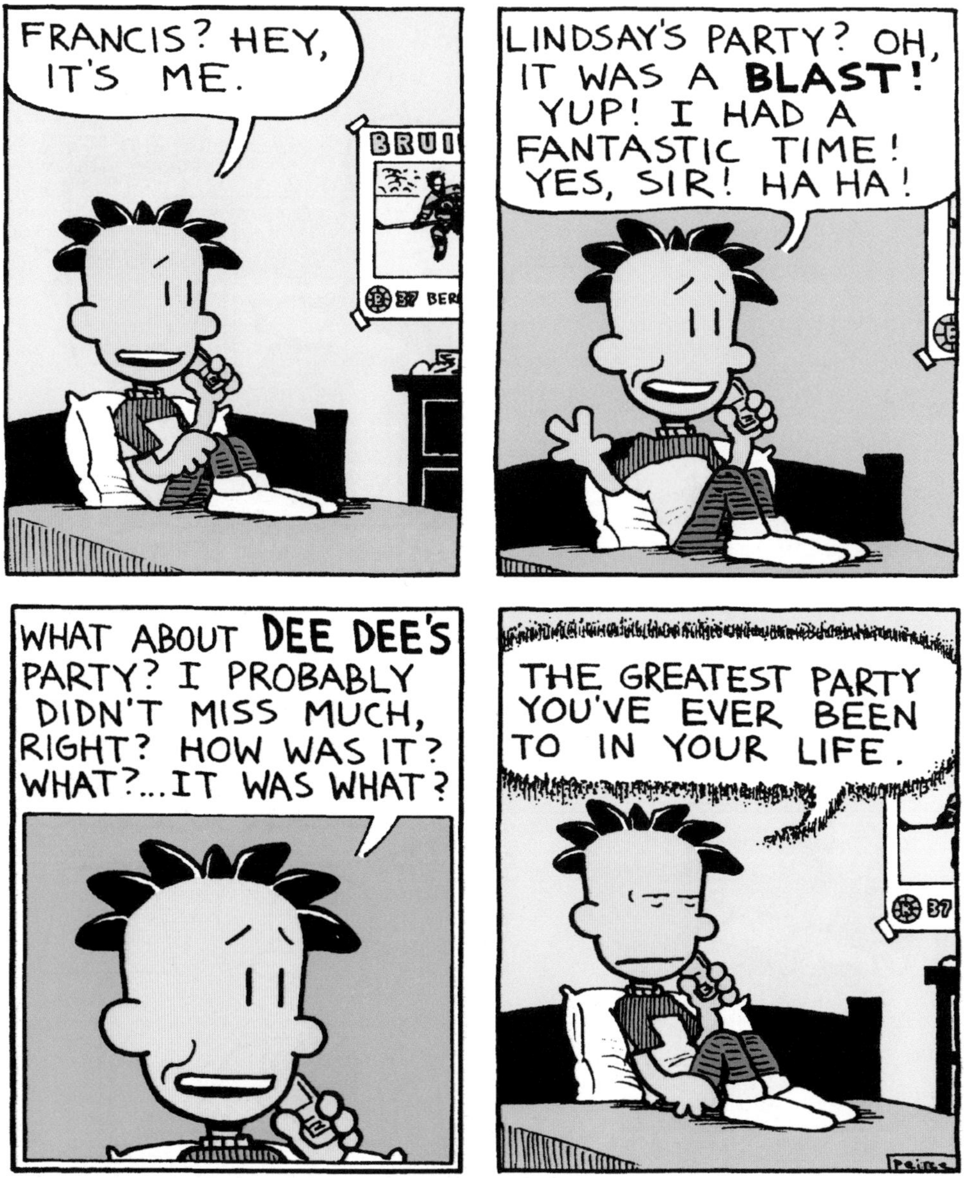
FRANCIS? HEY, IT'S ME.
LINDSAY'S PARTY? OH, IT WAS A **BLAST**! YUP! I HAD A FANTASTIC TIME! YES, SIR! HA HA!
WHAT ABOUT **DEE DEE'S** PARTY? I PROBABLY DIDN'T MISS MUCH, RIGHT? HOW WAS IT? WHAT?...IT WAS WHAT?
THE GREATEST PARTY YOU'VE EVER BEEN TO IN YOUR LIFE.

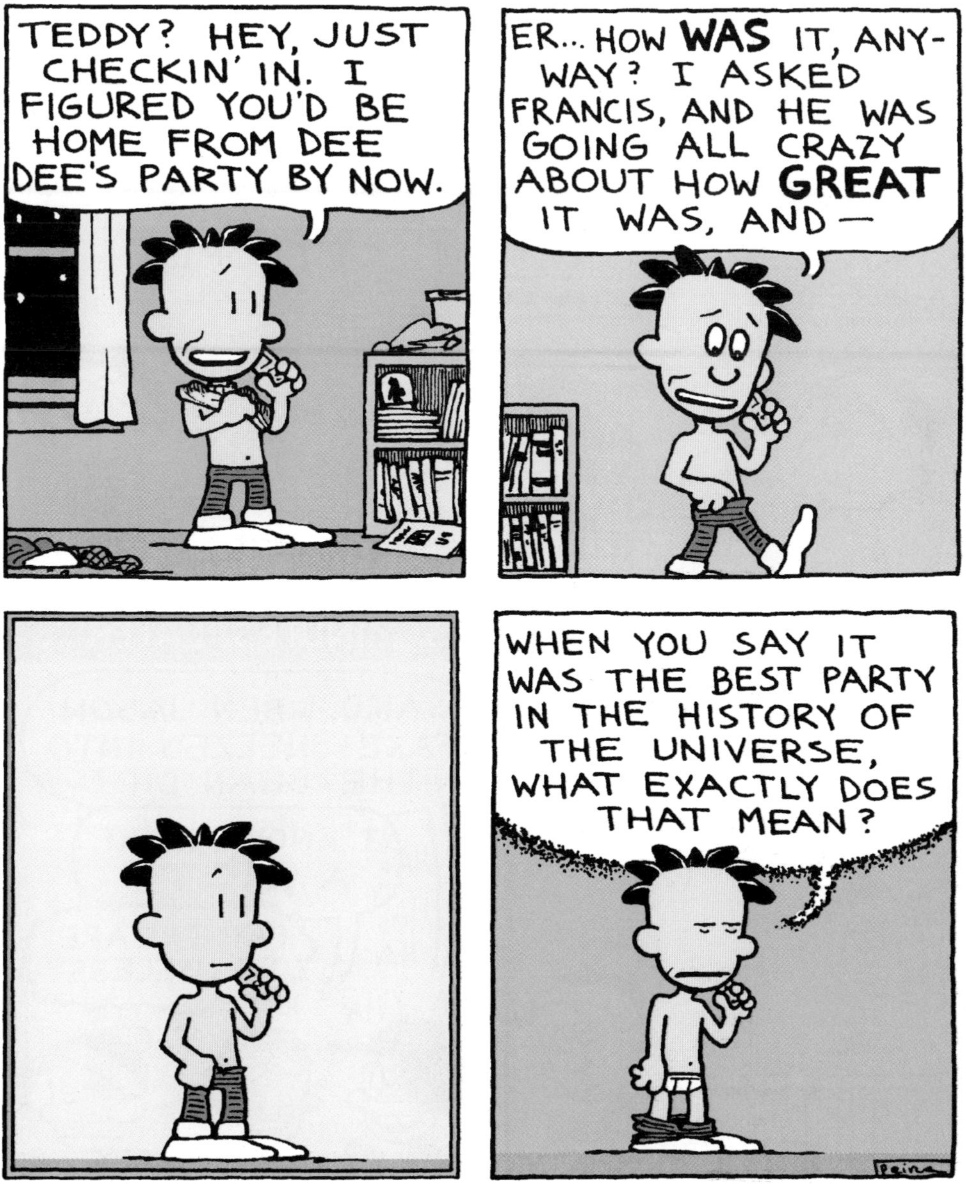
TEDDY? HEY, JUST CHECKIN' IN. I FIGURED YOU'D BE HOME FROM DEE DEE'S PARTY BY NOW.
ER... HOW **WAS** IT, ANY-WAY? I ASKED FRANCIS, AND HE WAS GOING ALL CRAZY ABOUT HOW **GREAT** IT WAS, AND—
WHEN YOU SAY IT WAS THE BEST PARTY IN THE HISTORY OF THE UNIVERSE, WHAT EXACTLY DOES THAT MEAN?
Peirce

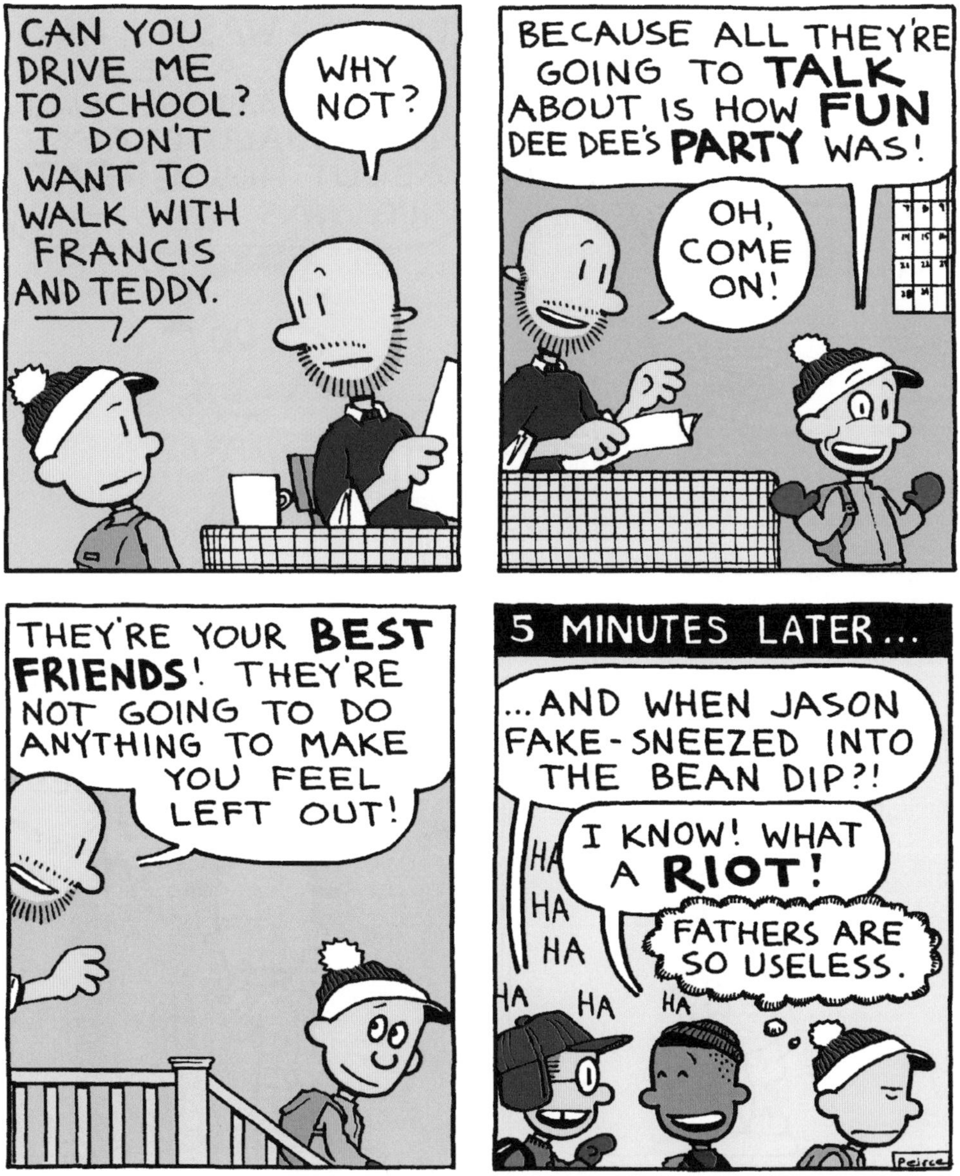
CAN YOU DRIVE ME TO SCHOOL? I DON'T WANT TO WALK WITH FRANCIS AND TEDDY.
WHY NOT?
BECAUSE ALL THEY'RE GOING TO TALK ABOUT IS HOW FUN DEE DEE'S PARTY WAS!
OH, COME ON!
THEY'RE YOUR BEST FRIENDS! THEY'RE NOT GOING TO DO ANYTHING TO MAKE YOU FEEL LEFT OUT!
5 MINUTES LATER...
...AND WHEN JASON FAKE-SNEEZED INTO THE BEAN DIP?!
I KNOW! WHAT A RIOT!
HA HA HA
FATHERS ARE SO USELESS.
HA HA HA
Peirce

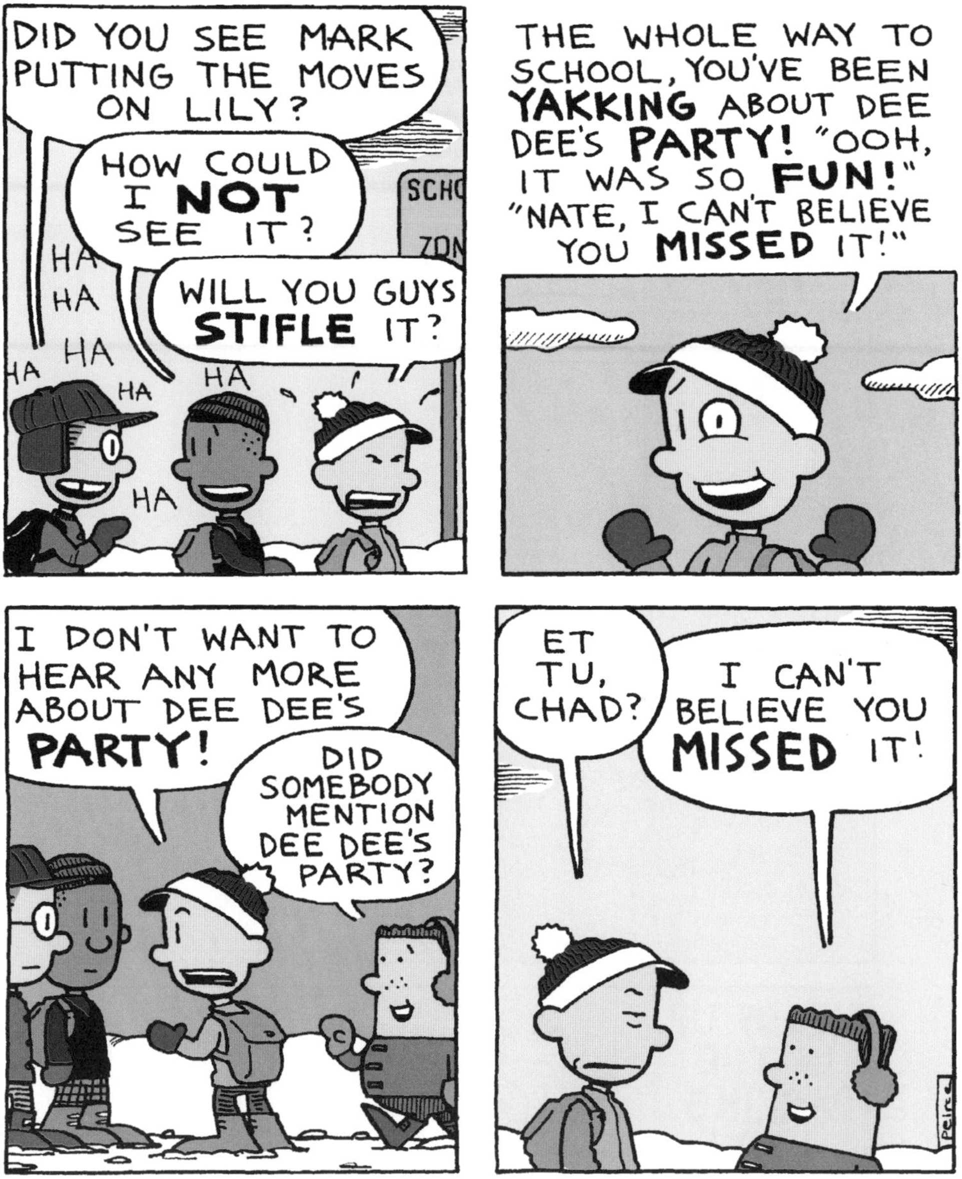
DID YOU SEE MARK PUTTING THE MOVES ON LILY?
HOW COULD I NOT SEE IT?
HA HA HA HA HA HA HA
WILL YOU GUYS STIFLE IT?
SCHO
ZON
THE WHOLE WAY TO SCHOOL, YOU'VE BEEN YAKKING ABOUT DEE DEE'S PARTY! "OOH, IT WAS SO FUN!" "NATE, I CAN'T BELIEVE YOU MISSED IT!"
I DON'T WANT TO HEAR ANY MORE ABOUT DEE DEE'S PARTY!
DID SOMEBODY MENTION DEE DEE'S PARTY?
ET TU, CHAD?
I CAN'T BELIEVE YOU MISSED IT!
Peirce

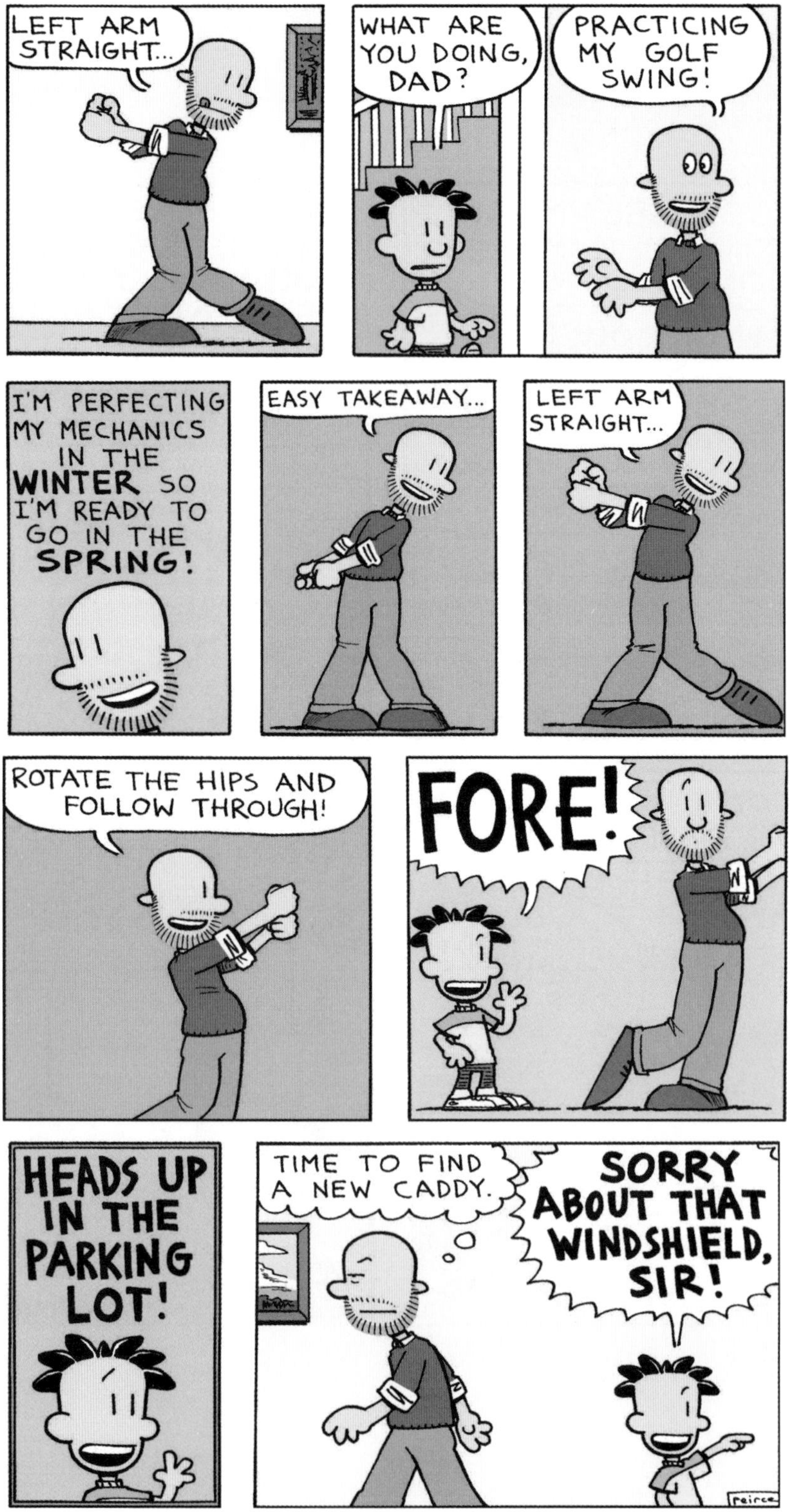
LEFT ARM STRAIGHT...
WHAT ARE YOU DOING, DAD?
PRACTICING MY GOLF SWING!
I'M PERFECTING MY MECHANICS IN THE WINTER SO I'M READY TO GO IN THE SPRING!
EASY TAKEAWAY...
LEFT ARM STRAIGHT...
ROTATE THE HIPS AND FOLLOW THROUGH!
FORE!
HEADS UP IN THE PARKING LOT!
TIME TO FIND A NEW CADDY.
SORRY ABOUT THAT WINDSHIELD, SIR!
peirce

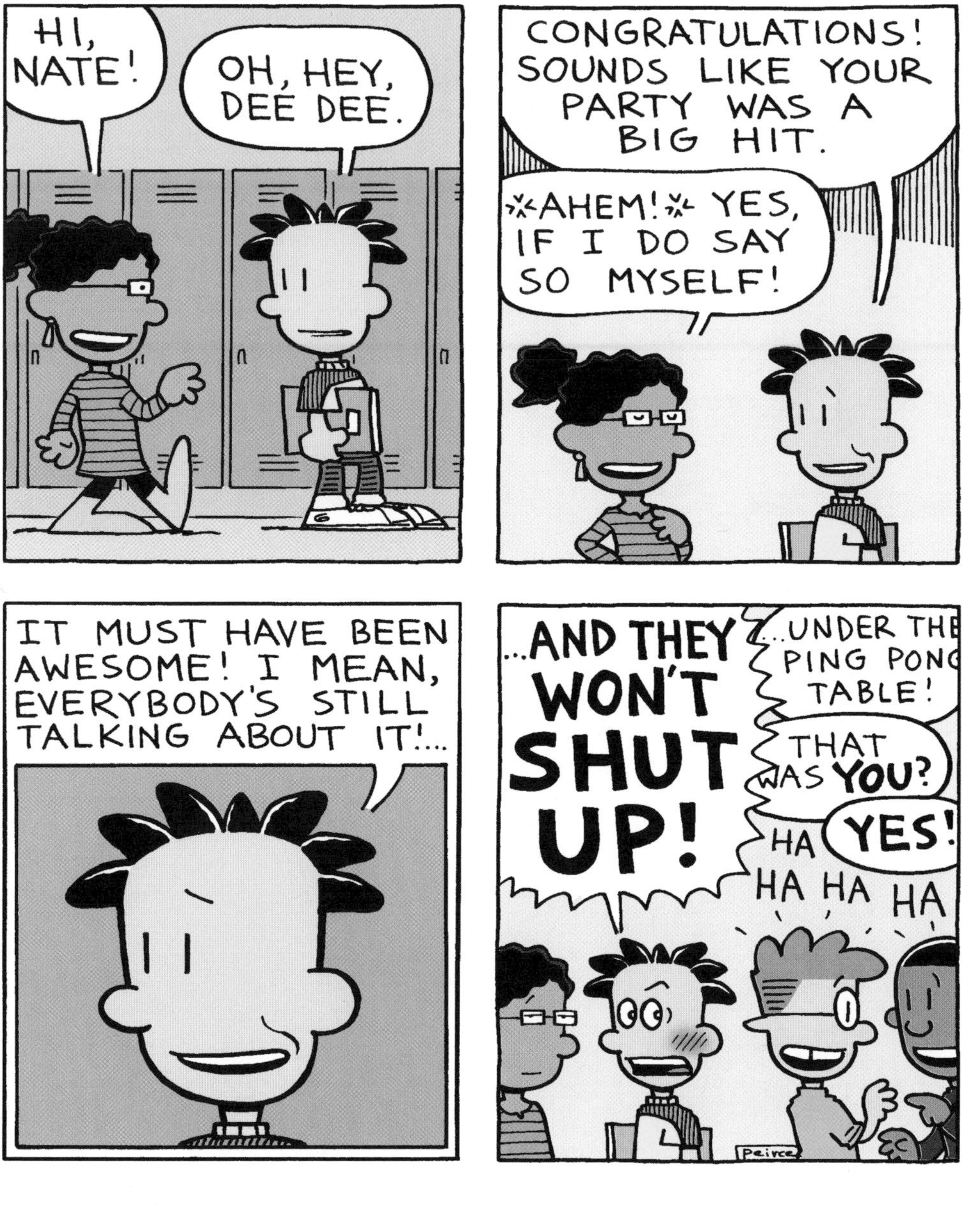
HI, NATE!
OH, HEY, DEE DEE.
CONGRATULATIONS! SOUNDS LIKE YOUR PARTY WAS A BIG HIT.
AHEM! YES, IF I DO SAY SO MYSELF!
IT MUST HAVE BEEN AWESOME! I MEAN, EVERYBODY'S STILL TALKING ABOUT IT!...
...AND THEY WON'T SHUT UP!
...UNDER THE PING PONG TABLE!
THAT WAS YOU?
YES!
HA HA HA HA HA
Peirce

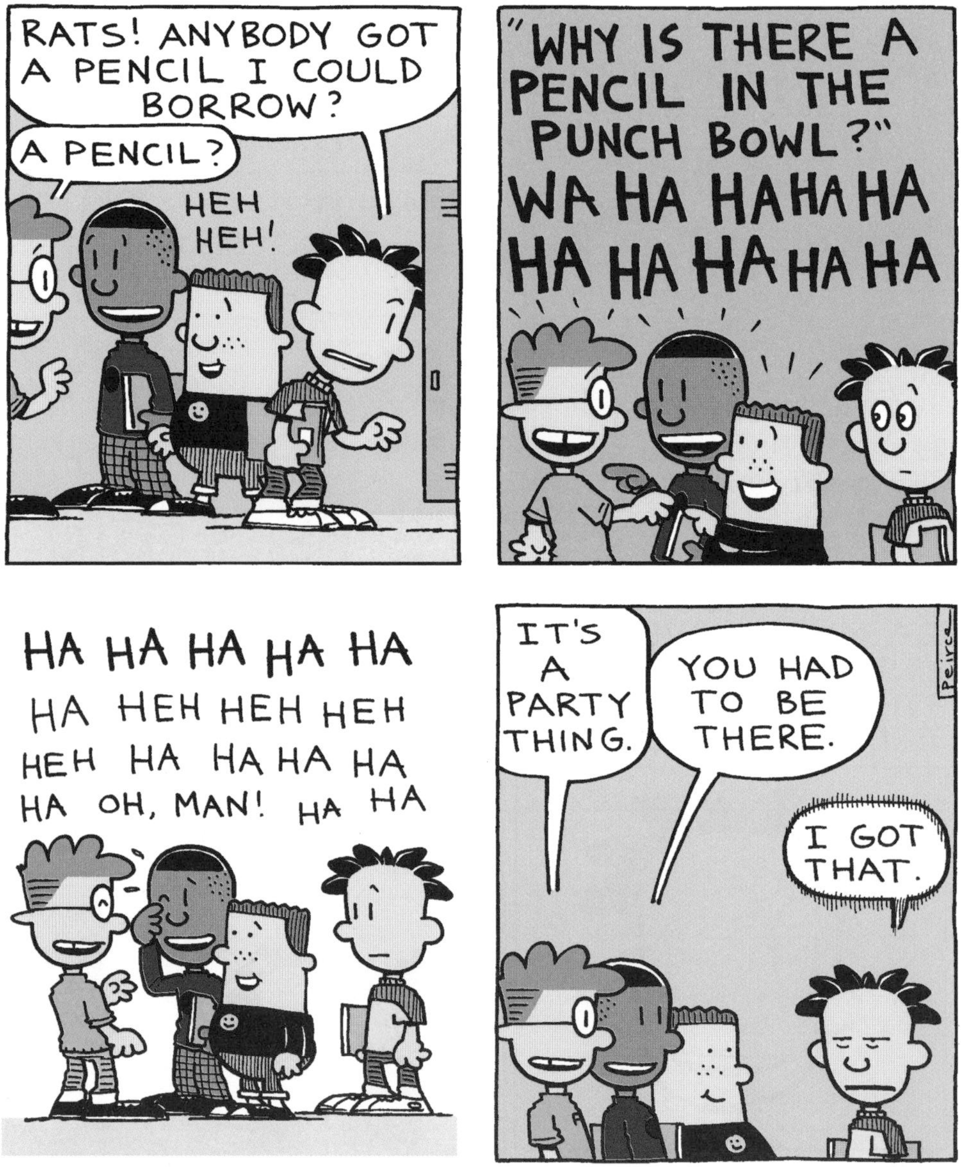
RATS! ANYBODY GOT A PENCIL I COULD BORROW?
A PENCIL?
HEH HEH!
"WHY IS THERE A PENCIL IN THE PUNCH BOWL?"
WA HA HAHAHA HA HA HA HA HA HA HA
HA HA HA HA HA
HA HEH HEH HEH
HEH HA HA HA HA
HA OH, MAN! HA HA
IT'S A PARTY THING.
YOU HAD TO BE THERE.
I GOT THAT.
Peirce

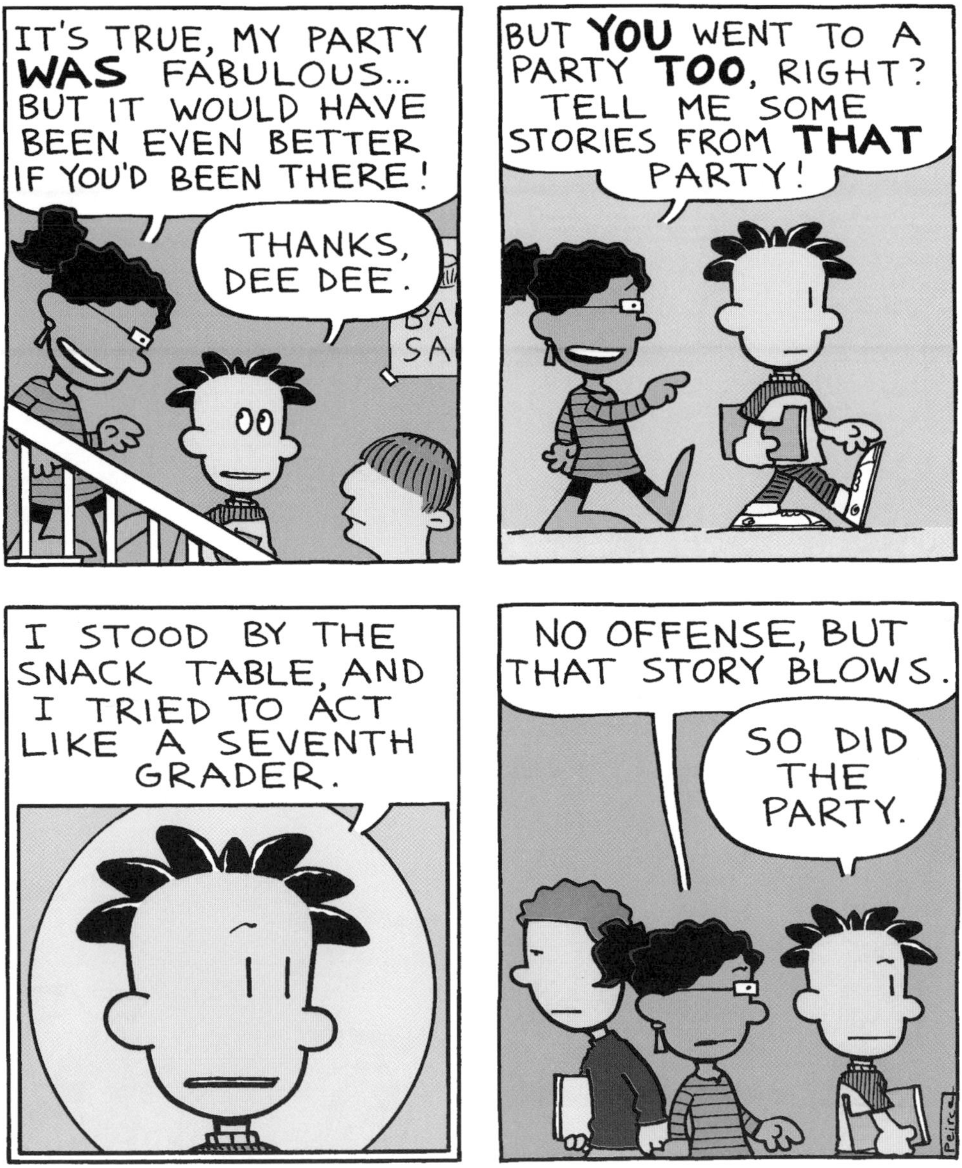
IT'S TRUE, MY PARTY **WAS** FABULOUS... BUT IT WOULD HAVE BEEN EVEN BETTER IF YOU'D BEEN THERE!
THANKS, DEE DEE.
BUT **YOU** WENT TO A PARTY **TOO**, RIGHT? TELL ME SOME STORIES FROM **THAT** PARTY!
I STOOD BY THE SNACK TABLE, AND I TRIED TO ACT LIKE A SEVENTH GRADER.
NO OFFENSE, BUT THAT STORY BLOWS.
SO DID THE PARTY.

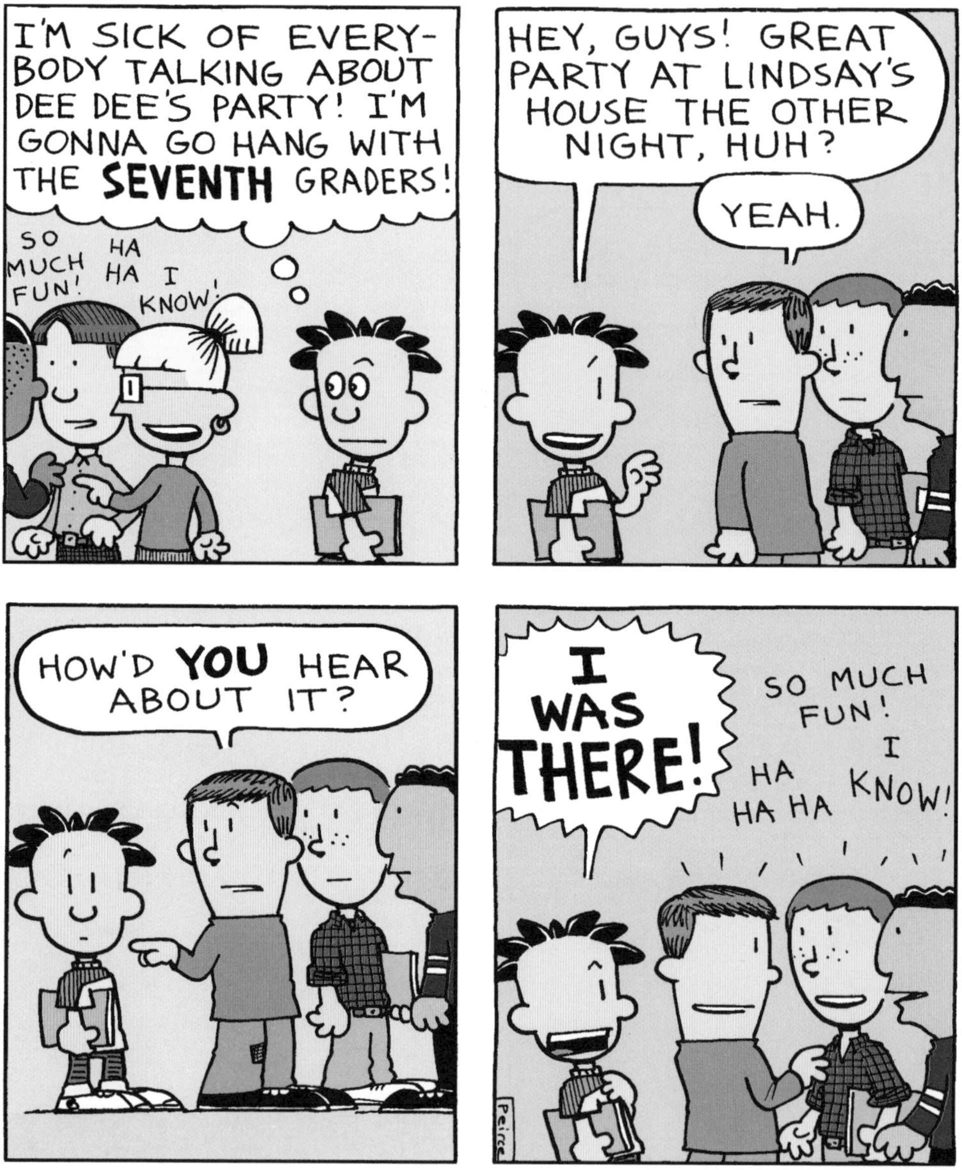
I'M SICK OF EVERYBODY TALKING ABOUT DEE DEE'S PARTY! I'M GONNA GO HANG WITH THE **SEVENTH** GRADERS!
SO MUCH FUN!
HA HA
I KNOW!
HEY, GUYS! GREAT PARTY AT LINDSAY'S HOUSE THE OTHER NIGHT, HUH?
YEAH.
HOW'D **YOU** HEAR ABOUT IT?
I WAS THERE!
SO MUCH FUN!
I KNOW!
HA HA HA
Peirce

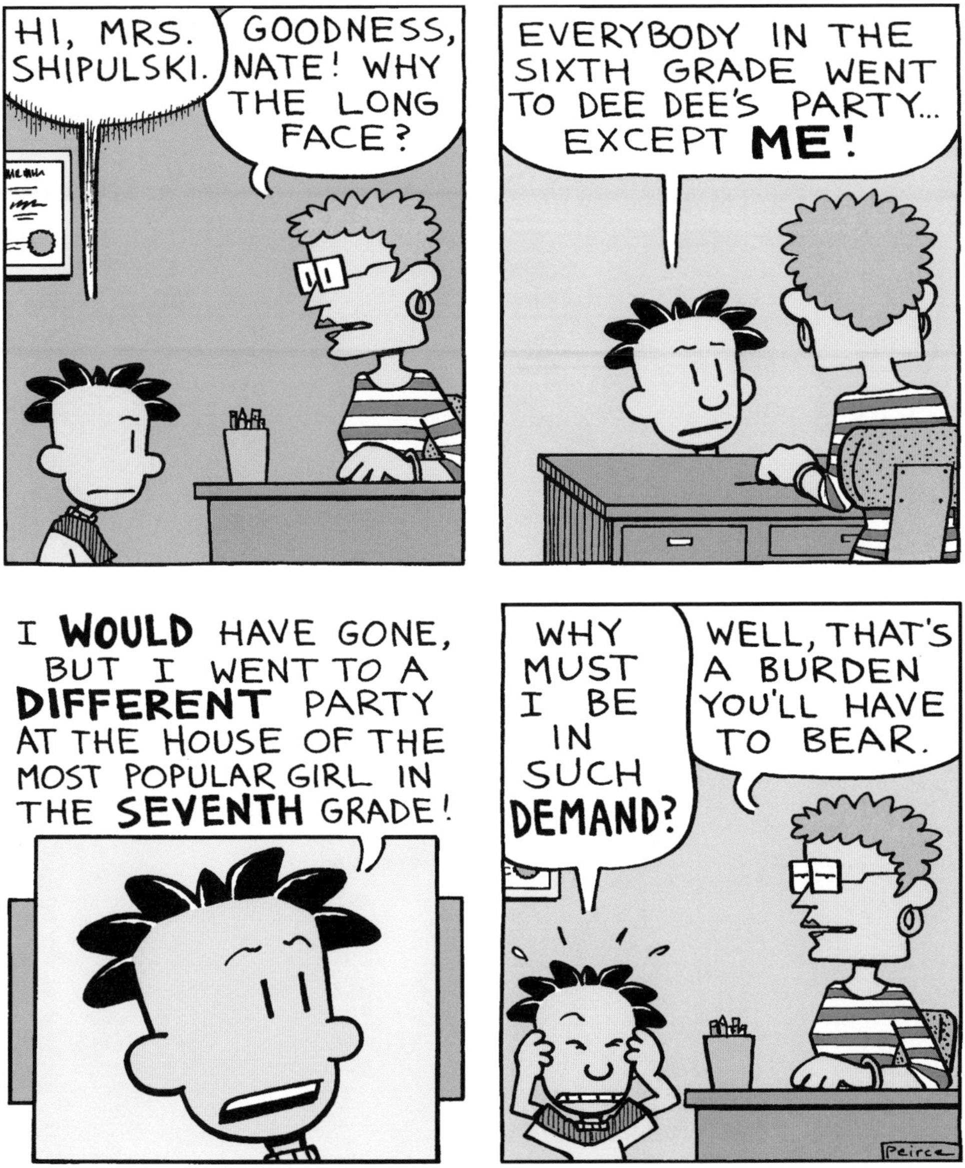
HI, MRS. SHIPULSKI.
GOODNESS, NATE! WHY THE LONG FACE?
EVERYBODY IN THE SIXTH GRADE WENT TO DEE DEE'S PARTY... EXCEPT **ME**!
I **WOULD** HAVE GONE, BUT I WENT TO A **DIFFERENT** PARTY AT THE HOUSE OF THE MOST POPULAR GIRL IN THE **SEVENTH** GRADE!
WHY MUST I BE IN SUCH **DEMAND**?
WELL, THAT'S A BURDEN YOU'LL HAVE TO BEAR.
Peirce

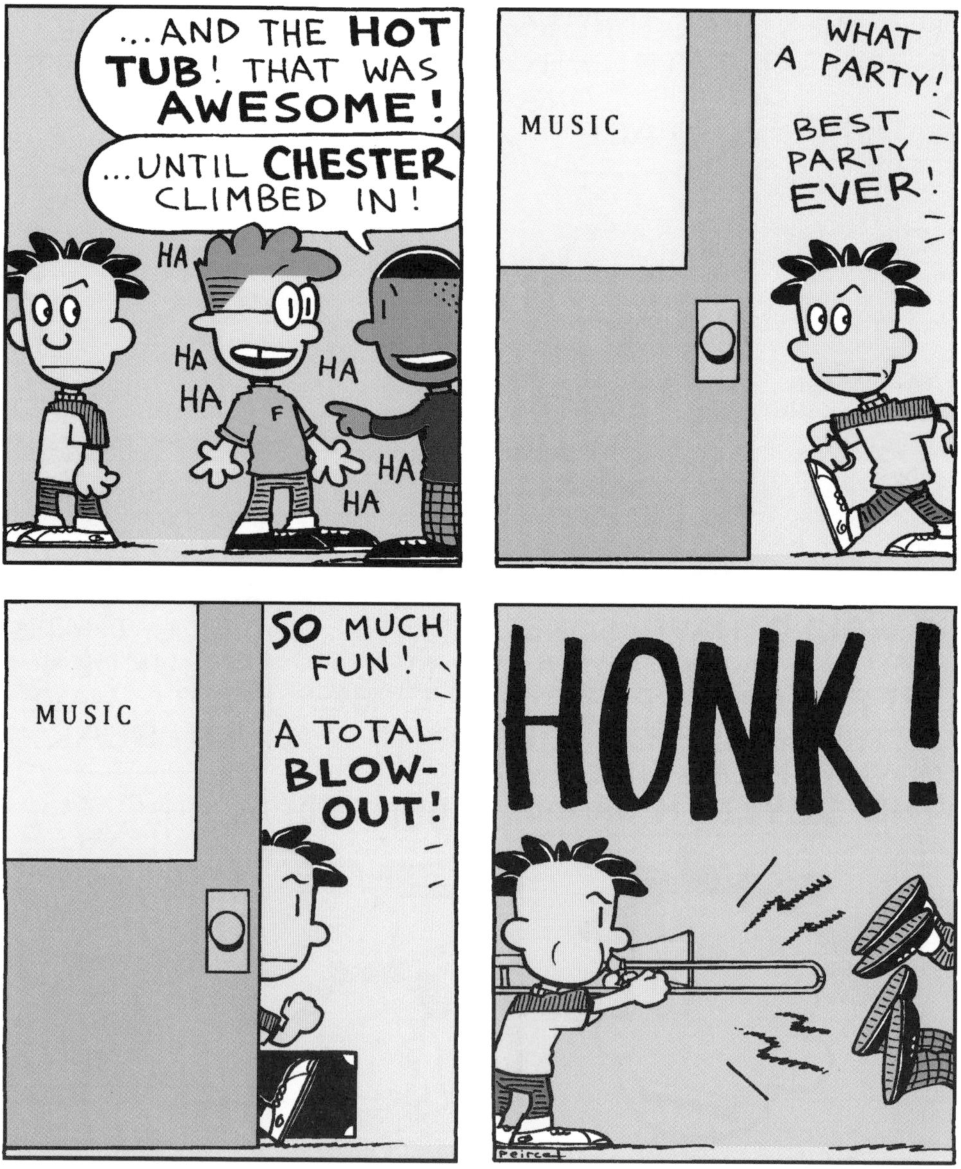
...AND THE HOT TUB! THAT WAS AWESOME!
...UNTIL CHESTER CLIMBED IN!
HA HA HA HA HA HA
MUSIC
WHAT A PARTY!
BEST PARTY EVER!
MUSIC
SO MUCH FUN!
A TOTAL BLOW-OUT!
HONK!
Peirce

Check out these and other books from Andrews McMeel Publishing

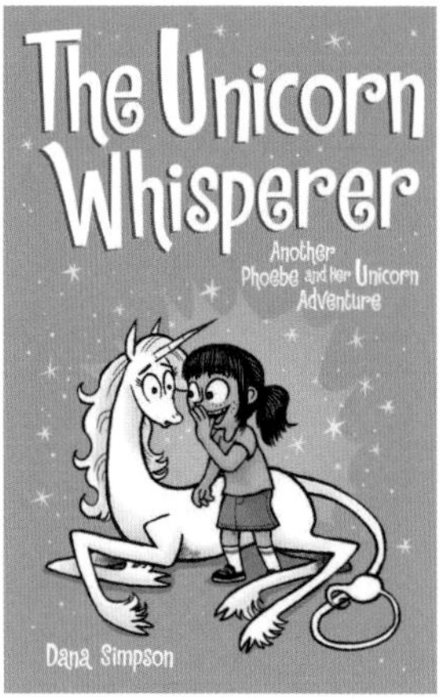
The Unicorn Whisperer
Another Phoebe and Her Unicorn Adventure
Dana Simpson

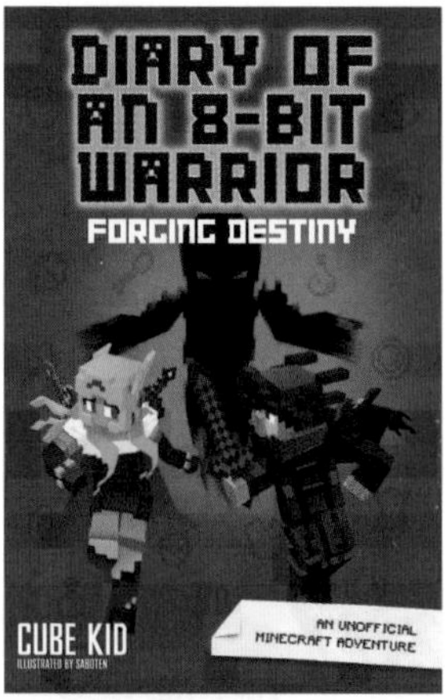
DIARY OF AN 8-BIT WARRIOR
FORGING DESTINY
CUBE KID
AN UNOFFICIAL MINECRAFT ADVENTURE

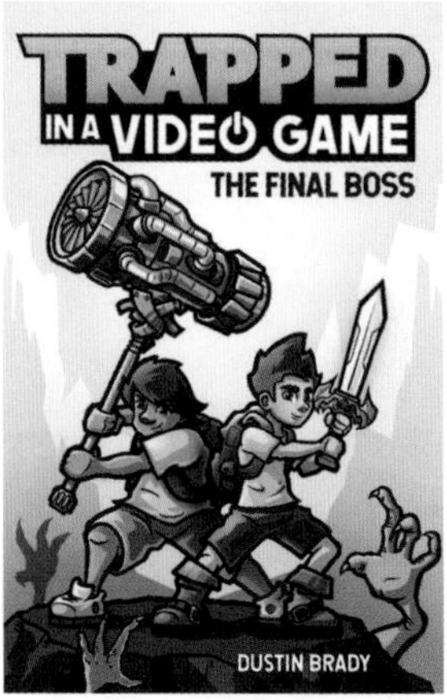
TRAPPED IN A VIDEO GAME
THE FINAL BOSS
DUSTIN BRADY

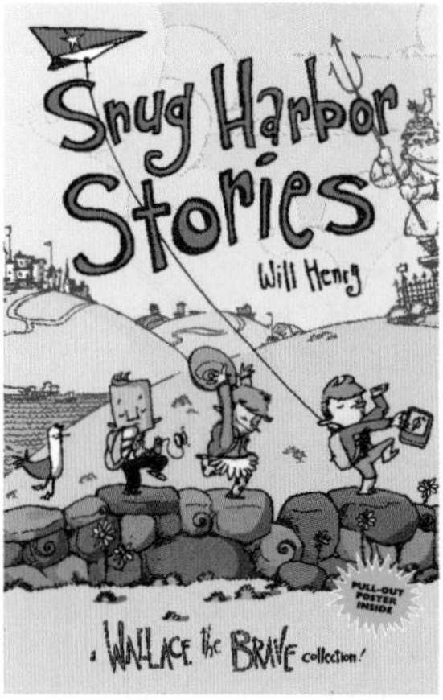
Snug Harbor Stories
Will Henry
FULL-OUT POSTER INSIDE
a WALLACE the BRAVE collection!

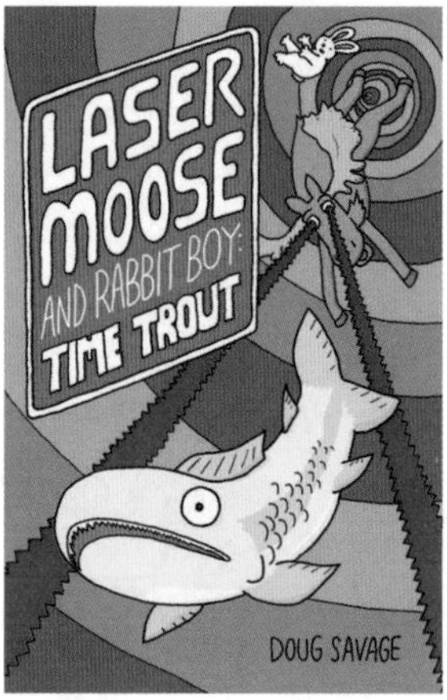
LASER MOOSE AND RABBIT BOY: TIME TROUT
DOUG SAVAGE

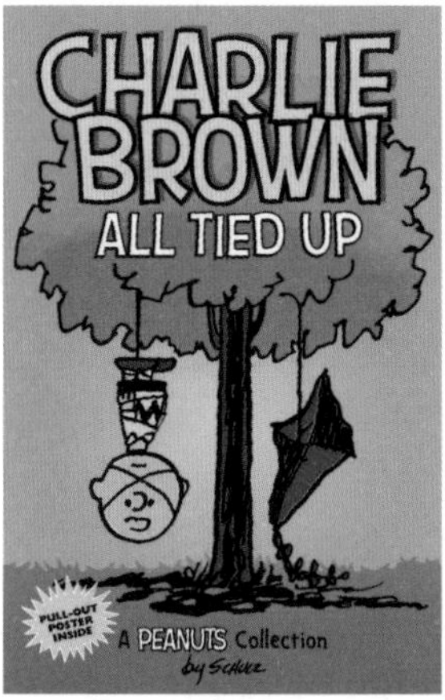
CHARLIE BROWN
ALL TIED UP
FULL-OUT POSTER INSIDE
A PEANUTS Collection
by Schulz

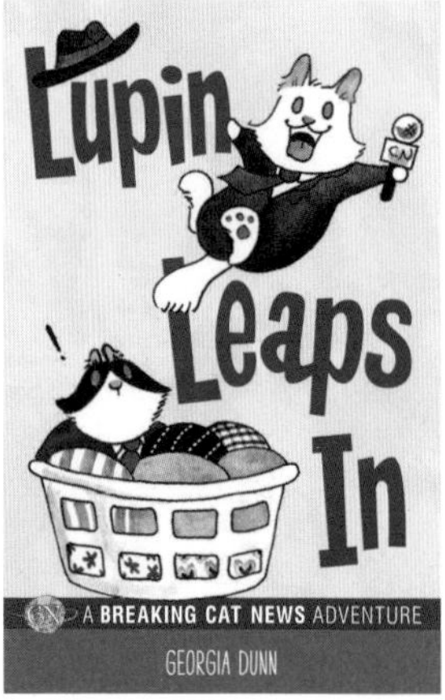
Lupin Leaps In
A BREAKING CAT NEWS ADVENTURE
GEORGIA DUNN

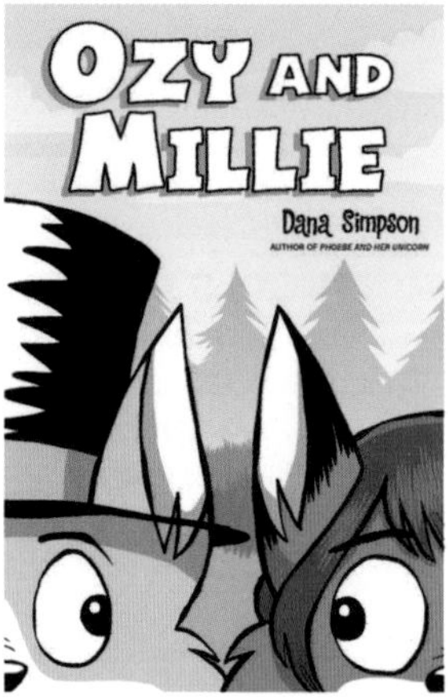
OZY AND MILLIE
Dana Simpson

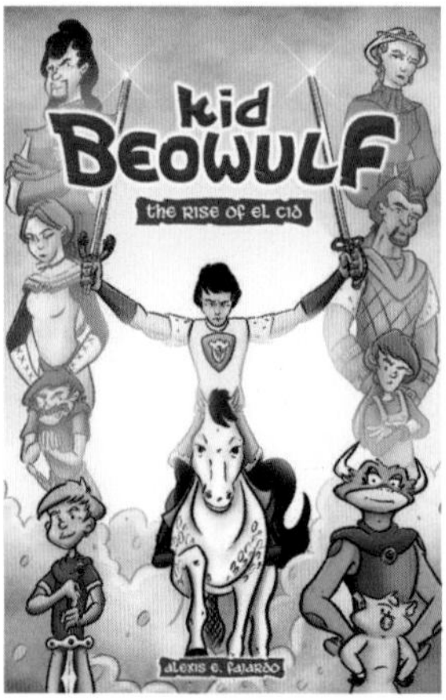
kid BEOWULF
the rise of el cid
alexis e. fajardo

Big Nate is distributed internationally by Andrews McMeel Syndication.

Big Nate: Blow the Roof Off! copyright © 2020 by United Feature Syndicate, Inc. All rights reserved. Printed in China. No part of this book may be used or reproduced in any manner whatsoever without written permission except in the case of reprints in the context of reviews.

Andrews McMeel Publishing
a division of Andrews McMeel Universal
1130 Walnut Street, Kansas City, Missouri 64106

www.andrewsmcmeel.com

20 21 22 23 24 SDB 10 9 8 7 6 5 4 3 2 1

ISBN: 978-1-5248-5506-2

Library of Congress Control Number: 2019945395

Made by:
King Yip (Dongguan) Printing & Packaging Factory Ltd.
Address and location of manufacturer:
Daning Administrative District, Humen Town
Dongguan Guangdong, China 523930
1st Printing—12/9/19

These strips appeared in newspapers from
September 14, 2015, through February 28, 2016.

Big Nate can be viewed on the Internet at
www.gocomics.com/big_nate.

ATTENTION: SCHOOLS AND BUSINESSES
Andrews McMeel books are available at quantity discounts with bulk purchase for educational, business, or sales promotional use. For information, please e-mail the Andrews McMeel Publishing Special Sales Department:
specialsales@amuniversal.com.